The Heart Remembers

Also by Margaret Redfern and available from Honno

Flint
The Storyteller's Granddaughter

The Heart Remembers

by

Margaret Redfern

HONNO MODERN FICTION

First published by Honno
'Ailsa Craig', Heol y Cawl, Dinas Powys, Wales, CF64 4AH

1 2 3 4 5 6 7 8 9 10

ISBN 978-1-909983-32-8 paperback
978-1-9099830-33-5 ebook

Published with the financial support of the Welsh Books Council.

Cover image: © Shutterstock
Cover design: Rebecca Ingleby
Text design: Elaine Sharples
Printed by Gomer Press

as always, to both of you, of course

Acknowledgements

Once again, grateful thanks
- to the Internet and its ever-increasing book-hoard and *bona fide* websites
- to the writers of books that have delighted, instructed and inspired me
- to the staff of Lincoln Central Library for their generous help
- to all at Honno for their patience, help and guidance

also:
- to Debbie of Lincoln, herbalist and wise-woman, and the joyful expeditions into the lime-woods of Lincolnshire
- to the Roving Apothecary, historic culinary and medicinal herbalists, the very best part of Lincoln's Christmas Market
- to the unknown, chance-met thatcher who patiently corrected my erroneous notions of thatching
- to my walking boots, the trusty companions of many years tramping

And to so many more chance-met folk who provided just that little extra fact (or fiction)

1

Venezia

Late autumn, 1336

No ship, beaten and conquered by the waves,
ever made land more happily than me
(Petrarch: 14thC)

Thick fog stifled all sound save slap of waves and crack of rigging and shouts from sailor to sailor, from boat to boat, swinging the lead, checking depth, checking channels, but all sound disembodied, souls of sailors lost at sea, not flesh-and-blood-and-of-this-earth. There was urgency in their calls: they must not run aground on the mudflats, not now, not so close to journey's end.

Shapes rose up out of the nothingness, resolved themselves into reeds, a bank of mud and silt, the bow of a boat sailing too close alongside. From somewhere came a bleating of flocks of sheep kept on the salt marsh. Without warning, the mass of a building ghosted before their eyes. It floated in fog, miraculous and disturbing. A sudden clamour of unseen bells close at hand. Another, further off. Another and another until the air was crammed with the clamour of invisible bells, some clangorous, some melodious, some cracked, some near, some far off and faint and all deadened by the clammy, salt-laden fog that drowned the lagoon.

As if the bells had power over the elements, the fog shifted and lifted infinitesimally and the prows of the fleet were visible at last. To the watching girl it seemed ominous, eerie. What was this watery world they had entered? It was different from rough seas and crashing waves; different from becalmed waters and jagged reefs that threatened to tear the fragile hulls plank from plank; different from the friendly wind that kept them on course, hour after hour, day after day, night after night, past a coastline of rearing white-rock mountains and the days when swags of cloud squatted on mountain tops, such heavy-laden cloud it seemed the mountains were crushed by the weight. There were times when harbours beckoned, safe and sheltering, stout fortresses guarding their entrance, where fresh water was taken on board, and fresh food, and a chance to stand on solid ground, though it felt strange after the lurching, shifting boards of the boat.

The 'berths' they had been promised were on deck, and the *patronus* was reluctant to take them when he realised two young women were of the party. He had to yield to Francesco da Ginstinianis, whose father knew the Welshman and whose family were of the elite, the inner circle of Venetian nobles. He smouldered; he was of noble family too, he, Marco Trevior, the younger son maybe but he was ambitious. One day, he promised himself, one day he too would be one of the Forty that ruled Venezia. Perhaps, even, if he played the game right, he might be elected one of the Council of Ten, the supreme ruling party, only last year declared a permanent office. His family was eligible, after all, and would be even more so if his brother Jacopo stirred himself to make sure of da Ginstinianis' vinegar-faced sister. A connection with that family would be useful. Very useful.

He contemplated his passengers: three tough-looking men well used to handling themselves, used to travelling, with the scars and bruises to prove it – a recent sword slash marked the face of the Welshman. There was a slim, blue-eyed younger man as well, with a mop of golden curls. A thin, dark youth without the power of speech. A simpleton. What had he to do with the world of money and merchandise? And the two young women, one with hair like pale gold, the other whose hair shone gold-copper-bronze in the early morning sun and whose dark eyes met his brazenly. She was too bold by half, this one. Such manners would not be tolerated in Venezia. If he had his way, he'd soon tame her. Both wore the clothing worn by the peasant women of Attaleia; loose breeches, a long tunic, a kaftan over that. Shapeless clothing. Nothing like the beautiful young noble women of Venezia. Not even like the working girls, who had their own attraction. He smiled to himself, remembering the way thin material ripped away to reveal rounded breasts and soft flesh yielding under his busy fingers. He promised himself another night out with his friends, like last autumn, when five of them had climbed over the wall of one of the nunneries. Nuns were willing enough, once they realised they had no choice. Good hunting, good sport, and a clean escape – not like his friend Moreto who was caught in bed with five nuns and a huge erect member as red as his face, and a fine to pay.

But that was for later; now he was a *patronus* with the fleet, his first command. On a cog, he sternly told his passengers, the cargo was stowed below deck and passengers had to take their luck in the open air, whatever the weather, sunshine, rain or storm, sheltered only by sleeping bags made of hide and pelts, leather-side outwards. It was no place for any woman. There was one latrine, over there on the starboard side, jutting out over the sea and open to view. He couldn't make special provision for them. Sior da Ginstinianis had not thought of these things, this lack of comfort, of seemliness, but since it was agreed…he shrugged.

The girl didn't mind. It was preferable to being entombed below deck. Here on deck she could see the stars and the moon, she could feel the wind and spray on her face. Their horses had been stabled on the capacious round boats, their baggage crammed into whatever space was available on this alum-carrying cog; alum as ballast, destined for the glass-makers of Murano. She had got used to the smoking, round-bellied cooking-pot and the open fire that was so carefully guarded. She had got used to the jutting public latrine on the starboard side, and the makeshift canvas sheeting which two of the crew rigged up for them. When a white-faced Agathi tearfully confided that her monthly time had started again, after barren months when she was taken as slave, it was the girl who had begged the Welshman to find linen for them, these two, the only women aboard the cog. She remembered his moment of silence, the deep flush that rose in his throat and travelled up into his cheeks.

'I should not speak of such things to a man, I know this, but what am I to do?'

'Exactly what you have done, *cariad*.' He was gone for no more than two gusts of wind that rolled the ship to leeward; he returned with a small roll of fine linen.

'This is too much and too fine.'

'Happen so. It's what I could get.' A sidelong glance. 'For you as well, Kazan,' he said, awkwardly. She in turn had felt her face redden. This was talk that should not even be between man and wife. 'Thank you,' she said, as awkwardly. They had not spoken of such things again. Instead, they had been anxious for Edgar-the-seasick, pale and feeble at the start of the voyage, staggering onto the quay at Candia, the first port-of-call, listless and helpless at sea, clinging to the railing and gazing wistfully at the beyond-reach land. How had he ever travelled so far from home? He never did find his sea legs, as the sailors promised him, but the wretchedness and vomiting subsided.

It was when they were harboured in Candia that the strange thing happened. Two Venetian galleys were due to join the fleet. Damaged by the *meltemi* on the outward journey, they had needed repairs, and Candia had an efficient *arsenale*. Several of the crew had stayed behind and now there was a re-shuffling and re-appointing of crew-members. A well-built young sailor was one of those to join their own cog. He came on board cheerfully enough, swinging his kitbag from one hand and lithely leaping the last few feet.

'It is Radovan,' someone murmured, and there were expressive looks one to the other. A too-hearty voice welcomed him, and another. Curly-haired Rizo blew out his cheeks but he was the one who reached for him and hugged him.

'We thought you had gone back to Spalato,' he said.

'No such luck. I need the work.'

It was then the *patronus* appeared. He stopped dead in front of the young sailor, his eyes disbelieving.

'What is this? What are you doing here?'

The young man Radovan reddened, deeper and deeper, then the colour drained so that his brown face seemed yellow. His body, that lithe, agile body, stiffened into stillness.

'You,' he said. 'I was not told that you were the *patronus* of this ship.'

'And I was not told that you were to be my extra crew.' Marco Trevior was furious. This man was trouble. He was a man of Croatia come to Venezia for work; the son of a carpenter, he was a mean deck-hand, one of those who lived in the poor quarters of the city, and as arrogant as if he were one of the nobles himself. 'I shall see about this.'

Trevior stalked back to the quay. Dai could see him in angry conversation with Francesco. He gesticulated towards the cog, raised a fist, turned and strode about the quay before he came back to Francesco. The Venetian authorities took seriously the Crime of Speech, that intemperate, angry speech that could lead to violence, to disruption, especially amongst the nobles. This must be a serious problem, if a noble was so openly disturbed by the presence of a worker. Usually, their paths would not cross. The officials were the ones who bore the day-to-day brunt of the poor, and their anger and frustration. The nobles were out of reach. Whatever the cause, Marco Trevior was storming back to the ship, his face as black as the winter clouds over the Mawddach. Radovan was to stay: Trevior had to accept it, and there would be tension the whole of the voyage. Not good. Dai had hoped for a peaceful journey though, truth to tell, he did not like this Marco Trevior. Why, he could not say. He was a polite young man, true; brusque, but that was no fault. He was good at his job, respected as a *patronus*, though it was clear he was not liked. More than that, Kazan did not like him.

'His eyes,' she said, 'they watch us, me and Agathi, as if we were vermin. As if he searches beneath our clothes for our skin.'

Dai was alert at once though he did not tell her why. He made sure the two young women were with them always, slept close to their men, were flanked by them, were accompanied whenever they reached land. He made her promise to stay always together with Agathi, never to stray far from himself or Twm or Giles or Edgar. What, he wondered, was the quarrel between these two men from such different backgrounds?

After that, it seemed things settled. Either that, or Radovan kept out of the way of Marco Trevior. There was only one more incident, a strange encounter between Dai and the young Croatian.

They had harboured in Spalato, with its new city centre and ancient fortified palace. It was good anchorage, and good to be on dry land. The warmth of Attaleia had long gone but this was a fine autumn day with clouds scudding before a freshening westerly. The man Radovan approached him carefully.

'A word, *sior*,' he said quietly. Dai nodded, and without speaking they both moved into the dark shadows of the harbour buildings. 'I must speak quickly,' the young man said. 'Trevior always keeps watch on me. It would not look well for you to be seen with me but I must warn you.' He looked around him, at the quiet quay. Nothing. 'Your two women – look after them well in Venezia. This man, this noble, Trevior.' He spat. 'He is not to be trusted, especially where women are.'

'This is a grave accusation.'

'Not in Venezia. A small fine is all that is demanded, and a woman's life is ruined, and that of her family.'

'Tell me.'

'We came from this town, from Spalato, my papa, mama, my sister, me. We are of a decent, hard-working family. We looked for work in Venezia. My papa, he was a carpenter, a fine craftsman, and they are much in demand. I have no such skill, though I tried hard to please my papa. Instead, I took work on board the fleet. Our plan was to invest our wages in goods. Perhaps I could have an education. Venezia was our great hope. Then that monster came. He saw my sister and lusted after her. He raped her. For such as him it is a petty offence, and the Venetian laws do nothing. If she had been a *puella* – a young girl – then it would have carried weight, but a young woman of marriageable age? That counts as nothing. A fine that these nobles can well afford. That is all their punishment. For us, it was dishonour. I was not there to protect her. I was away with the fleet. When I returned home my family was destroyed. My father died of grief and shame. My mother could do nothing. My sister has no chance of marriage. I am the sole wage earner and I do what I can to keep a roof over our heads.' He gazed fiercely at Dai.

'A terrible thing to have happened, and it's sorry I am for your family, but there is nothing I can do,' he said.

'I know that. I do not ask you for anything. I only warn you. I have seen the way this man looks at your women. They are safe enough now. I have friends on this ship. We will look out for your women, and shall do what we can when we reach Venezia, but after that it is you who must keep them safe.'

'I thank you, Radovan.'

The young man laughed without merriment. 'You know what Radovan means?' Dai shook his head. 'The joyful one. This is the meaning. Someone somewhere got it wrong, I think.'

'There is always room for faith.' Dai grimaced. How simple-minded that sounded to the Venetian religion of money and commerce. The world of the Sufis was far away. He knew a pang of loss. He sighed. 'An old friend of mine always says this. He looks at death but still he says there is always room for faith.'

'I shall remember this,' Radovan said, gravely. He looked about him again. 'Now I must go. If he sees me talking to you he will say that I am speaking ill of Venezia and I shall be punished and you will fall under suspicion.'

'But I am your witness.'

'You are a foreigner.' He paused on the point of leaving. 'Your Kazan – she is a great marvel. We love her very much. We shall take great care of her and so must you.'

He was gone, and that was the last time Dai had speech alone with him.

Two months it had taken the fleet to sail from Attaleia to Venezia and now here they were on a damp, fog-ridden November morning, a whole month behind the usual schedule.

'The camels are coming,' he said, the quiet brown man, the Welshman, standing next to the girl at the rails. 'Look there.' Towards them came a small fleet moving spirit-like across the waters of the lagoon. 'Camels they're called,' he said. He gave the local word: *cammelli*. 'They'll cradle us, keep us buoyed up, and take us into safe harbour – flat-bottomed, see, get us across the shallow water and up the *Canalazzo* to the quayside of Rivo Alto.'

They turned past the island of San Giorgio, where the walls of the Benedictine monastery loomed so ominously out of the fog and the bells of the newly built *campanile* clanged out the morning call to prayer. It still seemed strange to the girl, these bells, and not the call of the *muezzin* from the giddy height of the minaret. The shadowy shape of land took form. They were entering a broad channel, the *Canalazzo,* which wound its way through the whole of the floating city. They had told her about it but even so she stared in amazement. 'Where are the city walls and gates?' she asked and the sailors chuckled, true Venetians proud of their watery empire.

'There are none,' Sanuto declared grandly. She had learnt their names, the little names they called each other. Sanuto's was easy;

when he smiled, and he often smiled, his teeth showed large and white in his mouth. 'We have no need of them. The waters of the lagoon are all the walls and battlements we need. Kings and princes cannot touch us unless they come by sea and these waters have protected us from the first, by God's will. He has preserved us so that we may live in these watery marshes. He has enabled us to raise a new and mighty Venezia.'

They had filled her head with stories of this city of miracles, talking in the harsh, fast sing-song dialect of true Venetians that was at first so difficult to understand. They told her which ships carried ballast of precious stone. 'Venezia, she is a city born of the sea. She has no stone.' There was pink granite and porphyry from Egypt to be used in the new buildings that were replacing the old wooden city. 'To front the bricks,' Rizo-the-curly-haired explained. 'All stone is too much money and even our miraculous floating city must sink under the weight of it.' Other stone was bought or stolen – a flash of Sanuto's grinning teeth – from Carrara, from Verona, taken from the old buildings of the lagoon islands. Other stones were taken from the Padova hills that once used to spit fire, and these were used to pave the *campi* and *calli* in place of grass. There were even marble bridges crossing some of the canals in place of the wooden spans. 'And some say there is to be a stone bridge across the Canalazzo, a stone bridge high enough for all ships to pass under it but I do not see how this can be.' Zanino shrugged. 'The bridge we have is a wonder. It is wood, true, but its middle can be raised so all sailing craft can go through and dock at the Rivo Alto quayside. That is where we shall go.'

Radovan was loitering close by. 'A great bridge,' he murmured. 'At night it is where the vagabonds and the displaced sleep, and there are many such.'

'Rado speaks true.' Sanuto lowered his voice. 'It is said that there are so many crowded there under the bridge that late arrivals are tossed into the Canalazzo to drown.'

'Is this true?' Kazan exclaimed.

Radovan's mouth tightened. 'It is true, little one. There are many dangers in this city.'

Sanuto hushed him quickly and cast an anxious glance around the deck. He hurried on. The stones of Venezia, he said, were miraculous. There was much evidence of this. 'Do you know that here in our city is the rock from which Moses drew water? Do you know that there are the stones on which Christ walked? On which his blood was spilled?' Kazan's head reeled with the stories of sawn-apart marble that revealed the image of a hermit – a bearded hermit – whose hands were folded in prayer. There was the weeping stone, the bleeding stone, the stone where, if you held your hand just so, just there, you could feel its beating heart.

'And the lions, don't forget the lions,' Rizo insisted. His face was serious, full of awe at the wondrous thing he was telling them. 'At night the stone dissolves and the lions come alive and wander the *calli* of the city. It is true! Me, no, I have not seen them. I would be afraid to look on them. But others have said so.'

Dai glanced across at Twm. 'Better than the men whose heads grow beneath their shoulders,' he murmured.

'Do you believe any of this to be true?'

'They believe it,' said Dai. 'What I believe does not matter. This is their city, these are their miracles.' He paused, his face impassive but Twm knew there was more to come. 'A city that floats on water, Twm; a city of brick and marble floating on streets of water. Isn't that miracle enough?'

'A miracle, maybe, but so is water piped across ravines and into the *hans* and cities of Anatolia. Men had a hand in these miracles. These Venetians, they must sink their foundations deep in the mud and silt.'

Marco Trevior was nearby. The closer they came to journey's end, the more he found a reason to stand near them, near enough to overhear their conversation. Dai wondered if it had started after Spalato, and if that conversation between himself and Radovan had been observed. 'You are an unbeliever, *sior* Thomas,' he said now. 'You must allow us our miracles. These seagulls travelling with us,' he waved a hand at the swooping, screeching gulls, 'these are also little miracles. It was flight of such as these that led our forefathers from the plain of the Veneto to safety in the islands of the lagoon when the marauders came. But it is true that the buildings rest on good, strong foundations – no less a miracle for that, as *sior* Davide says. We have learnt how to drive huge wooden stakes deep into the clay and pave the surface with oak timbers.'

'Like a raft?' said Dai.

'Like a raft. Like a huge ship anchored in the lagoon, an Ark filled with all forms of life. If Noah's Ark was a miracle, why not this city of ours?'

'You are right, *sior* Trevior,' Twm said. 'I have seen nothing like Venezia. It truly is a marvel.' He smiled, his dark, handsome face less taut than it used to be. 'It is a miracle of God and men; will you allow me that?'

'Indeed I will. We of Venezia are miracle workers.' Trevior smiled frostily. 'It is not true what the proverb says.'

'Oh?'

'Venetians are born tired and live to sleep. How could we build our city if we are so tired? How could we make money?'

'And money is your second blood,' Dai said and the man laughed again but his laughter was strained. He did not like this self-assured Welshman who behaved as if he were an equal, who guarded his women as if they were daughters of nobles, though he was nothing but a peasant.

'I see you know our proverbs. You have travelled this way often enough, I think.'

They would have passed on but Marco Trevior touched Dai on the shoulder. 'A word, *sior* Davide,' he said.

Dai waited.

'If you'll take advice from a Venetian, *sior?*'

'What's to do?'

'It is a city of miracles, true enough, and no man is allowed to speak ill of it.'

Dai considered. 'Punishable, you mean?'

'Since the Council of Ten was made permanent last year.'

Dai nodded. 'I'll see to it. Thank you for the warning.' He waited: there was more.

'Your womenfolk…'

'Oh yes?'

'I am sure they are good and virtuous, the fair one and the bright one. But Venezia – I love my city, you understand *sior?*'

'*Wrth gwrs.*'

'She likes her women to be discreet. Obedient. The bright one lets her tongue trip heedlessly.'

'She will be heedful of this.' He waited.

'The sailor Radovan. He is a rogue. The Ten has warned him already, and fined him. Do not be taken in by him.'

'I am not.' Dai's mouth smiled. 'I am not taken in by anybody,' he said, blandly. 'Excuse me, *sior.*' He walked away. Trevior glowered after him.

They sailed up the great street of water, passing other narrow waterways branching off from it, fog clinging to them, curling and licking the houses and gardens and monasteries and nunneries and places of business, the palaces and rich houses. A city that had once been wood and mud huts perched above the treacherous waters was now the grand home of the rich merchants of Venezia. There'd be great relief and rejoicing at their arrival. 'Not for our safety,' said Rizo of the curly hair, 'but for the safe arrival of the goods we carry.' They had no illusions, these Venetian sailors, despite their miraculous stories.

They were past the Arsenale, the great ship-building yard, bigger by far than the one they had seen in Candia; past the great basilica of St Mark, with its high domes shadowy in the fog; past the Palace of the Doge that was being rebuilt in grand style. It was the place of government where the Ten met weekly; it was the place where men vanished into dark prisons. The *piazza* was already crowded with the curious; rumours of the returning fleet had already spread across the city – a fishing boat, maybe, or a herdsman. Who knew? Rumours spread like the fire all Venetians dreaded.

Two tall pillars stood sentinel on the *piazza,* one surmounted by St Theodore, the other by the great winged lion of Venezia: between them hung two wretched men. 'Another execution,' muttered a sailor, and crossed himself. On the far side, another Benedictine monastery. 'In Venezia there are all denominations,' said Brother Jerome. 'I shall stay with my brothers in the friary of Saint Francis on the Rivo Alto.' He glanced towards Thomas, dark and handsome, his gaze fixed on the waters of the *Canalazzo* and the rich buildings that fronted it. 'Thomas and I shall stay there,' he said.

Dai nodded. It was as he had thought when they left Attaleia, and the journey had only confirmed it: Twm intended promising himself to the Order of the Franciscans. Thomas turned towards him. 'I have promised to accompany you to Ieper,' he said, 'safe to Heinrijc Mertens. I shall honour that promise, Dafydd.'

Dai shook his head. 'There's no need, my friend.' He used the words of his own country. *Fy gefeilliog.* 'You know now what it is you want with your life. Start now. No more waiting.'

Thomas stared, pale-faced. 'All my life, Dafydd, I have blamed you for my failure. I was wrong.'

'Indeed you were. You are no failure, brother. You are at heart a peacemaker, a lover of peace, and yet you have lived too long at war with yourself. So few peacemakers amongst us. We need you, and people like you. If, as they say, England is to be at war with France as well as Scotland, we need you more than ever.'

'You are a good man, Dafydd ap Heddwyn ap Rhickert.' The dark man gestured towards the girl in the bow of the boat, her gold-copper-bronze hair bright against the pale gold of Agathi's. 'Take care of her. She is a star come to live amongst us.'

'I know. I shall.'

'You love her.'

'Always. But she is not for me.'

The dark man stared at him, incredulous. 'God made you for each other.'

'She is not for me,' he repeated. Even so, Kara Kemal's words came into his mind: *My son, who are you to decide what is and what is not to be? Only Allah the all-compassionate, the all-knowing decides.*

The bells were still sounding. 'That is for us, for the fleet,' Trevior told them. The first time he had been trusted with the command of a ship, so many delays, so many anxieties but at last they were here, sailing up the Canalazzo, all secure. If only the man Radovan had not appeared! But now they were about to dock, and the threat of the Croatian would soon be gone.

They were approaching the bridge that spanned the Canalazzo under whose shelter the dispossessed slept and drowned at night. Its entire length was thronged with people cheering and shouting and crying with relief. Here was the fleet! Not lost but safe, and intact. Here was the fleet! The people welcomed the safe arrival of the men. The merchant-nobles thanked heaven for the safe arrival of their goods and their sons.

The fleet sailed on under the bridge and into the quayside of the Rivo Alto. The *cammelli* herded them to docking point. On the quayside an imposing welcome committee was hastily gathering: the Doge Francesco Dondolo, his followers, the priests, the important men of the city. Here they were to greet the late arrival of the eastern fleet. Trumpets blazoned and were muted by the damp, foggy air. Soon, the ramps would be let down and the noble sailor-merchants would walk in state towards the waiting committee.

Fishing boats were already docked at the quayside, their slithering, flailing cargo unloading on to mule carts and into baskets, slipping on to the ground where the city's cats, the little lions of Venezia, lurked in the shadows waiting their turn. Turbot, sturgeon, red mullet, flounder, all the riches of the sea harvested for the pleasure of this sea-city. There was a lucky haul of bream and sea bass that always found a ready market with the rich. The poor contented themselves with small, silvery *marsoni*, cheap enough to be sold by the basketful. There were eels.

'Good Fenland fodder,' Edgar said. 'Blue should be here.' It was a restored Edgar now that he was so close to dry land. 'I'm ravenous!' He sniffed. Over the pervasive smell of fish was that of fresh-baked bread.

'Ravenous? Aren't we all!' Dai looked more closely at a wooden tub being hefted on to the quay by a sturdy fisherman. 'Now there's lucky. Soft shell crabs still to be had this late in the autumn – and *schie.*' He pointed to baskets of the heaped small grey shrimps that were local to these islands. 'Best eaten live, shells and all.'

'You and your stomach, Dafydd.' But Twm knew now the reason for Dai's obsession with food: the story he had told of his childhood, growing up as best he could during the terrible years of famine, his father dead in Llewelyn Bren's revolt against the English overlords, his grandfather sacrificing himself so his grandson could eat, so that the young boy he was then could forage and steal to provide for the family. The head of his family at eight years old, desperately trying – and failing – to keep them from starvation. It was a heavy burden to bear, and he bore it lightly.

Dai grinned. 'As bad as Edgar, isn't it? Ah well, our stomachs must come later. First we must take our belongings and our cattle in charge, and find our lodgings and our merchants.'

Kazan tugged on his sleeve. 'Agathi and me, we wish to spend some time in the *hamam.*' She pulled a face. 'So long a journey. We are not clean.'

Dai exchanged rueful looks with Twm. 'There is no *hamam*,' he said.

'What do you mean? How can there be no *hamam* in such a great city?'

'It's what I say. Nothing like it here, Kazan. No fresh running water, no piped hot water…not here, nor in England.' He sighed. 'And certain it is there's none in my country. Here, there's no fresh water, see, except for rain water that's stored in cisterns.'

She shuddered. 'They are *barbar,* these Venetians.'

'I cannot agree, *siorina.* It is true we must collect rainwater but now the *bigolanti,* the water carriers, you would say, bring fresh water from the mainland. We are very well served, even if we have no *hamam.*' Trevior's gaze flicked over her, from her head, down her body, to her feet in her soft-skin boots. He said nothing more but she shivered, hating the way his eyes raked her body. He swept past them, down the gangplank and on to the quay. There was cheering. Dai gripped Kazan's shoulder.

'Best stay quiet,' he said, 'and keep out of his way.' He felt her eyes on his face. 'This is not a man to be trusted,' he murmured. He watched the man's progress, his swagger down the gangplank on to the dock. He was greeted by a group of young men. He was laughing and smiling, at ease, relieved to be here in Venezia, his home, with his ship and cargo safe and with an idle winter to look forward to.

Sailors were coming down from the ship ready to unload the cargo on to the quay. Radovan and Rizo and Sanuto drew alongside Trevior. Dai saw Trevior's sneering smile; he made some comment to the young nobles standing next to him that brought from them a burst of laughter and burning blood to Radovan's face. He turned away from the lounging group of young nobles but Trevior laughed aloud contemptuously.

It was all so quick. Trevior glanced up at the cog, his gaze locked on Dai's. He scowled and turned back to his friends. He must have made another jibe because Radovan swung round, fury in his face, and Dai heard him shout, 'Not even you have the right! You have destroyed my family. You think you have escaped punishment. You are wrong.' The next instant the Croatian had drawn a blade, his bread knife; it flashed up and down as he stabbed Trevior, once and once again, before he vanished into the crowd, swallowed up by the lingering fog. It had been the work of seconds. Trevior collapsed, blood seeping from the wounds, held up by the young men who were exclaiming with alarm and anger while his family still rejoiced at his arrival and the arrival of the goods. Then the outcry and the realisation that he was wounded and shrieking cries of lamentation and anger overrode the daily routine. It was tumult, an immediate order to hunt down the sailor who had dared strike a noble. A contingent of armed men set off into the crowded streets.

Rizo was there, Dai saw, and Sanuto, and they could have stopped Radovan but they didn't. Justice, Dai thought, as claimed by the workers when nobles look after themselves. Like the *Cymru,* now the *Sais* were in charge. Only way to look after affairs was to take them in hand yourself. As for him, he hoped Radovan reached safety. He saw Trevior taken away, bleeding. He wouldn't die. The knife thrust was not enough despite the blood. He'd seen such wounds before, with not enough force behind the blows to properly penetrate a man's thick jacket. He wondered about Radovan and his dead father and the girl who was raped and the mother who was without hope. But it was not his business, he reminded himself; he had best set about keeping his little party safe in this city of splendour.

Francesco da Ginstinianis was waiting for him on the quay. He said, 'You saw what happened?'

'Some of it. The young man Radovan was provoked but I do not know what was said.'

'He should never have been under Trevior's command. I advised against it. Now he will be hunted and punished, this foolish young man. This is a serious crime, a worker to assault a noble with a weapon, and blood drawn.' He was impatient. 'Violence is an action that disturbs the peace and the honour of the state.'

'The honour of his family was in his mind,' Dai said, drily, 'and the harm done to his sister.'

'You know of this?' Da Ginstinianis' voice was sharp. 'Of course. Gossip. Always there is gossip. But that was dealt with long ago, and Trevior fined.' He shrugged. 'After all, it is not a serious crime. Not for the workers. As they say, it is only placing the woman a little sooner in the state she would become by marriage and love.'

Dai said nothing. He wondered if da Ginstinianis would be so tolerant if it concerned his sisters but Dai had no wish to quarrel with him, and it was clear they would never agree on this. The Venetian sighed again. 'It is a bad affair.' He glanced at the Welshman, would have said more but hesitated.

'It's nothing you need say, Francesco. I'm knowing to keep my mouth shut. I'm a foreigner in your city and I don't know its ways.'

'I am glad to hear you say this, my friend. Would you accept other advice?'

Dai nodded. He wondered if it would be the same that was offered by Trevior.

'You are here for some days, I think?'

'Only as long as we need for business. It's across the mountains we want to be before the winter weather blocks the Pass.'

'Even so, it would be well if your two young ladies were more appropriately clothed.' He pulled a face. 'This is a city where much store is set by appearance. All must be correct.'

'*Sior* Trevior has already offered us this advice.'

'Ah, my friend, please do not be offended by my plain speaking. It is practical advice I offer.'

He smiled. '*Sior* Marco is not always discreet, I know, but he would not wish your ladies to be open to comment and insult, as I do not. I realise it would be impossible, in a few days, to choose material and have clothes made.' He hesitated again. When he spoke, it seemed to be at random. 'You have met my two sisters.' Another pause. 'They are much the same small size as your Kazan and Edgar's betrothed. I wonder…'

Dai looked at him.

'…would your ladies do my family the honour of accepting gowns? Not new, you understand, and not of the latest mode, but of good quality. I would not offer your two ladies anything other than that.'

'It's very generous you are, Francesco. Do you think your sisters will be happy to be equally generous?'

'They will be more than happy to be of help. Especially,' he added, 'when they know they will have new gowns in the latest fashion to replace the ones they give as gifts.'

Dai chuckled. He recalled Kazan preening in Rémi's best clothes that first evening she had arrived at the *han*. What would she make of these western gowns with their long flowing skirts and over-dresses, she who was used to the freedom of *şalvar* and *gömlek*?

The day was full of business. It seemed like Attaleia all over again. Edgar was packed off to the merchants' *fondaco* to book lodgings. He took with him Kazan and Agathi. Dai had stolen moments to speak with Kazan, to order her not to go out alone, as she had done in Attaleia, with such disastrous consequences. He knew his anxiety made him abrupt. He gritted his teeth. Tried again.

'It is what I am wishing, Kazan. I beg you to stay safe indoors.'

Kazan laid her fingers on the scar that ran from cheekbone to jaw, healed after two months at sea though it would never fade, as the memory of that last terrifying night in Attaleia would never fade.

'Do not beg me,' she said. 'It is not fitting. Of course I shall do as you wish,'

'*Diolch yn fawr, cariad.*' He couldn't help himself. He turned his face and quickly kissed her hand where it had rested against the scar. 'Now, go with Edgar.'

They said goodbye to Brother Jerome who set off for the friary. Twm was to join him later.

'First I'll come with you to the Bank, Dafydd, in case there are messages to read.'

It was for Giles to stable and settle the horses. 'Fresh air first, Giles, and some exercise.'

Giles gestured towards the Rivo Alto Bridge and the loud clattering of hooves and high-pitched neighing. Two horses were being raced across it, pedestrians leaping out of their way and cursing loudly. Behind the riders, a pack of hunting dogs, tails flowing behind, mouths open, red tongues lolling. 'Like that?' He grinned.

'Not like that! It's time that was outlawed.'

Dai and Rémi had business. After amassing the baggage, there was the Bank and accounts to be settled. Dai thanked God for Rémi and his skill in numbers. There was a letter as well, from Heinrijc Mertens. Dai held it up in front of his face. 'He knows I cannot read.' He was exasperated. 'Rémi is better at numbers than lettering. What shall I do without you, Twm?' He watched Twm's grave face. 'Well?'

'He knows the fleet is late and hopes you are safe though he does not doubt it. He says you have five of your nine lives left to you.' Twm raised an eyebrow but didn't comment. 'He says you are to finalise the contract with Francesco Corner. He says ten years as a shareholder is enough.' Twm exclaimed. 'England has forbidden export of fleeces to Flanders! This is worse than we thought, Dafydd.' He read on, silently, his face serious. 'There is much written here that I do not like to speak aloud.' He looked about him. 'He urges you to destroy this letter at once, as soon as you know its contents.'

'Yes?'

'Corner is flying close to the wind. Before long he will lose money – this year, next year, maybe even the year after. Heinrijc does not think it advisable to renew a contract.'

'What else?'

'He has heard that his friend Pietro da Silvano, the glass-maker of Murano, was arrested this autumn.'

'*What? Sior* Silvano?'

'Hush Dafydd. This is Venezia, remember. There were accusations laid against him. Heinrijc didn't know the outcome when he wrote this but he is worried because you always trade with da Silvano. He says to make enquiries first, if he was found innocent or guilty.'

'What accusations? Does he say?'

'Revealing secrets of the glass trade.'

'But *Sior* Silvano would never reveal the secrets of glass-making!'

'Heinrijc Mertens is worried enough to write this, Dafydd.'

'If he were found guilty it would be a heavy punishment.'

Twm thought a moment. 'Where would it be safe to ask?'

'There's always gossip in this place. Keep our ears open, isn't it? Maybe the Friary will know. If not, Murano will have the answer.'

Twm nodded. 'I'll bring word as soon as I find out anything. Tread carefully, Dafydd.'

'Send Heinrijc a message to say we've arrived and are safe. Soon on our way home.' The message would arrive in a month, he knew, as long as the weather stayed well enough. They'd be following soon after. Under two months, they'd be in Flanders. If they were lucky they'd be there before the new year. Over-winter in Ieper then spring would see him and Kazan in England. God willing, her grandfather would be living still. After that? He refused to think.

They were well lodged. Kazan and Agathi were glowing with cleanliness and content after bathing in a tub of warm perfumed water provided for them by the *patronus* of the *fondaco*. 'He fell in love with Agathi's beautiful face and golden hair, I think,' Kazan chuckled. 'It is not like the *hamam*, but it is good to be clean.' She sniffed. 'You are also much in need of hot water, Welshman.'

He flicked her cheek. 'Impudent wretch.' He knew he smelt rank after the months of voyaging. 'Later,' he said. 'Let's see what's for supper.'

It was an evening of listening to news and gossip. Venezia always had news and gossip. There had been a storm in Paris that August. Thousands of trees uprooted in the woods about Vincennes. The Scots had attacked an English merchant ship in the mouth of the Seine. Edward, the third Edward, had retaliated, attacking the Moray Firth, his soldiers pillaging as they went. Now there were rumours the French were raiding the Channel Islands. King Edward had asked for money from the Pope to fund a Crusade and had been refused but he had taken it anyway from St Mary's Abbey. The talk went back and forth, but most of all it centred on Venezia, even amongst these foreign merchants, and the imminent threat of war. City states had formed allies, each with each and against others. The balance of power was strong on both sides; strong enough, perhaps, to avert war but now, at the closing of this year 1336, the prospect of peace was fragile. If there was war here, and war between England and France, what hope did honest merchants have of making a profit? Nobody spoke of Pietro da Silvano. Whatever had happened was old news. Best not ask questions in this crowd of strangers. Too much gossip, see, in this sea-city. He hoped Kazan and Agathi were comfortable in the women's quarters. His mind drifted to the time when she slept next to him in the *han*, woke in the morning next to him, so that, if he chose, he could have stretched out his hand to hers. He loved her then; how much more he loved her now, knowing her, living with her. He realised the man next to him was asking a question, forced himself to focus, answer.

2

You'd fancy she had wintered, sure enough,
Where icebergs rear themselves in constant snow:
And Lord! if in mid-August it is so,
How in the frozen months must she come off?
(Dante Alighieri: 1265 – 1321)

Kazan was awake before the *Marangone* bell rang out to announce the beginning of the working day. The shifting light woke her, glimmering through the slats of the shuttered windows. The wind had risen sometime in the night, dispersing the fog. Today the sky was the light, clear blue of late autumn and it threatened rain. She opened a shutter and looked through the window on to the canal, already busy with boats, buildings reflected in the water and shadows rippling across the surface of the buildings. She had never seen anything like this. A broad street of water with buildings rising out of it, arches on the ground floors because this was the place of business and where boats could unload. The *fondaco* might be for visiting merchants but it was the same for the noble families living in great houses they called *casa* along the length of this waterfront. There, too, the ground floor was given over to business and the families lived above. Some buildings had a third floor, and everywhere the huge chimneys of Venezia were already smoking, fires lit and the business of the day begun.

There was more business for Dai and Rémi. 'But later you will take me on the *Canalazzo* in one of those strange black boats with the prows like galloping horses?' Kazan begged. 'It is perfectly respectable. I have seen the women who travel in these *gondola* and they are very handsome and very rich.'

Dai smiled at her innocence. 'But not respectable, my Kazan,' he said.

'No? Is it so?' She chuckled. 'But all the same…'

'Will I take you in one of these black *gondola*? Do you trust yourself to me?'

'Always,' she said, very serious. 'Always I trust you.'

It was late morning when a messenger arrived from the sisters of Francesco da Ginstinianis inviting them to the *casa*. It was a very formal, very polite invitation and Kazan wrinkled her nose.

They do this because the brother says they must, she thought. She sighed. These noble Venetian women, they were very correct, very beautiful, very obedient. Very foreign.

Edgar was to accompany them, and the servant who had brought the message. He was an austere man dressed in severe black with the blazon of the da Ginstinianis household on his cloak. He made her a stiff bow. 'I am sent because I am a trusted servant who has been with the family for many years,' he said. 'You need have no fear, *siorina*. You are well protected. *Sior* Francesco has sent his private *gondola* for your use so there is no need to walk through the *calli*. Our ladies do not ride on the public boats.'

She flushed but lifted her chin. 'I am not afraid, *sior*. It is only that I gave my promise to *sior* Dafydd to stay indoors, and a promise is a promise.'

The servant hid his surprise. This was not how the ladies of Venezia spoke, and certainly not to a servant, but this young woman stared boldly at him, though what she said was honourable and obedient. Edgar said, 'Dai meant only that you were not to go out alone, Kazan.'

'You think so, Edgar? I would not want him to be disappointed in me.'

'He would want us to go.'

She smiled suddenly, her face lighting up. 'I would like very much to ride in this boat of *sior* Francesco on this street that is water. And you, Agathi, you would like this?' She chuckled. 'We shall have adventures to tell Dai after all.'

Agathi nodded, her eyes wide with pleasure and excitement. They wrapped themselves in their cloaks, as much to hide their shabby clothes as to keep themselves warm. They went down the stairs of the *fondaco* and out on to the *fondamenta,* the pavement beside the canal. The arches of the building cast shadows over the *gondola* bobbing on the water. It was dark green, with the same blazon of colours. The servant handed in the two young women and their escort and stepped in beside them. Kazan and Agathi exchanged startled glances; the inside of the gondola was richly painted in reds and golds and the seats were well cushioned in brocade. This was a sumptuous floating palace.

'It is a short distance only,' he told them. The boatman poled them away from the side. Kazan watched him, dazzled by the ease with which he handled the long, thin boat, the sinuous movement of the pole in the water. Sunlight reflected off the water and on to buildings which themselves reflected looking-glass images on the water. It glanced off glassed windows. It struck the pale stone. A city of light, except that the water of the Canalazzo was dark and mysterious. The seas at home revealed the pebbly bottom and small fish swimming in beams of sunlight. It glistened. Here, nothing penetrated its dark surface. A city of contrasts, of light and dark. The dispossessed slept at night under the Rivo Alto Bridge whilst the nobles slept in grand houses. A city of marvels and miracles, of saints and churches and monasteries and nunneries but its true worship was commerce. Better to be a *yürük*, and free to move from winter dwelling to summer pasture than a vagrant in this city. She wondered where Radovan had slept. She wondered what would happen to his mother and his sister, who would look after them. His father was dead and they were alone, as Agathi and her brother Niko were alone. Now Niko had a new family in Attaleia while Agathi…she glanced at the girl, her pale gold hair gleaming. She was smiling, touching Edgar's hand to bring his attention to something on the further bank of the *Canalezzo*. Lucky Agathi, she thought, to be betrothed to the one she loves, and who loves her. She remembered the pale shivering girl they had rescued from slavery, despair and hopelessness in her face. Now, Agathi smiled and sometimes laughed. That is Dai's doing, she thought. It is because of him that Agathi is free and can smile and laugh. And Niko and Hatice and pale, dead Asperto, all rescued by Dai. And me. Such care he has taken of me. Such a worry I have been to him. She looked at her hand, the hand that had stroked the scar on his face. She felt again the light warm touch of his lips.

'I am sorry. What did you say, *sior*?'

'I said only that we are coming to the ca' Ginstinianis. See?'

It was a grand building indeed, set back from the canal side with steps leading up to the *fondamenta* and the arches of the ground floor. There was a grand entrance, with skillfully carved stonework and heavy wooden doors. The first floor projected over the ground floor, protection from sun and rain. A row of glittering windows ran along its length, the stonework casement shaped to arched points. They did not enter through the great doorway. The servant led them into a narrow *calle* that ran alongside a smaller canal that he called a *rio* and through an archway into a courtyard where a huge cistern head of carved stone sat in the centre. Steps led up to the first floor. Their cloaks were taken from them and they were ushered into the *salon*. Kazan looked about her curiously. It was a large room lit by the windows she had seen from the canal. At the further end, close to a huge fireplace, were ornate carved chairs where the sisters of *sior* Ginstinianis were seated. At their feet sat a bright-eyed, black-nosed little dog, a jewelled collar glittering against white fur. His ears were cocked, his eyes inquisitive, his whole body quivering with friendly curiosity.

Not so the sisters. They rose in unison and glided across the length of the salon. Their gowns trailed behind them, the folds of gleaming soft scarlet and pale blue whispering and rustling on the polished wooden floor. Their hair was elaborately plaited and pleated over the crowns of their heads. Kazan saw the startled look that passed between them as they took in the foreign women strangely clad in garments that were so indecently masculine. Beside these dazzling rich noble women, they looked wretched indeed – plucked crows to glistening plumage.

'I am Elizabeta da Ginstinianis, and this is my sister, Alegreza,' said the older of the two. 'We welcome you to our home. We are pleased to be of service to you.' Her voice was polite and as cold as the mid-winter ice on the mountains; her smile stretched her mouth in a thin, tight line and did not reach her eyes. Kazan's heart sank. Out of the corner of her eye she saw Agathi looking nervous and ill at ease. She smiled shyly when Edgar introduced her as his betrothed.

'Your *promessi sposi*?' Elizabeta raised politely incredulous eyebrows. This girl who looked like one of the dispossessed betrothed to this handsome young man with such golden curls and eyes as blue as the summer skies?

So this is the welcome Venezia gives to its strangers, Kazan thought. Better to be a *yürük* who knew how to give proper welcome. She raised her head. 'We are grateful to you for your welcome,' she said, haughtily. 'We are strangers here in your city. To be welcomed into the home of such a noble family is an honour.' Her voice was as dry as ever Thomas's could be.

'You must first have some refreshment,' said Elizabeta. She clapped her hands and a servant appeared at the doorway with a tray that contained glass beakers chased with gold and silver and an ornate honey-coloured glass jug enamelled with scarlet berries and green leaves and blue-clad huntsmen on prancing white horses. Kazan eyed it curiously. This had been brought from the east. She recognised the style of workmanship. The servant poured light wine and proffered sweet sugar cakes. They nibbled and spoke in stilted voices. At last, the sisters rose. 'You will come with us, *siorinas*.' Elizabeta looked towards Edgar. Her voice was noticeably more affable when she spoke to him. 'My brother will be here shortly and will bear you company, *sior*. We trust your wait will be worthwhile.'

Kazan and Agathi followed the two women through dim corridors into a chamber that contained a huge carved chest and a large bed hung with deep red damask curtains. Gowns were spread out across the bed.

'We have made a selection for you. We hope you will think it appropriate.'

Kazan and Agathi looked at each other. These were beautiful gowns. 'But how can you part with them?' Kazan asked impulsively. 'These are too beautiful and too costly to give to us. It is too much to ask of you.'

The first genuine smile touched Alegreza's lips. 'It is our pleasure. Besides,' she added naively, 'these are not in the latest mode. The new fashion is for the cloth to be cut close and shaped to the body and this is what we shall have to replace these gowns we give to you. Perhaps it is better these are not so.' She cast an experienced eye over the two girls. 'My brother said you were of our height and size but you are smaller than either of us. Fitted gowns would hang loose. First, though, you will wear the *chemise*. Come, let Cristina dress you.' A stern-faced elderly maidservant came forward. She held up loose shifts of soft linen and waited until Kazan and Agathi shyly undressed.

'Hm,' said Elizabeta, 'no need for breast bands for either of them, sister.' A flash of cruel amusement came and went in her face at their embarrassment. She pointed at a fine woollen gown that was the green of fresh oak leaves in spring. 'See, sister, this green is just the colour for the dark one, I think, with that russet over-gown that never became me. It will bring out the colour in her hair. Such short hair.' She frowned then smiled and nodded. 'See, sister! Am I not right?'

She spoke across Kazan. As if I am a poppet for the dressing, Kazan thought. The over-gown was high waisted with long folds dropping away beneath her breasts. It was heavier than she had expected, she who had been used to the freedom of cotton *şalvar* and *gömlek*. She lifted an arm experimentally and felt the material of the long sleeve pull and drag.

'And for the other, this blue will match her eyes, do you not think, sister?' Alegreza said. The older sister nodded. 'Let us see.'

Some of the stiffness was gone. The sisters were absorbed in the business of dressing their living poppets. Elizabeta looked critically at Kazan standing in front of her in the russet and green. She twitched a fold into position, arranged the sleeves. 'Yes,' she said, 'this is very good.'

'Let them see for themselves, sister,' Alegreza said, eagerly. 'The looking-glasses that are made by the glass-makers of Murano are the best in the whole of the Veneto,' she told them, adding with simple pride, 'and ours is the best in Venezia.'

'And the last,' Elizabeta said, 'now that traitor da Silvano has been put to death.' Cristina pulled away a draping and a looking-glass stood clear and bright. Kazan had seen nothing like it. Agathi was closest, her shape reflected in the looking-glass, with the sun streaming through the window directly on to her. Her pale gold hair shimmered and the blue folds of the gown gleamed. Kazan gasped. 'You are so beautiful!' she exclaimed. 'Agathi, you are like an angel come to earth!'

Agathi looked wonderingly at herself. 'Is this me?' she asked. She looked across at Kazan. 'You too, Kazan, you are very beautiful, like a garden. Come and see.' Kazan walked across the room feeling the unfamiliar drag of skirts, lifting the material to make movement easier. She stared at herself in the looking-glass. 'Where is Kazan?' she murmured.

'Your hair,' Elizabeta said, addressing the girl directly for the first time, 'why is it so short?'

'I cut it when I ran away,' Kazan said calmly. 'It was better to travel as a boy.'

'Run away? Travel as a boy?' She was shocked into genuine emotion now. 'What can you mean?'

'I promised my grandmother I would travel to the country they call England to find my grandfather. It was her dying wish. But to do this I had to travel the merchant road through my country to Attaleia and from there by ship to Venezia.'

'Alone? You did all this alone?' There was no admiration in her voice.

'Until I found *sior* Dafydd and his caravan on the road to Konya.'

'And then you travelled alone in the company of men?'

As if I were one of the women who haunts the Rivo Alto, thought Kazan. She said, '*Sior* Dafydd knew my grandmother. He kept me safe.' Her head tilted up in the way Dai would have recognised as a battle sign. 'He is a man I trust with my life.'

'I have met *sior* Davide. He is a friend of my brother and known to my father through *sior* Heinrijc Mertens.' Elizabeta stumbled over the foreign name. 'He is a man of few words.' Her thin lips curled in that tight smile. He had not found favour with her, Kazan realised.

'He is my good friend.'

Alegreza tittered in a way Kazan found maddening. Elizabeta said, 'Your good friend? But that is not possible. No man can be the "good friend" of a young woman. Never. This is why our fathers and brothers keep us safe, from the young men especially, and their appetites.'

'In my country,' Kazan insisted, 'it is possible. It was the young men of my tribe who taught me to ride and shoot with the bow until I was better than any of them.'

'Ride and shoot? You did these things?'

'Of course. But not in clothes such as these. It would not be possible, not even to mount a horse.'

Elizabeta had frozen into outraged condemnation. Alegreza rolled her eyes at her sister, open-mouthed, avid with curiosity.

'Were none of these young men in love with you?'

Kazan chuckled. 'There was one but Nene – my grandmother – sent him away.'

'Your grandmother did so? But what of your father?'

Kazan hesitated. The dark waters of the *Canalazzo* came into her mind. This was too deep to explain to these disdainful women. 'I have no other family and now my grandmother is dead I go to my English grandfather. *Sior* Dafydd escorts me.'

'When *sior* Davide came here two years ago, a very handsome man came with him. He was tall and dark haired with very dark eyes and long lashes, like a girl's. Did he travel with you?'

Kazan recognised Alegreza's description immediately, and her interest. 'You must mean Thomas,' she said. 'Yes, he travelled with Dai. He is very handsome, as you say.'

'You must be a little in love with him, I think.'

Kazan shook her head. She grinned. 'It is lucky I am not. He has promised himself to the Friars of St Francis.'

Alegreza pouted. Elizabeta's laugh was mocking. 'Now you have broken my poor sister's heart. She was much taken by this young man but, as you say, it is lucky he has promised himself to God. My father has a husband in mind for her.'

'But he is old and ugly,' Alegreza complained.

'He is rich,' Elizabeta said. 'A man without money is a corpse that walks, as the saying goes.' She turned to Agathi. 'What of the young man who has escorted you here today? Your *promessi sposi?*'

'He takes her now to his family in England where they will marry.' Kazan smiled at the blushing Agathi, determined to say nothing of Edgar's past to this calculating woman. 'I think Edgar will fall in love with you all over again when he sees you looking so beautiful.'

'Are you also betrothed, *siorina* Elizabeta?' Agathi asked in her soft, shy voice.

'Yes, of course. We shall be married soon, before the winter, now that Francesco is home. It is the duty of the older sister to marry before the younger one. My home will be with my husband's family in the ca'Trevior.'

'Trevior?'

'Yes. I am to marry Jacopo Trevior, the older brother of Marco who was the *patronus* of your ship.'

'He is not as old as the *sior* Guiseppe,' muttered Alegreza. 'Nor as ugly.'

'Nor as rich,' responded Elizabeta. 'Not yet,' she said confidently.

Kazan said, '*Sior* Francesco did not tell us of this.'

'He did not know.' Elizabeta smiled. 'He was away with the fleet when we exchanged our promises. And now our brother has gone to visit Marco, to see how he is recovering from the wounds inflicted yesterday by that madman.'

Cristina had been busy plaiting and looping Agathi's hair. She threaded a gold-spangled blue ribbon through it. Elizabeta nodded approvingly. 'Now see what can be done with this short-haired one, Cristina.'

'If the Signora agrees, perhaps a green ribbon?'

'And then let us show our handiwork to your *promessi sposi* and our brother, if he is returned.'

He was. The sisters entered the *salon* first and clapped their hands for attention. 'See what a miracle we have achieved, brother!' exclaimed Elizabeta. She stood aside and beckoned Kazan and Agathi forward. Kazan, behind Agathi, saw Edgar's eyes glisten with adoration. Lucky Agathi. *Sior* Francesco came forward, raising Agathi's hand and bowing over it. '*Bella bella*,' he said admiringly. He turned to Kazan. 'And you also, *siorina* Kazan.'

She smiled. 'Not so *bella bella* as this angel, I think, but,' she sighed, 'I am no longer Kazan.'

'Then what should I call you?'

She paused, shrugged. 'I was named Sophia after my grandmother

but I have never been called by that name. It sounds strange to me.'
She thought of the image in the looking-glass that was not her. I am a
stranger to myself, she thought. All these reflections in this city hide
truth. She shivered.

'How did you find our brother Marco?' asked Elizabeta.

'A slight fever. The wounds were not fatal, thank the good Lord.
I shall return later. I wished to see that all was well with our two
guests.'

'It is a disgraceful business!' Elizabeta said viciously. 'When that
murderer is caught, he should have his wicked hand cut off and hung
around his neck and then be strung by his neck for such a crime. A
worker to attack a noble, to draw blood!'

'Hush, sister. Such hasty words are not becoming to a noble lady.
Marco is alive yet, and the surgeon says he is strong and healthy in
spite of the fever. No murder has been committed but it is, as you
say, a disgraceful business. The Ten will have justice, no fear of that.'

'Has the man been found?'

'Not yet. They are searching.'

Kazan's mouth opened to protest, to say what she had seen and
heard from the deck of the boat; she caught Edgar's warning look,
the slightest shake of his head. She lowered her head, kept her mouth
tight-shut.

Afterwards, in the gondola, this time with only Edgar as escort,
she said, 'Why did you wish me to stay silent? Should we not try to
help Radovan?'

Edgar sighed. 'Venezia has its own laws and strict regulations. We
are strangers here. We do not understand their ways.' He
remembered what Francesco had told him when they were alone
together; how there was talk that the Croatian had been hired as an
assassin. Nonsense, of course, but it worried him. 'Let's ask Dai,' he
said. 'He'll know what best to do. He knows this city.'

He had not returned. Rémi was there. Dai, he signed, had gone
to the island of Murano to find out for himself what had happened

to a glass-maker he knew, one Pietro da Silvano. He knew the glass-makers there; he would ask them. Kazan was disappointed. She had wanted to walk in and surprise him in all her finery but Thomas was there, sitting with Giles over a jug of wine. He looked at them, astonished and laughing.

'You are transformed into a girl at last, Kazan,' he teased her, as an older brother would. 'You too, Agathi. Whoever would have thought a slave girl and a *yürük* boy would turn out as Venetian ladies of fashion?' He grinned. 'I'd give good gold to see Blue's face.'

'He would still call me Fustilugs,' said Kazan.

Thomas laughed outright. 'I expect he would. Now, sit down and listen, Kazan. I've been waiting half the afternoon for you. I have news for you.'

'News for me?' Her face paled.

'Good news, I think. The brothers at the friary know of the great artist Giotto of Padova who has done much for the Franciscans.'

Kazan and Agathi looked at him, puzzled. These names were nothing to them. 'This is good news for me?' she asked doubtfully.

'The *Sior* Giotto uses real people to paint the figures in his *frescoes*. Many years ago he met your grandfather, Kazan.' He sat back and waited for her to comprehend his news.

'He knew my grandfather?'

'And he painted him. The friars said it was the year of the great comet. One of them, an old man now, takes great pride in remembering the friendship between the storyteller and the painter.'

She drew an ecstatic breath. 'Can I meet this *sior* Giotto? See these paintings?'

'See the paintings, yes. They are in the Chapel built by the Scrovegni family in Padova. It is not so far from here – a day's travel by horse or by boat along the river. And it is on your way to the mountain road. But meet Giotto? No. He is an old man – and a rich one – and lives in Firenze.'

She drew another breath. This grandfather, known only through

Nene's stories, was becoming real. They would stop in Padova, she knew Dai would agree, and she could see her grandfather's likeness in these paintings, see the young man her grandmother had fallen in love with. 'That is wonderful news you bring me, Thomas.' She glanced at him through lowered lashes. 'I would like you too to see my grandfather's image. Are you sure you wish to go with the friars?'

'I am sure, Kazan.' He suddenly stretched out his hand to cover hers. 'I do not like bloodshed, Kazan; I never have done. Now I feel free to be my true self, a man of God.'

'Then you are right to go, Thomas. Dafydd will miss you. We shall all miss you. We do already,' she said, sadly. Our tribe is breaking up, smaller and smaller, she thought.

She walked down the steps with him to the Canalazzo, They stood together in the shelter of the *portico* where goods were being unloaded from laden cogs. A musty, stale smell came from the water. One of the monastery pigs was snouting into a wooden crate. They roamed freely over the city, protected by law; the sailors shrugged and ignored this one. Thomas pulled her aside to make room for a young sailor panting under the weight of the heavy barrel he shouldered.

'Do you care for what Dafydd thinks, Kazan?' he asked, suddenly.

'Yes, of course. How could I not?'

'He loves you. Do you know that?'

'As a man loves his horse or his sister.'

'No, Kazan. He loves you as a man loves his woman. He would have you to wife but he thinks you can never love him.'

She stared at him, her face pale. 'No. You are mistaken. He has never given me any sign.'

'He wouldn't. He is honourable. He thinks he must protect you, and that means from himself as well as others.'

'He does not love me.'

'I say he does. Do you love him?'

'I do not know. It is not as my grandmother told me.' *What was it then that tore my heart and soul? Who can tell, girl? When you feel this, then you will feel love and you will give your heart and soul and life for your beloved.* 'I do not know.' She was agitated. 'He is my good friend.'

'I'm sorry. I've upset you but he will never speak and I could not leave you without speaking for him. No,' anticipating her question, 'he has not asked me to do so and he would be very angry if he knew I had said so much. Don't hurt him, Kazan. He is the best of men.'

'I know that. I would never hurt him. Never.' She was passionate, rejecting what he said, and he sighed, his dark face all angles and planes and so handsome. She wondered how she could ever have imagined herself in love with him.

'No. I don't think you would ever intend hurting him.'

There was no place in this *fondaco* to be alone, to be quiet, to think. Always there was coming and going, and she and Agathi were the centre of much exclaiming and admiration. One man produced a fiddle, another a pipe, and they played cheerfully and discordantly until their friends begged them to stop. 'A donkey is trying to sing my song – he gives a donkey's bray,' one man warbled the lines from an old song and there was a burst of laughter. But here was Evrat le Breton who played the lute like a *troubadour* and who sang with the voice of an angel; not loud and harsh like these donkeys but soft and sweet and melodious as was fitting for two such beautiful ladies. Now listen!

Sweet noble heart, pretty lady,
I am wounded by love
I am sad and pensive,
I have no joy or mirth,
for to you, my sweet companion,
I have given my heart.

Evrat le Breton's pure tenor voice rose high and fell and rose again; the strings of the lute rippled in unison. *I am wounded by love.* Was it true, as Thomas had said? *I have given my heart.* He had given no sign; he had never given any sign that she was anything other than Kazan. True, he called her *cariad*, but that was what he might call a loved child. She was so lost in thought she didn't see him arrive but suddenly there he was, dusty and tired and hungry and with such a sternness about him that she dismissed Thomas' words as nonsense. He came over to their small group and sat down next to her.

'Very fine plumage it is, Fustilugs.' He watched her face a moment. 'Well, Kazan, what troubles you?'

'Am I Kazan? Me, I do not know who I am.'

I am Çiçek, granddaughter of Sophia-the-Wise
I am Çiçek, granddaughter of Will-the-Wordmaker

'You are you, always and only you. Your name does not matter.'

'And these clothes?'

'You look very fine in them.'

She waited.

He sighed. 'You are always beautiful. In these fripperies, of course; the colours suit you. Those sisters of Francesco have chosen well. But,' he smiled, reminiscing, 'Rémi's best clothes suited you just as well. And your blue *şalvar* and *gömlek.*' He paused, thought of his own fraught day. 'Is that all that troubles you, *cariad*?'

Am I truly your cariad? she longed to ask. Instead, she said, 'Those sisters, they said no man could be a friend of a woman.'

Those sisters, he thought irritably, should be boiled alive in their own olive oil. The older one especially. 'They are Venetian,' he said, 'and noble and sheltered. You are wiser than that.'

She sighed. 'The older one – Elizabeta – asked me why my hair was so short so I told her I travelled as a boy.'

'I expect,' he said, calmly, 'she was very shocked.'

'She was. Dai, you should have seen her face – like a landed fish gasping for water! Then stiff like a corpse.' She lifted her eyes to his, shaking her head. 'I should not say such things when they have given Agathi and me such beautiful gowns to wear.'

'I remember the *siorina* Elizabeta,' he said. 'It seems to me you have earned them now, isn't it?'

'But Dai, what do you think? She is betrothed to the brother of that slimy sea-snake, that Marco Trevior.'

'Is she now? Francesco didn't tell me that.'

'He did not know until he returned. I think,' she added thoughtfully, 'he is not pleased by this.'

'Hm.'

'*Sior* Francesco was at the ca'Trevior. You should have heard the things they said! It is not fair that Rado is the villain. Marco Trevior is not a good man. I heard Rado, Dai. He said Marco Trevior had ruined his family. What did he mean? You must tell me.'

'Hush – speak quietly. Tell me first – did you say any of this to Francesco or his sister?'

She shook her head. 'Edgar would not let me.'

Dai sighed in relief. Sensible Edgar. He considered; better if she did know, now they were no longer confined to the boat. 'Marco Trevior,' he said slowly, 'raped Radovan's sister.'

'But that is terrible!'

'Not in Venetian law. It would have been more serious if she had been a young girl…'

'Or one of the noble ladies?'

'Exactly. He was fined and so justice was seen to be done.'

'But Rado does not think so. And he was provoked. You saw as well.'

'True, but nothing can come of bearing witness. Venetian law is strict, especially when it concerns a worker who attacks an official, let alone a noble. That is a serious crime.'

'That Trevior is a snake, a slug. He is not fit to live.'

'Do not say this to anyone else, *cariad*,' he said, urgently. 'It is not safe. Better we leave as soon as possible.' He looked at her. 'Perhaps I should teach you how to defend yourself against these young nobles.'

Unexpectedly, she grinned. 'There is no need. Before we left Attaleia, Blue told me what I must do. He showed me how to hit where it hurts men most.'

'Did he indeed?'

'Like a felled ox, he said, even for a man his size. I wish I had known this when that donkey Veçdet and Big Aziz captured Niko and me.'

'You never fail to surprise me, *cariad*. I hope you will not practise on me. And I trust you will not tell the icy Elizabeta.' He grinned. 'Though I'd give a lot to see her face if you did. Come, I am hungry and dirty and you and Agathi should not be here in company with all these men. You will shock all of Venezia, *cariad*. Time you were in your own quarters.'

She pulled a face. 'It is dull there. The women talk of clothes and conquests.'

'All the same, go. There's a group of merchants leaving for the north. If they leave tomorrow we should try to leave with them. Could you be ready?'

'Of course. I shall be glad to leave this place.' Where nothing is as it seems, she thought. Here, I can trust nothing.

'Take this.' She stared down at the object he held out to her. It gleamed in the lamplight.

'What is it?'

'A trinket to wear with your fine new feathers, my peacock.'

She felt the coolness of metal, gazed at the round of bracelet cunningly worked in twists of gold and silver and copper, recognised the workmanship of the country she had left behind. 'For me?'

'Of course for you. Come – take it.'

'I shall treasure it always, Dafydd. It is a beautiful gift.'

He grunted. 'Now *nos da, fy nghariad*. Go.'

He watched her pause by Agathi's side, saw the long look Agathi and Edgar exchanged, and sighed. He watched both girls leave the room to a male chorus of regrets, then beckoned to Giles and Edgar.

'Where is Rémi?'

'Gone to check on the horses. He should be back soon.'

'Is there a problem, Dai?'

'I don't know, *bach*. I hope not.' He waited until he had been served with wine and a platter of steaming clams. For once he was uncaring what he ate, as long as he filled his belly. It had been a long, hard day. 'Best we leave as soon as possible, all the same.'

'With the German merchants?'

Dai nodded. 'And they have two women in their party.'

'What's happened?' Giles asked. Dai looked about him. They were in a shadowy corner and no one within earshot. 'The glass-maker I've traded with before, Pietro da Silvano; he was arrested early this autumn. Heinrijc wrote to warn me that he was accused of betraying the secrets of glass making. It is a very serious crime in this city.'

'Go on.'

'Today I went to the island of Murano to find out the truth.' Dai remembered the averted faces, the silence, the hard looks. A beggar tugged at his sleeve, a hunched, fetid, hooded creature whining for alms. Dai palmed money into the man's filthy hand. The beggar mumbled his thanks. He tugged on Dai's sleeve again. 'The *basilica*,' he muttered, 'of holy Maria and Donato the dragon slayer. I can tell you what you want to know.' Instinct warned him to go as quietly as possible to this ancient *basilica*, all dark red brick, on the side of a canal.

'He was imprisoned while the Ten made their *inquisito*,' Dai told them. 'Da Silvano was found guilty. There was too much evidence against him and no one dared speak in his defence. They were all too frightened. The beggar said men came to threaten them and their families if they spoke for him. He didn't know who had set them on.' He was grim faced. 'It is unthinkable that he should have been found guilty. Da Silvano was known as an honest man, a man of great honour. '

'Was?'

'He was executed last week – the two men hanging in the Piazzetta of San Marco were his men, and found guilty with him.'

'What happened to him?'

'Oh, an honourable death,' Dai said. 'He comes of a noble family and to save the honour of the name he was taken by boat into the lagoon and drowned.'

'May God rest his soul,' said Edgar. He was profoundly shocked by the contradictions in this sea-city, a city where it was accepted sport for the young noble men to invade the nunneries and monasteries and cause havoc. A fine, a minimal fine, Thomas had told them. No wonder this city had been excommunicated.

'Da Silvano's young nephew has vanished. They still search for him, and for da Silvano's contacts: I am one of them. You must leave as soon as possible, get Agathi and Kazan to safety.'

'I for one will be glad to leave,' said Giles. 'Give me the open spaces of Anatolia any day. Too much gossip and secrecy here for my liking. It seems to me any man can be accused behind his back, whatever the law states. Anonymous letters burnt unread? I don't believe it. Word of mouth straight to the inner ear more like.' He screwed up his face at Dai's warning glance. 'I know. Crime of Speech.' He thrust out his tongue and mimed cutting it off. Edgar shuddered.

'Settled then? We leave tomorrow?'

He didn't tell them the secret he had uncovered, there in the shadows of the *basilica,* how he had spoken with a hunched, ragged old man who had the rounded arm and supple hand of a young man and a face he recognised. And behind them, the relics of the dragon slain by Donato.

3

He stopped attentive, like a man who listens,
Because the eye could not conduct him far
Through the black air, and through the heavy fog.
(Inferno, Canto 1X, Dante Alighieri: 1265 – 1321)

It was only when she and Agathi had reached the women's quarters that Kazan realised she had not told him of the man Giotto and her grandfather's likeness that they would see in Padova. Time enough. Tonight, he was tired and hungry and, she thought, downcast. She remembered guiltily that she had not asked him about his own day. The only other occupants were the two German women, already in the bed they all shared, and sleeping. One snored quietly; the other, Kazan knew, later in the night would grind her teeth. The girls were about to undress each other, take off the beautiful gowns and prepare for bed, when there was a discreet tap at the door of the sleeping chamber. A dimpled, blushing maidservant stood there.

'There's a young man wishes speech with you, *siorina,*' she whispered.

'A young man? What is his name?' Kazan's heart lurched. It could not be Rado. He would not do anything so dangerous.

'He did not want to give it but I know him from childhood. It is Rizo, the curly-haired sailor.' She flicked curious eyes at the small foreign girl who looked so beautiful in her new gown. A romance here, she thought, and felt sorry for the quiet brown man. 'What shall I tell him, *siorina?*'

'Nothing. I'll come myself.'

'He says be very quiet.'

Kazan glanced at Agathi, raised her eyebrows. Agathi said, 'Should you do this, Kazan? Meet with Rizo at night, and alone?'

'He means me no harm. He may have news.'

She walked quietly down the steps to the courtyard. It was shadowy, deserted, the arches black. For a moment it seemed she was back in Attaleia and her heart raced. 'Rizo?' she breathed.

A dark shadow detached itself from one of the pillars inside the covered way.

'Is that really you, *siorina* Kazan?'

'It is – in new feathers, but Kazan for all that. Why are you here and like this?'

'I have news. There is danger for *sior* Davide.' He jerked his head towards the busy, noisy men's quarters. 'It is too crowded in there. I must not be seen talking with him.' A burst of laughter and the start of drunken singing. A bawdy song.

She drew a breath, kept her voice calm and quiet. 'Tell me.'

'Marco Trevior's father is to lay an accusation against *sior* Davide tomorrow. He will accuse *sior* Davide of setting Rado on to assassinate his son. He says he has evidence.'

'What evidence can he have? Such an accusation is not true!'

'Rado took *sior* Davide into his confidence.'

'I know only that they spoke together.'

'That's it. They were seen. Marco has spies everywhere. He says they were conspiring against him. That is not all. He says also that *sior* Davide was part of the conspiracy to betray the glass-making secrets of Murano. He knows that *sior* Davide was at Murano today asking about da Silvano.'

'I know nothing of this.' Da Silvano. Where had she heard that name? She looked up at Rizo's face. It was in deep shadow. She could see only the whites of his eyes gleaming in the dark. 'How do you know all this?'

'I have a cousin who is employed in the ca'Trevior. He heard the father talking with the son. When my cousin heard the names of Radovan and *sior* Davide he listened.' She felt him shrug. 'This is how it happens in Venezia. The street urchins know the name of a new *doge* before it is announced. He came to me as soon as he could and now I come to you. You must warn *sior* Davide.'

She nodded. 'What of Rado?'

'He is safe, *siorina*. We shall get him away tonight. He is not a murderer but for the attack on a noble, an attack that drew blood...' he shrugged. 'His hand cut off, perhaps two years in prison. He will be banished from Venezia for sure, so it is better he goes now and keeps his hand and his freedom. It is my belief *sior* Davide should come away with us, out of danger.'

She stared at him in the darkness, her head spinning and bile gripping her stomach. Dafydd in danger? Her hands clutched his. His grip tightened on hers. 'Listen! There is someone...'

'Indeed there is now, Rizo. This is not what I expected of you. It is Kazan's reputation you put at risk, meeting her alone like this, at night, in a deserted place.'

Dai's voice was cold, quiet, level. He couldn't believe it when the returning Rémi had signed to him that he had seen Rizo waiting in the courtyard, that Kazan – Kazan! – was hurrying to meet him. He had come down the stairs quietly, unobtrusively, swallowing his jealousy and anger though it choked him to see them there, clasping hands, murmuring together. He wanted to kill this curly-haired Venetian sailor.

Rizo had released her hands at the first words. 'I know what you are thinking, *sior* Davide, but you are mistaken...'

She brushed aside the words of both men, didn't register, as Rizo had, the aggressive stance of the man he had recognised in Attaleia as dangerous.

'Dafydd, he says you are in danger. Let him tell you quickly but be quiet. We must not be seen or heard.' And Kazan, who never cried, who had braved so many dangers, who was indomitable, leaned against his body searching for comfort. He felt her trembling, saw her hand come up to scrub away tears. His arm came round her, pulling her hard against him.

'What is this? What have you told her?'

So Rizo told his story again. He finished, 'I could not come to you in a crowded room, *sior*. I know I am wrong to speak so with the *siorina* but I did not know what else to do.'

'He risks his life, Dafydd.'

'They know I went to Murano today?'

'*Si, sior.* Spies everywhere.'

Had they seen him meet with the beggar? He prayed they had not.

'They said no one in Murano would talk with you, *sior*, because you are known as a traitor to Venezia.'

'And I was seen talking with Radovan?'

'In Spalato, by those who are loyal to Marco Trevior.'

'Damning evidence, then?'

'It would seem so, *sior.*'

'Is Radovan safe?'

'Yes, *sior.* We keep him hidden.'

'His sister and mother?'

'Safe also. I shall take care of them. I shall marry Bianca and take them both away from this city. Radovan we shall get away to safety this night.' Rizo was very serious. 'You should go with him, *sior*. You should go now, at once.'

'Tomorrow, Rizo. I must make arrangements.'

'Go now, Dafydd. Please. I beg you.'

'Tomorrow, Rizo.'

'As you wish, *sior.* Tomorrow.'

'There is the curfew, Rizo, and the *custodi*.'

'So there is, *sior*,' he said, blandly, and then he had slipped away into the shadows.

'Do not cry, *cariad*. All will be well.'

'I am not crying.' She drew a shaky breath. 'A little at first but not now. What must we do?'

'You and Agathi and Giles and Rémi and Edgar will leave tomorrow for Ieper.'

'What about you?'

'Better for me to be alone, *cariad*.'

'Safer, you mean?'

He hesitated. 'Safer, yes.'

'Then I shall do as you say.'

'Does Agathi know you came to meet Rizo?'

'Yes. She will be anxious.'

'Then you must go back to her now. The German women…'

'They are asleep. They know nothing.'

'Good. Best they don't.' He shook his head. 'You should not have come to meet him, Kazan.'

'What else could I do? I knew he would only come at this hour if it was something very important. I thought he would have news of Rado.' She looked at him in her candid way. 'What would you have us do, Agathi and me?'

'Go to bed, Sleep. Be ready to leave early in the morning.'

'And you?'

'I must talk with Giles and Edgar. And Rémi.' He sighed. Rémi would be difficult. They had always been together, ever since Dai had found him begging on the streets of Ieper with his hare's lip distorting his face and making eating and drinking all but impossible. 'He must go with you, Kazan. You must make sure he understands.'

'I shall do so. You must not worry.'

'Good girl. Come – you must leave tomorrow, early.'

Black night. Black water. The smell of algae and seaweed was heightened at night. Sounds were amplified. Water was lap-lapping and slapping against stone. Deep, dark, threatening water. This is where you came from, city, remember that. I can return you to the deeps whenever I choose.

The narrow streets funnelled sounds. Footfalls. Voices echoing. Three drunken figures stumbled into view, German, from the sound of their obscenities and snatches of bawdy song. They were out well after curfew. The maze of streets reminded Dai of the maze he had seen drawn on the great Mappa Mundi that was housed in Hereford's cathedral. So many *calli* criss-crossing each other, and then a dead end, or a bridge over a narrow canal. He had lost track of the route Rizo was taking, except that it was towards the northern *sestiere* of Cannaregio. It was where many of the workers lived, away from the upper sweep of the Canalazzo and the grand houses, in mud and straw hovels on land that had been drained many years before but where there were reed beds still. It was here they would hide, where hard-won land gave way to water, where Sanuto would bring the boat.

They were still far from safety, close to one of the great *rio* that drained the area, when Rizo's hand came down on his arm. He jerked his head towards a narrow entry. Two *custodi* of the Signori di Notte were heading towards them. The three drunken Germans wandered aimlessly into view, rowdy, shouting abuse. Rizo and Dai heard the warning: 'You have already been warned this is not the time to be out of doors, *signori*. If you do not go home you could go to jail.' One of the *custodi* raised a sheathed sword in warning. In answer, there was a stone flung so hard that the man it hit fell backwards clutching his head and shouting with pain. The second *custodi* chased after the stone-thrower.

'Let's get away from here,' said Rizo. 'This could finish badly for someone.'

They edged out of their hiding place and into the shadows of the *calle*. Behind them came a cry of pain, an alarmed shout, a splash.

'We must not interfere in this,' Rizo whispered. 'The *custodi* make searches for illegal weapons. If they stop us, we shall be arrested as well as these drunken fools.' Dai thought of the *falchion* knocking against his side, the broad bladed dagger he carried, and grimly acknowledged the truth of this. He remembered what Rizo had also said: 'Sanuto and me, we shall be called as witnesses but there are those who will bear witness against us, those who are in the pay of Marco Trevior and his family. It will go hard against us, *sior.*'

Dai remembered the two forlorn creatures hanging between the pillars of the *piazza.* 'You think torture, now?'

'That is possible, *sior.*'

'Best leave, then.'

'That is my thought also, *sior*, though it distresses me not to speak out in your defence.'

'No matter, Rizo. You have risked everything to help me and Rado.'

No, best leave her, make sure she was away to safety, take shelter until he knew the lie of the land.

Leaving. What is that? While the heart remembers, there is no leaving.

It was what she had said, facing him, those gold-flecked eyes on his. 'My Nene said this. It is truth, Dafydd.' And all the time her heart had cried out the other truth. *What was it then that tore my heart and soul? Who can tell, girl? When you feel this, then you will feel love and you will give your heart and soul and life for your beloved.* This was her beloved, she knew it now; his life mattered more than her own. She would in truth give her heart and soul and life for him but it would do him no good. Now, he must leave, hide, escape to save his life.

'Keep safe, *cariad.* Go with God.'

'Keep safe, my dearest friend. Go with God.'

'Giles…'

'I shall take good care of her, Dai, of them all.'

Dai watched her into the flat-bottomed boat that would take them up the Canalazzo and across the lagoon and up the river to Padova.

'Here, *sior*. We must wait here for Sanuto.'

It seemed an endless time. No moon. Night cries of birds and beasts. Reeds and canes rustling and rattling. Water. Always water. Always the salt-water air and seaweed and algae, and water trickling and murmuring and oozing between the stalks of the reeds, soaking them. Fog settled over the lagoon as it settled over Venezia, obscuring truth, creating illusion.

'It is lucky there was *la guerra dei pugna* – the fight of the fists – today,' Rizo said. 'Every autumn this happens. The Castellani and the Nicolotti. You know this?'

'Yes. I have seen it before.'

Impossible not to witness these brawling *battagliole* if you were in Venezia any time after Lammas and before Epiphany – but nothing religious, now, about these encounters. This one had erupted out of nowhere but others were planned weeks in advance, smiled on by the Forty who doubtless saw it as a way for rivalries and dissatisfactions to be resolved. Today, a scuffle in the fish market had started it, insults exchanged, and sharp words, a blow then someone had brandished a *pistolese* that they called here a cow's tongue, and one of the gondoliers raised his spiked boat pole. And suddenly chaos, disruption, baskets flying through the air, slap of fist on flesh and pushing and punching and kicking and a writhing entangled mass falling into the canal only to be replaced by other brawlers. So much noise that it brought the Council to see what was going on. From the safe shadows came a hail of stones that had, Dai supposed, been stuffed inside roomy work aprons. As if they had known, he thought suddenly, as if they had come anticipating trouble. It was in the midst of the uproar that Rizo and he had slipped quietly away. He glanced across at Rizo.

'Very lucky for us it was…' he said.

'It is good sport, *sior*. Me, I support the Nicolotti, but most I like the dumplings and chestnuts that are for sale on the Canalazzo.' He met Dai's eyes with the bland look Dai was beginning to recognise. His head came up. 'Listen!'

A splash of oars, a low whistle, and Sanuto was with them. Not long after, they were pulling the boat on to the shore of a desolate island. Reeds, sand, little else. Sanuto whistled again. 'Rado?' he called softly.

'Who is with you?' The low voice came from the darkness of the reeds.

'*Sior* Davide. We'll explain on the way. Time to get out of here.'

Radovan was consumed with guilt. 'I never wanted anything like this, *sior*,' he said again and again. 'I wanted only to protect your ladies. Now Kazan will be so angry with me for putting you in this danger.'

'Kazan is angry, but not with you.' He sighed. 'I hope she keeps her anger quiet, Rado. She wants Marco's blood.'

Unexpectedly, Rado said, 'She is a wonder, your Kazan. I have never known any woman like her. So honest, such a way of looking you in the eye and yet she brings peace and harmony amongst us all. Is she safe? And your friends, *sior* Davide?'

'I sent them away. They should be in Padova by now; setting out on the mountain journey tomorrow. Keeps them safe from questioning, doesn't it now?'

'You will join us in Padova,' she had said and he had not replied. Let her believe that or she would never leave. Not lies, but not the truth. Was there ever truth in this place?

Leaving. What is that? While the heart remembers, there is no leaving.

Kazan. Çiçek's daughter. *Fy nghariad.* Keep safe. Go with God.

The brown-robed brother tried to hide his amazement. He was a stunted little man with a snout of a nose. A monastery pig, thought Francesco, intent on rootling out juicy gobbets of gossip. 'Of course, *sior*,' he said smoothly. 'Your visit will be in the strictest confidence, as you ask.' He looked around the bare little room, chill on this morning of November fog. There was a wooden bench. He gestured to it. 'If you care to sit, *sior*, I shall find the one you seek.'

Francesco da Ginstinianis nodded impatiently. It seemed a long time before Brother Jesolo opened the door and ushered in the man he had come to speak with so early in the morning.

'Not in monks robes yet, *sior* Thomas?'

'Not yet, *sior* Francesco. I may need these clothes and this life a little longer, if the rumours I hear are true.' His dark face seemed more hard-angled than ever, his dark eyes alert and watchful.

'They are true. *Sior* Davide is to be arrested this morning.'

'Accused by the so noble Marco Trevior.'

Francesco inclined his head. 'For plotting the assassination of said Marco Trevior and for conspiring with Pietro da Silvano to acquire the secrets of the glass-makers of Murano.'

Tom uttered a sound of scorn. 'And you who know him can believe Dafydd guilty of such crimes? He is falsely accused.'

'The Ten will conduct the investigation. Witnesses will be questioned. Once an accusation is made, especially one so serious, you know that the law must follow due course.' He paused. 'As it did with the *sior* Pietro. You knew of his execution?'

'The friars spoke of it last night but yesterday, no. That he was arrested, yes. Heinrijc Mertens sent a letter. It was waiting for us at the Bank. It was…unlooked for news. Dafydd could not believe it of *sior* da Silvano.'

'Nor can I. He was a man my father trusted absolutely, and his nephew was a good friend of mine. Now da Silvano is dead and Guiseppe nowhere to be found. It is a sad homecoming.'

'He was proved guilty beyond all doubt?'

Francesco hesitated. 'It must be so,' he said at last. 'The Ten do all in their power to investigate.'

'Including torture?'

'If they have to. They dislike to do so but it loosens men's tongues.'

'But not always to speak words of truth.' Tom closed his eyes against the thought of Dafydd, his friend, arrested and imprisoned, tortured to force him to confess. Impossible. 'He is innocent,' he said again, 'and that is what he will say. There are those who will speak in his defence.'

'There is a problem.'

'Oh yes?'

'Witnesses who could speak for *sior* Davide have vanished in the night. The sailors Rizo and Sunato cannot be found.' He paused again, stared intently at the dark faced man in front of him. 'Neither can *sior* Davide.'

Tom stared back. 'What do you mean?'

'I went early to the *fondaco* this morning, as soon as I heard of Marco's intentions. My father spoke with his late last night. My father, you recall, is one of the Council of Forty. It worried him. Like me, he has much respect for *sior* Davide. It is not perhaps correct but I wished to speak with *sior* Davide before the *custodi* came to arrest him. He was not there.' He stared intently at Tom. The silence lengthened. Tom raised an eyebrow.

'You imagine him to be here, taking refuge in the Friary? He is not. I wish he were. What news of the others?'

'They left with the German merchants at the time of the *Marangone*. They were lucky. They left before the *guerra dei pugna* made travel along the Canalazzo impossible. Impossible even to walk along the *fondamento* when such fights take place.

Tom grimaced. 'He has got them out of this city. That is Dafydd. He will get his people to safety first. Then he will offer himself to the Ten.'

'You are certain of this?'

'Yes.' *You and your conscience, Dafydd. It will be your death.* 'I believe he has some days of Grace, according to your Venetian law, before he must give himself up.'

Francesco da Ginstinianis nodded. 'Normally seven but I think it may be less than this because of the seriousness of the accusations.' He looked down at the unevenly paved floor of the small room. 'I agree with you, *sior* Thomas,' he said suddenly. '*Sior* Davide I know as a man of honour.' He raised his head, looked Tom in the eye. 'He would never commit an act of treason. Never.'

Tom stared back. 'Your sister is betrothed to Jacopo Trevior?'

'Yes.'

'Yet you put more trust in the man who is accused of attacking your family?'

'They are not yet my family, *sior*. I say these things in confidence, you understand?'

Tom's eyebrow lifted again. He nodded.

'My father agreed this betrothal while I was away with the fleet. I did not want it. There is bad blood in the Trevior family but they are becoming rich and my father is failing and wants his daughters settled well. You understand?'

'Yes.'

'But these Trevior…I do not know, *sior*, if I wish my family to be so connected.'

'Why not?'

'Jacopo, he is decent but weak. Marco is wild, as so many of our young nobles are wild, but I tell myself it is only the foolishness of youth.'

'The truth is,' Tom said with deliberation, 'he rapes the nuns and the young women of the workers and considers it sport. He would rape the noble women, if he could.'

'How do you know these things?'

'The monks. It is known in the city. The sailors Radovan and Rizo and Sanuto.' He flung the names in the face of the man. 'They know the truth but dare not speak out against him. They protected our Kazan and Agathi on our journey here. Radovan told Dafydd of the rape of his sister. He urged him to protect our women. This is the truth of the conversations between Radovan and Dafydd. We did not tell Agathi and Kazan. It was enough for them that they were two women alone on the ship.' He thought a moment. 'Kazan did not like Marco Trevior. She is an innocent. She did not know why.'

Da Ginstinianis was silent. Tom waited. At last da Ginstinianis said, '*Sior* Davide must be proved innocent.'

'Yes. And returned to his home and *sior* Heinrijc Mertens who loves him as a father does a son.'

'What can we do, *sior* Thomas?'

'I do not know, *sior* Francesco. We must stand as witness but we need more than that.'

'We must find him. These friars – they would give witness?'

'Perhaps. They know the monasteries and nunneries raided by Marco and his friends. But this is seen as a minor crime by your Venetian law.' Tom turned impatiently in the small room. He strode to the door, not even head height, and leaned against its frame looking towards the main door of the Friary, closed on the street beyond. Faintly came the city sounds of cartwheels grating and mules' hooves clopping on stone; snorting, marauding pigs; the hoarse shouts of traders and workers. Overhead were wheeling, screeching gulls and clamorous pigeons in a sky that was steadily darkening. More rain, more fog. In the distant mountains, there would be snow. He hoped Giles had the sense to provide them all with furs for the journey. The cloaks they had were well enough for a summer journey, even the autumn chill, but not for the bitter cold of a winter journey through the mountain passes. What it must have cost Dafydd to let them go with only Giles to protect them. Edgar would do his best but he was no swordsman, not after monastery life. Then there was the danger of rock falls, avalanche, wolves and bears, snow storms, robbers…and here he was, safe in the friary, a new life of peaceful reflection ahead of him. No. He needed these clothes and this life a little while longer. He turned. 'He sent Rémi back to the *fondaco* yesterday afternoon. Dafydd intended going to the island of Murano to find out what news he could of da Silvano.' How he wished he could have spoken with Dafydd last night. 'He must have discovered something to send him into hiding and the rest to safety.'

'Then we should go there as well.'

'You?'

'Of course. I am known. You are a stranger.'

Tom nodded. 'I should be glad of your company.' He looked at the sad-faced Venetian. 'They looked so happy and beautiful in their new finery. I haven't thanked you for that.'

Francesco sighed. 'I saw them. As you say, very beautiful.' His mouth lifted. 'I think perhaps Kazan was not so comfortable. I think she would prefer her peasant clothes.'

Tom's face softened. 'I am sure of it.'

'She is…' The Venetian hesitated. 'Unusual,' he said at last.

'She was brought up by a Christian grandmother who made her home with one of the *yürük* tribes.' Tom saw Francesco's startled expression.

'But she has an English grandfather?'

'She has – none other than Will-the-Wordmaker. You have heard of him?'

'I have *heard* him! Many years ago now when I was a small boy.' The man had magic in his voice, he remembered; young and old alike listened open-mouthed with wonder.

'The brothers told me he knew *sior* Giotto – and that *sior* Giotto painted his likeness in one of the chapels in Padova. She was so excited when I told her. She would have had me go with them just to see her grandfather's image.'

'But you would not?'

Tom shook his head. 'I believed my life was here.'

'And now?'

'It is still here, until Dafydd is proved innocent. When do we go to Murano?'

'As soon as you are free to go.'

'I am free now.'

Rizo stared at him in horror. '*Sior* Davide, if you give yourself up it will be your death.'

'You are safe here,' Rado said. 'It is outside the city boundaries.'

They were huddled in the small space of a mud-and-reed cottage on the marshes of the Venuto. A hearth in the centre of the room puthered thick, choking smoke but it was warm, steaming their sodden clothes to dryness, and the pot balanced over the fire bubbled promisingly. Eels were easy come by in these marshes.

Eels: Fenland fodder. Years ago, another life it was. *Taid* had told him of the Fenland eels, long before ever it was he met Blue. *Taid* heard it from the young boy, from Will, see, who grew up and became the Wordmaker in search of his lost brother. *Taid* it was who told him the story of the man who filched eels from the Abbot's own fishery and who was with Will on the long walk from *Lloegr* to *Cymru* to build castles for the first Edward. Who, that first night in strange places, brought out a wad of dried eels and how it brought to them all the smell of home, the far off land. What was it that brought home to his mind the bright citadel land, the country of Dafydd where Welsh freely flows? A buzzard wheeling over the Mawddach? Black storm clouds piling higher and higher, sweeping in from the western sea? The smell of damp earth and moss and perfume of blossom and the flowers of spring bright to the eye – daffodils and celandines and burning gorse? Or was it blackened buildings with no roof, ruined by fire and desolation? A hearth with no light, no candle, no songs? An old man's gaunt face and ruined body, starving himself to death for the sake of his grandson?

Rado's mother smiled toothily, free now of anxiety. Her son was safe, her daughter promised to this curly-haired sailor; best of all, they had left the sea-city that had killed her husband and all but destroyed her son and daughter. 'You must stay, *sior* Davide,' she said, awkwardly. Her language was that of Spalato. She had never mastered the harsh, sing-song Venetian.

'I must go back,' Dai said. 'To prove my innocence and that of *sior* da Silvano.'

'But he is dead. What does it matter to him?' Rizo was above all a practical man who had learnt the art of staying alive.

'It matters. And there is his nephew to consider. He has lost his inheritance and the good name of the family as well as his freedom.'

'And you say you know where to find him?'

'I have spoken with him and promised to return. If I can borrow your boat, Sanuto, I shall make sure of its safe return.'

'I shall come with you, *sior* Davide.'

Dai shook his head. 'Best not. No need to risk your neck, is there now?'

The old beggar was sleeping. He was curled against the pillar in his usual place, his ragged cloak huddled about him, the hood pulled forward over his face. 'Wake up, old man,' said the youth. He shook the old beggar by the shoulder. 'Come on, wake up. Here's a man wants to talk with you.' He stopped, stared. Something was not right. When he let go of the old man's shoulder, he slithered to the ground. The hood fell back. 'May God and his Son and all the saints protect us.' The youth crossed himself. The old beggar was dead, his throat sliced open. Where he had leaned against the wall were blood smears. Now that he was disturbed the youth saw he was lying in a congealed pool of his own blood, thick and black. The youth gasped for breath. 'He's dead. Murdered.' He turned to the man behind him. 'See for yourself.'

Dai stared thoughtfully at the dead beggar, at the wrinkled, sunken face, short grey hair and stubbled jowls. If he pulled back the cloak, looked at the man's hands, he knew they would be weathered and gnarled, not young and supple.

'Strange, to murder a beggar,' he murmured. 'What has he to give?'

The youth was looking more closely. 'But this is old Tonso,' he said. 'This is not his usual place.'

'Who is here, usually?'

'I don't know his name. He has not been here long. He came from across the water, I think.' He gestured in the direction of Venezia. 'Perhaps he has killed the old man.'

'Why should he?'

'To take his place back again.'

'Why leave the body?' The youth was silent, taking in this idea. 'You must tell the *custodi*. I shall light a candle for this poor old man. Go now.'

He watched the youth out of sight. He looked about him. The street was quiet. If anyone was following, watching, they would be hidden in the shadows. He moved quietly towards the *basilica*. Inside, he walked towards an altar in a side chapel where he had talked the previous day with the old beggar with the young arms and hands. He knelt before the altar and rested his head in his hands. A whisper came from the shadows behind the altar.

'You have come back.'

'Yes. And it's you should be dead, Guiseppe da Silvano, not that poor devil of a beggar.'

'I saw what they did to him.'

'You saw who committed the murder?'

'Yes. I do not know them but I have seen them before. They are the ones who have threatened the workers of Murano.' He shrugged. 'They are hired killers. It is the ones who give the orders who have done this.'

'You know who they work for?'

'I suspect but have no proof, and without proof what can I do? A rich and powerful family can buy its own truth.'

Dai nodded to himself. It was as he had suspected.

Guiseppe said, 'There were others who came yesterday asking questions. One I recognised: Francesco da Ginstinianis. He was my friend. Now, I do not know. There was another with him, a tall, dark man, a foreigner like yourself. Francesco called him Thomas, like the saint.'

Dai was silent, pondering. 'I know Francesco da Ginstinianis. I think the other is my good friend.' Twm, who should have left the city by now. 'What did they want?'

'Like you, asking for information about my uncle. No one was willing to speak, and I dare not. You, and these two, and later that day the *custodi* came. Now, the old beggar is dead. Poor old Tonso. I feel it is my fault. I dared not sleep in my usual place. He must have seen the empty place and decided to sleep there where it is warm against the wall of the furnace.'

'No use blaming yourself, is it now? Best come with me to a safe place. Soon they'll realise it's the wrong man they've killed and come back again.' But best make sure they were not followed, he thought grimly, not until he'd decided what best to do to cut through this tangle of lies and treachery.

4

Ieper
Late January 1337
Where have you gone leaving me alone,
my soul, my warrior?
(The Book of Dede Korkut, c. 9th C)

All day it was dark. So dark neither candles nor lamps nor hearth fire could penetrate the gloom of the hall and chambers. A pale sun dragged itself across the sky in a low arc, weighted down by leaden clouds. *A howry winter's day.* That was how Blue would describe it. *Just when winter's at its bleakest and it seems spring's never going to come.* Snow in the air but no snow as yet.

'But it's coming,' Heinrijc Mertens said cheerfully. 'One last blast, dear girl, and then spring will come again. You'll see.' He rubbed his hands together and held them out to the glowing fire burning in a hearth that was larger than most; a modern hearth built against a wall with stone hooding and huge circular chimney. Glazed windows and bright tapestries blanketed the room against draughts. There were chair covers and cushions artfully embroidered but with warmth and comfort in mind to keep out the bitter winter weather, and bitter it was. Bitterer than the coldest winter on the Çukarova coast. Warm was how he liked it, and he had need of warmth and comfort, this old man whose outstretched hands showed transparent against the flames. 'Before nightfall, I say.'

He was right. By dusk snow was falling, thick flakes that settled on pitched roofs and cobbled streets and spiralled over the dark waters of the Ieperlee canal that flowed through the town, past this brick-built merchant's house with its stepped gable and tall round chimney, past the great church, past the jetty at the western end of the huge magnificence of *lakenhalle,* the cloth hall, with its high belfry and four sharp turrets, and miles away to Nieuwpoort on the coast, the trading route to England. A canal, like Venezia. Same but different. Different, and not the same at all. Water, certainly, in this low-lying country, water that constantly encroached on the hard-won land. Marshes and lakes and waves beating constantly on the coast, and clouds hurrying across the sky, and rain, constant rain, beating down on the sodden land until rain turned to ice and snow. But its soil was fertile.

Neither land nor sea, this was a country that had flourished. Men had won land from the sea, had built towns, free men who traded with many countries, whose coins circulated as far as the Black Sea and Caucasus. There was no weaving like Flanders weaving, no cloth like Flanders cloth. But those who worked were kept in a state of near slavery, threatened constantly with unemployment until there was no bearing it, and a fierce civil war erupted, workers against patricians. The Men of the Claw against the Men of the Lily: *Clauwerts* against *Leliaerts.*

Heinrijc Mertens spoke of it in the dark of the winter evenings. He told how the Men of the Claw, the workers, rough sons of the people, fought against the *Leliaerts.* He told how the terrible Philip le Bel, King of France, Isabella's father, brought knights from Picardy and Normandy and Artois; from Hainaut and Brabant. And the Men of the Claw armed only with weapons of iron-headed clubs stuck with hooks or spikes. Heinrijc Mertens chuckled. 'We called them *goedendags. Good mornings,* dear child,' he explained, and laughed at her expression of horror. 'Only a handful of knights to command them, my own father amongst them. And they won, these *Clauwerts.* Impossible, you'd say. But you must remember, child, they knew their country, its marshes, their countrymen. They took no prisoners. How could they? Who could guard them? No prisoners and no booty. That was the order. Anyone picking up treasures was to be killed as the enemy was killed. Even the nobles. Not one was spared. Not even Robert d'Artois, crying his name aloud as he was dragged from his horse, surrendering. 'We do not understand French,' they said, and killed him. Desperate times, child, and desperate deeds, but they won us our freedom. For a time.'

He was silent, gazing into the burning hearth fire. 'It couldn't last. What does? There were the terrible years of famine and then the French attack that cut our men to bits. That was not even ten years ago. And now no one remembers the names of the *Clauwerts* and *Leliaerts*. All of Flanders surrendered and the captains tortured to death.' He sighed. His father had been one of the captains. 'They made up songs about our *kevels*, our workers, mocking them but we are proud of these songs. We sing them ourselves. Listen.' He sang off-key, with flamboyant gestures to emphasise the words, this ancient scarecrow of a man who had once been well-fed, plump and who was now hunch-shouldered and shrunken. Still he delighted in fashionable clothes, the most sumptuous to be had. Today, he wore a gown of fine crimson wool edged with furs and embellished with golden embroidery.

Let us sing of the churls
their ragged clothes are fit for the sty
their hats are too small for their heads
their hoods are all awry
their hose and shoes are worn to shreds
with bread and cheese and curd and gruel
they all day stuff their guts
the churl is such a fool he never eats but gluts

'There was more of the same. Your grandfather would remember the words, I'm sure.' He stared for so long into the fire she was sure he had fallen asleep. 'He would have approved,' he said suddenly. 'Your grandfather was always one for the little people, the workers, the ones of no account. And now, child, it begins again. Not that it ever went away. There has been simmering discontent in this land ever since suppression. It is thanks to the goodness of our Countess of Flanders that we still have our independence but she bought it at a great price. Now the English king has forbidden the export of English wool, who knows what will happen? It seems he has ambitions to create a textile industry of his own. They say he plans a blockade as soon as the winter weather lifts. And of course France will retaliate and attack the English ports. What it means for us, God help us, is no work and starvation. England may be our ally but our neighbour is France. And a cruel neighbour she can be. There'll be trouble, child.' He sighed again. 'Always trouble.'

She stirred. 'If that is so, Father Heinrijc, then I must go to England before this blockade. Before the French attack. Winter will soon be past and I made a promise to Nene to find my grandfather.'

They were silent.

'He will come, my daughter. Have faith. He will come.'

There is always room for faith. Allah's will – God's will. Two old men, one Muslim, one Christian, who had both lived through desperate times and yet their mantra was the same: *keep faith.* Her grandfather would have said it was in the gods' hands. For herself, she dared not think. Sometimes thinking didn't do you any good.

It was in Padova she had known for certain he would not come. The German merchants went on ahead after all, and their own small party waited for two days. They went with her to the chapel of the Scrovegni family, Giles and Edgar and Agathi and Rémi. One of the monks led them in and smilingly watched their awestruck faces as they stood in the infinity of the blue space around them. Figures moved before their eyes, so real did they seem, so different from the stiff, expressionless faces they had seen in the churches on their journey to Venezia. Here, agony and anguish, love and forgiveness blazed from the painted faces of the Christ and his mother and Mary Magdalene. There was the birth in the stable with the great comet blazing overhead and there – just there – was the youthful, well-knit young man who was her grandfather, curly brown hair and wary eyes. Wary as a child, wary as a man, Nene had said. She stared at him but saw only another brown man with dark, inscrutable eyes. To go on to the cold country where her grandfather may or may not be alive? To go back to Venezia where her soul's mate may or may not be alive? Don't think. Thinking doesn't do you any good. There was no choice. She had made her promise to Nene and her promise to Dafydd. She must go on.

The old men of the town had urged them to leave: could they not smell the storm that was brewing? The *marroniers* – the guides – gravely nodded. It was true: travel now or wait out the winter. Dai's instructions in his ears and the dour advice of the old men and *marroniers*, Giles rented mules from the *hospitallars* and bartered for thick furs. The mountain tracks were too steep for horses; they must be led. Safer to travel on mules. It was a long, bitter-cold journey into the heights of the mountains where fragile wooden bridges crossed chasms too deep for reckoning. The flimsy structures swayed and jolted under the weight of the pack animals and their human cargo. The mountains were higher than any in Anatolia, their tops reaching into the heavens, lost in mist. Lodgings were at flea-ridden *hospices*, each one dedicated to a saint, and run by monks, and no charge for these wayfarers. The wind whistled through cracks in doors and walls and windows and there was not the comfort of hot water baths at the end of the short, exhausting day. It was Agathi, so frail-seeming, who was most stoic. She never complained, not of fatigue nor cold nor hunger. 'She learned how to endure when she was taken as a slave,' thought Kazan. 'It is how she survived.' There was a memory of cold night and falling water and danger; the time when Kazan first met Niko, Agathi's young brother. He had helped her escape from the slave traders, hidden her behind the waterfall, brought her what scraps of food he could pilfer, and a ragged blanket to protect her from the wetness and the chill night. What was it he had said of his sister? 'I wish my sister was brave but she cries all the time.' You were wrong, Niko, Kazan thought. Your sister is brave but it is a different courage from yours.

The *marroniers* told them stories; one of a young man who was engulfed by an avalanche. His wife was with child and she refused to believe he was dead. One day in the spring he came back to her. He had made an air hole through the snow and so survived, on breath and water from handfuls of melted snow. He said his unborn child spoke to him in his icy prison and it was this that gave him courage and faith. She refused to believe he was dead. *Even when it seems all hope has gone, there's always a thread.* And so do I refuse to believe you are dead, Dafydd, Kazan had thought. I cannot think of you as other than alive. My heart would surely stop beating if you were dead. So you must be alive.

After the frozen heights came the slow descent and the transfer to water and then again to road and another slow journey through forests ravaged by wild boar and wolves and then into garrisoned towns where tolls were charged and searches made because this was a country on the brink of war. To Troyes, where the roads met and parted, one heading towards Paris, theirs towards Rheims and Bruges, and the last few miles of the long journey through the dead of winter in a landscape bleached of colour and shuddering cold such as the girl had never known.

Rémi had led the way into Ieper, past the new earth-banked defences, through the great gates, into the town and to Heinrijc Mertens' brick-built townhouse. And his welcome – such a welcome. Arms open to catch Rémi close; a welcome for his friends; a check when he realised 'Davit' was not there. Those pale grey eyes could not quite hide his loss. The frail voice trembled on a note of regret. 'But he will come, no fear of that. He is a cat with nine lives, and five are left to him. He will come.' Mertens' gaze rested on the girl with empty, exhausted eyes. He rested a hand on her bright head. 'He will come, dear child. Do not fear.' He raised his brow when told of Thomas' choice. 'A Franciscan?' he murmured. Then he nodded, perhaps not so surprised. When Rémi revealed his hidden cache of treasure concealed in the padded jerkin – the little things Heinrijc Mertens loved – then the pale eyes bleared and the old man's fingers trembled as he lifted the objects one by one. There was a strange two-pronged device he had longed for, ever since he had heard of it. A *barjyn*, he said, that was sometimes called a *furca* or fork, used by the Musselmen but despised by the Christians but mark his words; this would be as much used as the daggers men kept about them for eating at table. See how useful it was? For keeping meat still and so make slicing a morsel neater and easier; and how much more seemly than fingers dipped in the common bowl. So useful. And this small goblet of carved rock crystal. Davit must have bartered well for such a work of craftsman's skill. Did they know the Ancients believed rock crystal to be alive, taking a breath once every hundred years? 'It is said to be an incarnation of the Divine.' He chuckled. 'If you believe such things. Ah, and this.' He breathed deeply and reverently turned the leather-tooled binding of a small Koran. This beauty, this God's Word though another's God. How splendid. How rare. He gave thanks to his son Davit for such gifts. He would thank his son when he returned. 'In the spring, dear child. Do not look for him before the spring.'

The new treasures were ranged alongside other treasures brought back from other journeys: glass from Murano that made Kazan remember the night-time meeting with Sanuto, and her fear for Dafydd. There was ancient glass, tiny stoppered flasks that were almost opaque yet had a rare delicacy; a brass bowl inlaid with gold and silver and with a pattern of mounted huntsmen running just below its rim, with lean hounds running alongside, forever and forever encircling the bowl; a painted silk robe from the Far Country; fragments of fabrics that were very old and very precious. 'See, my child; these carpets are said to have knots two hundred to an inch. How splendid is that? See – this one – brocaded with gold and silver thread and studded with jewels and pearls. Such working we in these low lands never dream of, though we are master cloth makers.' Stars and octagons on a pale green ground of worked silks; a procession of horses on a madder background. There were books of great beauty: a bestiary, a copy of the Gospels, a psalter. 'And now this Koran,' said Heinrijc Mertens, and laid the precious book down next to its Christian neighbour. He loved these treasures not for their monetary value but for their learning and craft.

'And now there are plans for a new Guild for our own painters and sculptors,' he said with satisfaction, 'but not to work alone in monastic cells. No. Our craftsmen live with their fellow man, in the daily coming-and-going of our lives. This is the way it should be.'

'I think perhaps I saw something of this in Padova.' Kazan told him of the seeming-living figures in the Chapel of the Scrovegni and he nodded his head. He had heard of this great artist. But here, where there were the most beautiful of cloths, the most delicate fabrics, the richest weaves, the finest dyes…how much more beautiful would the painted figures be? The light and shade that caught the garments draping the body; the dignity of the wearer; the nobility! 'And drawn from living people, my dear girl, from life itself! One day we shall be renowned as the greatest sculptors and artists the whole world has ever known.' He nodded his head with sober certainty.

There were jade figures that made her cry out in amazement. She showed the old man her own jade axe. He fingered its smoothness. 'This is a great treasure, my daughter.'

'My grandfather will know me by it,' she said, 'but after that, after I have shown it to my grandfather, I would like you to take it for all your great kindness to me.'

He shook his head. 'It is yours, my daughter. You must keep it close.'

'But I have this.' She lifted her arm to show him the bracelet cunningly worked in twists of gold and silver and copper. 'Dafydd gave me this beautiful thing.'

The old man smiled and shook his head. 'A fitting gift from my son to you but even so, dear child, keep the jade. Do you know what they say of this jade, these people of the Far Country?'

'Nene told me it would protect me.'

'Let me tell you what a great man from the Far Country said many, many years ago. Many hundreds of years ago. He was a man of great wisdom. He said that this is a stone that is soft, smooth and glossy, like benevolence. It is fine, compact and strong, like intelligence. It is angular but not sharp and cutting, like righteousness. It hangs down like humility. When struck, it yields a note so clear and prolonged but finishing suddenly, like music. Its beauty does not conceal its flaws nor do its flaws conceal its beauty. Like loyalty. It has inner radiance, like good faith. It is bright like a rainbow, like heaven. It is exquisite and mysterious, appearing in the hills and the streams, like the earth. It stands out against all ranks, like virtue. It is esteemed by all under the sky, like the path of truth and duty.' The old man stopped, catching his breath. 'Truly, this is a great gift. To give such a gift to your grandmother tells me he loved her deeply.' He stroked the girl's cheek. 'She gave it to you. You are like this jade, my daughter. You are bright and true and loyal and loving and virtuous. I am very happy to give you to my son Davit.'

She lowered her gaze. 'Father Mertens, we are not betrothed.'

'Perhaps not before the priests but in your hearts I think you are, my daughter.' He touched the bracelet. 'Does this not tell you so?'

'He called it a trinket to wear with my new fine feathers.'

'He is a man of few words but with much in his heart.' He traced the interlaced pattern. 'Precious metals woven together with such delicacy and craft – and as carefully chosen to be a gift for you. Perhaps this is what he wishes to say but cannot find the words. Hm?'

She liked it best when he told stories of Dafydd. He told the story of their first meeting and she thought how strange it was to hear the same tale but on another man's tongue.

'Such a scrawny little creature they brought to me!' Heinrijc Mertens shook his head over the memory. 'Starving thin and stinking like a midden. Crusted all over with blood. Oh, he'd taken a beating had the boy, from those street thugs. He could barely stand but he still had fight in him! I can see him now. He must have felt fear but he gave no sign. He gave me back look for look.'

'He said you sat him down and gave him meat and broth.'

'Of course. The boy was half starved. To throw him out on a night like that would have been the end of him. There is too much hunger in this world. No one should go hungry.'

'That is what he says.'

'Well then.' He sighed. 'Such a boy – he has never given me cause to regret that night. He has been like a son to me – and like a father to this one.' He ruffled Rémi's hair. 'Rémi is the first he brought home to me. My good friend Jehan was alive then, and still practising his skills. A clever man, a brilliant *chirugien*. He is with the angels in heaven now, these three years past. It was Jehan who was the miracle-worker with this one. But so much pain you suffered, little one. So much. Too much for me. It was Davit who helped to hold him down though it was as much agony for him as for the child. He wept afterwards, asking me again and again if he had done right after all. My poor Davit.' Always there was a place at the board kept for the absent one. 'And what a hungry stomach he will bring! Always the hungry one, my Davit. Forever in the kitchens sneaking chewets of beef and dipping his fingers into the sauces and the coppetts of raisins and figs. Sniffing at the spices – he said that cinnamon and ginger and cloves and saffron were sent by Heaven to be united with toasted bread and wine and sugar and sharpened by wine vinegar. Grains of Paradise! He'd a passion for those. And the long black pepper that's going out of fashion these days, I fear. We always use it in this household. Davit's preference, you see, and always he brings a bundle back with him. Always there when the pies were baked, he was, forever under Karel's feet. But he was a good boy for lugging the bundles of faggots to the bread ovens. That's heavy work, girl, but he'd not complain. And he'd spike them. He had a real knack for that, spiking the faggots on to the oven fork and thrusting them right to the back of the oven when they were alight, right to where they were most needed. Inhaling kitchen smoke until his nostrils were twitching and his eyes shed burning tears and still he didn't complain.

'He'd been a kitchen boy in England. Did he tell you that? In the great kitchens of the castle at Hereford. Feeding the fire: that was one of his jobs and he said it was worth all the hard work for the fragrant hot loaves that came out of the ovens. Said he was clumsy in those days, forever in trouble for misplacing spices in the wrong jars. He said he grew so red-hot turning the spits he didn't think hell-fire could be any hotter so he'd nothing to fear in the next life. Such blasphemy, the wretch,' Mertens said, cheerfully.

He'd said more than that, remembered Mertens: that the place itself was a hell created by Queen Isabella and the hated Mortimer. The execution of De Spenser in the market place, the boy said, had sickened him to his soul. He spoke just once of another boy, a squire's son, who had screamed with night terrors because of what he had witnessed, and who could blame him? Such wickedness – worse than anything he had been threatened with. It was then Davit had decided he could no longer stay in that place and so had quietly escaped a country that reeked like a slaughter house and came to one where he was set on and beaten almost to his death.

'Did I tell you about the time he brought home a slave from your country? Amit, who you've met – another treasure! It is wonderful to see how he cares for the animals! Wonderful! It was when Davit was acting as interpreter for that strange traveller from some outlandish place...what was his name now? Rémi, what was his name? Ah, I have it! Battuta. Ibn Battuta, the young man from Tangier who had set out to travel the world. He's travelling still, for all I know. He made Davit a gift of Amit as a slave. Davit never was one for slaves but he said the man was better with him than another. Amit and a fellow slave escaped – took the horses they were charged to take care of. Of course, they were caught and recovered. Punished, Davit said, severely punished. When he left Ibn Battuta he took Amit with him and gave him his freedom. And would you believe it? Amit chose to stay with Davit, chose to leave his country and come here to the low lands. He has learned to speak our language but he told me he was glad to have conversation with you, dear girl, in his own tongue.' He sighed. 'Another who will be glad to see Davit home. In spring, dear girl, in spring!'

Long before spring Edgar and Agathi were made man and wife in the porch of St Martin's church. It was a Benedictine monastery and this troubled Edgar. It was gentle Agathi who urged him to make confession to the Father Abbot and seek his advice. 'It will ease your soul,' she said. The Abbot was pragmatic. 'You have done no wrong. You made no vows. Even so my son, go to your abbey and offer penance.'

Heinrijc Mertens grunted. 'A bag of silver coins should accomplish that.' He came of the long tradition in this country of distrust of Christian ceremonies. One of the leaders of that long-ago revolution had declared he wanted to see the last of the priests hanging from the gallows, and Mertens' father had more than once said the same. But now, with this golden, innocent couple standing before God making their vows, his eyes were bleared with tears. 'Ah my dear girl, when my boy comes home, then it will be your turn and we shall have such rejoicing.' He rubbed his hands together in anticipation and refused to heed Kazan's repetition that she was not promised to Dafydd as he refused to consider that his boy would not come home.

All winter long they waited. All the long holiday of the Nativity, though some days before Epiphany Edgar and Agathi left for England in a brief, calm spell before the snow-storms closed in again. There came news of them: Edgar's father was dead. His brothers were overjoyed to see him safe and well. They welcomed his foreign wife for his sake, but who could not love gentle, beautiful Agathi? More, Alfred, the eldest, had made him reeve of one of his manors. True, it was a small manor with an old-fashioned hall built long ago but it was built of good stone. The service buildings were badly in need of repair, and the manor had been as badly managed, but it was a living and in a good part of the shire, not on marshy ground but higher, yet not so high as the unworkable heathland. With hard work, it could be reclaimed and its people given a better living than the miserable state they were in now.

'So overjoyed, these brothers of his,' muttered Giles, 'they make a reeve of him and set him to work.'

'Now you sound like Thomas,' Kazan told him. When he didn't answer, she rested her head against his arm. 'You miss your friend,' she said. 'Always we speak of Dafydd, and when he will come home, but you must wonder what has become of Thomas, and if he is safe in the friary of the Franciscans. He will send you word, Giles. He will not forget you.'

'I know he will not.' They were in the solar, watching the snow falling on the town. 'I miss them all,' he said. 'All our brave company. Don't you?'

'Yes. Yes, I do.' It seemed so long ago, that late summer journey from *han* to *han*, across the great plateau and down the treacherous mountains to Attaleia. So many adventures, such danger, such friends; and here they were, the sad remnant: she, Giles and Rémi, and now Father Mertens, all mourning the loss of their loved ones.

5

Attaleia
Late January 1337

If there is love, the heart burns; it softens like a candle
(Yunus Emre, 14thC)

Like a hundred harvest moons they were, swollen round and ruddy, hanging from the green branches: fruit of the orange tree, sweet as honey once the bitter skin was fetched off, just like Sakoura had promised. Like the setting sun back home in the fens, a burning blaze sinking into the darkening marshlands. Not like that here. A blink and darklins was gone. Howry enough it was here in the winter months, with the sea turned iron grey and waves crashing into the harbour mouth and rain clouds smowered over the mountain tops and a snide wind whipping round the smootins and streets of the town in spite of its great high walls. Other days, fair enough, it was blue skies and a warm wind. Never snow. Never a good, sharp frost biting at toes and fingers and noses. Snow was up on the mountains, and bitter cold. Not down here on the coastal plain. But it was wrong of him to grizzle when he'd known many a drear winter's day when it seemed spring was never going to come. All lowering grey skies and vicious rain that drenched you through to the skin and your belly groaning with hunger.

Not like that here. Plenty of belly-timber here. A good man to work for, Sakoura, and Hatice more like a friend to that pretty wife of his than a servant. Easy work with a cosy home to come back to. Bath house just around the corner, hot water piped. He'd never been so well fettled in all his life. Not never so sober, stone cold, not even sheep drunk, and not wanting none, neither. Yes, it was a good life here for himself and Hatice, and the boy Niko was content.

Blue heaved a sigh. Content enough. The boy missed his sister. He missed Kazan and Dai. Didn't they all? He'd caught Hatice pink-eyed just this morning. Nothing, she said, just a lash caught in her eye. Nothing. But he knew she grieved for Agathi, just as he missed the boy Edgar. And that fustilugs, that cheeky boy-girl Kazan. And Tom and Giles and that mumbling boy Rémi who had them all beat with his finger signing. All of 'em, truth be told. He'd never had friends like them, not never in all his born days, and now they were gone. Had they reached safe landings? May'appen, come summer, there'd be news. Until then, swallow down grief like it were gristle. They'd chosen to stay, Hatice, Niko, him. Beds made. All the same.

Then Mehmi's *abi*, his eldest brother, came with news: Kara Kemal was dead, and not long after they had left him. 'But no fault of yours, young Mehmi. Our father said to tell you this. He spoke of you even in his pain. He said it was time for you to be a bird of heaven, and like them make beautiful music for all to hear.' Aksay bent his head. 'He spoke the Mevlana's words right to the end. This is what he said:

There is neither death for us
Nor sorrow, nor care, nor grief,
In this ocean, which is one vast love;
This ocean of love and generosity.

'It was our great honour to have had such a man for our father, Mehmi. He was truly a great man.'

Mehmi wept. 'I have money now,' he said. 'When spring came, I was going to bring it to our father, with gifts of all the foods he loved most to eat. You must take it, *abi*, and when I have more I shall send more. There must be no more poverty in our father's house. As for me, I shall do as he said; I shall become a bird of heaven.'

That evening, Sakoura gathered the household for a feast in honour of Kara Kemal. After, there was the telling of the Hoca stories, and laughter, because this was a man who had loved laughter and family and friends. Then Mehmi played for them, a mournful song first in the fashion of the old days of the Oghuz because Kara Kemal was a hero amongst heroes, as great as Bamsi Beyrek of the Grey Horse; as great as Prince Kazan; as great as Dirse Khan.

My father, oh my father,
my white-bearded father
I am separated from you by death.
This black earth will eat us too.
The end of life, even a long one, is death
When the hour of your death came
It did not find you apart from the pure Faith
I shall pray for you, my father.
May your place be Paradise.

After, Sakoura said, 'Now you must sing the song of the white horse, Mehmi. That too will honour your father.' Mehmi balanced the *tanbur* in one hand, its long neck leaning against his shoulder, his right hand whispering the strings. He began to sing the story of Karoğlu.

Let the white horse come
Let it go free
And let go of your grief
Set that free as well...

Listening to the notes trickling from the tanbur, and to Mehmi's true voice raised in song, with lamps flickering and casting shadows over the gathered household, warmed by the high-leaping fire, Blue remembered that evening in autumn when they had found shelter with Dai's friend Kara Kemal, and they had feasted together, and talked, and told stories, and Mehmi the youngest son had played this same song, and they had been lost in wonder, all of them. A day later, Mehmi had joined them at the han, and with him came the boy-girl Kazan who had cozened their stories from their souls. Let go of your grief...

It was Kazan who had insisted on the rescue of the boy Niko, and it was Dai who had saved Agathi and Asperto and Hatice from slavery; and so he, Blue, had found his mate in honest Hatice, and golden-haired Edgar his beautiful silver-haired Agathi. Their lives were bound together, tied up tight. *Let go of your grief.* Dai should be told of the old man's death.

He turned to Hatice, opened his mouth to speak but she was there before him.

'We must travel to your country. We must find our friends for they are truly our own dear family. What do you say, husband?'

The big man felt his eyes burn and brim with tears. 'A says yer a rare woman, Hatice my lass, the bewtifullest as ever was, that's what yer be.' He wiped his sleeve across his face. 'Look at me, blubbing like a bairn. Best see what the boy says.'

'He'll say yes, and gladly,' Hatice said with certainty.

She was right. The boy's dark eyes sparkled. 'We shall be with Agathi and Edgar and Kazan? And Dafydd and Tom and Giles?' He mouthed the names lovingly.

'Yer right, Niki boy, we'll be with them.'

'And Mehmi comes with us?'

'A doesn't know about that.'

'But I do,' a voice broke in. Mehmi, the *tanbur* slung across his shoulder as if he were ready for travel that moment. 'Mehmi comes with you to this infidel land you miss so much, big man. May the good Allah help all true believers!'

6

Rochby Manor
Mid-January 1337

…would you go mine errand
To the lord of the house, harbour to crave…
(Sir Gawain and the Green Knight, 14thC)

It was just as he remembered it: the old, straight road, rising-falling-rising for miles, as far as the eye could see; the dark holloway where branches curved overhead then the slope upwards and out from tree shadow into open land; gentle, rolling hills covered in abundant woodland stretching down through folds and dips to the stream running through the valley bottom.

'You should see it in summer, Agathi,' he said, 'when the sky is blue and the sun is warm and all these woodlands are green and loud with bird-song.' He smiled ruefully. 'It's not at its best, midwinter.' The trees were bare now, black against the iron grey of the sky, branches clattering together. A murder of crows lifted and circled in a solid black cloud, their harsh cries raucous in the freezing air.

Agathi shivered despite her warm travelling dress and fur-lined cloak. To her, it was bleak and cold. Not even in the high mountain passes had she been chilled to the bone as she was here but she would not complain: this was her husband's land. Drifting snow was thick on the ground and heavy on tree branches. At times, her mare stumbled and slipped so that she had to cling tight to keep from falling off. The sky was leaden with the threat of more snow to come and soon the short day would end. 'We'll be at my father's house long before dark,' Edgar promised.

Would they be welcome? Surely his father would not turn him away, nor his young, tired wife, not on a wintry day like this one, and Epiphany just gone? He watched a kestrel hovering, wings fluttering then swept back as the bird plunged earthwards. He hoped it was not an ill omen. Superstitious nonsense, he told himself; he was getting as bad as Blue. He pulled on the leading rein of the horse plodding patiently behind him, heaped with baggage, so much of it gifted by Heinrijc Mertens. 'You cannot arrive penniless at your father's house after such a long absence,' the old man had said, and Edgar had protested that he was not penniless. Indeed, Dafydd had insisted on Edgar's share of profit, though he'd done nothing to deserve it.

'But you did, Edgar,' Kazan had said. 'You rescued Agathi, and then you helped to rescue me and Niko, and now you have helped Giles bring us through the high mountains of mist and ice and snow to the home of Father Mertens. We shall be always in your debt, dear Edgar.'

'Besides, you are a married man now and must take care of your beautiful young wife – isn't that so, Rémi, my boy? Giles?'

And because they were all agreed, and he was a man with a wife to protect, he had become a man of substance – some substance, anyway. Enough to be independent of his father should he and Agathi not be welcomed.

How familiar it all was, despite his seven-years' absence: those five long years at Croyland and two years of travelling in strange lands. The manor village was tucked into a fold of the hills, sheltered from the biting north-easterlies. The road dipped down past the mill and joined another road coming in from the east. Both were heavily rutted with wagon wheels and horse-traffic; frozen solid now but they would be churned mud come the thaw. The roads joined just before the stream crossing. A new stone bridge, Edgar approved, supported by a neat pointed arch; though it was not so fine and elegant as the bridges that sprang across the gorges in Anatolia, he thought, and smiled to see how his world view had changed. Wood smoke curled out of the holes at the ends of the thatched roofs of the village houses; light flickered through cracks and gaps. From the barns and sties and over-wintering pens of the demesne farm came the subdued sound of pigs and cattle settling for the night. A buxom young woman chased the last of the hens into shelter, safe from foxes, safe from the bitter night. She looked up at the sound of their approach, horses' hooves and jingling harness, then dipped her head and pulled her shawl more closely about her head and shoulders. A glimpse of her face only, but Edgar did not recognise her. They rode past the smithy and Edgar looked for Jack-Smith who had always had a welcome for the youngest son of the squire but the man hammering sparking metal on anvil was a stranger.

They rode on to the protective moat and wall that surrounded the hall and its service buildings; on to the gatehouse. The stout wooden doors were open and through them Edgar could see the stone-built hall with its high roof rearing over all the other buildings. It was oak-shingled, not the thatch he had expected to see. And there was new stone-build, halted now until the spring, the last courses of stone protected against ice and snow. From the look of it, the hall house would be doubled in size.

There was great activity in the courtyard and he remembered that Epiphany was only just past. Horses, sweating and steaming in the chill winter afternoon, grooms at their heads, and hounds, wet and panting after a day's hunting. A group of young men was disappearing into the open door of the hall and their voices came cheerfully on the air. There must be guests here still. A man-at-arms stood to attention.

'Is the master home?' Edgar asked.

'He is.'

'Tell him Edgar, his youngest son, is come home with his wife and asks for shelter.'

The man looked perplexed. 'His youngest son, sir? It must be the old master you speak of. He's been dead nigh on these last two years. It's his son Alfred who's squire now.'

'My father is dead?'

Agathi grasped his hand. She had barely understood the man's speech but Edgar's words were clear to her.

'Aye, sir. I'm sorry it's news to you. Shall I tell the master you're here?'

'Yes…yes…tell him.' Edgar looked at the man again. 'I don't remember you.'

'No sir. I came with the mistress, sir. With the Lady Philippa.'

'Lady Philippa?'

'Yes sir. Lady Philippa. The squire's wife.'

More changes than he had anticipated, Edgar thought. He squeezed Agathi's hand. 'My brother is the new squire and it seems he is married.'

It was a happy meeting with his brothers. Both brothers, for Eric was here as well with his family. A seven-years-older Eric, married and the father of three clamouring children, but the same cheerful, careless Eric of his boyhood, boisterously overjoyed to see his youngest brother again – and a married man! 'A pretty wife indeed – worth running away from monkhood, hey, Edgar?' Alfred frowned at the reference to his youngest brother's past and hushed his tongue-tripping younger brother, but Eric laughed loudly and hugged Edgar to him again and again. 'We searched for you all over,' he said, 'when they brought the news you'd flown the cage. Not a sign! Not a whisper of a rumour! Father was gnashing his teeth and pulling his hair out – wasn't he, brother? You must tell us how you were spirited away. What stories you must have to tell, hey?'

'But not in company,' Alfred said, austerely. 'Edgar's story is for the family only.'

'Hey, long-mouth, you never used to be such a dull dog.'

'I am Lord of the Manor now, Eric, and have a position to keep.'

'Well, you kept your position with magnificence these past fifteen days and nights.' Eric was unabashed. He said to Edgar, 'He promised Matty and me all the feasting and carousing we could wish for. Nothing like the old days. Father must be burning in hellfire at such profligacy! The best food, the best wines, the best company; music and dancing and games; hunting and a tournament, Edgar!'

It was the custom at his father-in-law's manor, said Alfred. His wife had determined to introduce the custom here at Rochby, though it was not as grand as her father's. 'I think it was successful.'

'To be sure, we had a good day of it. A pity you couldn't secure that dancing bear for your guests.' Eric's eyes were blue, like Edgar's, though lighter, and mischief sparkled in the glance he flickered towards his younger brother. 'My daughters had high hopes of seeing a cavorting bear. But we had sport enough with the guests. You couldn't move without bumping into priors and chaplains come from over three counties.' He would save 'til they were alone the titbit that not an archbishop nor a bishop swelled the number of guests. Plenty of minor knights and squires and their ladies, to be sure, with greedy eyes on the tasty morsels set before them, but no one of real importance. City reeves, sergeants-of-arms, merchants and franklins, gentlemen and gentlewomen of the same standing. 'We had trumpets announce each course, and pipes and rotas, and a whole choir of cherubs. Still, you'll see for yourself at supper, brother. Where is that magnificent wife of yours, Alfred? And mine, come to that? I thought they'd be here by now to greet these new guests. Matty!' he yelled, and to a passing servant, 'Find that wife of mine and tell her – no, request her – to come here to me. There's a surprise waiting here for her.' He was grinning like the boy he used to be. 'Philippa tells me proper husbands must request, not command.'

A plump-cheeked, smiling woman arrived in the hall, two young girls following her on short, stubby legs. Eric's wife was a plain girl but serenely good-natured. 'What's to do now, husband, with your "request"?' You are as demanding as your son!' She was shaking her head at him, not deceived by the words of the message. Then she saw the golden-haired man standing there, a beautiful, slim girl next to him, silver-blonde hair shining in the light from the sconces and candles. 'Edgar! Is it really you? Are you come back to us?' She rushed at him, her arms flung round his waist, hugging him to her, laughing with joy. 'Eric has worried so much about you! You naughty boy, Edgar, to torment us so. Not a word from you for years, and now you arrive here and we must leave tomorrow! This is not well done, my brother.' She turned to Agathi. 'And welcome to you, my dear.'

'This is Agathi, my wife.'

'Your wife! Now you bring us a wife! A sister for us!' She clasped bewildered Agathi to her, kissed each cheek. Edgar said to Agathi, in Turkish, 'My brother Eric's wife, Matilda. As mad as he is, and as generous.'

'But your wife does not speak our language?'

'A little,' Agathi said in her careful French. 'I can understand if you speak slowly. And Edgar helps me.'

'I'm sure Eric has been chittering on like crickets in summer.' She used the local word, Edgar noted: chittering. He remembered her as a no-nonsense girl, honest and loving. Blue would like her, he thought suddenly, and his heart lifted. He smiled at the two little girls standing by her side, thumbs in wondering mouths, hands clutching their mother's skirts. 'And these *dwts*, these are your daughters?' He used the Welsh word without thinking.

'Dots, Edgar?'

He laughed, shrugged, exchanged glances with Agathi.

'A friend of ours,' she explained, 'he says such words. It means "little one". We have another friend who comes from your fen land. He would say "recklins", I think.'

Eric laughed in his loud, infectious way. 'May'appen,' he said, 'but more likely "bairns". Yes, these are my two tiny tormenters. My little recklins. Little Matty, named for her mother, and Margaret, named for her grandmother, though we never call you that, do we, sweetheart? It's Greta.'

Two girls and, at last, a longed-for son, though Eric loved his daughters as much as he loved his infant son, and he beamed on the girls as they romped about the hall though Matilda frowned and chastised them and said they were not fit to be in polite company. Edgar heard his brother say to his wife, very quietly, for her alone: 'Tomorrow, sweetheart, we shall be in our own home. Have courage.'

Into the clamour swept Philippa, Alfred's wife, and she was magnificent. Some years older than Alfred, she was a tall, thin woman with a proud bearing, a beak of a nose and pursed lips that mouthed words of welcome. She was dressed richly, in high fashion. Elizabeta da Ginstinianis, Edgar found himself thinking and, after that, he silently thanked Heinrijc Mertens for the gifts of clothes he had made to Agathi. She would have need of them here where such things mattered as much as they had in Venezia. One thing good about his father, Edgar thought, he had cared little for social advancement. Land, yes, and profit, but he was a fair lord, if cheeseparing. Make do and mend, he said; look after the pennies and the groats would take care of themselves. Alfred had made a good marriage, if you counted lands and riches. He had married the daughter of a southern lord of good birth and with several profitable manors in the southern counties. Alfred was fortunate to have secured her as his bride, though she was some years older. 'Our fathers worked hard for this,' he told Edgar later that evening. 'With our joint lands, we can plan for a profitable future. We are to be at war with France, it's rumoured, and that gives me the opportunity to be recognised at court. This is a great time.'

Edgar remembered Heinrijc Mertens' resigned acceptance of war and death and destitution. A great time? He said nothing.

He tried to be generous but it seemed to him that the Lady Philippa was proud and haughty and had nothing but contempt for these cold, north lands and countrymen. Contempt, as well, for the returned brother, the runaway. Worse, she showed her contempt for Agathi. She smiled, true, but there was ice in her smiles, and icicles dangled from her lips when she spoke. She cast her eyes up and down the fashionable winter gown Agathi wore but her only comment was, 'Now so many of our guests have left us, we are few women here, and tonight we dine in the new chamber that has been built for our use. You will join us there for tonight's meal.'

'Philippa, of course you won't!' exclaimed Eric. 'What? Our brother and his wife just arrived, he long absent and she a stranger to us? And you say we don't all eat together in the hall? Alfred, tell her this can't be!'

Alfred winced. He forced a smile at his wife. 'Indeed, my dear, I think it would be thought more fitting by all if you women joined us in the great hall tonight.'

Philippa inclined her head. 'As you wish, husband.' To Agathi she said, 'Perhaps you do not have appropriate dress for tonight? Perhaps I may help you?'

Agathi said, 'There is a gown in the baggage. I think it will be adequate.' To Edgar, later, she said, 'This one is so much like Elizabeta da Ginstinianis. I like your brother Eric's wife more.'

'So do I, sweetheart. I'm afraid we have an ordeal ahead of us tonight.'

Agathi smiled. 'Worse than the donkey Veçdet and Big Aziz?'

'Same but different,' said Edgar.

Trestle tables were set out, with the top table raised on a dais. 'Father didn't bother with a raised top table but Philippa considers it of utmost importance,' Alfred told him. 'It is what she was used to in her father's house. You will join us there. The prior had to leave this morning but we have his chaplain still with us, and Lord Geoffrey of Irnham has condescended to join us tonight. We have knights and masters-at-arms still with us. My *mareschal* is supervising, as you see.' He waved a hand towards the harassed man instructing his men to turn out the dogs. 'We have a groom of the hall who should,' he frowned, 'have tended the fire long ago. Why this delay, man?' he shouted, and the groom cringed and hurried to the hearth in the centre of the hall. 'Philippa would like to have a wall hearth built into the side wall,' Alfred said, 'but there is so much building work going on elsewhere she has agreed to wait a while. Besides,' he added wistfully, 'I like a central hearth. It is very cheering.' He cleared his throat. 'Edgar,' he said, and stopped. Now what, thought Edgar. He waited. 'Philippa – my wife – she likes everything to be correct. Her family, you know. Everything of the most tasteful.'

'Speak out, Alfred. What's the problem? Your runaway, renegade brother? Be assured, I shall make my peace with the good brothers of Croyland.'

'Not that, though of course tongues will wag.' The thought of wagging tongues tightened his mouth. He started again. 'Actually, we wondered – Philippa wondered.' He stopped again. 'Your wife, is she Christian or…'

Edgar smiled politely. 'Or…?' he prompted, and watched Alfred's face mottle with deep purplish red embarrassment.

'It's the blessing, you see, at the start of the meal. And the prayers at the end of it. And,' he continued desperately, 'mass tomorrow morning. Philippa means only kindness.'

'Calm yourself, Alfred. Inform your wife that mine is a good Christian. A Greek Christian, but Christian for all that. She's no heathen infidel.' He saw the relief in Alfred's face. What would he think if he knew that beneath Edgar's calm words lay burning anger? What would he think if he knew that Edgar counted amongst his friends Muslim and Christian alike? Aye, Jews as well.

The wall behind the top table was hung with a splendid wall hanging, rich with red and black colour, and run through with gold thread. 'We had it put up for Christmas but it must be taken down tomorrow,' said Alfred. 'It's too precious to be ruined by fire smoke.'

The gold thread gleamed in the light from the sconces that flanked the wall hanging. Edgar looked again: not the wrought-iron sconces he remembered, forged long ago by Jack-Smith. These were beautifully crafted pieces, engraved and tooled in gilt copper; the four evangelists, seated, leaning slightly forward, holding a writing tool, about to scribe, it seemed, words spoken by the Holy Spirit. The evangelists were paired, so that St Luke solemnly regarded St Mark, and St Matthew stared at St John, from either side of the wall hanging. The twelve apostles sat facing towards them along the adjacent walls.

'Very fine, aren't they,' Alfred said complacently. 'A gift from Philippa's father. He – er – rescued them from a ruinous French church. Ancient craftsmanship – just look at the detailing of hair and beard. I assumed we would gift them to our church but Philippa said they might have been made for this hall. Their presence would remind us to thank the good God and his Son Jesus, especially at meal times. And the ones father had Jack-Smith make, well, they were rather crude, weren't they? He always was one for penny-catching.'

'What's become of Jack Smith? When we passed the smithy there was a stranger working there.'

Alfred scratched his nose, embarrassed. 'Philippa took a dislike to him. Said he was rude and bumptious – and he was, Edgar. You know he was.'

'An honest man for all that, and a good smith. What happened?'

'She had him turned off. Her father sent a smith from one of his manors, a far more civil churl.'

'But is he as good a smith?'

Alfred didn't answer. The servants had arrived with ewers of water, towels draped over their left shoulders; time for those at the top table to wash their hands.

The trestles were set with pewter at the top table; wooden trenchers elsewhere, thick slices of bread set to the left. Now that the great feasting of Christmas and Epiphany was over, there was no trumpet announcement, and Eric mouthed his disappointment but with such a glint in his eyes that Edgar had to turn away. The Marshall of the Hall was much in evidence, and there was a yeoman usher, and gentlemen of the hall serving on them. 'Though they are mostly sons from the other side of the blanket,' Eric murmured in his ear. Edgar tried not to laugh: he concentrated on pottage that had been set down before them. It was boar in a sweet and sour stew redolent with ginger and cloves and cinnamon, almonds and currants, sweetened with honey and sharpened with red wine vinegar. Edgar dipped his spoon in to the communal bowl, careful not to overfill it. Shame on him if he spilt any and soiled the tablecloth.

The pottage was removed, spoons wiped clean with a morsel of bread and the bread eaten. 'Tell your stomach to prepare itself,' murmured Eric. 'The meal is only just begun.' Roast haunch of venison was set down before them, sprinkled with salt and cinnamon; a capon with a sauce of sprinkled verjuice; the wing of plover with a camelyne sauce; roast rabbit; baked eel…the dishes went on and on, into the next course, and he thought of the simple food served in the *hans*, where all ate together regardless of rank, right hand only, because to use the left was a great impoliteness. There, the company was ranged around a communal serving board. No status there, no false pride. He remembered Dafydd's pleasure in the meal, and how he had been starved when he was a child. He remembered how Agathi had told him of the slaves' meagre food, how they were always hungry. He wondered what she thought of such excess, so much flesh and fish. There was a monstrously ornate salt cellar prominently displayed, and a silver boat-shaped dole vessel ready for the uneaten food that would be passed on to the poor.

Here, dining daggers were used to slice a bite-sized piece of meat and then its greasy blade was set down on the trencher to keep the tablecloth clean. Thumb and two forefingers of the right hand to raise the pieces up to the lips. A little salt taken on the point of the knife and placed on the trencher. He had all but forgotten the protocol. He looked towards Agathi and saw she was delicately raising a morsel to her lips. She was calm and quiet as always. Then he looked again. Her gaze was fixed downwards, at the table, but he saw the way her lips twitched. She was struggling to stay solemn. He wanted to laugh and cram his mouth with gobbets of meat and behave badly here in his brother's so-polite hall. But he didn't. Eric tried to catch his eye once more. Edgar smiled blandly at him and sliced another morsel of venison.

He thought about his brothers, and their welcome. They had thought him dead, and now he was alive and returned to them, but no prodigal: he had come from the east with pennies in his pocket, and a beautiful Greek Christian bride and, thanks be to Heinrijc Mertens, a dowry for his wife. He was no longer the timid youngest brother but a man, with a man's experience. For reasons he could not explain to himself, Edgar did not tell them the extent of his wealth, nor of his new sword-fighting skills, though he would never be as expert as Giles or Thomas or Dafydd. Nor did he tell them how Agathi had been captured as a slave to be sold to the highest bidder. He did not think his brothers would understand. The masterful Philippa would never understand. When he told the story of their journey through Anatolia and down the mountains to Attaleia, he was careful to keep Agathi's story from them. But he told them of Kazan, the boy-girl who had joined their caravan, the expert rider and archer who had fooled them all until the terrible avalanche that killed good Asperto and injured Kazan.

'And then you found out he – she – was a girl after all?' Eric was open-mouthed.

'Yes, but Dai had always known. He helped her.'

'That is most unusual,' Philippa said.

'She's an unusual girl,' said Edgar.

'She is our sister and our very dear friend,' said Agathi,

unexpectedly bold. 'We wish she were here with us now. We miss her, and all of our dear friends.'

'She is coming to England? To Lincolnshire?'

'In search of her grandfather, the storyteller, Will-the-Wordmaker. Perhaps you have heard of him? He is a Lincolnshire man.'

'Heard of him? Of course we've heard of him! He's well known in these parts. Or he was. He's dead, Edgar. Word is, he died this winter, out on the Fens. They found him frozen stiff in the morning mists. Your Kazan has a wasted journey.'

Edgar shut his eyes in agony for the bright girl he knew. Her grandfather dead. And Dafydd? Only God knew what had happened to him. The poor girl. Poor Kazan, bright warrior, bright star. He hoped Giles was with her still. He prayed for Dafydd's safe return. Agathi wept. 'But she will come to us, husband, wherever we may be. She will find us.'

Later still, in the new, quiet chamber that had been built for the family's use, he spoke with his eldest brother.

'Our father was adamant to the end,' Alfred told him. 'You were dead to him. We are sorry for it, Edgar, but so it is.'

And so it was. Foolish to hope for more. When had his father ever spared a thought for him, the youngest son? He dared the question that was tormenting him.

'How did he die, brother?'

Alfred sighed, gustily. 'Nothing to do with you, Edgar, be sure of that, though he was much afflicted by your flight. No, this was a hunting accident late in the year. We were all there, Philippa as well. It was a grand chase but suddenly Oswald stumbled – you remember his black stallion? Father was thrown headlong. He was badly injured; he lingered for some days in great pain and the doctors said there was nothing that could be done only give him poppy to ease his suffering. Tell truth, it was a relief when he died. We had the horse slaughtered, of course.'

Why 'of course', wondered Edgar. The horse had done no wrong. His father was a stern man who could not love him but who was, after all, a man who cared for his people and lavished love on sturdy black Oswald. He was a man who had died in agony. That must surely be cause for grieving; and grieve he did, standing in the chancel of the church before his father's tomb. His effigy was life-sized, the stone and paint still glaringly new-worked. A pillow supported his head held up by angels. His feet were supported by a dog and a lion. Next to it was Edgar's mother, another life-sized effigy though the years had softened and deepened the colours on the stone. Hand-to-hand, palm-to-palm in eternal prayer. Had she really looked like this? He didn't know, had never known. It was a thing not talked of.

Outside, grey mist settled on the manor, snow quietly falling on deeper snow.

The next day brought worrying news. Mass was done and they were in the courtyard bidding the guests farewell when a messenger arrived from Bradwell Manor. Bedraggled horse, bedraggled rider, both exhausted by their frantic journey to bring dire news. 'I didn't expect trouble from there,' Alfred said. He was shocked. 'Philippa insisted I set up a reeve of her own choosing there, one of her father's men. He is totally dependable.'

But there was a serious problem: the reeve had been found dead in the icy pond the day after Epiphany. Not found till the morning because of the festivities. Everything pointed to unnatural death, said Alfred. To murder. And the murderer? Cedric, hayward and pinder, had accused a villein called Bernt who, he said, had good cause to hate John Reeve. Bernt had been robbing the copses of good timber. Cedric had seen that underwood was cut from elm and maple and hornbeam. He had reason to believe Bernt had plans to fell two of the full-grown black poplars that had been marked out as timber for the new building work here at the Home Manor. The reeve, honest man that he was, had found it out and had saved the trees. Now, John Reeve was dead. Bernt was stubborn and silent but Cedric had arrested him, and confined him in the narrow cell in the undercroft. 'It's a plaäce with a great-big oak door and a listy lock John Reeve had made to saäfen the valuable stores, maäster. Now it keeps Bernt kibbled an'all. Cedric said I was to stuttle mesen and ride here fast as I could, even though there wasn't a glimmer o' daylight, because yer'd be wanting to know straight off.' The man stopped for breath. He daren't say how frightened he had been, riding alone through the dark; his fear of dead and living alike, especially the wild gangs that haunted the High Dyke road; relief when the first pale light glimmered in the eastern sky; his gladness when he reached Rochby, even though he had no good news to bring.

'You've done well,' Alfred told him, and the messenger heaved a great sigh.

'But what a time to bring such news!' Alfred fumed. The messenger had been sent to the kitchens, the horse to the stables, both to be given fodder. Eric and his family were long gone. Alfred had spoken with Philippa privately for some time; an altercation, it seemed. Edgar heard Philippa's voice raised: 'You are a fool. You owe nothing, husband.' Alfred's answer was inaudible but Philippa snorted with contempt. In the end, she had swept Agathi away to the new private solar.

The brothers sat together in a window embrasure in the hall. 'I have not the time now to go to Bradwell. I wish to God I had listened to Philippa and got rid of the manor! Leased it at least! There've been poor enough returns these past two years.' He gritted his teeth, sucked in angry breath. 'We plan to remove to her father's manor when he dies, and leave this wretched northern holding. Oh, I'll set a reeve in charge but I'll be glad to leave this place. Nothing but misery after mother died. Before that, it was a happy home. She was beautiful and joyful – but you won't remember that. She died giving birth to you.' For a moment, Edgar was reminded of his father's anger, then Alfred was sighing and brushing aside his bad temper. 'Not your fault, brother,' he said, but Edgar was sure that Alfred thought that it was. His brother was frowning, thinking. 'There are problems, Edgar, serious problems, but I think you are the man to resolve them.'

'Me?' Edgar said, startled.

Alfred nodded. 'I must stay here at Rochby. Plough Monday's come, and though the reeve here is an excellent man, I like to be on hand; see all are back to work. After all, I am in authority here now. I have other plans that I hope will serve Rochby well: I intend calling on the retainers for fighting service. Father insisted on paying retainment service to gentlemen only, and I have kept to this. With my riding household, I can muster a good number of fighting men to serve our young King Edward. The young men here, our guests, will be part of that. The tournament was only a beginning.' He smiled, anticipating reward. What a king to serve! Youth, vitality, so handsome that women adored him. Such an athlete, such prowess at the tournament; a hunter, whether boar or venison; falconry, fishing…was there no end to this king's virtues? And best of all he valued valour and virtue, not birth. Now there was Edward's courageous determination to confront Philip of France for what was rightfully his…if, Alfred thought, he served loyally, and with courage, surely he should be rewarded?

'I need someone to go as proxy to Bradwell, and immediately. Edgar, I ask you to be that person. Would you become the reeve of the manor at Bradwell? With the old reeve dead, the manor is much in need of care. Tell the truth, it is Philippa's idea. She has a clever head, my wife.' He glanced sideways at his brother. 'But perhaps you do not care to take on such a role?'

Edgar wryly acknowledged that this brother of his would not gift him a manor, not even a small, unprofitable manor that he wanted to be rid of. Alfred was his father's son, and money and land mattered more than anything. Maybe, Edgar thought, he could lease the manor later, after these problem times – maybe buy it. For now, it was enough to be reeve and discover what was amiss. But was he really the man to resolve these problems? Dai was the man for that, and Dai was only the good God knew where. Venezia? Escaped? Worse than all, was he captured and convicted of crimes he had not committed, condemned to death like the unfortunate innocent glassmaker of Murano?

It was a heavy start to a new life in England.

'You must discover the truth, Edgar, and bring the murderer to justice. Perhaps this thief Bernt is the murderer. It seems likely. The sokemen are loyal enough, and bound to the land.'

'Not free men?' Edgar was surprised. He had always supposed they were.

'Not entirely. They are bound to give us fifty-five days' work each year. It suits us better that way. However, there are only six families to help stave off the threat of revolt amongst the villeins.' He shrugged at Edgar's surprise. 'I told you, the manor is much reduced in lands and in tenants. As for the villeins, they must be kept well under the thumb. Find the murderer, bring him to justice, and the manor will once again be productive.'

'Have you considered making your villeins freemen?' Edgar asked. 'Free men, with a share of the land?'

Alfred snorted with derision. Where was the economy in giving freedom and a parcel of land to ten rebellious villeins and their families?

'They would work all the harder,' Edgar said, 'if they were working for their own livelihood. There would be no opportunity for rebellion, and no cause. And hard work it must be, if this manor is as hard-set as you say, and must recover.' He did not say that he disliked the idea of serfs. They had rights under the law, true, but they were bound men for all that, and therefore little better than slaves. His head swam with memories of the lakeside at Beyşehir in the high plateau of Anatolia where he had first seen Agathi, pale and wretched slave, but so beautiful she had stolen away his breath and his heart. Slave through no fault of her own but taken by force. These villeins were bound to their lords through no fault of their own.

'Is that what the monks taught you, little brother?' Alfred asked. 'Make all men equal? Where is the wisdom in that? God decrees order. Each man in his place if we are to keep the country secure. Every right-thinking man knows this.' When Edgar didn't answer, he continued: 'The tenants – the sokemen – would not think kindly of land being handed out willy-nilly to wretched villeins. Then we'd have a different rebellion on our hands. Or hadn't you thought of that? Maybe you'll think differently once you've seen it, brother.'

7

Attaleia
February 1337
I am not permanent here; I came here to leave…
(Yunus Emre, 14ᵗʰC)

Winter voyages were hard come by but there was a man who said there were passages to be had. 'An Arab ship, *efendi*. Perhaps your Christian friend does not like this?' He was a small, wiry, dark man from the countries east of Anatolia.

'Muslim, Christian, it's all the same to us. And to the Mevlana,' Mehmi added.

'The Mevlana?'

Mehmi's thin, fine-boned face was lit by his smile. 'My father was a fervent believer in the wisdom of Jalal al Din Rumi, the Mevlana, who is buried in Konya. Many people from my country are followers of the Mevlana. My Christian friends also honour him, and find comfort in his words.'

The man's face brightened. 'This is good to hear. I know of the Mevlana. My wife is from Urgüp where people carve their houses out of the rock itself. Her father was a follower of Jalal al Din Rumi, and his father before him.' He was himself a devout believer in Allah and his prophet Mohammed, and followed the Shi'a way of Islam, and a line of Imams appointed by the Prophet Muhammad himself. Or by Allah. Not elected leaders, as the Sunni would have it. As the captain of the ship believed. No, when the Great Prophet died, leadership should have passed directly to his cousin. But in the end, all Muslims were brothers who shared the same faith. 'There are berths, *efendi*, for you and your friends, and the captain will make the *hanım efendi* comfortable.'

'We thank you, brother.'

A winter voyage. Mehmi wondered if the Fenman was crazy after all, as Thomas had said. And to risk their lives in the winter weather was the desperate act of a crazy fool. But there was Blue's woman, Hatice, once a slave, now turned driver whipping him on, and the boy Niko just as eager, just as crazy. As if, thought Mehmi, time were the enemy. And maybe it was. May'appen, as the Fenman would say. Enemy to him whose father was dead, his beloved father, none better. What should Mehmi do now but travel on, take time as it chanced? These friends of his, friends who longed for their companions, he would join them. After all, they were his friends as well, his good friends, born out of conflict and trouble and trust and loyalty. It would be a blessing to be with all their good company again, even if it were in the dark, cold country beyond the holy land of Islam. He wondered what the golden girl was doing, the sharp, bright warrior Kazan. And Dafydd, the quiet brown dangerous man his father had loved as a man loves his son; and Dafydd in his turn had loved Kara Kemal as if he had been his own father, with no difference of race or religion or blood. Dafydd, his brother-in-love, who did not know of their father's death.

'Tomorrow, then, *efendi*. Be early. The ship sails at dawn and the captain is a man who likes all to be ready before time. The weather-wise men say there should be a calm voyage for some days at least, and he wishes to take advantage of this.'

'We shall be there. Early, tell him.'

Another leave-taking, except that this time Sakoura and his wife stood on the quay and the four of them, Blue, Hatice, Mehmi, Niko, were the ones to stand on the swaying deck of the ship watching the figures grow smaller and smaller on the quayside until they were swallowed up into blue distance.

It was a *baghlah*, with lateen-set sails. 'A mule,' Mehmi told them. 'That is what *baghlah* means in their language.' It was a deep-sea dhow, and heavy enough to need a crew of thirty. He prayed this mule would be stubborn enough to kick against the winter storms. But now, the weather was set fair and soon the sun would break through the early morning mist and light the sea in dazzling, glinting flashes of silver and blue and green. This was how he was leaving his country of nineteen summers in search of the friends he had found on that journey through the high places of Anatolia.

8

Bradwell Manor, Lincolnshire
February 1337

Wind sharp, hillside bleak, hard to win shelter;
Ford is impassable, lake is frozen;
A man may near stand on one stalk of grass.
(Anon: 10th-11^thC)

The low sun was dropping fast behind a cover of dark cloud. Time they downed tools and got back to the village. Light enough to see by still, but a day's work was a day's work, and the men had worked with a will. Darkening land below, dark rim of cloud above and, between, like a strip of bright ribbon, the orange-golden glow of the setting sun. A spinney of thorns was outlined in black against the brightness, as clear as if it had been drawn by Brother Hibald, the best of the Croyland scribes. A shift in the cloud and the round orange-gold sun appeared, pouring its rays through the cloud gap; no warmth in it but no smell of snow in the wind, though it was a snide east wind at that. Snide, he thought, what Blue would have said. What they all said in these parts. Here he was back in Lincolnshire and Blue far away in Attaleia. How he missed him. How he had need of him, of his physical strength, the way he could turn his hand to any task, his fenland speech that all here would understand. Not like his own polite Norman-English. Most of all, he missed Blue's easy friendship, his coarse humour. Even that annoying greeting: *Another howry day, altar boy.*

Edgar stood upright and stretched, his fingers finding and easing the sore places. His back was aching from a hard day in the woodlands. They were repairing the fencing that protected the coppiced trees. 'Dead hedging', they called it here: stakes set two feet apart and interwoven with long, flexible *ethers*. Nothing permanent about it but at least it could be made on the spot and it did its job. Make sure bushes and trees grew up around the gappy hedging and then it would be sound. 'Drive stakes in first,' he ordered. 'Without stakes, it's no good.' They said there was an escaped boar hereabouts, a bad-tempered, vicious beast that had smashed through the flimsy palisades of the sty. Edgar hadn't caught sight of him; not a whisker, not a twitch of curly tail, no signs of rooting. They must be mistaken, he thought. Another crime to lay at John Reeve's door.

John Reeve. Now there was a story.

Those first days – all but a full moon ago – were chaotic. He and Agathi, with the servants Alfred thought necessary, had come to the manor on the dankest and dreariest of winter days. They travelled along the High Dyke, the King's Highway, a worthy procession of outriders and baggage carts because Alfred had said they must arrive safely, and with dignity. They travelled along a road built long ago by the Romans and still in better repair than many modern roads, though stretches of it were renowned for bold gangs of robbers. It would take them to Lincoln but they turned aside and followed a lane that was deeply rutted, treacherous with ice and snow. It led down the slope of the hill into a shallow valley and to the frozen beck and rickety, slithery plank that was the bridge. In front of them was the village. As they came closer, the stench of shit came to their nostrils. Agathi flinched. The outriders blew their trumpets to announce their arrival. Ensigns fluttered. A grand arrival indeed, Edgar thought. It was not what he would have chosen; nor, he knew, would Agathi. There was no one to greet them because he had insisted on setting out at first light the next morning, not waiting for an out-rider to go on ahead. The hall would not be prepared for their arrival, Alfred protested. If the hall was ill prepared, said Edgar, well, they had met with worse on the journey through Anatolia. On board ship for Venezia, truth to tell, was the harder life. Alfred nodded, muttered; he had no experience of travel and foreign ways. He insisted Agathi travel in the Rochby carriage but she had already seen the cumbersome, covered vehicle with its great wheels and shook her head: she preferred to travel on horseback by her husband's side. 'That carriage,' she said privately to Edgar, 'would surely shake the bones out of my body.' And so Edgar and Agathi had set out before dawn the following morning and arrived at Bradwell early in the afternoon, though the day was so dank and the sky so lowering it seemed daylight never truly dawned.

A lean, pock-faced man was summoned to greet them. His eyes flickered when he saw strangers, not Squire Alfred nor his lady. 'Wot's dis 'ere, den?' he muttered under his breath. He smiled ingratiatingly at the visitors. 'Squire Alfred's yer bruvver, den?' He couldn't keep the surprise out of his voice; a younger brother sent to do a reeve's work? Interesting. A cock's egg of a bruvver, 'an 'all, from the look o' fings. With a flick of his wrist, he summoned boys to hold the horses' bridles while the visitors dismounted; he gave orders to take the horses to stable, to groom them, water and feed them. It was Cedric, the hayward and pinder, the man who was useful to John Reeve, and who was now useful in keeping the prisoner in close captivity. Alfred had told him, 'He knows how to keep order. Rely on him.' There was disdain in the smile he turned on Edgar. 'Book learning won't be much help to you there, brother; what you need is a strong sword arm and that, I can promise you, is what Cedric Hayward has. John Reeve and his man Cedric were my wife's choice to replace the old dodderer left in charge by my father. You will see how the manor suffered under him, and how much remains to be done to set all to right.'

It was the reeve's responsibility to maintain the manor and its well-being. If he shirked his duty, how could the sokemen and villeins do their work? Perhaps the former reeve had been an old dodderer, as his brother said, but little ditching and delving had been done here this past year, from the look of it, and now the manor was reaping the rewards of sloth. Edgar checked himself. Unfair. It was not the fault of the villeins, whatever his brother might say. Perhaps it was not the fault of the reeve nor the hayward. It seemed that much of the year's harvest had been sent to Rochby manor, together with slaughtered animals, for the Christmas feasting. Edgar remembered the silver dole ships laden with food for the poor. He looked at the village folk hastily assembled to meet him. The sokemen and their wives and children looked lean enough but the rest – the rebellious villeins, Edgar supposed – shivered, stinking skinny bodies in threadbare tunics and kirtles. The dole ships would have found a better harbour here.

Cedric called a servant to him and instructed fires to be lit and a meal to be prepared. The kitchens had not been much used, Master Edgar must understand, and the hall had stood empty. Hif there 'ad been warning of their arrival…

Edgar did not like this Cedric. He did not like the way the man swaggered about the place. A hayward, he thought, no more than that, then memory kicked in. Cedric was a bully. Agathi edged close and whispered that he reminded her of Big Aziz, the thuggish, terrifying righthand-man of fat Veçdet the slave trader. This man was not huge and muscular, like Big Aziz: he was whippy-lean; his face was thin, wedge-shaped, pock-marked; his eyes a watery pale-blue that never quite met your own. But there was about him the same love of cruelty for cruelty's sake. Edgar paid heed to her, this one-time slave who was now his wife. Her instincts were always right. Besides, he was himself remembering Venezia, and how Dai had returned from the glass-making island of Murano saying that no one would talk to him; all were sullen and silent, intimidated by someone powerful enough to keep them from talking. These villagers when he met with them, sokemen and villeins alike, listened in sullen silence but they would not talk to him.

He and Agathi made an inspection of Bradwell village. The land must wait until next daybreak, and before that he needed to talk with the leading men of the village, and with Cedric Hayward. They started with the hall, since this was where they must live and sleep and Edgar was anxious for Agathi to have as much comfort as possible in this neglected place.

It was old-fashioned, built in the old Norman style, with outer stairs leading up to a stout wooden door, that much he remembered from childhood, but now he saw it was a good stone building for all its age, with solid shutters to the windows and, in the solar's round-arched windows, parchment had been added made from oiled goatskin thin enough to let light through but strong enough to keep out the icy wind and swirling snow. With wall-hangings and warm cushions, the solar would be a cosy place where Agathi could find some peace and privacy. The hall rose up to the usual trusses and beams but, instead of a central hearth, there was a wall-placed hearth such as Philippa coveted, with a great cylindrical chimney climbing the outer wall and rising high above the thatched roof: a thick thatch, re-laid in time for winter. On the ground floor was the undercroft for storage of beans and fruit and grain – animals, if need be. Cedric pointed to the bolted and locked chamber where the villein Bernt was held. ''At's 'im in 'ere, Master Edgar,' he said. ''Ee'll keep. 'Ee's snug as a flea in an 'owd cat's fur. I'll check on 'im layter.' And Edgar, berating himself for a coward, agreed, 'Later.'

Nothing wrong with the hall nor undercroft nor, across the yard from it, the thatched, timber kitchen with bakehouse and brewhouse backing on to it. The dairy was ranged around the same side of the open court. On the third side were stables for the hall horses, and a lean-to timber building with a thick plank door, another that was well secured. Across the bare-branched orchard was the church, a small, simple building of stone, no tower: a single bell hung in the bell-cote. The thatching was in need of repair, Edgar noted. Further off was the great granary but there were gaps in its sides and the thatch was rotting on that as well. Easy pickings for vermin. They had passed one of the sokemen's farms on their way down the rutted track to the plank-bridge; two more were in the valley bottom and another part way up the opposite hill where the track climbed up towards the ridge. The sixth was out of sight but, since all were on the land that was left to the manor, he supposed it must be beyond the church. The rest were now the property of adjoining manors. These sokemen's farms were more dilapidated than he liked to see but spring repairs would see them sound enough. It was the villeins' cotts that shocked Edgar. They were opposite the manor house, on the other side of the track, each with its croft extending towards the beck. From most of them, no smoke rose, and wisps from only a few. They were all unkempt, dilapidated, meagrely thatched with last year's rushes; all stank of shit. The villeins looked gaunt and hungry. Worst of all, beneath the sullenness was an undercurrent of unrest and hostility that worried him. Then there was the shocking dilapidation of the land: signs of neglect and disrepair everywhere he looked.

He remembered it from seven – maybe eight – years ago, before he was sent to Croyland, when he had visited in company with his brothers and his father, that stern, rigorous lord, but a fair one. Edgar was a young boy then but he remembered that the manor had been well administered, well husbanded and returning a good profit. A good reeve was in charge, whatever Alfred might say; an elderly man but much respected. Summer time, and the manor lands sat well in their shallow valley. A peaceful place, and he was content to spend day after day proddling in the beck for small fish, and riding over the open lands and through woodland. Higher up the cliff was heathland, wild and uncultivated. Lower down the Fens began, those great watery tracts brimming with fish and fowl.

'It's not profitable now, Edgar,' his brother had said. 'That's the truth of it. Father should never have sold land to the Templars, and that was before you were born, when the Templars were still powerful. They had a huge holding higher up the heath, a great temple, and lands abutting Bradwell. He said it made sense to sell to them, if he had to sell at all, since the lands roundabout were all Templar held.'

Since then, the Templars had been finished by the second Edward, after Philippe le Bel had organised his rout of the sect in France. Their lands were forfeit to the Crown; the great temple was desolate, abandoned to whoever cared to seek shelter under its roof. And not many dared. It was hag-ridden, they said, a cursed place. Its great domed temple was visible on the winter skyline. Edgar had seen it as a young boy, and its towers, but now the wind whistled around it and, if it were not cared for, would sink into decay. Alfred had said there were rumours that the Hospitallers at Eagle were to establish a Commandery there, and Edgar hoped that would prove to be true. Better by far bring the lands back into order, life into the temple, than have this perpetual reminder of a brutal act.

Since land had been sold to the Templars, this manor had shrunk even more. Since then, Alfred had leased or sold huge amounts of what land remained – woods, arable, pasture – to other manor holdings, and with them the sokemen's farms and villeins' crofts and tofts and, of course, their legal service to the running of the manor.

But it was big enough still to make a living for those who lived here, thought Edgar, if it were efficiently managed. If the leased land could be brought back into its care. If – small hope – some of the sold land could be bought back. It was well watered by springs and a beck, and the land was fertile red-brown earth up to the eastern boundary with limestone gravel that made the earth rough but good for all that; sandy land at the western boundary, ideal for the warren, and he remembered seeing black rabbits when he was a boy, bred for their pretty, valuable fur as much as for their flesh. The manor still retained the warren, and there were limestone seams that could be quarried for boundary walls and building, if he'd a mind to build more in stone. If Alfred didn't quarry out all the good stone in this ambitious building scheme of his; it seemed the stone he was using came from Bradwell.

Edgar thought of the accused man Bernt held in tight bonds in the undercroft in the cold and dark; of his wife Ellen, a pretty young woman as silver haired as Agathi though her hair was a tumble of curls where Agathi's was shining straight. Ellen's face was haggard where it should have been smooth and smiling. There was a son, Oluf, barely nine summers old, with his mother's silver-fair curls. When Edgar looked at the boy, he imagined a son of his own; he saw Niko and the way his long lashes would quiver and cover the mischief in his dark eyes, though little mischief there was in these hazel eyes. But this boy looked him full in the face, as Niko did, and his chin was raised in that proud way Niko had, beaten but not cowed, daring this new-come stranger, this brother of the Lord of the Manor, to call his father murderer.

Edgar was consumed with worry and, truth be told, guilt. He thought how Dai had stayed behind in Venezia though he knew he was a hunted man. 'Get them all to safety,' he had told Giles. Edgar had heard him. Yes, Dai knew Edgar was as much in need of protection as Kazan and Agathi. A runaway novice, a young man unused to the wide world, even after two years' journeying; a novice sword-fighter. How could he restore order to this manor with its undercurrent of violence? How could he protect Agathi? As well as Blue, he needed Dai here, a dangerous man but one to give him good counsel about this death, the man accused, evidence of theft, a cruel bully against whom no man was willing to give evidence, and such a gap between those who lived in comfort and those who struggled to survive.

Agathi was disturbed by what she saw. While Edgar discussed the terrible business with the hayward, Cedric, she explored the place.

There were pitifully few barrels of salted meat and fish stored away; remnants of cheeses on the shelves in the dairy; sacks of coarse flour in the bakehouse. She thought of the lavish banquet that had been served the night before at Rochby and wondered how much provision had come from this poor manor. She watched women come with pitifully small quantities of mixed barley and pea meal to be baked on the bakehouse stones. They had no fire in their own homes but even if they had these wretched creatures were obliged to use the manor bakehouse, and pay for the privilege. One of the sokemen's wives was escorting her, and explained this to her and yes, she had understood the woman's words. They were speaking in laborious French; Edgar had taught her that language and her understanding was good enough but she did not have the words for what she saw now.

The same woman escorted her round the manor cotts. Agathi was shocked by the stinking poverty in which the villeins lived. There was an old grandmother, rheumy-eyed and blue-cold in a cott where there was no bright hearth, no food, no warm blankets, and young children crawled about the filthy earth floor, their teeth chattering with cold. The thatch had mostly blown away or rotted. Green mould seeped down the walls. 'She must be taken into the hall,' Agathi said, and her speech was painfully slow and halting. Rémi's signs, learnt from Edgar, conveyed as much as her words. 'They are making a good fire now in the hall. It will be warm there tonight, and there will be food for the grandmother.' She looked at them, this pitifully underclad, underfed family, and she in her warm travelling gown and fur-lined cloak. The rest of the villeins' wives crowded outside the opening of the cott, agog for a sight of this foreigner. Agathi spoke to them all: 'Will you all live here in the hall this winter? In spring we shall repair your homes. Make them good.'

The sokeman's wife frowned, wondering if she had understood this foreigner's meaning. It was the young woman Ellen who understood and translated. The village women looked frowningly at

Agathi, suspicion on their faces. The young squire, for squire he was though his brother had made him reeve, had brought a heathen wife back from the Holy Land, and one who couldn't speak Norman-English, let alone good Lincolnshire.

Agathi regarded their faces: they were like Hatice, she thought, so harsh-seeming but inside wanting the best for their men and children and nothing to give them in way of comfort, neither a warm hearth nor a full belly. Little wonder they mistrusted her, with one of their own bound hand and foot in that dark, cold cell and like to die unless Edward could save him.

'Please tell the women, Ellen, whoever wishes may sleep in the hall this winter. They may sleep there tonight. The men also. We shall be many but there will be fire and food enough and a warm place to sleep.'

'Does your man agree to this?' Ellen asked.

Would Edgar agree? Agathi did not know. She had not stopped to think. It seemed so long now since Edgar had rescued her from wretched captivity, and Edgar had been pleased to allow her to make choices. He valued her thoughts and opinions. But this? 'Yes,' she said with certainty, 'my man will agree.'

Ellen nodded. This could only be good.

Ellen seemed to like her well enough, one of the women muttered, and Ellen with most cause for distrust. Besides, she was a gentle little thing, said another, nobbut a bairn herself, and for sure she thought the world of her handsome husband. Not like that vemonous beezum Lord Muck had brung back from southern parts, Hilda said, that toad dressed up in silks and damask. But Hilda was always brazenly outspoken. Got her into trouble with John Reeve, that tongue of hers, and a lashing from that brute Cedric.

Agathi caught at some of what they said. If only she could speak their language! She scrabbled in her memory for Blue's words. 'We can tent best for the abless and bairns like this,' she told them, each word quaintly precise. They stared at her, astonishment all over their faces. She heard Blue's voice in her head as clear as if he stood next to her. 'It is doable if we remble ourselves.'

Hilda started to laugh, a wheezing laugh but laughter all the same. 'Then let's git agaäte o' moving our tuts, lass,' she snorted. 'Yer heard the mistress,' she said to the rest. Ellen smiled though there was sadness in it. 'They will come,' she said. 'It is a good thing you do, to give them warmth and comfort for the winter. The bairns will be healthy and the old grandmother will live, and the rest of us will have food in our bellies.'

Agathi felt tears misting her eyes: she knew who Ellen was. Generous, graceful Ellen, wife of Bernt-the-villein who was imprisoned in the undercroft. How cold it must be there, this drear dark day. The curly-haired boy was their young son; as many curls as Edgar but as silver fair as herself. He glowered at her, reminding her of Niko, her brother, though he was as fair as Niko was dark.

Perhaps the child she was carrying would have silver-fair curls like this child. This third week in January, their first day in the manor, she was sure she was with child. Part of her was elated, longing to give her husband a son. Perhaps a daughter. What did it matter? A man like Edgar would welcome boy or girl child. How lucky she was to be the wife of such a man. But he was worried, she knew, because this was a dangerous place. She felt it. It reminded her of the slave camp, and the way Veçdet controlled them all with the help of his guard, Big Aziz. John Reeve was dead but his man Cedric Hayward controlled the village. This she knew without being told. She had sensed it from the moment of meeting him earlier that afternoon. But what proof did she have? No one would dare speak out, as no one dared speak in Veçdet's camp. She frowned, thinking hard, staring through the thin parchment that protected the window at the growing dark beyond. Niko, my brother, she thought, if you were here you would not allow this. Kazan, bright Kazan, boy-girl, warrior and maiden, you would not allow this. Dafydd, strange, frightening man that you are, you rescued me and Niko and Hatice and Asperto. You grieved for the death of the child Hatice loved. You grieved for poor, drowned Asperto. You hate slavery, and these villagers are slaves. They live in fear, as we did. Edgar, my gentle husband, you hate injustice and you will not, must not, allow this.

She went down the outer steps from the hall and across the yard to the kitchens. The ground was frozen now but come the thaw it would be a morass of mud, unless they found a way to make it firm. She should see what food was being prepared, and if there was enough to feed all, not just the newly arrived reeve and his wife and servants. Perhaps there would be those who would talk to her. Talk to her! How could they talk to her, she who spoke Greek and Turkish and a smattering of the Venetian language, and the pitiful French that Edgar had painstakingly taught her? She needed Blue's language that even Dafydd could barely understand. But Edgar knew it. Edgar knew these people. He came from here. This was his country. She felt calmed, confident.

Inside the kitchens was clamour and alarm. The new reeve was here without warning, and he a brother of the squire! There must be a meal fitting for him, and what was there to give him? The bulk of it had been sent to Rochby, and salted meat needing soaking overnight before it could be cooked, what was left of it. There were provisions John Reeve had stashed, they all knew that, but no key to be found.

'Now then,' said an under-cook who had been spared from the Rochby kitchens to come with the party, 'yer telling me yer can't organise an 'arvest supper for a fambly o' fieldmice? What matter that the best provisions have been sent to Rochby? Surely there must be something left for the young maäster? Yes – the young maäster! Don't yer 'member the young maäster?'

The older men remembered the young boy with the curling golden hair and eyes as blue as the bluebells that grew in the woods in spring. A gentle boy, the young squire, clever and gone for book-learning to the abbey at Croyland, and now he was here to restore order and harmony to this sad manor. Nothing had been heard of him for a while now. It was said he'd turned runaway, and his stern father like to one mazzled by it all, and dead now, too late to see his recklin returned with a pretty young wife, a foreigner but Christian, they said. And now she had sent orders that the whole village was to share in the evening meal! And without her husband's permission. Should they follow her orders?

'Yer mun do as the mistress says,' said William Cook. 'She's a quiet-spoken one, fer sure, but she's a good woman, wi' 'er head screwed on, and a good wife for our young maäster, and 'ee thinking the world o'er. Yer mun tek 'eed o' me. Even if we served up oatmeal gruel, I think yer villagers would be greätful, from the look o' them.'

The stories went round, licking the servants as the hot fire licked the cauldrons. Oluf was there, the silver-curly-haired son of the villein Bernt and his wife Ellen. He was tending the bellows where the fat-bellied cauldrons were sitting on their brandreths over the fire. He saw the woman Agathi come into the kitchens, walking calmly, quietly about the place, stopping to talk with this man, that boy, until she came to him. He glowered at her. A good woman, they said, but his father was bound and imprisoned in that dark cell, and that pretty young husband of hers was doing nothing to help him. He'd believe Cedric Hayward. Like his brother the Lord of Rochby, and that woman he'd wed who ruled him.

'Tell, Oluf,' he heard her say, slowly, carefully, quietly. 'What here? Tell to help you baba. Help baba and tell.'

Oluf shrugged. Her words were difficult to follow, this strange, beautiful, foreign wife of the new reeve. She was fair and fragile, the women said; how could she cope with managing a manor? But she had taken care of the old grandmother, taken care of them all, given them a warm place to sleep over the cold winter. She had sent the tiny bairns to the warm kitchens so that they were not out in the freezing wind and ice-cold cotts. She had set pert Joan to watch over them, make sure they didn't get into mischief while the women and older bairns moved what they needed into the hall. A stringy-haired, mucky-faced pest, Joan was, an orphan taken in by big Hilda, and look at her now, sticking her tongue out at him. And Hilda had called her a sensible body, well able to look after the bairns! He ignored her and concentrated on the bellows he had been set to blow. Now the new mistress had come to see how the preparations for their supper went. His mouth watered at the savoury, herby, meaty smells drifting through the kitchen then he heard her quiet voice asking questions that should never be answered, and yet there was no other way of saving his father. 'Help baba and tell.'

He looked about him. That Joan was trying to stop a quarrel that had erupted between two of the bairns. Pinching each other, he knew that's what it would be with those two. Mawks in her head if she couldn't see it. Needed a wap on their arses; that would sort 'em. But there she was, playing on that elder pipe her da had made her, and thinking that would fettle 'em. That interfering beesom of a wife of greasy Hugo-the-sokeman had her sticky nose in a pan. He hoped the steam scorched it off. Cedric was nowhere to be seen. This gentle woman was kind, though she was a strange one who spoke in a strange language that only his mother could understand. 'He'll kill me if I tell.'

'Kill? Who?' She looked at him, at his frowning face and rigid body. 'Cedric Hayward?' she asked quietly.

'How d'yer know?'

'I know.' She nodded. 'Not good man.'

His face flushed red with anger. His chin came up in the way that reminded her of Niko. 'John Reeve was a cruel man, and Cedric is just as cruel. They were the thieves, not my father, but there is no one to believe us.'

She frowned, trying to follow his rapid words. He sounded like Blue, and though she could not speak his language, at least she could understand some of it. 'John Reeve is thief?'

'Yes – and Cedric, but no one dare say a word. All of them are cowards. I am not a coward. But if I tell my mam will suffer and my da will surely die.'

'You must tell, Oluf. Truth must tell.'

He wasn't sure he had understood her. She spoke some French, and he knew a few words, but his own language she spoke badly. A few words here and there. He eyed her, wondering if he dared trust her.

'Soon my man come – you tell him truth. He know what to do. Yes?' She was very certain of herself, of her young husband, and somehow it calmed him. Perhaps there was hope, after all. Slowly, he nodded.

'Yes.'

'Good.' She patted his hand and moved away to where William Cook was cherishing the biggest pot-bellied cauldron sat over the fire, flames lapping around its base. 'Clingard' they called it, he'd been told, and it had not been used in years, not since the old days when the lord would arrive with his retinue and friends and there would be a banquet in the hall for all the grand people. And now who would be the guests seated at the trestles in the hall? Sokemen and villeins and cottars and their miserable families! It was unthinkable! Yet this gentle mistress was a woman of sense, and these villagers were desperate. Even the sokemen were at their wits' end, taxed as they were, and winter provisions sent to the Home Manor. He'd seen for himself how much was wasted, how much dole was given to the poor of Rochby, though they were not as poor as these villagers of Bradwell. Lean times here, sure enough. Well, new customs now the young master and mistress had arrived. Or maybe not. His father had told him of the ancient custom of boon feasts; protection and food given in exchange for labour. Out of fashion now, but perhaps a good idea here in this starved manor. He smiled on the little, fair mistress. She wanted to taste the pottage? Let him take the lid off the pot and give her a spoonful. He'd given orders to wring the necks of a few old hens, hastily plucked and pulled them, carved them into gobbets, used what herbs there were, flavoured it well, though it was nothing more than the ordinary, and likely the flesh would be stringy. Take care now, mistress. It's hot.

'Is good,' she said approvingly. 'Very good.'

He preened. He tasted. Yes. It was good. He hoped these wretched villeins knew how good it was.

Oluf watched her as she walked out of the steamy kitchen and into the yard. He saw her walk across the yard to the big oak door of the undercroft, saw her struggle with its weight and open it enough to enter. He frowned, puzzled. Was she going to see his father for herself? Oluf glanced at Joan and the little'uns, sprawled all anyhow on sacking and fast asleep in the kitchen warmth. Safe to leave for a while. He beckoned young Alwyn to take his place and crept quietly after the mistress.

Agathi had intended doing just that: seeing the prisoner for herself. She heaved open the heavy door enough to let her inside. It was then she heard voices, and groaning. The door to the cell was open, and Cedric had half-hauled the man Bernt out on to the cobbled floor of the undercroft. He was thrashing him, thrashing him with a length of knotted rope. Ellen was there, sobbing, pulling on his arm, begging him to stop. Cedric smashed out a fist. It caught her across the cheek so that she reeled and slipped heavily, crashing against the stone walls.

'Yer'll keep yer norf an' souf shut if yer knows wot's best, yer scummy bastard. If yer don't, remember wot I said to yer? John Reeve promised yer missis to me after 'ee'd finished wi' 'er, and I intend to 'ave 'er, as promised.'

'Never,' groaned the beaten man.

'Oh yes,' Cedric sneered. 'One word out of yer beak an' I'll 'ave 'er, right here in front of yer. Yer'd like that, wouldn't yer, yer scummy serf? Yer'd like to watch me rut yer wife?'

'Let her be!'

'Or wot? Yer'll stop me?' He laughed, and the sound of it was chilling. 'Who'll believe yer wasn't trying to escape, and yer woman 'elping yer? Dat fool of a wench-faced bruvver dat's been made reeve? 'Ee didn't choose to see yer, did 'ee? 'Ee's a coward. 'Ee shouldn't 'ave left yer unguarded. So I'll tell me Lady an' she'll see to it 'ee's throwed out.'

'Mistress Agathi is your lady now, and she won't believe you.' Ellen had pulled herself upright. She was trembling and white-faced except for the bright red weal across her cheek.

'Mistress Agathi!' he sneered. 'I suppose yer'll be calling that recklin "Maäster Edgar."' He imitated the villagers' speech. They hadn't noticed the part-opened door, nor Agathi squeeze inside. Cedric raised the heavy, knotted rope again. 'What's yer choice, woman? Yer husband's life is in your 'ands, not mine. Tell 'im to keep 'is mouth shut. Isn't an 'ard choice, is it?'

Agathi was shocked into stillness. She was back again in Veçdet's camp, and Big Aziz punishing the slightest fault, but this wasn't Big Aziz, though he was as cruel, and she was no captive slave. She had heard her name, and Edgar's, and understood the man's sneering laughter. She understood as well the famished leer on his face when he looked at Ellen. She'd seen that look before on the faces of the men who guarded the women slaves. It was why Hatice had ordered her to keep her head down and keep from notice.

How could she let this happen? She was the wife of the reeve of the manor. She was carrying Edgar's child. Edgar had a right to govern this manor, to maintain it as he saw fit. Not be at the mercy of a cruel bully. She had to protect her child and Edgar; this young boy Oluf and his mother Ellen; the man Bernt, sprawled on the cold stone cobbles, close to unconsciousness and innocent, of that she was sure. It was no longer the time to keep her head down, to keep from notice; no longer the time to be gentle and complaisant. She set her shoulder to the door and hefted it wide open. A crimson pool of light from the setting sun turned the cobbles red. Agathi walked into its path. Unseen behind her, Oluf struggled to keep the door from swinging shut. He heard Cedric's voice, and his mam's, and groans that could only come from his da.

'What you do here? Stop now.' The mistress, for all she was so gentle and soft-spoken, sounded fierce. Out of the corner of his eye, Oluf saw pert Joan trailing him across the yard, the sleeping children left behind, mazzled wench, and still playing on that pipe.

'Joan!' he screeched. 'Joan! Get the women. Run. Quick. Get the women!' Joan stopped dead, staring at him. Mawks in her head, thought Oluf. 'Get Hilda – now,' he hissed. Joan stood still a moment longer then scurried towards the stairs that led up to the hall. Oluf breathed a sigh of relief. He leaned back on the door and managed to wriggle into place the big stone that wedged it open. He followed Agathi inside.

'What you do here? Stop now.'

'It's de pris'ner, mistress. 'Ee's trying to escape, wi' dis woman's 'elp. It's lucky I'm 'ere ter stop 'im.'

'I don't believe you. You are a bully who beats innocent men and threatens their women. You must come out of here now!' She spoke in Turkish but so sharply the man's mouth opened but no sound came out.

'Come out. Now.' She spoke in careful English.

The man laughed. 'Yer don't mean dat.'

'Out. Now.'

He slapped the rope against his free hand and slouched to where she stood by the door. 'Yer making a big mistake, mistress.' He sneered. 'Dis is a murd'rer. Alfred who is Lord of dis manor will 'ave somefing ter say abaht dis. Leaving dis fief an' murd'rer alone, unguarded? I 'spect our new reeve will be dismissed. 'Ee's a recklin, and recklins are of no use 'ere.'

She didn't understand half the words, only the intent, and she was back again in Veçdet's camp with the massive presence of Big Aziz threatening them all; gentle Asperto drowning in his fits; brave Hatice, desperately caring for the child too young to know his own name; Niko fighting for freedom. All the men and women and children so unjustly captured and enslaved. All these villagers living in fear and poverty. And Edgar, her own dear Edgar, her husband and the father of the child she carried, a recklin? That word she understood. He was not. He never had been and never would be. He was brave and kind and honest.

'You wrong, donkey,' she said. 'You bad man.' And she swung at him with the short, thin log she had picked up when she entered the building. Swung up between his legs, as Kazan had instructed, as hard as she could. She felt the log snap but it had done its job and the man-weasel Cedric fell to his knees, as Kazan had said he would. As Blue had said he would. He wheezed, gripping his groin. She glanced down at the broken length of log in her hand and swung again, across the side of his head. Blue hadn't recommended that but it seemed a sensible thing to do. Cedric collapsed on the stones of the undercroft. Oluf and Ellen stared at her open-mouthed. Hilda hurried in, with Joan cantering beside her. Hilda took one look and bawled for the rest to come, as quick as they could, and soon they were all crowding into the doorway. Oluf pushed his way to where his father lay, eyes closed, arms and legs tight-bound. 'Is she safe, boy?' he muttered. 'Is your mother safe?'

'Yes da. The mistress saved her.' There was wonder in his voice. Whoever would have thought a frail young woman could fell a man like Cedric?

Agathi dropped the stout stick. 'Have I killed him?'

'No, mistress, you've not wapped him hard enough for that. He'll be stirring soon enough,' Hilda said, grimly. The little lass was white-faced and shivering now it was all over, and who could wonder at it? 'Best get him fast bound, while he's out to it,' she said briskly, and reached for the coil of rope Cedric had dropped. 'Come here, Janet, get a hold of his arms. You get his legs, Martha.'

Ellen struggled to her feet and the two young women clung to each other. 'How did you know to do that?' Ellen asked.

'Our good friend Blue told my friend Kazan, so that we would know how to look after ourselves if we were threatened by bad men.' She blew out a long breath, felt her shoulders sag. 'I must tell Kazan it is true, what Blue said. It is…' she blinked, 'astonishing.'

Ellen stared at the prone Cedric, already stirring and making whimpering noises, one hand still clutching his groin until hefty Janet pulled both arms behind his back. Ellen started to laugh, until the laughter turned to sobs.

Hilda turned to the women. There was Mary, young and fleet enough. 'Run to your father, girl, and the young maäster. Get them here as fast as you can.' To Ellen she said, 'Yer mun take care of your man. He's hurt. Get them bonds off of him an' all.' She looked down at Joan and fondled her head. 'Eh but yer a good 'un, little lass. You an' all, Oluf, doing as what yer did.' She turned to Agathi, reached for both her hands. 'Yer'll do us, mistress.'

When Edgar arrived, it was Cedric who was tight-bound, Bernt freed. They took him to be bathed and salved where the heavy, knotted rope had gouged flesh, and set him in front of the blazing hearth fire. Most of the village was gathered there by now, and the dark night was closing in. Agathi and Ellen were jubilant and fearful by turns. Agathi clung to Edgar. He grasped her to him, tight, tight, his wife, his warrior-maid. His conscience.

'Did I do wrong, husband?'

'You were right, my Agathi. But,' he strained her tighter still, 'do not ever take such risks again. I cannot lose you now, my Agathi, my life, my soul.' He kissed her, and kissed her again. 'What should I do if I lost you?' He asked, bemused, 'How did you know where to hit him?'

'Blue told Kazan, after she and Niko were rescued from Veçdet, and she told me.' She was suddenly prim. 'I did not expect it to be so true, husband.'

'Lucky for you it was, wife.' He sighed. 'So Kazan and Blue protect us still. I miss our friends, Agathi. I wish they were here with us. We need them.'

'I think,' she said, carefully, 'I have much need of Hatice and Kazan. I am carrying our child, Edgar.'

Later, when all had fed plainly but well, and all had a place to sleep, the eldest of the sokemen came to Edgar. The men were bemused by the sudden turn events had taken, the way the women had taken charge, moved their families into the hall at the bidding of the unknown mistress. And she, frail foreign woman, more child than woman, had defeated the terrible Cedric. The men were ashamed of themselves and ready to speak out now.

Edgar invited the older man to sit and he did so, perching himself uneasily on the edge of a bench. He folded his hands one over the other where his paunch used to be in the days when the manor was fruitful; he was nothing now but wrinkled flesh and guilty conscience. He looked at the young man sitting opposite, golden curls a nimbus round his head. They had thought him weak when he arrived, a puling younger brother with a pretty, foreign, frail young wife. They were wrong. This young couple was strong and united. The young master was determined to set this manor to rights, and his mistress determined to see him do it. Determined now to know the truth, and fight for it to be known.

'Bernt did not steal, master. He did not kill. This is how it was.' Ever since Squire Alfred's wife had set him up here, anything John Reeve wanted he thought he could have. The timber? That was his doing. He had men he dealt with, a gang that hid out in the woodland along this stretch of the High Dyke; they ambushed unwary travellers. They'd been seen in this village doing trade with John Reeve and Cedric Hayward. The conies in the warren – the black ones especially, the ones whose fur was valuable – those had been caught and sold to the gang. Nobody here dared speak out. Risked a slit throat or tongue cut out, speaking out. And Bernt's wife? John Reeve wanted her. He arranged for Bernt to be accused of stealing the timber. Easy for him and who would listen to a villein? Who would listen even to sokemen when John Reeve was the choice of the Lady of the Manor? The night of the Epiphany he was drunk. He was always drunk. This night he was staggering outside Bernt's house, shouting to Ellen to come out or it would be the worse for her and her man.

'Bernt would not let her go. She is a good wife and mother, master, but she knew what trouble there would be for her family. She thought, if she gave herself to John Reeve, it would be enough but Bernt said no. He had rights like any other man, and his wife was not for bartering. So they did not open the door. We all heard John Reeve shouting and bawling for long enough. It was a bad end to the feast day. Then all went quiet. We thought he'd gone home, fallen asleep, drunk as he was, but some of the young 'uns were still out-and-about and they came to tell me they'd seen him cursing and swearing down by the cattle pond. I went out to look and that was when I saw him tipped arse-end-up in the pond. He was alive, master. He was gasping and flailing like a landed fish. And I didn't help him. I watched him. I let him drown and no priest there to hear his confession. I condemned him to eternal darkness, master. There you have it. If anyone must be accused, let it be me.'

Edgar sat still. This had the sound of truth, a terrible truth.

'But you did not kill him, Luke.'

'I let him drown, master.'

'There is a difference. This man was evil. He deserved to drown. He was bound for hell, confession or no. You should not chastise yourself. It was God's will.' Edgar looked in the face at the anguished man in front of him. 'There is something you should know, Luke. My father promised me to the monks at Croyland when I was still a young boy. I did not want such a life and so, after five long years, I escaped and fled to the eastern countries. I went on pilgrimage to atone for my sins but my life changed when I was befriended by a Welshman. He made me part of his group of merchants and I travelled with him to the port of Attaleia and from there to Venezia. From there, to Ieper and so here to Lincolnshire. A circle, you would say, but my life is changed. I am no longer promised to the Abbey life; I have my wife; I have made many mistakes but the good God has protected me, and given me dear friends, though we live far apart from one another. I have fought to protect them, and would kill to keep them safe and think myself right to do so. Thanks to God, I have not had to. You, my friend, have no need to berate yourself. This John Reeve was not a good man.'

'No, my lord. He was not.'

'Then go in peace, my friend. You did not kill him. He killed himself and that is what I shall tell my brother. There is no more to be said.'

But that night, with the windows shuttered against the cold night. Edgar couldn't sleep. He lay with Agathi in the small inner solar with its flimsy door and listened to the breathing of the sleepers in the hall. His villagers. Snores and grunts and farts that reminded him of nights in the *hans*. But this was different. Edgar thought hard and long. Was it the best decision, to bring Agathi to such a place? To more problems? She was too gentle and beautiful, though she had been as brave as any man this day. She had astounded him with her courage, her recklessness. She deserved better than this. He should protect her but he was no warrior. He did not have Blue's strength nor Dai's quick-witted, dangerous ruthlessness and bandit-learned cunning. He did not have the sword-skill of Thomas, nor Giles. He was a monk-raised weakling who knew only book-learning and crop-tending. Agathi stirred against him. She, too, was wakeful.

'What troubles you, husband?'

But when he murmured his doubts, she surprised him by saying they had a duty to the manor, to its sokemen and villeins and cottars. They had a duty to reveal the truth of what had happened that winter. 'And who better than you, husband, to know what to do for this land, these people? Who better than you, with your book-learning, to know how to sort truth from lies?' She snuggled closer to him. 'Fighting with swords and daggers and arrows; this is not always the best way, beloved. Violence brings more violence. A peaceful way is best. You can do this for us, my altar boy.'

Edgar chuckled at the name given him by Blue but he sighed as well. 'It's a poverty-stricken place, sweetheart. It's been plundered, and not only by John Reeve and Cedric Hayward. My brother and his wife have used it as a pantry.' He heard the bitterness in his voice.

'A reeve should look after his tenants better than this, shouldn't he, husband?' insisted Agathi. He was reeve now, and should do his best to restore the manor, create harmony where there was dispute; protect the villagers from his own brother, if need be. Food might be scarce; couldn't Alfred supply them this winter? Return part of what he had taken? And there was firewood enough. She had seen it with her own eyes, in the barred-and-bolted lean-to by the stable. Huge logs, bundles of faggots laid by. 'But, husband, there is one thing you must do. This village, these people, how they stink! They must bathe, and have better arrangements for their bodies' needs.'

Yes, for sure his gentle bride was becoming a true lady of the manor. Perhaps it was because she was married, and carrying his child. It gave her dignity and confidence. 'We stay, then, wife, if you say so. And,' he promised her, 'I shall find an answer to the problem of our stinking village.'

During the long, dark night, Edgar made his choice: he was here as reeve, as Agathi had said, and his first duty was to the manor and all its people. The villeins' first need was warmth and food; the land's first need was heart. It was what Brother Peter had always said: put heart back into the earth. It could be exhausted, as any man could be exhausted, and needed tending. It was what he knew. The monks had taught him well, land-craft as well as book-lore. Besides, he needed to know his men better, and what better way than working with them?

He'd ordered the men out, not caring if they were sokemen or villeins, not caring for grumbles or sullen faces, not caring that it was bitter cold. Best if all worked together, if this manor was to recover.

But the men were happy to follow him. They had hated and feared John Reeve and his man Cedric. Bernt was popular, a good-natured man, ready to lend a helping hand to any and all. His wife was respected for her skills in healing. Their young son – well – always into mischief but a likeable boy for all that. When Bernt was imprisoned, it seemed impossible for any of them to protest. Impossible! Now it seemed there would be justice and they thanked God and this gentle, golden-haired son of the old squire. And his young wife, the women reminded them. A foreigner she may be but a good woman for all that.

He'd had them draw lots to see who were unlucky enough to be set to clear the middens and gong heaps that had accumulated in the village. They would have to cart it far enough away for now for the stench not to cause nuisance and sickness. Later, when the thaw came, it could be buried deep in the earth. He pondered. The monks had used fast-flowing water to carry all away but they couldn't do that here. The beck was not big enough, and the water was used for washing; the animals drank there. He'd seen the women dip pitchers in, though there was a well of water that was sweet enough, if brackish. No, best dig a trench, plank it, make sure all knew to cover their shit with earth after they had eased themselves. Build a wall around it, when the thaw came, and thatch a roof. He tried to remember how the *han* privies were built, but sighed when he remembered the piped water for drinking, for the *hamam*, for the latrines. Best he could do for now.

The rest of the villagers he set to hedging and ditching, lopping and coppicing. The hazel undergrowth was thinned and stacked into faggots and bavins ready to be carried to the barn. The spikey thorn bushes were best as hedges against the young trees where the deer had eaten away the lower shoots. The trees should have been better pollarded long since, he thought, exasperated. The beck was cleared so that it would run free when better weather came and snow and ice melted. With the water drained away, crofts and fields would recover in time for spring ploughing and harrowing and sowing, God willing. He blessed the monks at the abbey for teaching him these skills, and smiled to think he, the rebel, the runaway, was grateful for his cloistered life.

Alfred came to the manor in answer to the urgent summons Edgar had sent. The hearing proved that the guilt of theft lay with John Reeve and his man, Cedric. As for the accusation of murder, there had been no murder: John Reeve had been falling-down drunk. It was his habit. Only this time he had done his falling-down in the pond and drowned. Alfred's wife glared but there was nothing she could do. Every villager was willing to swear on the Bible, swear on pain of death, of the never-ending horror of Hell, that what they said was solemn truth. Cedric Hayward was caught in his lies, and blustering did him no good. Death by hanging was inevitable. Alfred had the power to serve such a sentence but Edgar was glad that permission to set up the gallows was given only for Rochby, not Bradwell. He did not want the dead man haunting this place.

There was the matter of provisions for the winter as well, Edgar said. As reeve, it was for him to represent the villeins and cottars – the sokemen as well. Truth was, Rochby had taken more than its share. For sure, John Reeve had been seeking favours of his Lord and Lady, and had given them to suppose that the harvest and beasts had been better than usual this year. Add to that the stores John Reeve had kept for himself, sold off for profit, and the end-up was starvation for Bradwell Manor.

'It deserves better than this, brother,' said Edgar. They were speaking privately together; Edgar blessed Agathi for taking Philippa out of the way. Let Alfred speak for himself as Lord of the Manors of Rochby and Bradwell, without Philippa's spiteful intervention. 'I know you say you want to be rid of it but it could be a prosperous place again. The land you sold to Roger de Langton? I thought we might try to buy it back. It's good arable land, fertile soil, up beyond the Long Wood, over a hundred acres of it, and the services of the sokemen as well as the villeins. I cannot see why you sold it. With it, Bradwell can double its yield.'

'But the money from the sale is worth as much as worked land. Philippa says so.'

'What is a manor without its land?' Edgar asked. 'I always had a liking for this place. Summer comes late here but it stays longer. Remember how we proddled for fish in the beck when we were young?'

Alfred nodded. He smiled wistfully. 'It was a lovely place then. We rode up into the heathland and pretended we were brigands. We killed Eric. Do you remember?'

Edgar couldn't help but laugh. 'Now that I had forgotten. They were good times, brother, and I have you and Eric to thank for that. I wish the children here could have the chance to play make-believe. Instead, they are little old men before they've reached six summers.' They were in the neglected herb garden. He reached down to pluck a lavender spray, woody and winter-dead but the sharp tang of summer fragrance was there for all that. 'Bernt's son, Oluf, he's about Niko's age. He puts me in mind of Niko.'

'Niko? Your wife's brother?'

'Yes. Niko is as dark as Oluf is fair but they have that same look about them.'

'Why didn't the boy come with you?'

'He stayed with our friends Blue and Hatice. They took him as their son. It seemed for the best. Agathi and me, we didn't know what lay ahead. We wanted Niko to be safe and loved.'

'And now you wish you had him with you,' Alfred said. It wasn't a question.

'Yes. Yes, we do.'

'God and his son Jesus know what is best, brother.'

My son, who are you to decide what is and what is not to be?

'Only Allah the all-compassionate, the all-knowing decides,' Edgar murmured.

'What's that?' Alfred asked, sharply.

'Something a great man says. A tribal chief and a devout Muslim, one Kara Kemal, a man of compassion and wisdom.'

Alfred moved uneasily. 'I think you have been amongst strange people, brother.'

'I know I have been amongst good people.' He looked his brother in the face. *There is always room for faith.* 'About this matter of the leased land, and provisions until we can fend for ourselves…'

It was easy if you had dogged determination, he realised. Was this what Dafydd knew? Stay calm, determined, resolute, and in the end you had your way. No loud wrangling, no skirmishing, no need for brute force. Agathi was right, again and again: *Violence brings more violence. A peaceful way is best.*

9

Ieper
February 1337

My love cannot be reached,
My pain be healed...
(Yunus Emre: 14ᵗʰC)

Another message arrived: Agathi was with child. Kazan stared out of the window at the swirling snow, turning and turning the bracelet that never left her wrist. Edgar begged her to come and stay with Agathi. 'But I know nothing of children and childbirth,' she thought. Just once, she remembered, she had helped Nene with a birthing. Such pain! Was there always such pain? 'She needs Hatice, not me.' It seemed so long since they had left Hatice and Blue and Niko behind in Attaleia, watching their figures grow smaller and smaller on the quayside until they were swallowed up into blue distance. 'We should never have left them behind,' she thought. 'We need them. They are our family.'

She was in the inner solar. It looked out onto the snow-covered herb garden and orchard at the back of the house. Winter was not over, in spite of Heinrijc Merten's optimism. Below the window a small figure darted out from the cross-passage into the garden. Matje's son escaping again from the kitchens, his mother's voice shrilling after him. Outside, he flung his head back and screwed his eyes shut. He thrust out his tongue to catch snowflakes. He reminded her of Niko and she braced herself against the sharp pain of remembering. Matje shouted again and the boy opened his eyes. He saw her at the window and grinned saucily before shutting his eyes and thrusting out his tongue again. He was round faced and red cheeked and ecstatic in the late afternoon gloom and swirling snow. Matje erupted from the passageway, scolding loudly. She grabbed the boy by the scruff of his neck and cuffed him soundly. The boy waved to the girl in the window. He was cheerful, secure because his mother loved him dearly and her plump hands fell lightly. Another of Heinrijc Mertens' rescued souls. This was a widow whose husband had been drowned at sea. She and her young son faced a life of poverty and destitution until Mertens had brought her into his household. 'She is a treasure,' he said. 'A most wonderful cheese-maker. All the luck is mine.'

And this was another astonishing thing about this land won from the sea: same, like Venezia, but so different. Here, the rich women were not guarded, as property was guarded. Here, there was no casual rape of poor women that carried a minimal fine. Here, they had rights in law: any man who struck his wife had to pay a heavy fine to the court, and larger sums in damages to his wife, whatever her status. Rights in business; some women in charge of cloth-making – some even were weavers. Sometimes, entire workshops were in charge of women. Not the fulling, nor the cropping. That was strenuous work, beyond a woman's strength. Rights in education because the Countess of Flanders had introduced free education almost a hundred years before. This was indeed a remarkable country and yet Kazan yearned for the spaces of her own country, and the freedom to gallop across the open land. She had never before lived without sight of high mountains, and the flatness of this land sat on her spirit.

She walked every day to the monastery church to pray for Dafydd's safe arrival. And here was another difference: the great cupolas and domes of the eastern churches, though so many had become mosques, were light, with huge open spaces. Here in this northern town were high, vaulted, cross-shaped churches. Shadows where there had been light; pillars and arches where there had been space; wall paintings that told of death and damnation and hellfire. Fearsome sights. Where did they find comfort, these Christians of the western world?

Rémi went with her, Rémi who missed Dafydd with the same sharp pain. Besides, he liked to sign-talk with the monks now Edgar was gone. It had been Edgar, the runaway novice, who first taught him sign-talk. More than that, Rémi liked to talk with the young daughter of a cloth maker, a pretty young girl who blushed and sign-talked. 'She makes many mistakes, Kazan,' signed Rémi. He was smiling his lop-sided smile.

'Then you must teach her,' Kazan said, 'though I do not think you care about the mistakes.' She watched the bright red rise up in Rémi's cheeks. She laughed. 'She is beautiful, and good-natured.'

Rémi sighed, shrugged, signed. 'But what am I? Who am I to ask for her? I cannot even talk to her.'

'You are a wonder, you are amazing. You understand numbers and commerce. Dafydd relies on you. Father Mertens relies on you. You have travelled the eastern countries. You are handsome and so very smartly dressed. Father Mertens has seen to that. How could her family not see this? You have money, from Father Mertens and Dafydd. You are – what do you say here? – a good catch? Like a big fish. Her family will think so. You must ask for her, Rémi, if you love her.'

'I do love her. I always have. For years now. But she does not love me. She likes me as a friend. That is all.'

'She tries to sign-talk with you. She looks for you when we pass by. I have seen this, Rémi. You should talk to her. Know her better.' She sighed. 'Rémi, you must know that Dafydd is my dearest friend and I love him so very much. Thomas says Dafydd loves me. If that is so, we have wasted precious time and it may be too late for us. You must not do this. Speak to her, dear Rémi.'

Rémi caught her hand, squeezed hard, signed to her: 'He is alive, Kazan. I know it. He will come.'

Her eyes misted with tears. 'I think it is so. I cannot feel he is dead. But you, dear friend, must not waste time.'

'And you, dear Kazan, how good you are, how well you make it all seem for us. God willing, it will be well for you.'

And so Rémi was slowly, so slowly, courting Enna, the daughter of a Flanders cloth-maker.

They passed by daily, and always she was there, watching for them. They passed, as well, the workplaces where the cloth-makers were hard at work. They were jealous of their reputation for producing the best cloth, these low-landers, and kept their secrets close guarded though it was known that they always separated the wool, English from native and sort from sort, according to the town and province. The wool of live sheep separated from the dead carcasses, old from young animals: it was strictly forbidden to mix any of these kinds. Then each separate stage was in the hands of different craftsmen. Not the wool-workers who washed, combed and sorted the wool – these could be anybody, Mertens told her, women or boys or strangers or unemployed weavers – but there were the fullers, the spinners, the croppers. 'We have as our motto: let one man help another as his brother.'

Let one man help another as his brother. She liked that. The words sang to her. Wasn't that what they had done, their little band of travellers? *Let one man help another as his brother.*

Heinrijc Mertens said, 'We have very strict laws to make sure our cloth is always the best. Fulling, now; Flemish cloth must have a smooth surface, completely smooth. Ah, so smooth. And before that, all the fats and dirt are so carefully removed. But not with piss, as the rest of the world is foolish enough to use. Oh no, not here in Flanders. Such barbaric customs! Here, it is punishable by imprisonment.' He raised his eyebrows in that unintentionally comic way he had, and raised his arms and spread his hands and waggled thin fingers. The rich folds of his own gown fell in sumptuous folds from elbow to near hem; warm red today. 'And these *ramscheerers*, the croppers; simple work on damp cloth but so necessary for the good finish. For our finest, best quality wool – like this of my gown – the cropping is done on dry wool.' He stroked the folds with innocent complacency. 'Your gown too, my child, is of the finest, and it becomes you very well, does it not?'

It was a new gown and surcoat that had been a gift, an extravagance that had taken her breath away. It was in the new fashion, fitted close to her figure and at first she blushed to see her shape so revealed. The surcoat was deepest indigo, purple-blue, like rich, ripe grapes, but the over gown was full rich scarlet with bands of red gold and rich stones; rubies as red as any hot coal, green beryls, burning blue sapphires. For Agathi there was a gown as blue as the hyacinths that grew in the springtime in Anatolia, and edged with ermine that nestled soft against her own soft skin.

'This is too much for me, Father Mertens,' Kazan had exclaimed.

'Nonsense, my dear daughter; it is but a setting for your own beauty. Come, give me a kiss and wear it to give an old man pleasure.' He chuckled and rubbed his thin hands together, the skin rustling like thin parchment. 'See! Agathi knows the art of graciously accepting a gift from an old man. She knows what pleasure it is for me to give you trifles. Learn from her.'

Learn from her. Learn how to endure when life is unendurable. *There is always room for faith.* And now Agathi was long gone, to the cold lands – though could they be any colder than these lands of Flanders?

'Of course, it is the secrets of dyeing, the secrets of weaving, these are never revealed.' Father Mertens' voice brought her back to the present, and the falling snow and the crackling hearth and guttering candles. 'Always the craft is passed on through practice and teaching but nothing is ever written down. If it were put into writing then comes the danger of it becoming common knowledge.' And now, he thought sadly, the English Edward is starving our fullers and our weavers and dyers of the fleeces they need to work their magic. Why should they leave their own country for foreign lands?

'It is what our friend, Blue, said of the dyers,' Kazan told him. 'He came here to learn their art.' It was a night for memories, a winter's night when stories were shared. She saw again the big fen man's plain face transformed as he recalled the moment when the cloth was lifted from the noxious, steaming vat.

Lifting the cloth bright green and dripping and seeing it turn all shades of blue right there in front of your eyes. Like a miracle, out of all that filth and stench and back-breaking work and then that. Makes you believe in summat, that does.

'Your friend is a poet,' Mertens said. 'He should have come home with you. There is work here for such a man.'

'I think this also. I am sorry they stayed behind. Sorry as well for Agathi. She has never said so but I think she misses her brother and her great friend Hatice very much. Hatice was like a mother to her, and Agathi has much need of her now.'

'Have faith, dear child. Who knows? Perhaps they will realise this for themselves?'

She shrugged, spread her own hands in unconscious mimicry of the old man. 'Perhaps. Tell me about the weavers of this wonderful cloth.'

Scantily dressed, barefoot, even in the chill weather, and like to be near naked in the summer months, the weavers were absorbed in the secret, closely guarded craft of cloth-making. They worked at treadle looms with a horizontal warp. There were complicated methods of raising and lowering the rollers. 'You understand of what I speak, dear girl?' She nodded but, tell the truth, she found it difficult to comprehend. It was not the simple arrangement of the *yürük*, and that had been mystery enough for her.

She was back in memory to the summer camp and the time when she too had taken her place at the loom. 'Fumble fingers!' Aysel had screamed. 'Botcher! Go and shoot arrows with those useless boys!' And she had been sent back to Nene in disgrace, a girl who could not weave without making costly mistakes. Nene had laughed. 'Each to his own, child,' she had said. 'Do as the good Aysel says. Shoot your arrows. Hit your target, whatever it may be.'

They would be in the winter camp now, the girl thought, and remembered how the rain beat down and white-capped waves tore at the shore and how they crammed together in the smoky, steamy winter houses and the old ones told stories of past times, of the great warriors, of things that happened long before the girl was born, long before she and Nene came to live with the wanderers, the *yürük*. Did they miss her? Did they tell stories of the Christian grandmother and her granddaughter who had lived with them for so many years? Did they tell how the granddaughter had disappeared one summer's night, taking the mare Rüzgar, leaving no trace? It was another world, a lost world, and no good came of remembering. She hoped Sakoura had returned the mare to the tribe, as he had promised.

How they longed for this long winter to be over. With the thaw, hundreds of flat-bottomed boats would travel constantly up and down the canal coming to dock at the jetty close to St Martin's where they unloaded goods for the great *lakenhalle* warehouses and markets amid a babble of languages: English and Welsh and French and Italian and German mixing with the Flemish. Strangers from the northern lands as well, bringing thick, warm furs. There were always cats prowling. Sleek cats with tubbed-out stomachs from mousing and ratting in the storehouses, they still could not resist the tempting whiffs from barge-loads of meat and fish. Fleeces as well, despite the heavy import tax. Kazan felt sorry for the cats; Heinrijc Mertens had told her what their fate would be, come Ascension Day. 'It is not a custom I approve of but it is our way. They have a glorious autumn and winter, they are warm and happy, glutted with their catches and have done their work in ridding the wool houses of vermin. When the cloth has been sold, then the cats will be thrown from the high belfry of the *Lakenhalle*. Before the belfry was completed – and I remember that day of celebration – they were thrown from the tower of St Martin's.'

'Thrown?'

'I am afraid so, dear child. They say it is to rid us of evil spirits but in truth it is the only way to keep their numbers down. They breed so fast, you see. Our little one, Stoffel, was a lucky one. He escaped with just a broken leg and Davit mended that. He is supposed to be our mouse-catcher but I suspect he prefers his food to be waiting for him on a platter.' Kazan exchanged a grin with Rémi; that was true enough. They had watched Stoffel lurking behind a bench, his tongue showing pink, his body rumbling with purrs, creeping towards the place where a platter of juicy gobbets of chicken had been left unattended. Neither had stopped the thief from snatching a mouthful.

She wondered if cats lost all nine lives at once. Was that possible? What of Dafydd's five lives left to him, if that were so? No thinking. Sometimes thinking doesn't do you any good.

10

Journey to Venezia
March 1337
No matter how strong the wood
The sea can smash the ship
(Yunus Emre: 14ᵗʰC)

They'd left Candia and were crossing the great expanse of water before steering into the route that would take them up the jagged coast to Venezia. Endless sky above; endless sea below. Blue remembered it from before, the long journey from Venezia to Antioch, and from there overland eastwards. It was a long time ago, and truth tell now, how much did he remember of it? On his ownsome then, and one, long, drunken haze. Different this time round. This time he had his family with him: Hatice, young Niko, and Mehmi, more like a son to him these days. And look at 'em, bedazzled by it all. Not never been on any sea voyage, never in their lives, mebbe never ever seen the sea, before Attaleia, and all three of 'em as steady on their legs and sturdy in their stomachs as if they'd been born to it. For himself, he wasn't so fond of deep water. A good enough sailor, not like Edgar, but he didn't like thinking of what might lurk below in the darkness. Different, now, if it were salt marshes where land and sea mingled till you couldn't tell one from t'other and yer felt like yer were walking on water. May'appen that was how Jesus felt, walking on that lake when he were out on the boat with the fishermen. Blasphemous talk, he supposed.

Captain Abu Hazim halted by his side. He had been reluctant to take these strangers, especially the woman and this mountain of a man who looked trouble; the young boy must learn not to be under their feet, getting in the way of ship-shape work. The handsome young Muslim, pear-bellied, long-necked *tanbur* strung across his back, if he had sea legs, he would be welcome. If he truly could play the *tanbur*.

But the days passed and there was no trouble, not even when they berthed in Candia. A sober Christian, the captain marvelled. A Christian miracle. The woman kept herself to herself, and the man-mountain kept a jealous, vigilant eye on her, as if she'd been a great beauty, or young, at least. As for the boy and the music player, they were a marvel. The *tanbur* sang and whispered and pulsed; this Mehmi's hands blurred with the speed of his playing, his fingers tapping rhythms on the sides of the belly of the *tanbur*; yes, and the singer's voice was pure. His music tore at the heart or quickened the pulses or brought laughter. But the boy! Who could have dreamt it? He had taken the rim of a barrel, stretched goatskin across it, secured it, wet it, dried it, turned it into a *daf* that he played rhythmically, mesmerizingly, keeping pace with the *tanbur* player, pattering out counter-rhythms, having them all beating time, clapping, singing with the chorus. Abu Hazim could not remember another voyage so full of life and laughter. And the woman and man-mountain, how they beamed with pride. As if these two were their very own sons. He knew the story by now: their journey in search of their companions and the boy's sister; how Mehmi's father was dead and so he had chosen to go with his friends, the friends of his father, even to the cold, dark lands of the infidel.

And so Captain Hazim halted beside the man-mountain who spoke a language he could not understand. He gestured to the wide ocean. 'The sea is a boundless expanse where great ships look like tiny specks; nothing but the heavens above and the waters beneath,' he said.

Blue gazed out at the wide sea and said to the captain who spoke a language he could not understand: 'We're nowters in this stretch. Great-big-huge sky an' sea an' all. Nowt but spelks.'

They stood side-by-side a moment longer, neither understanding the other's tongue but their thoughts united, the two men on the great *baghlah*, tiny in this huge expanse, dipping and lurching through the wide waves. Abu Hazim was proud of his ship and proud of the crew that sailed her, this two-masted Arab vessel with large, triangular sails and a high, raised prow that reminded Blue of some of the ancient hulks that he'd sometimes seen wrecked along the Fen shore.

Those were bright days with clouds scudding high above though the nights were cold enough to freeze the blood in your body. Then the good weather failed. Contrary, roaring, howling winds drove them up and down the coast for days and nights, and there was no sun, no stars to steer by. Behind them, foam-flecked waves reared high over the stern of the ship. The captain and his crew were skillful sailors and the ship rode the waves but Blue didn't look, not after that one horrified glance. He'd be frittened, and that wouldn't not be doing no good, not fer any on' em. He'd seen waves breaking white out to sea but surely that was the dark shape of land and they were close to shore. Were waves breaking there on rocks? If so, two chances: ship rock-driven and wrecked or foundering on a sand spit. Either way, drowning in this wild water. They were sounding the fathoms, as well as they could in this tempest. The mainsail was hoisted – that lateen-set triangular Arab sail. Order was given to lighten the ship – cast out the tackling – throw overboard the cargo, their precious cargo. They tossed with the tempest. Blue squinted at the white foam ahead of them, staggered as another wave lifted and dropped them, grasped the mast. Yes, a shore line for sure. Abu Hazim grasped him by the arm, gestured towards the land, shouted incomprehensible words that were wrenched away on the screaming wind. Mehmi was there, yelling into his ear.

'He's aiming for the long island – sandy bay he's used before in rough weather – narrow – sharp rocks either side – thinks it's possible, *İnşallah*. Run the ship aground – swim for it.'

Swim for it? Could she swim? Could young Niko? He looked about him, saw a coiled length of rope and swung it round his body; grasped at broken pieces of the ship; grabbed hard hold of them, his family. He would never let them go.

The ship lurched and jolted. Its bow sank into sand but its stern was afloat, battered by the storming waves. Only moments now before it broke to pieces in these frantic seas. Blue tightened his hold on Hatice, on Niko. Where was Mehmi? A voice in his ear, a pat on the shoulder, Niko taken from him and held securely. 'Always room for faith.' He caught the words, blown by the wind, as they toppled into the foaming surf.

11

Ieper
March 1337

Lenten is come with love to toune,
With blosmen and with brides roune
(Anon: 14ᵗʰC)

And at last came Heinrijc Mertens' last blast. Spring arrived in a rush as if to make up for its late arrival. Overnight frost and ice were gone and the sodden land steamed in the sun. The promise of new growth was everywhere. In Heinrijc Mertens' orchard, apple and pear trees showed tight, tiny buds, barely formed. The elm trees along the Ieper River, so valuable to the lowlanders, were timidly showing shoots growing from the suckers of older trees.

Strange, then, that one morning she felt such suffocation. She could not breathe. She fell gasping to her knees, pushing at air that thickened and overwhelmed her. She felt she was dying. Such a weight toppling over her, and all about was blinding white. 'Dafydd,' she whispered. '*Sevgilim. Canım. Fy nghariad.* Beloved.' Slowly, so very slowly, her breathing eased. Her heart stopped pounding. She sipped cold air into her. Freezing cold. The whiteness dissolved. She felt weak and was trembling. So strange. It was all so strange. She did not tell anyone what she had experienced.

On a blustering day of sharp blue sky and billowing cloud she and Rémi walked together to St Martin's. She knew her own time of hibernation was over. 'I must keep my promise to Nene,' she said to the boy. 'My grandfather is an old man and this winter has been harsh. Perhaps it is already too late.' Rémi rested his hand on her arm. He smiled his snail-trail smile but it was wistful. 'You must stay here and wait for him. He will come, Rémi, as Father Mertens tells us. You must believe this. Besides, Father Mertens has need of you.'

A nod, thumbs up. He will come. I shall stay. Unmistakeable message.

'And there is the lovely Enna.'

Thumbs down. She laughed. 'Trust me, Rémi.' She watched with satisfaction the bright colour rush into his cheeks.

Another leave-taking. Heinrijc Mertens and Rémi and the whole household watching until the brick-carrying barge was out of sight. It was another day of scudding clouds and blue sky, a fair wind and a spring tide. Kazan-the-bright travelled with Giles-the-protector to the Flanders coast and from there to Boston and Swineshead. After that, if all was well, up the Witham to Lincoln and from there along the Cliff road to where Edgar and Agathi held their small manor.

'Any news, my daughter, I shall send there.'

Giles had plans to travel home to the Marches. It was time to be reconciled with his father, he said. Besides, there was a girl there, a cousin of sorts, part Welsh. He'd a mind to see how she had grown. Best as well, he thought to himself, to get thoughts of Kazan out of his mind.

And so the barge left Ieper in the early dawn, and the old man and the young boy stood watching, watching until it was long out of sight.

12

Bradwell Manor, Lincolnshire
March 1337

Whole be thou Earth
Mother of Men
(Anglo-Saxon ploughing charm)

The snow and ice that had fastened on the earth for weeks on end, gripping too hard for ploughing, were gone. The frozen ponds and ice-fast beck were flowing free now. It was good to feel warmth in the air again, good to feel the tilth turn under the plough, know that spring was come again. The ploughing was late this year. Winter had lasted long. It had seemed that it would last forever, and the whole village in desperate need of food and warmth and sound roofs. Alfred had been as good as his word, and provisions had been despatched to Bradwell, though they were meagre. More substantial were the supplies sent from the manor adjoining their own, from Roger de Langton. A wagon arrived one day laden with sacks of grain and dried pease and flitches of salt pork. Edgar sent back messages of thanks. He had vague memories of his father's friend, a jovial, sardonic man saddened by the death of his wife. A message came back: 'You must visit me but not now. I am indisposed and the doctors tell me I must keep to my bed and rest. A tedious prospect but I shall do as they say. I hope you will find some use for the victuals.' Some use! Edgar sent a messenger blessing the old man and wishing him a speedy recovery.

The fair at Welbourn was timely, held as it was that first week in March. He picked his strongest, fittest men to act as guard, mindful of the woodland gang. Eudo's gang. He had a name for them now, though there had been no sign nor sound of them for weeks now. He hoped they had moved on, now John Reeve and Cedric Hayward were gone. A guard first, all the same, and after he had the men draw lots, see who would go to the fair. 'And the next fair, those who don't go this time are first in line for next,' he promised. He was humbled by their excitement; this was a rare treat. 'They are like children, Agathi.'

'But of course, Edgar. They are not allowed to go anywhere without permission. Of course they are excited.' She chose not to go, though she would dearly have loved to be free of the manor, just for one day. 'I shall rest here, and Ellen and Hilda are to go in my place, husband,' she said firmly. 'They will know what cloth to choose.' For she and Edgar had agreed that they would make a gift of new clothes to their villeins and sokemen in time for Easter celebrations. Rightly, it was the duty of the Lord of the Manor but Edgar could not see Alfred recognising it. Agathi watched the procession leave, the horses and carts and men, and women and children shrill with excitement. She watched them return, late in the evening when it was long after sunset, saw the flares of the torches that lit their way, and breathed more easily because they had come home safe, carts heaped with provisions and sleepy bairns. Ellen was starry-eyed, pink-cheeked, ecstatic. 'Mistress, if only you had been there…'

'Next time, Ellen. There will be next times. And other fairs in other places.'

'Mistress!' Other places? Maybe Stow Fair. Ellen had heard tell of the great Stow Fair. She'd never dreamed of going there. Ellen had never thought she would travel beyond the manor. The mistress, now, for all she was so young, she'd travelled across countries, across seas. Little wonder she was fearless.

There were still stretches of dirty snow in the sunless banks but the snow storms had at last given way to gales and torrents of rain that swept away the snow and ice but caused as many problems as it solved; the sodden land squelched underfoot, thick mud that sucked a man down knee-deep. The swollen beck overflowed, despite their efforts to clear it of weeds and debris. The water flooded the pasture and crofts, coming too close for comfort to the tofts. The storms brought down branches, both rotten and green, and trees were uprooted, some well grown. The best of the timber they could keep for working but the rest, well, good for firewood and God knew they needed all the firewood they could get in this shivering place. The great black poplars remained undisturbed along the edges of the water meadows.

Edgar remembered the first day of ploughing. They had an ancient custom here, surely of the old religion. He didn't argue blasphemy though the priest, Father Emanuel, tutted. No, he liked this ceremony, this kneading of bread with milk and holy water, reluctantly given by the priest, and the whole laid under the first-turned turf.

> *Acre full fed;*
> *Bring forth fodder for men!*
> *Blossoming brightly,*
> *Blessed become;*
> *And the God who wrought the ground,*
> *Grant us gifts of growing,*
> *That the corn, all the corn,*
> *May come to our need.*

Seed in the earth, and seed of his in Agathi's belly. *Blossoming brightly, blessed become.* God bring her safely to childbirth, and this land to harvest.

Now the fields were ploughed and harrowed and sown, and soon bright spears of barley and oats would push through the red-brown earth. The boys shouted and whooped at flocking crows and seagulls, defying them to steal the seed. They knew they were not allowed to kill the pigeons because these belonged to the lord and the church, but Edgar laughed and urged them on. 'That's our dinner, boys,' he said. 'Greedy creatures! Make your shots count.' Their eyes glistened. Pigeon pie! And the Maäster said so!

The men worked together to sow all the fields, all working together, sokeman and villein, to make this year a good harvest, and the next winter bearable. Edgar promised the villeins help to tend their own crofts, if they would gift him more days' work than they were bound to, and they agreed. Agreed, as well, to working on one man's croft, then another's, and another's, one by one, until all were ploughed and harrowed and planted. Never before had they worked land in this way but the Maäster said so!

It was a different place from the one Edgar and Agathi had come to in January; different because its people were different. There was no more hostility and sullen reluctance to work. No sudden eruptions of anger and resentment. No fear of wrongful accusation and harsh punishment. No empty bellies and shivering nights. With the coming of the new young reeve and his gentle wife, the manor was once more well administered, even if the young couple had strange ideas. The trench latrine, now that was a good idea, they agreed, but bathing in great wooden cauldrons that were more like to cook them for pottage? The women lined up with the girls and very young children; the men and boys in another line, with the bathtubs housed in separate huts hastily built just for this.

'Heathen,' they muttered, but emerged from their soaking and scrubbing clean and pink and sweet smelling. Even their clothes, new-washed, were clean, lice-free and mud-free. And there were new clothes, the woollen cloth gifted by the master and mistress, to be kept for Holy Days. An early Easter gift. Doff an' don, just like rich folk; clothes to put on and clothes to put by. Dyed cloth as well, in blues and yellows and a small quantity of madder that the women declared was for Ellen. The women preeked and preened. They combed each other's hair, and plaited it and pleated it and wove ribbons in and out as the sokemen's wives did. The children were rosy-clean, and the young girls shiny like new coins. Joan emerged with her hair copper-bright. Agathi found a green ribbon for her and fastened it round her glinting hair. It reminded her of Kazan, and that day at the ca'Ginstinianis, when they had looked at each other in the mirror and wondered at their changed selves, and the miracle of rich robes. Now little Joan looked and wondered at herself in a new yellow kirtle. Her eyes were the colour of catkins before they burst into yellow tails. 'Pretty girl,' said Agathi, and kissed her. From a distance, Oluf glowered in silence. Mazzled wench. Prettier than he'd reckoned. Who'd ha' thought her hair so bright? He flexed skinny shoulders. He wasn't so bad-looking himself, now he were cleaned up, and in clean clothes. Smelling sweeter than a tussie mussie. He swaggered across the yard in front of Joan. She didn't poke her tongue out at him now, he noted with satisfaction, but the trail of notes on her elder pipe followed him across the yard, clear and bright in the spring morning.

This was a different life from that they had been used to, said the women. This strange young mistress with her outlandish ideas… baths every week…well…this was one change they were happy to make. And their complaining men? They'd best get used to it. Stinking brutes.

'Foreign,' the men said, darkly, but they shrugged and carried out requests. That was one of the strange changes: no orders but requests that all were unwilling to refuse. Once, old Luke politely asked to speak privately with the Master. It seemed that he disagreed with something the Master had said, and the Master had listened, and bowed to Luke's greater knowledge of the lie of the land, and told them so, publicly. After that, he referred to Luke in meetings and nobody thought any the worse of him for it. They were heartened by it.

Before the thaw, snow kept them from ploughing but, Edgar said, it gave them the chance to make repairs closer to home. There was threshing to be done, and what was left of the seed corn to be separated. There were repairs to be made to the villeins' cotts. These were not as bad as feared; Edgar blessed his father for an honest man. He'd had the cotts built well. The thatching was blown and the earthen floors gouged and fetid. In some cotts, slimy damp smeared the walls but that was as easily dealt with as the floors. Thatching now, that was different. Old Andrew had taken a fall and his son was simple-minded. Couldn't be trusted up the ladders, see, not on his own. Still, if he spared even one man to watch the boy, they could make a fist of it; and they did. One by one, the cotts were rembled and the families re-homed. Summer, may'appen, he'd hire a better thatcher, make the roofs right before the latter-end. He smiled to hear his thoughts falling into the pattern of the villagers' tongue. Blue's tongue.

All the tackle for the plough horses was checked for damage, repaired or replaced. The smithy was busy, its anvil ringing throughout the day, new hubs for wheels, the blunted, bent ploughshares good as new. Not only that, Jack Smith was here. The young, barely-apprenticed smith had been left on his own when the old smith died. Edgar found out where Jack Smith was eking out a living with his grand-daughter and brought them both to the manor. Young Jack Smith and Old Jack Smith, they called them, though the young man's name was Mark. The young man and the grand-daughter were much taken with each other. A wedding in the air, come summer, and the master wanting no fee for arranging the marriage, though it was his right.

Father Emanuel was a happy man now, with order restored and regular worship in the church. He was promised a new thatch for the church this summer – perhaps even shingle – and candles lit for all the saints and martyrs, and black cloth for Lent. 'I tried to do my best for these villagers but it was not easy. I did what I could for the comfort of their souls.'

'They needed comfort for their bodies as well, Father,' Edgar said. He thought, I sound like Dafydd. 'Why didn't you tell my brother there was trouble here?'

'I should have spoken out, Master Edgar,' the priest said, 'but if I did they would have got rid of me. And what would have been the good of that to these poor people?

'"They"?' asked Edgar.

Father Emanuel dipped his head. 'Maybe I should have said "she".' He sighed. 'The new lady of the manor, Lady Philippa, she put her own men in charge,' he said reluctantly. He shrugged. 'I do not like to say these things. The good Lord says we should not.'

Edgar silently thanked the good Lord that it was not his brother the priest spoke about. 'But I think you must explain if we are to have justice in this manor, Father. Tell me now.'

The priest sighed and folded his hands inside his sleeves. 'Your brother's wife comes of a good family,' he said. 'She wants only the best. That is well enough. But the best has to be taken from somewhere, and that is the problem. She doesn't understand the land, Master Edgar. She thinks she can draw on it, and it is inexhaustible. You and I know this is not so but she will not listen.'

'And Alfred listens only to her,' said Edgar. The priest inclined his head. He was unwilling to commit himself in honest speech. Well, thought Edgar, so it always is. Timorous priests. God take the lot of 'em. 'Give me Thomas,' he found himself thinking. 'Now there's an honest soul who wants to do the best for his fellow man. And he knows how hard the world can be.' He laughed at his thoughts. Blue and Hatice and Niko here, part of their family, and Thomas their priest? What wild thinking was this? Add Dafydd and Kazan and Giles. And Rémi and Mehmi. Why not? Why not have them all here, safe in the manor, their company complete again? He paused inside the porch and the entrance to the church; facing him was the huge wall painting of St Christopher, the giant who wished to serve the greatest king in the world, the man who lived on the edge of a dangerous river. One day St Christopher crossed the river carrying not a man but a child who became heavier and heavier, as heavy as the world, and on the other side the child revealed himself as Jesus Christ. And so St Christopher was the saint of travellers. And of the unconfessed. Any sick man on the point of death, if he saw the image of St Christopher, this man would be confessed. And so the saint was painted large opposite the entrance so that he might never be missed.

Now, on this fine-and-blustery March morning, here he was, Edgar, stretching and bracing himself for his turn at the plough. It was good to be in his own country again, making a difference to his land and people. He sighed. If only they were his lands, his people. He had grown fond of his motley villagers, sokemen and villeins alike – and the cottars, the poorest of them all, every one of them eager to be of use, whether it be bee-keeping or swine-herding or – surprising them all – old Herbert who had learned reading when he was a boy and who now schooled the children, boys and girls alike, on Sundays. Edgar took the older ones, and any man or woman who wanted schooling. Agathi joined them. She could read and write but now she wrestled with this strange new lettering and strange new language. Not French. Edgar decided to follow Robert Mannyng of Brunne's lead, the monk of Sempringham. Edgar had read 'Handlyng Synne' when he was at Croyland, astonished then because it was not written in Latin, nor French, but English. Better by far for these villagers and their children. Not that they were all eager to learn. Oluf was one of the reluctant and he only attended because Joan was a star pupil. He couldn't bear to let a girl – and that girl Joan – better him. He wanted to be out in the woods, hunting down the escaped boar. Now it was coming on spring, there were signs of rooting and trampling. Perhaps it was true, after all, and there was a fierce-some boar loose in the Long Wood.

They had all stopped for a bite mid-morning, oatcakes and cheese, and Edgar crumbled the last of his oatcake. There was a robin flitting about the branches of thorn bushes that sang with hedge sparrows and was bright with blossom. He'd seen it earlier. He held out crumbs in the palm of his hand. The robin hopped closer, its head tilted. Bright, brave bird. Come on. Come closer. The bird hopped to a nearer twig. It regarded him with bright eyes, hesitated, then hopped on to his outstretched hand and pecked from his open palm. He stayed stone still though his mouth curved into a smile. The men about him stayed still as well, wondering at their master's strange ways. 'He's one for the birds right enough,' they told each other, but secretly they were amazed at the trusting robin and admired their master for it.

A messenger came from the manor abutting Bradwell with a summons from Roger de Langton. 'Bring your young wife,' he'd added. 'I've a fancy to see you both.'

Agathi was working in the herb garden. Its woven hurdles were falling apart, no longer keeping out hens and dogs and cats, nor foxes; some plants had perished in the bitter winter, like the bay tree that should have been lifted at the first sign of frost and replanted in one of the many wicker baskets there for just that purpose. Other herbs had survived: bright green chive shoots were already poking through the earth; there was rosemary and rue, thyme and sage, wild garlic and borage yet to come; violets and celandines already budded; lemon balm and mint that were so good for strewing showing shoots above the earth. There was straggling lavender that Agathi was clipping into shape with a pair of precious scissors. Here were herbs for cooking, for strewing, for physicking.

Ellen and Hilda had chastised her: no digging or raking, they told her. Keep to the raised beds so there was no bending nor lifting. She had a bairn to think of now and, these first months, care was always needed. She had given in to them, wanting the best for the boy she was sure she was carrying. The two women had taken over the heavier jobs, wielding axes and spades and shears and heavy, clumsy wheelbarrow with the familiarity of long usage. Hilda knew the Nine

Herbs Prayer, learned from her mam when she was a bairn, and her mam from her own mam. 'The prayer tells of the best and most useful herbs for all complaints,' she said. 'Mugwort, plantain, shepherd's purse, nettle, betony, crabapple, chervil, fennel...' she ticked them off on her fingers as she recited their names. 'And here they all be, working their magic over us.' She half-sang, half-muttered the prayer in her throaty voice as she worked amongst the herbs: snatches of it came over the garden to Agathi's ears:

nettle she is called
dashes she against poison
she drives out wretchedness
throws out poison

Agathi laid aside the scissors she was using when she saw Edgar. 'By summer this garden will be very useful, Edgar, as well as a great delight.'

He smiled at her, kissed the palm of her hand, kissed her sweet mouth. 'As you are to me, sweetheart.'

'Husband!' she said, reproachfully. 'We are not alone.'

He glanced across to where Ellen was filling the wheelbarrow with wind-snapped branches of crab apple. Hilda was crouching over the bed where nettles and plantain grew.

shepherd's purse this plant is called
she on stone grew.
stands she against poison
she drowns out pain

'They are happy to see us happy, sweetheart.' He tugged at the sleeve of the simple woollen kirtle she wore; her fashionable gowns were laid down in the great oak chest in the solar. 'You'll be needing your fine feathers,' he said, 'if they still fit you.' He placed his hand on her belly, felt the smallest of swelling there. 'We're going visiting the neighbours. Sir Roger de Langton, who sent us provisions. He has invited us to visit.' Summoned, more like, he thought with a quick chill of anxiety. No need to say so to Agathi. 'Well, I hope it may be profitable. He knew my father. He bought the lands above the Long Wood, and all the South Wood and South Fields. Over a hundred acres of good land. I hope to persuade him to sell some at least back to us. What do you think, sweetheart?'

'I think that would be very good for this manor, Edgar. And,' glancing at him from under lowered lashes, 'I want to meet this man who was your father's friend and who knew you when you were a young boy.'

'He may not remember me, sweetheart. I was very young and very shy.'

Now strength have these nine plants
against nine who from wonder flee
against nine poisons
and against nine infections

Edgar caught the last of Hilda's song. 'What is she singing?' he asked.

'It is the Nine Herbs Prayer,' Agathi said. 'It is to give all who live here protection from evil, and from all poisons that may harm us.'

'As much protection as Blue's shivery spiders?' he teased. 'Or better still a live spider rolled in butter and swallowed?'

'You should not make fun of these matters,' she told him gravely. 'You do not know how much truth is in them. Hilda says the ash tree has great powers. She says there is one on this manor that used to have a split in the trunk and one winter many children had the coughing sickness. Hilda says they were passed through the split and then it was bound up and it healed itself, and the children were all cured.'

'I've heard that tale told before,' said Edgar, 'except the child died though the tree healed itself.' He saw the anxiety in her face and could have kicked himself for his stupidity. 'Perhaps there is truth in it, sweetheart, but I'd sooner put my faith in these healing herbs growing here, and those who know their mysteries. Luke says the nuns at Catley Priory are skilled in the use of herbs and medicine – birthing too. I'm sure they will help us.'

Her gaze was reproachful. 'Hilda and Ellen are both skilled in the use of herbs, husband. You should not mock the wisdom of women.'

'I am chastised,' he said. 'I am sorry, Agathi. I should have known better.' He hugged her. 'Come, change this gown. We're going visiting.'

Roger de Langton did remember Edgar. 'Like your mother, boy. Spitting image. She had the same golden curls and blue eyes. Hm.' He had an open, broad face with double chins and fleshy neck; his cheeks and nose were red-veined with good living; his eyes like currants pushed into dough. He patted his belly. 'Didn't have this last time you were here. The good Prior of Catley tells me too much good living will be the death of me. I tell him good living makes for a good death. Enjoy this life, boy, just in case the next one is too hot for you.' He looked across at Agathi. 'My, but you're bonny,' he said. 'Struggling to know what we're about? Let me see, now, bonny lass, what I remember from the old days.' He sat a moment, screwing up his mouth, flaring his nostrils. 'I am very pleased to meet you, pretty wife of Edgar,' he said haltingly in Turkish. He watched with pleasure as Agathi flushed and smiled.

'I am very pleased to meet you also, Father Roger,' she replied in the same language. 'I would like you to tell me what Edgar was like, what you remember of him when he was a young boy.'

'Now, now,' he said in the French they had been using. 'I remember only a little of your language. I did some merchanting in my youth. Not so long after the last Crusade. That's how I learned a bit of your language.' He smiled again. How good it was to be in the company of a pretty young woman once more, and a gentle little thing. Gentle? What had his bailiff told him? She'd felled that fellow Cedric like an ox, smashing a great log into his balls. What a woman! Just the sort to suit Edgar. Keep him right. 'You must teach me, Mistress Agathi,' he said in Turkish. 'Come here sometimes to keep an old man company and we shall speak in your language.'

'It will be my pleasure, Father Roger,' she said.

'You want to know about young Edgar, hey?' He reverted again to French, and spoke to Edgar. 'Told your father it was a foolish idea to send you off to the Abbey. Your mother liked her freedom and open spaces and so did you. Always out and about in the fields and woods, I remember, you and those brothers of yours. Up to mischief in the beck.' He chuckled. 'I remember how it was. Drove Simon Bailiff mad, you did. Ridiculous idea, cooping you up in holy piety. One for his own way, your father, and he was desolate without your mother. Don't be too hard on him, boy. Realised he was wrong-headed when you ran away. Settled Bradwell on you. Told me so. "Not much of an inheritance," he said, "but he always liked to visit there and it's well enough for a runaway, should he ever come back. If he can make a go of it, then he'll prove himself worthy." Now here you are and making a good fist of it, from what I hear.' He frowned. 'Took me a while to realise it was you. My men talked about a new reeve. Never said you'd come to claim your inheritance.'

Edgar stared at him. 'I am the new reeve,' he said. 'Alfred asked me to take care of Bradwell for him.'

'You? Reeve? Nonsense, boy. Don't know what maggots Alfred has in his head. Your father bequeathed you Bradwell. Since he died – well – it's been let go to rack and ruin. Land sold off or leased out. Catley runs sheep on some of the pasture and for sure they can't pay the bills. Can't pay the tax they owe, poor devils. In a bad way, they are. Good folk as well, monks and nuns both, and our own St Gilbert's. Not like some of them foreign abbeys…ah well, shouldn't speak ill of any of God's chosen, hey?'

nettle she is called
dashes she against poison

Edgar sat stunned. His father had given him Bradwell Manor? But Alfred had asked him to be his reeve. What did this mean? Agathi looked anxiously at him, not sure of her understanding. Edgar was lord of the manor? Not a reeve? Is this what the old man was saying? She leaned forward, summoning words that were elusive.

'You say Edgar has this manor? It is his?'

'Yes. His father wanted it so. Ah, boy, how he regretted what he had done. A hard man but a fair one, and he loved you as much as he cursed you. Forgive him, my boy. Saw your mother in you. He loved her very much.' The old man shivered with memories. 'Enough of that. Now, these lands I've bought from you...' He had no sons to inherit the manor, only rascally, grasping nephews. 'I'll not give them the pleasure of fleecing me,' he said. 'I'll return the land to you. What do you say to that?'

'It is Alfred's land.'

'My dear boy, haven't you heard what I said? It is yours. Your father told me so. Made it all legal and such and had me sign to make all right-and-tight. Had Prior Hubert sign as well, and the papers are safe with him at Catley. Your brother has a second set.'

'Alfred said nothing.'

shepherd's purse this plant is called
she on stone grew.
stands she against poison

Roger de Langton frowned. 'That brother of yours diddling you, hey? Wouldn't put it past him, nor that new wife of his. Airs and graces – that's what's running Bradwell to ruin. Not content with leasing and selling land. The quarries have been robbed for all that new build going on at Rochby. Taking more than their share of rent and harvest. Think I hadn't heard? Talk gets around, boy. Summoned me to the Christmas feastin', y'know. Didn't go. No taste for such things. Your father, now, honest-to-goodness he was, for all his failings. No pomp for him.' He was frowning still, chewing at his fleshy lower lip, his face so suffused with red that Agathi was alarmed. 'Wouldn't surprise me one bit if it was all done deliberately, cheat you out of Bradwell.' He grunted. 'Must have given them a shock when you turned up alive and well and wed. What you going to do about it, boy?'

Edgar sat back, thinking. He wondered how much Agathi had understood. 'I must explain matters to my wife.'

Explain to his wife? Valued her thoughts, then. The old man watched the girl's face as Edgar explained in Turkish that was fluent enough. No squeaks and shrieks for this lass. Like his own wife, clever woman. Missed her still, truth be told. Ah well. This girl, she sat still, hands folded across her belly. Giveaway sign, that. Brat in her belly for sure. Better for that. She'd do much to keep her husband and child secure, this one. Then the to-and-fro of their discussion in Turkish too rapid for him to follow; too many words he didn't know. What were they thinking, these two young 'uns? Looked like angels, the pair of 'em, but they'd a head apiece and together they had the strength of ten. And the boy, sitting straight and dignified. Like his father, thought Roger de Langton. Just like his father; with his mother's eyes and hair but with his father's chin. Hadn't noticed that before. Iron under the gilding, this boy.

'Well, young Edgar?'

'Sir, we need to see this document you and Prior Hubert have signed your names to. After that, we can consider what is best to do. Not immediately. I would like to know more of the circumstances. He is my brother. I cannot believe such ill of him. He was a good brother to me when I was young. We were raised together. We played together.' He was silent for a long while. 'I need to discover what

Eric knows of this. But first, most important, it is necessary to make this manor secure for the sake of the sokemen and villeins and cottars. Agathi is with child and I would not wish her to be worried, and that she must be, were I to challenge Alfred and his wife.' Edgar heaved a sigh.

Roger de Langton sank his chins into his chest. He looked down at his clasped hands. He nodded. 'Perhaps that is for the best, for now, as you say. But not for long.' He looked up with currant-dark-eyes that were suddenly piercing. 'Meanwhile, take back the lands I bought from the estate.'

'I have money enough to buy them back from you, sir.'

'Have you, stiff rump? That's good news but keep your gold. I said take back and I meant take back. When I saw the lie of the land,' he smirked at his own joke, 'I bought what I could solely to keep it safe for you, should you return, and out of the greedy hands of my nephews and your dear brother and sister-in-law.' He smiled on them. 'It is my wedding present to you both. My men shall work the land this year but the harvest is yours.' He chuckled. 'My men? The men are yours, boy. They came along with the land, as you know.' He lifted his heavy hands, turned them palms out. 'No need to let your brother know our arrangement. He has his secrets; you have yours. Hey?'

Edgar nodded. He was reluctant to practise any subterfuge but Dafydd would be the first to say it was sometimes necessary. He thought of the young men Alfred had called to him, a private army. 'You are very generous, sir. We cannot repay such—'

'Good good. Enough of thanks, young Edgar. It's as much for your father as for you. He's been tossing in his tomb at all this, I shouldn't wonder. He'd a rare gift for managing his manors. Seems you've inherited his gift, if all I hear is true. You've need of a thatcher, they tell me. Old Andrew can't do the work anymore with that bad-set leg of his, and his son is simple, even for thatching. I'll send Peter over, with the means for thatching. Good sedge for the ridge and reeds for the thatch. That should see you through a few seasons. No, I've said, away with your thanks. Have done. If you must thank anyone, let it be Catley – came off their fens, and they'd be glad of an offering. Glad to see you back, boy, and more like your father than you'd like to admit. A brat on the way? Well, young mistress, that is good news indeed. Work to be done this summer, hey? But remember you've promised to keep me company.'

He sighed with pleasure when she put her young arms about his neck and kissed his cheek. Ah, if only he'd had a daughter like this. Or a son such as Edgar. God had not smiled on him and his wife, as they had on his friend Alfred. Foolish Alfred, putting his faith in his firstborn, never knowing that his youngest was pure gold, from his curls to his heart.

Now strength have these nine plants...
...against nine poisons
and against nine infections

13

Swineshead
April 1337
Have pity on me, full of mourning
(Anon: mid 14ᵗʰC)

She was too late, after all.

The journey through cold country and rough, dark seas had been too late. She was bludgeoned by the flat, dark land merging into water. Land and sea, sea and land; where did one end, the other begin? She who had roamed the high mountains and tumbling crags was overwhelmed by this flat, watery place. They'd waited for the tide to turn before they could sail up the Haven to Boston. These tides! She had seen nothing like it in her life; the sea covering the land, deeper and deeper, trickling at first into creeks and mud banks then a swirl of treacherous water rushing into the dry places.

A channel was marked with posts. 'Keep getting moved, those,' the steersman said. 'Have to keep a good lookout this past year. Silting up, see. Goes on like this, won't be able to get the big boats up here. Then what will Boston be without its sea trade?' He shook his head. 'Doesn't bear thinking.'

She wasn't sure what he meant. All this water. Surely any ship could sail up here?

'We're in the Deeps now, miss,' said the captain. 'Don't you be afeared. Soon as we're in the Haven, soonest we'll be in Boston.' But wherever she looked was brown sea, mud and saltmarsh and creeks and channels of brown water and flatness. Even the lowering clouds were brown-tinged. She was deafened by the din of birds, flustered by their swooping and swirling through the rigging and sails of the cog. So many; she had never seen so many flocking together, shrieking like lost souls.

'Back along, miss, there's the Abbey of Freiston. Benedictine, that is. And there's salt workings right along the marshes.' He laughed his loud, sailor's laugh, happy to be home. He liked the little lass, though she were frim folk from far away. She'd been brave as owt on the high sea, and now she were frittened by the sight of the land. 'It's a good living here, miss, for web-footed-uns like we be. My brother, he's comes fra well into the Fens, he does. Wouldn't not never live nowhere else.'

'Web-footed?' she asked faintly.

'That's how they knows us Fen men.' He laughed again, showing blackened teeth and gaps where some had been drawn. 'There's some as think we really do 'ave web feet. It's the watter-land. Marshes fed by salt watter and the Fens by fresh watter.' The cog dipped and jigged in a sudden gust of wind; sails flapped and cracked. For a moment, the heavy swags of cloud shifted to let through late afternoon sun; a shaft of brilliant light silvered down on to the watery land so that it gleamed with dazzling intensity. 'See that? Watter-jawelled, we call it, the way it shines i' the sun. Bewtifullest as ever was.'

She was reminded of Blue's face when he spoke of the Fens, the sadness he tried so hard to hide, standing there on the wharf at Attaleia, staying behind for the sake of Hatice and young Niko, and all the time consumed by longing for this flat, brown, waterland. 'Yes, beautiful,' she agreed, for Blue's sake, and for the kind captain who loved his fenland home. But it was beautiful, she thought, this great sky-light beaming on to the water and lighting up the afternoon, just not the same as the high mountains and bright blue sky and sea.

The captain took Giles to one side. 'Yer'll be needing a plaäce to stay the night.'

Giles was startled. 'We'll stay at the Abbey, surely, as travellers and guests.'

'You, mebbe, but not the maid. Won't not never have females at the Abbey, those Cistercians. 'Specially not the new Abbot. Abbot John. It were different in the old days. If it were a Gilbert house, now, that's different again. Built for monks and nuns both, they are, though they're kept well separate, one from t'other. The village is big enough – has its own fair – but best you come back to Boston. There's a fine guesthouse run by the Shodfriars. Quiet, it is. I'll show yer its whereabouts, and yer can leave yer tuts.' He nodded his head at Giles' expression. 'Yer right to be wary, it being a port and you strange folk, but yer needn't worry yerself none about the Shodfriars' place. They'll see yer right.'

'Is the Abbey far?' He gestured towards Kazan who was still gazing out over the brown water of the Haven. 'She's a rare one, the best, but she's tired, though she'll never say so.'

'I can see that.' The Captain shot a swift, shrewd look towards Kazan, back to Giles. 'Only a short stride from town to Abbey. Mind as 'ow yer keep to the tracks. There's pools as 'ud swaller an 'orse an' rider.' He shot another quick look, curious this time, asked the question that had been in his mind since the pair boarded. 'She your missis?'

Giles shook his head. 'She's a sweetheart, but not my sweetheart. Her man had to stay behind in Venezia. We're worried for his safety. There's been no word all winter. But the girl promised her grandmother she would come to find her grandfather, and she's a girl who keeps her word.' He smiled ruefully. 'Many don't.'

'Yer right there.'

'And I promised Dafydd – her man – to keep her safe so here I am, though I'm a man from the Marches. That's in-between country as well, neither one place nor the other.'

'Oh aye?' The Captain knew only coastlines and watery places. 'Tell yer what, best send Simon Salter with yer. Knows the ways through these Fens. Back of 'is 'and. He's known by the soldiers as they've got patrolling the coast, an' all. Not good ter be frim folk these days, what with this war coming.'

The Captain was a man of his word as well. Rough-talking, rough-seeming, but honest. He sent a boy to find Simon Salter. 'He'll be home this weather.' He led them to the guesthouse that belonged, it turned out, to the Dominicans, and it was a comfortable lodging. More comfortable than many of the mountain passes of the High Alps, Giles acknowledged. He wished that Kazan had agreed to bring a female with her, someone to keep her company, but she had been impatient, declared they were all townswomen and would moan and complain and drive her distracted.

'I shall keep my dagger by me, Giles. Do not worry so. Besides, all the women in the sleeping chamber, they are comfortable matrons. I do not think they would know how to stab me, even in my sleep. It is you who must take care. Now, if we are to go the Abbey, and come back here before dark, let us go straightway. That Simon is here.'

Now that she was so close to finding him, she was nervous. Her stomach and throat were tight-knotted. Suppose he would not recognise the green jade? Suppose it was all so long ago he had forgotten? She had only Nene's memories, and Nene had been a young girl in love. But Nene was always right, she thought: if she and Will shared a so great love, then this was truth, and he would be pleased to see the granddaughter of the child they had made between them.

And after all she was too late.

'Master Will? You say this is his granddaughter?' The very small, very young, white-robed monk had only today been trusted with duty in the gatehouse. He was chattering with anxiety. A woman at the Abbey gatehouse! Demanding admittance! And Brother Wilfred dead not even two months gone. 'I'll ask for the Prior. He will know best what to do. Oh dear.' He hurried away, leaving Kazan and Giles to wait outside the Abbey precinct. Not long to wait. The prior arrived with the little monk galloping at his heels, his robe billowing out behind him.

'You are welcome, sir, though not your lady. We do not admit any to this House of Prayer, and certainly not women. The new Abbot is very strict.'

'What does he say, Giles?'

'You can't come in. You'll corrupt them all.' He smothered a grin though he was tired with travel, full of anxiety for the girl. 'I'm welcome. I'm Adam – you're wicked Eve come to tempt them.'

She put a hand to her mouth. 'Oh no! Really?'

'Really. Better if you'd come in your boy's *şalvar* and *gömlek*.'

'But not honest, Giles. Have faith. I shall wait and you will find my grandfather.'

'Perhaps they'll let you into the gatehouse.' He engaged in energetic discussion with the prior, protesting that this young lady had travelled from a far-off land to meet her grandfather. Almost as far as Holy Jerusalem. And now she was to be denied? Not even allowed into the gatehouse on a cold March afternoon? Simon Salter would stay with her; he would protect the young monk from any temptation. She had never before heard Giles so burningly caustic.

The prior was heavy-hearted. He looked from the girl's anxious face to the young man's angry one. There was bad news awaiting her at the end of her long journey and he didn't want to be the one to tell it. He acceded at last that she wait in the gatehouse. 'But she must stay here, in this place. And you, Brother Jude, will not exchange any words with the woman. You hear?'

The little monk nodded and shivered and kept his eyes downcast. How bright was this young woman's gaze, her eyes gold-flecked like the Abbot's hunting hawks. Enough to make a monk regret his vows. He shook his head. He avoided her eyes, after that one look.

Giles was taken to the Abbot's lodging. The Abbot was not a man to be disturbed by even the most startling news. He took the sudden arrival of the tough-looking young squire and the foreign girl with equanimity, though he made sure the young female was kept at a distance. Even her presence in the gatehouse was bad enough. He yearned after the old Cistercian commands when all was clear, austere, pure. If he could, he would return this abbey to its true state of Christian virtue.

'I fear our brother Wilfred is dead these two months past. Come where it is warm. The air is cold, despite this welcome sun.' He indicated a bench close to the hearth. 'We had not expected the arrival of any family, least of all a grand-daughter,' he said calmly. 'Wilfred's family was killed in the Great Floods of 1282. He was not married. Yes, he travelled far and wide and men are what they are.' He pursed his lips, carefully tolerant of the ways of the world. He pondered. They had come a long way, these two. Should he? Brother Hugh was a steady soul but he had been too much moved by the Wordmaker's story, and distraught by his death and the manner of it. 'You say the girl has never known her grandfather?'

'She knows him only from the stories her grandmother told. And we have seen his image, Father Abbot, painted when he was much the same age as I am now.'

Faint surprise rippled across the Abbot's face; his expression became smooth again. 'His image, you say?'

'In the chapel of the Scrovegni family, in Padua.'

'Ah, the Franciscan chapel.'

'A man called Giotto painted people who look so real it seems they will walk off the walls and into the chapel.'

'I have heard of this Giotto. Very modern, of course. We are traditional here.' He was interested, all the same. 'And you say he painted the girl's grandfather?'

'Yes. In several of the scenes.'

'Nothing blasphemous or heretical, I hope?'

The question came sharply. Giles said curtly, 'Not at all, Father Abbot. He was painted as a bystander, one of the crowd, a soldier. Nothing that could offend a holy man.'

The Abbot nodded. He made up his mind. 'There is a Brother here who was with Brother Wilfred the night before he died; he listened to Wilfred's story and will swear to its truth. Perhaps you would wish to speak with this Brother?'

'Of course,' said Giles. He sounded abrupt. This smooth-talking, self-righteous abbot irritated him. He deliberately softened his voice; nothing gained by offending. 'It would be kind of you to arrange that, Father Abbot.'

Brother Hugh was brought to them, a pale, serious-faced man not yet in his middle-age. 'I do not know why he chose me, sir. I was honoured. We spent the night in the hospital. He was not a well man and he wished to make confession.'

'Confession, Brother Hugh?'

'Of a sort. He told me the story of his life. It was...' he paused, bewildered, at a loss for words, '...extraordinary,' he said.

'Did he speak of Mistress Kazan's grandmother?' Giles asked.

'No, sir. I am sorry.' He spoke quietly, barely above a whisper. 'He talked mostly of his brother, sir, and the Welshman, the music man, Ieuan ap y Gof, who was a renegade before the first Edward subdued the Welsh lands.' A hero, he thought, but that was wrongful thinking. 'They met him first here at the Abbey, before the First Welsh War. He had broken his leg and was resting until he was well enough to travel back to Wales. He taught the brother how to play music.' Sweet music; so sweet old Brother Matthew talked of it even now. That was in the days of the old Abbot, a man of gentleness and tolerance. Would that Abbot have allowed the girl entry? 'Your grandfather talked of how many *fossatores* – ditch-diggers, and experts, every man of them – were marched to the Welsh lands to build the first of Edward's great castles in Wales. Six were sent from the village of Swineshead.' He paused. 'If you wish, and if Father Abbot gives his permission and blessing, I can tell you the story as it was told to me. It is a story long in telling.'

Giles looked questioningly towards the Abbot who fixed a stern gaze on Brother Hugh's bent head. His tonsure gleamed pale in the light from the window; his lashes shadowed his cheeks. He stood quietly, schooled to patience, one hand cupped in the other. Giles wondered what his life was like, bound to his God and his Abbot, day after day, month after month, year after year. It was what Edgar had rejected. Was this truly what his friend Thomas had chosen for his life?

The Abbot nodded. 'As you wish. You will be our guest tonight and tomorrow you will meet with Brother Hugh.' He permitted a small smile to flicker across his lips. 'In our Order it is forbidden for women to live under the same roof as the monks. Even entry past the monastery gate is denied them.'

Giles shook his head. 'Thank you for your invitation but I cannot accept. I am Kazan's friend. I am also sworn to be her companion and protector. I cannot and will not leave her alone in a strange town, and a port at that, even if she should wish it, for the sake of the story Brother Hugh has to tell.' A look at Father Abbot's face told him it was more impassive than ever. 'This is hard news for her. Any true Christian would feel pity for her.' He was gritting his teeth with the effort of keeping his voice level and quiet but he had the satisfaction of seeing a dull red creep into the other man's face. 'We have lodgings in the Dominican's guesthouse. I'll return tomorrow to speak with Brother Hugh.' He thought a moment. 'Is the grandfather buried here?'

'Yes.'

'And I suppose it is not possible for her to see the grave?'

'I regret not.'

There's Christian charity for you, thought Giles savagely. He went back through the precinct to the gatehouse. Simon Salter was as good as the word he had given; he was waiting with the pleasure of a hard-working man not accustomed to taking his ease. He had got talking to young Brother Jude. 'But yer real name's Robin, innit? Godfrey Baker's boy?'

The young monk blushed and stammered that he was Brother Jude now; the other was as if it had never been.

'Ah well,' Simon Salter said, vaguely. He looked up as Giles strode into the gatehouse. 'Right you are, young sir? Let's be back to Boston, then, afore darklins.'

Kazan pushed her hand into Giles'. His own wrapped around her fingers and squeezed them. 'What is it, Giles?'

'He is dead, Kazan. These last two months.'

'Oh.' It was little more than a wisp of breath. 'I thought it,' she said. 'I felt it.' She was silent. Silent as she mounted Yıldız and they set their horses moving quietly along the causeway, Simon ahead of them, sure-footed. 'How did he die?'

'I'm not sure. Old age, probably. I'm coming back tomorrow to talk with Brother Hugh, the monk who was with him the last night of his life.' He sighed. 'Brother Hugh says your grandfather told him his story, and he will tell it to me.'

'Nene?'

Giles shook his head. 'He says your grandfather didn't speak of her. But,' he added, 'we must wait until I've heard the whole story.'

So he was dead, her grandfather, and all this long journey had been for nothing. She fingered the jade axe about her neck. All for nothing. Nene, I have kept my promise. You said he was alive. You said he would be here for me. No, she had not said that. Only that he was alive, then, at that time in the late summer in the high pastures. Since then, the old man had died and she would only ever know him through Nene's stories, Nene's eyes, and the eyes of the painter Giotto. No, not quite true; there were many others who remembered him for the stories he had told. And Dafydd's grandfather had saved her own from drowning in the Mawddach Falls. She must be thankful for all these memories. Her grandfather would never be forgotten.

'You must not be sad, Giles,' she said. 'Not be angry. It is.'

'I've failed you. I've failed Dafydd.'

'No! Foolish Giles. Of course you have not. How could I have managed without you?'

'These monks…' he said. He gritted his teeth. 'The Father Abbot says you cannot see your grandfather's grave. You're not permitted to cross the threshold of the Abbey precinct. It's as if you were unclean!'

'Well, and so it is with some of these religious men. Not all.' She smiled at him, a little crookedly, the gold subdued. 'You and I do better together, do we not?'

'Yes.' He flung his head back, breathed in the earthy smell of the marshland. 'Yes, Kazan; you, me, all of us. All our band of friends. We are bound together, male and female, Christian and Muslim, for all eternity, living or dead, wherever we may be.'

'But they are not dead,' she said. 'Not Thomas nor Dafydd. We shall see them again.'

'You think so? And what of Blue and Hatice and…'

'…Niko and Mehmi? Perhaps they are already with Edgar and Agathi.' She was smiling but he was serious.

'You make me think all things are possible.'

'But so they are, my very dear friend. Remember: "*Only Allah the all-compassionate, the all-knowing decides.*"'

'"*There is always room for faith.*"' He was smiling now, his anger receding. 'Thank God and Allah for men like Kara Kemal and Heinrijc Mertens. They're truly Men of God. Isn't it now, Kazan?'

'You sounded like Dafydd just then.'

'Did I?' He sounded pleased. 'Must be sitting on my shoulder.' He let the mare Yıldız step ahead of the brown stallion he was riding: Dafydd's horse, Sadık the Faithful. 'How are you so sure they're alive, Dafydd and Thomas?'

'I feel it is so.'

'As your grandmother felt your grandfather was alive?' It was a cruel question but she answered with tranquillity.

'When she told me so, it was true.'

He sighed. 'What it is to have faith, Kazan. I envy you.' The track widened and he drew alongside her again. Her profile was pure against the bleakness of the marshland and late afternoon sky. Her hood had fallen back and her hair, past shoulder-length now, was blown back. The setting sun caught the glint of gold-copper-bronze. A lucky man, Dafydd, to hold this woman's heart.

The next afternoon he was given leave to spend time with Brother Hugh. The monk was nervous, twitching and restless, but he told the story of how the brothers and the *fossatores* had journeyed to Flint, unspeakably crude, digging in dirt to make the foundations of the first of the new castles for Edward. 'It was a hard life. Very hard. Especially for a young boy such as her grandfather, as he was then.' How they had escaped, how they went in search of the Welshman, the music man, and made their way south-west to Cymer Abbey and were saved from drowning...'

'By the Welshman, Dic,' said Giles.

'Yes, brother, yes, that is so. How do you know this?'

'He was the grandfather of Kazan's beloved friend, Dafydd. He saved them and took them to the Abbey of Cymer. And there they recovered. This is true, isn't it?'

'It is true, brother. That is what happened.' Brother Hugh marvelled. 'It is what is meant to be,' he said, 'the granddaughter and the grandson. Truly God is great.'

'He'd be even greater if he got Dafydd safe to Ieper,' Giles said. Brother Hugh gulped at the blasphemy.

It was there Will-the-Wordmaker left his brother behind, the monk continued, and returned here, to Swineshead and his family, to his mother and sisters. Some years later, at the end of the second Welsh War it was, one winter, there was a great tragedy. A great storm swept away many towns and villages. The Wordmaker's family as well. After that, he became a travelling man, searching for his lost brother. He never found him. *I listen, and listen but cannot hear their music.* So he came home again, in his old age. *I came back home – not home, though I call it so. It suits me well enough. It's comfort you want when your bones ache and your sight's failing.* Brother Hugh sat a moment with his hands folded in front of him, remembering the old man, his determined manner, his voice lost in memory. 'He did mention, just once, perhaps he had children but if so he had never seen them.' *For all I know, I've a brat or two in this world. They've never seen fit to find me.* No, these were not words for this young man to tell the girl so anxious to find her grandfather. And yet…

'Well?'

'He said something…perhaps the girl would find it of comfort.' *There were women. Some for pleasure, that's true, but others because we shared our souls. I remember…*' He did not say what he remembered, Master Giles, but it is my true belief it was of the girl's grandmother he spoke. That is all I can tell you.' He hesitated, fluttering nervously. 'But there is something more.'

'Yes?'

'We found him amongst the reeds in the freezing cold. He had walked out there in the late night. I am sure he meant to die but I did not say so or he could not have had a Christian burial and his soul would have wandered for ever in Purgatory.' *Last night I wondered if I heard the swan pipe. Fleeting notes, sweet as only Ned could play them.* 'He held the swan pipe that had been his brother's. It was precious to him but Father Abbot said it was heathen to bury it with him and would have cast it away but I took it and kept it safe. He said it was Ned's soul that sang when the pipe was played, and the pipe was made of a swan's wing and they were fallen angels. Such a small thing to be so precious, but isn't that always so? Here it is. It belongs to his granddaughter now.'

He held it out to Giles. Smooth length of bone flute marked with little scratches. Whispering silent ghost sounds of sweet melodies.

The story of another time, another life. 'Thank you, Brother Hugh. Kazan will treasure this.'

The monk twitched again. 'I am guilty of a sin, Master Giles, and a sin I have not confessed. I have not told Father Abbot,' he confided.

'No, you're not guilty of a sin, Brother Hugh. You're guilty of,' Giles smiled, 'great kindness.'

'Thank you, Master Giles, but all the same I must confess and do penance.' His own smile held an unexpected flicker of mischief. 'But only after you and the swan pipe have left this abbey.'

Kazan fingered the smooth length of the bone flute that gleamed like moonshine. She held it to her mouth and blew into it but there was no sound, nothing, except for the hiss of breath between her teeth. It needed her grandfather to do that. No, not her grandfather but his brother Ned, the brother who was not a brother; the music man who had no voice of his own but who breathed life into the dead bone until it sang like the angel it had once been. So Nene had told her. It was how Will-the-Wordmaker had told the tale of the swan pipe to her grandmother. Now here was the angel-pipe in her hands and her grandfather was frozen to death in the bleak midwinter marshland by his own will.

'That is a terrible, beautiful story,' she said, and after that she was silent, holding the swan pipe carefully in her hands.

They stayed in Boston while rain and wind raged about the low fenlands. So much sky with massed dark clouds stretching across flat brown land that itself stretched away as far as the eye could see. Distant rain was tumbling out of cloud on to earth; it was moving quickly, and soon sharp hail was rattling against the shuttered window. She could hardly remember her own land: the tumbled, rocky coastline where they made winter camp; the high mountains of their summer dwellings. Her sea was blue, not this brown-grey mass that was half land, half sea. It was an in-between land, and she felt in-between. Where was Kazan? Gone, with Dafydd. This shell, this girl who used to be Kazan, journeyed on but her soul was gone from her body.

'There's nothing more here for us, Kazan,' Giles said. 'Let's go on to find Edgar and Agathi.' He was worried by her quietness. 'They may have news of Dafydd. Remember what Heinrijc said? He would send word to Edgar. Besides,' with a lift in his heart, 'it'll be good to see those two again.'

'Yes, let us do that,' she said, but there was no answering gladness in her voice.

Go by boat, they were told, up the Witham River to Lincoln. That is the easiest way. Brother Hugh had told Giles, 'It is the way Will-the-Wordmaker started his long journey to Wales.' And so, one April morning, they were at Boston Haven boarding the boat that would take them up the Witham to Lincoln. 'It's a fine town,' said Simon Salter, 'and a good road from there to your friend's manor. God speed.' The wind and rain had gone and that morning the great flat sky over the flat land was bright blue. As far as she could see was blue sky and white sheep grazing on greening salt marsh where there was sea in winter. Birds were everywhere. The air was full of their din. Their horses were brought on board the flat-bottomed barge. Yıldız was snorting, alarmed by another water journey, but she lifted her head and her ears pricked. Her eyes fixed on Kazan and she came quietly enough, following the girl on to the boards, nuzzling the sleeve of her kirtle. Kazan soothed her, whispered words of love into the mare's ears. Yıldız snickered and mouthed her bridle but she was quieted. Sadık the Faithful gave no cause for alarm. He followed the mare on to the boat boards and stood by her side, whickering gently.

The wharf faded out of sight. The salt marsh gave way to fen and the fen to green fields and long orchards, bare branched now. 'But spring is coming,' said one of the boatmen. His home was close to Bardney Abbey, and soon he would have leave to return there. 'It's a pretty sight in spring,' he told them. 'The lime woods smell sweeter than anyone can think and the ground is thick with white wood anemones. Later, there'll be daffodils and honeysuckle, and in autumn fat blackberries.'

'I think you love your home,' said Kazan.

'That I do, Mistress. There's no place like it in the whole world, I'll be bound.'

No place like it. She thought about the summer camp in the high valleys that bloomed scarlet with anemone and poppy, pale purple with crocus and white daisies with yellow eyes waving through grass that was lush and fresh; craggy mountain sides backed by range after range, all blurring into blue; steep-stepped half-circle of ruins climbing to the highest, loftiest, top-most point where, on a clear day, she could see the glittering blue of the sea far below, and the *yurts* sheltering in their own grassy harbour in the dip of the valley.

'No place like it,' she agreed. She slept after that, lulled by the suck-and-slap of waves against boat, the dip-and-pull, the quietness of it all. She slept past Barlings and Bardney, Steinfield and Bullington, past the great stretch of lime-wood forest where the 'Wild Man' lived by stealing cattle and sheep. Giles let her sleep on. That was what she needed most. There was another passenger, a man returning to his family in Lincoln. 'Business in Boston,' he said briefly. He roused himself to point out places they passed and told him the story of the 'Wild Man'. He nudged Giles and pointed in the distance to where a great building rose from a high cliff. 'That's the cathedral,' he said. 'We can see it well enough. That's good.' Giles was puzzled. 'It means mild weather from the west,' the man explained. 'If it's mist-shrouded, it means we're in for cold, wet weather from the east.' He smiled, the tight-lipped smile of a serious man. 'Spring's on its way at last,' he said.

Giles woke her in late afternoon.

'Lincoln,' he said briefly.

No need for warning. There was clamour enough: boats docking; wares unloaded; shouts and yells reverberating across the wharves; carts standing ready. And always the fetid stench that lurked in a city in this country. She rubbed sleep from her eyes, bewildered by the bustle after the quiet journey and her long sleep. Like Venezia, but not like: same but different. And so very different was the high cliff and, on top of it, pressing down into the earth, was the great cathedral, like a ship sailing out over the hilltop, proud and free, its high tower flaunting itself high in the sky. It seemed like it was the highest building in the world, towering into clouds that had massed again in the late afternoon, sharp angled light and dark by turn. It strode over the high cliff, dominating the little lives below. Kazan shivered. This was power indeed.

'There's time before dark to travel through the town to St Catherine's,' said Giles. *You'll be comfortable there, both of you,* the serious stranger had told him; *it's Gilbertine, for men and women alike, and it's on your road.*

Through the lower town, taking the High Road that led out of the city. It was still well paved, one of the old Roman roads. Some of it had been cut into, where the good stone of the road was used as foundations for buildings, like the guildhall that had once been a king's palace, but a good road for all that. They could follow it for miles, all across the country and down to the southern coast. Better still, for them, it met with the road they would need to take the next day, another good, straight road. But for now, no need to think about that. St Catherine's was before you came to Cross o' Cliff, near to where the first Edward had raised a cross for his dead wife, the Queen Eleanor. No need go so far as the joining roads. Malandry on your left, lepers' colony but hardly any lepers these days. The monastery was just through Great Bargate. No distance at all, and do the horses good after being cramped on the barge for so many hours. Watch out for pickpockets and vagrants at Swine Green.

She nodded, willing to have it all arranged. She felt limp and helpless, not like Kazan at all. She had done so since she was told her grandfather was dead. And before that? Without Dafydd she felt half-alive. I left him, she thought, and all for nothing.

'Now that's not true, *cariad*.' She heard his voice clear as if he had been standing next to her. 'You made your promise to your *nain* to go in search of him, didn't you now? You have done as you promised. There's nothing you have to regret.'

I have my grandfather's swan pipe, Dafydd, though rightfully it belonged to his brother. I have my grandfather's story. I have Nene's stories of my grandfather and the jade stone that he gave to her as a love token. I have the bracelet you gave to me, I think as a love token, and I long to see you, *sevgilim, fy nghariad,* beloved. Now we must go, Giles and me, to find Edgar and Agathi. That is our sworn promise. Our lives are all promises, she thought despairingly. When can we follow our own hearts?

14

Ieper

April 1337

*Often the wanderer pleads for pity
And mercy from the Lord; but for a long time…
He must follow the path of exile…
(The Wanderer, Anglo-Saxon)*

March became April. It was late evening and the lamps were lit. Heinrijc Mertens was nodding by the fire, Rémi frowning over a book of lettering. He heard a loud knocking at the outer door but no stir. Karel must have fallen asleep. He was an old man to be steward, as old as Heinrijc himself. The pounding came louder. The boy's head came up, alert. He stood up and stared across at the old man by the fire. Heinrijc Mertens opened his eyes and smiled.

'He keeps us waiting almost a six month,' he murmured, 'and now he's impatient to be let in. Best go, my boy, before he wakes the whole household.'

Rémi hurried out of the room, down the stairs and into the passage. He almost collided with Karel. They both hurried towards the outer door, barred now against the night.

'Who is it?' demanded Karel.

'Thomas Archer with a sick man. I have Dafydd-the-Welshman here with me but he needs help.'

A grating rasping noise of bolts drawn back and there was dark-faced Thomas, very thin, his face exhausted, holding up the gaunt, yellow-faced, drooping skeleton that was Dafydd.

15

The Island
April 1337

*The city which forgets how to care for the stranger
has forgotten how to care for itself
(Homer: Odyssey)*

He woke to whiteness. Was this death? Couldn't be, not for him a white death. Roaring hellfire, more like. He stirred, and the movement had him groaning. May'appen this was death, and he was damned and in hell, on the rack, some evil little demon tearing into him with red-hot pincers.

'Lie easy now,' said a voice. French but so heavily accented he could barely understand. Where was he? Who...

'Who are you?'

'Brother Francis. You were hurt in the shipwreck. Lie still. All is well. All are safe.'

The shipwreck. This wasn't death and damnation. It was here and now. 'Hatice? Niko?'

'Safe, my friend. All your friends are safe, and all the crew, thanks to you. Sleep now.'

Slipping into sleep. No pain. No thinking. Let everything go. All safe. Waking again to whiteness and the same voice, the same soothing words.

'Hatice? Niko?'

'Safe, my friend. All your friends are safe, and all the crew, thanks to you. Sleep now.'

The next time he stayed awake long enough. 'What do yer mean? Safe? Where are they? Where am A?'

Brother Francis was pleased. The big man's soul had come back to them. He smoothed the man's forehead with the sign of the cross, murmured a blessing. 'You are here in our Abbey. Your ship was wrecked in the storm but all – every soul – were saved. Your family waits for you to come back to them. They are well, thanks to you. The crew is safe and well, thanks to you. We have lit candles and offered our prayers for your safety and your soul these past two days and nights, and now God has heard our prayers. Thanks be to the good God and his Son and to the blessed Mother Mary. You are safe with us. God loves the stranger, and you were cast on to our shore cold and hurt. We shall care for you, and your friends, and rejoice that God sent you to us.'

Blue cast about in his battered skull for a memory of what had happened. The storm, and casting themselves overboard to try to reach the sandy bay. Hatice all but swept from him, and him clutching at her hair, yanking handfuls, then the relief of the sandy shore, staggering to safety, looking back at the foundering ship. Its lateen sails were ripped to shreds and the masts broken. He'd seen that in one quick moment. He'd uncoiled the rope and told Hatice to fasten it to a jagged rock. She'd clutched her head and cursed him, he remembered now. 'Later, my Hatice. There are souls need rescuing, woman.'

He waded out into the wild waters, stood braced, rock-solid as he could, while the spluttering, drowning, gasping crew grabbed hold of the rope tied about his broad girth, and from him they hauled themselves to safety on the shore line. The force of the waves crashing against him was too much, even for a man-mountain, and he was knocked backwards off his feet and under water, drowning and gasping and spluttering in his turn. Fleetingly, he thought he remembered a hard hand hauling him to dry land and sharp rock against his cheek. Now, here he was in a Benedictine monastery, in a white cell, and cared for. And so he had slept, woken, asked the same questions, slept, and now he was awake, wide awake.

Niko came to sit by his mattress, a pale ghost-boy haunted by the fierce storm and their fight to live and, yes, the resurgent memory of Asperto falling to his death in the landslide in the mountains. The mischief was gone from his eyes. 'I thought you were dead,' he whispered. He didn't sob; he sat head bowed, streaming silent tears.

'Well, A'm not, so stop yer snatterin and ditherin. We need to be out o' here and away on the next ship. And doön't yer tell me it int doäble.' He raised himself up, though his head swam. 'Come here, yer greeät daft lummox. A'm not to be drownded by a few splashes o' watter.' The boy threw himself at Blue's broad chest and the man wrapped his arms about the shivering child. He looked over the boy's head at Hatice. She was pale, as pale as the boy, with great purple shadows beneath her eyes. She looked haggled, she did. 'Eh, my Hatice, that were more close-run than A like. The priests tell us as it's a narrer, rough roäd to heaven, an' a stright, smoothe way to hell, but A reckon as they've not nivver been in no shipwreck. Rough roäd all the way.'

'May'appen we were on our way to heaven, husband.' She had started to use some of the Fen language Blue used.

'We've left our worldly goods be'ind, that's fer sure. All drownded with Hazim's ship. I've nowt to keep yer with, lass.'

'We're well enough, husband. We have our lives, and each other.'

'That's the truth on it. Where's the boy?'

She knew he meant Mehmi. 'He lost the *tanbur*. He says it is given to the sea as an offering for our lives, but I think he mourns it, all the same.'

It was a loss for him, more so since the *tanbur* had been a cherished gift from his father, and had belonged to his father's father before that; a beautiful instrument, its pear-shaped belly fashioned from mulberry wood. It should have been given to Aksay, the eldest son, but Aksay had declared he was no player, no singer of songs, no weaver of music magic. Let it be given to Mehmi, the youngest, the dream maker. And now it was gone. It had been strung around his shoulder but he couldn't hold Niko tightly enough and so he had let go the *tanbur*. He had gone down to the shore with the rest of the men to search the wreck for what they could salvage. He had found the *tanbur* – pieces of it, at least – washed up into the rocks and stones around the sandy shore. Its long neck was broken, its strings drifting in a pool of water like strands of silver hair, tiny silver fish darting through them. He lifted it out, cradled it in his arms. Al-Abjar, nicknamed for his big-belly, laid a heavy arm round his shoulders.

'Ah, my song-bird, this is sad. Very sad. You've had your wings clipped.'

'There will be another, Mehmi,' promised al-Muḥibb. 'Like women – there is always another.'

'But not when there is no other woman quite the same, as this *tanbur* was. *The* woman, *the tanbur*, Muhi.'

'*The* Niko, friend,' Muhi said unexpectedly. 'Only one of him. I saw what you did – save the boy not your *tanbur*, even if it were your soul, and the soul of your ancestors. You sacrificed it for a boy of flesh and blood, and Allah be praised for this. It was a good act, and shall never be forgotten.'

Mehmi sucked in his breath. 'What's this, Muhi? Next you'll be telling me there is *the* woman in your life.'

'And so there is. Don't drop your mouth open like that; it makes you look like Abjar when he's loading his mouth with *riza*. Who knows what a shipwreck can do to a man? I prayed to Allah, if he saved me, *Inşallah*, I would go home and marry the little brown mouse of a girl I nursed in my arms when she was an infant. There! Laugh if you like.'

'I am not laughing, Muhi. This is good, the best. I envy you. And you are right; the boy Niko was worth saving. There will be another *tanbur* for me, not the same but a *tanbur*, even so. There is no other

Niko. There can never be another Niko. His sister would be desolate without him.'

'Your friends Blue and Hatice also.'

'Yes. We are family now. Not through blood but through love and pain and struggle.' Mehmi looked down at the cradled *tanbur*, his long lashes casting little shadows on to his sharp cheekbones. 'I shall sing songs of this time, of the terror of storm and sea, and of how we escaped, each one helping his brother, whether Christian or Muslim.'

'What will you do now?'

'Go on to Venezia, and from there to England to find our friends.' He smiled. 'More like our family,' he corrected himself. 'Edgar is like a son to Blue, and Agathi a daughter to Hatice. Perhaps we shall find the rest of our companions. We have missed them.' His lashes flickered upwards. 'Our hearts are heavy without them.'

But we shall find them, he thought. Blue and Hatice are determined, and they will have their way, no matter what storms and tempests are tossed in their way. There is nothing as powerful as a heart filled with love. He thought again of his lost *tanbur*, and longed for it so that he could make a song fitting for his friends.

16

April 1337
Bradwell

...they feared
That fierce and frenzied boar
Whose tusks could slash and tear
(Sir Gawain and the Green Knight, 14*th*C Trans. Simon Armitage)

They had been tracking the boar all morning. First they had driven the sheep and goats up on to the common land on the high pasture close to the High Dyke, left the youngest boy to make sure they were secure. After that they had set about tracing the spores and rootings and droppings left by the escaped boar in the Long Wood. Thorns and thickets, that's what pigs liked best. They'd taken one of the dogs with them, an old bitch used to herding sheep but now too old for service.

'She's a good nose,' Oluf said. 'If she tracks the boar, then we can use our sticks to herd it back to the village. The Master will be grateful. He will say we are men, not boys.' His eyes sparkled. 'It will be a fine offering for Easter Day.' The group of small, eager boys clustered about him shivering in the sharp north wind. They grinned and nodded. The Master would be pleased. Everybody wanted to please the Master. He was a good man. Their das said so, and their mams. And Oluf said it would be a good thing to do; Oluf, whose da, Bernt, would be a free man because of the Master. He had promised so. And his mam, he boasted, was lady's maid and close friends with Mistress Agathi.

They'd seen signs the day before: broken branches; a whole stretch of earth ploughed up by powerful tusks; droppings of pig shit; a tuft of black bristle caught in a blackthorn bush, white blossom dying now. For sure, the boar had come this way. And then they heard it; a snuffling, whittling, snorting somewhere in the undergrowth. Grunting. Crashing of branches as the boar tussled its way through the woodland. Suddenly, it was there. They had not thought it could move so fast, leaping across ruts in the earth, powerful back haunches sloping down to a tail that twirled and twitched and twisted; a creature whose ears, snout, tusks threatened danger. It was more wild boar than farmyard escapee.

The boys fled, shrieking. Only Oluf was left in the clearing. He whistled to the old bitch but she sloped away, too old and wise for this. The creature stopped short, pawed the ground, sniffed the air, fixed its vicious beady gaze on the two-leg standing in front of it. Oluf grasped the stout branch tighter but suddenly it did not seem as strong as it had when he chose it. He had thought they would goad and steer the boar into the track leading down to the village. It was a boar from the sty, after all, and they would return it there. Not this one. This was run-wild, black bristled, black snout, black heart. He shook the staff, yelled and grimaced, as he had seen the men do. The boar did not move. It gathered itself, a hulking black mass of energy, and launched itself at the boy.

Edgar heard the shrieks of the boys. He was riding the bounds, checking hedges, coppices, palings, beck, the new bridge over it. It had become a daily round for him and the dependable rouncey mare he usually rode. And now what?

'Oluf, maäster, it's killing 'im!'

'It's the boar, maäster, Oluf's thrashing it.'

'No he's not. He's not got nowt but a piddling stick he took from the hedgerow. Can't not do nowt wi'it.'

Edgar didn't try to make sense of it; they'd garbled enough for him to know the fool boy was in danger, and his father on the other side of the village, gone up to the mill. He could just see its sails turning from here, the great wooden post keeping them turned into what wind there was now the too-strong gales had died down.

'Where is he?'

'Back there in the Long Wood.'

'Not far from the roaäd – that's where we was.'

'We dussn't go back.'

'Get the men. Any of the men. Quick now – be off.'

They scattered, two older boys outrunning the rest. Edgar wheeled his horse around, headed in the direction they had pointed, hoped the boys were right. The Long Wood was sprouting leaves amongst the bushes though the tall trees were still leafless this late spring. Low branches whipped about his head and he slowed the canter of the mare. Best not be swiped off. Then there was the clearing yellow with celandine, and a split second to see Oluf, and the boar crashing towards him. Somewhere, there were shouts and hooves thudding but he shut them out. Too far away to be of help.

'Oluf!' he shouted. 'Grab hold!' The rouncey jibbed but he held her steady and swept past the boy, yanking at his outstretched arm and twisting him up and on to the saddle. He pulled the mare up but even dependable, amiable Sorrel was nervous, whinnying and side-stepping and trying to rear up so that he could hardly hold her. He felt the boy slip from him, slither to the ground. He viciously pulled the curb, halted the mare, slid down from the saddle, dagger in hand. The black boar turned, only feet away. He saw its vicious little eyes, tusks protruding from black jowls, its massive haunches settling into a leap. He raised the dagger, all he carried, and a broad sword was little enough match for this fierce beast. If he could, he would pierce its throat.

His heart was thudding. Or it was horses' hooves? Sorrel was screaming with fear now. There were other horses whinnying and loud shouts of alarm. The whisk of an arrow whistled past his cheek and thudded into the beast's throat, stopping its leap on to him in mid-flight; a second arrow glanced from the black-bristled, thick-fleshed flank of the animal. It was squealing, high-pitched, splitting his ears. It dropped inches from him. He felt the ground shudder. He felt its rush of breath and the spurting spray of hot red blood from the pierced throat. He stayed still, dagger raised, while the enraged beast scrabbled to get back on to its feet, as Oluf was struggling to his feet, white-faced but stick at the ready. Bold boy! No need now. The boar was dying, shot through with another arrow piercing its eye; another aimed at its softer underbelly as it toppled. Arrows he recognized. He twisted and tugged one out of the flesh of the dying animal, felt the sinews give and tear and rasp a gaping wound. He stared at the flight feathers, disbelieving. *God's will?*

'Hoi! Edgar! You safe?'

Giles' shout. Edgar stared about him. Two riders were galloping towards him, reeling in their panting mounts.

'Edgar! Thought we'd missed the brute. Fierce stock you have on this manor of yours.'

'Giles?'

'And Kazan. The last shot was hers.'

'And the first, Giles! It was my arrow that struck the boar first. Yours did not even pierce its hide.'

'So it was, fire-eater.' Giles swung down from the brown stallion. Dafydd's horse, Sadık, Edgar realised, and it only added to the dream-like state he was in.

'What are you doing here?' he asked.

Giles grinned. 'Rescuing you from your own beasts, altar boy.' He held out his hand. 'Come on now, not a scratch on you or the boy. Kazan, next time, don't take so long. You had me in a rare sweat.'

'Edgar, it is good to see you. Take no notice of this *palavracı*. Without you and Dafydd and Thomas, his head swells so big! And his mouth grows even bigger.' She laughed, Kazan's joyful laugh, and she was joyful. Giles was right after all; it was good to be with friends, as it had been good to ride hard again along an open road, with land stretching about them though there were no high mountains. Sharp wind in her face, bright sky that became cloud covered. And it was good to shoot arrows again from her curved bow, hit a fierce-some target. It made her Kazan again. And perhaps there would be news of Dafydd. She felt so sure he was safe. It had come to her while she was galloping Yıldız the Star. He was well; he was alive. It was as if she had heard his voice carrying on the wind. She almost expected him to ride to meet her. 'Edgar, here we are, come to see you. You are pleased?'

'Oh yes. Pleased. Very pleased.' He released pent-up breath. 'How have you come here? Alone? There's a gang roaming these roads.'

'So they told us. We travelled with soldiers as far as Somerton Castle and then with merchants bound for Boston.'

'We have brought gifts from Father Heinrijc – if the packhorse has not run away. No – it is there.'

'I'll get it,' Oluf offered, and raced away. Two strangers come to visit, and one a foreign-faced woman who could shoot like a man with her strange curved bow! And from astride her horse!

'But now! You are here now, and have saved us from a severe mauling. Maybe worse.'

'God's will,' Giles said cheerfully. 'Edgar, you look mazed and I'd rather you said welcome and took us to your home, and food and drink, for we've had none today.'

Edgar laughed and shook his golden curls. 'I can't believe it,' he said. 'Here you are. Where's Dafydd?' He saw Kazan's mouth droop. 'Not here yet?'

'You've had no word?' asked Giles.

'Only that there is no news.' He looked again at Kazan. 'It's early in the year yet. He'd be held up by the snow, and the mountain passes may still be closed.'

'You are the same, good Edgar,' she said. 'Perhaps that is so.'

'I'm sure that's so.' His reeling head was settling. 'It will be so, Kazan.' He took her hands in his. 'But we did have news of your grandfather, Kazan. I sent word to Heinrijc but you had already left. I am sorry.'

Kazan said, 'You heard he was dead? I was too late, Edgar. He died only two months ago.' Her voice trembled. Edgar let go of her hands and hugged her to him.

'I am sorry you had such a cruel end to your journey.'

'It is not so bad now. Giles has been so very good to me.'

'Come home now with me. Tell us your story in warmth and comfort. We have missed you so much, both of you. All of you. Agathi will be so very happy to see you. Come. Let's take the boar. You've brought your feasting with you, except it's a fasting day and so we must only imagine roasted pig until Easter Day.' He turned to the boy who came slowly towards them leading the burdened packhorse. 'Oluf! Come! We have guests! These saviours of ours are my good friends Giles and Kazan. And this,' he ruffled Oluf's curls, 'is the daredevil who set the boar on! I hope your father gives you a good beating, devil-child. Still, you've got what you wanted – a great-big boar to take home. Think you can carry it? And skin it and butcher it? We'll eat it come Easter Day.'

Shouts reached them; the men of the village racing up the hill towards them, red-faced and breathless, Luke with them. Surely a man his age should not be running uphill like that? They stood panting, gasping, Luke clutching his side.

'Eh but Maäster the bairns said as yer were like to be killed – you and Bernt's young devil!'

'The women are frittened out of their wits.'

'Ellen was fer coming wi' us but Mistress said no, best be ready for you being browt back.'

'Your mangled bodies, I suppose,' Giles murmured.

'Ay, so we thowt, Maäster, from what the bairns were telling.'

'And so we might have been, except that God sent this valiant pair to rescue us!'

The men crossed themselves and fervently thanked God and the two strangers and His Son Jesus, all in the same jumble of voices so that Giles came close to laughter. Not Kazan: like Edgar, she was awed by the solemnity of this happen-chance.

'Not strangers!' Edgar said. 'That is what is so very remarkable.' And he would have explained again except that Giles cut him off.

'Finish the explanations later, for pity's sake, altar boy. We're half-dead from hunger! Besides, look at that sky! We'll be lucky if we're not caught in the rain.'

They made quite a procession, arriving back in the village, Edgar leading the way with Oluf high in the saddle in front of him, beaming with pride, all fear forgotten now. Giles and Kazan were just behind, flanked by the men, one of them leading the packhorse and two carrying the dead-weight black boar, its front and back legs hastily bound and secured to a sturdy branch, a makeshift carrying-pole. Storm clouds were rolling in behind them and the first of the rain was falling higher up the heath. Ellen was first to dash out and grab hold of Oluf to cuff him and cuddle him, fat tears rolling down her cheeks. Agathi was grave with worry for her husband but her face lit up when she saw who rode in with him. 'I have missed you so much,' she said. 'These villagers are very good, and I am very grateful for my Ellen and the good Hilda, but you are my family.' She kissed Kazan, and kissed Giles, and hugged them tight to her. 'Now, you must be tired and dirty. We have a sort of bath. Not a *hamam*, Kazan, but you can clean yourself in a great tub of hot water. Edgar has made it so. We say our people must wash once every week. The women like it very much and the men are learning.' She sighed. 'I wish we had the *hamam*. It is very harsh here. But,' she smiled at them, 'this is Edgar's country, and so I am content.'

Kazan looked at her friend. She was so different from the pale, frail, cowering slave of Beyşehir. Still the silver-haired, beautiful girl she remembered from Venezia but different. This Agathi was confident, sure of herself. She talked of the Lenten meal being prepared in the kitchens, of going herself to be sure of its preparation.

'We have fish!' she said, and it was clear this was a luxury, but she shook her head over the absence of *yoğurt* and olives and dried figs. 'This is a barbaric country, Kazan,' she confided, 'but it is Edgar's country and so I must learn to love it.' She shivered at the tale of the boar, and its death. 'You will never learn, my husband,' she said, exasperated, but her voice was loving. Edgar hung over her, kissed her hand. 'I am sorry, sweetheart. There was nothing else I could do.'

'Oluf must learn to be more careful,' she said. 'He must learn to know when he puts others in danger. I shall speak with Ellen. She will know what to do.'

Women's choice, Kazan thought. That is what is different. Agathi has power now, and uses it for good; and the women in this village, they take power from her, and use it to look after their men. No slaves here. She approved the way Edgar and Agathi had taken all the villagers into the hall to eat. Frugal meals at best, and more so now it was Lent. The fish Agathi had so proudly spoken of was no more than a mouthful for each person. 'But none of the sick and aging are required to fast,' Agathi said. 'That would be wrong, and against the teachings of Our Lord.' She smiled suddenly. 'And soon this never-ending Lent will be over. Two more weeks.'

'Too many villeins still,' Edgar told them. 'I don't have the right to make them all free men. Not yet. But I shall. There will be no serfs on this manor, Kazan. Dafydd would be pleased, I think?'

'Yes, my Edgar, he would be very pleased.'

She was slowly realising how much Edgar had done to bring this destroyed manor back into productivity. He and Agathi. They were united, master and mistress, a single voice, heart, thought and will, and the villagers were happier for it. But there was something – a rippling underwater current – something she could not comprehend but it teased at her.

Giles said, 'So your brother made you reeve.'

17

The Island
April 1337

The person who comes to this world needs to leave eventually.
He is a guest; he needs to travel to his hometown one day.
(Yunus Emre: ca. 1241-1321)

There was a ship, Hasim said. It would take them to Venezia; Blue, Hatice, Niko, Mehmi. 'I have agreed this with the captain. He is known to me, a fellow captain, though he is *infidel*. He will do this for you.'

'For you, I think, friend.' Hatice wanted to weep with gratitude but that was not her way. Her face was taut, her lips thinned. 'You are a good man,' she said brusquely. 'We shall not forget you.'

'You are a good woman,' he answered. He was not fooled by her austere face and harsh voice. He knew now how she looked and sounded when she was most moved. 'You are a good wife and mother. May Allah bless you and your husband and your children and your children's children.' He smiled as she would have spoken. 'They are your children, Hatice *hanım*.' He was again the straight-talking captain, though now without a ship to command. 'You must be ready tomorrow morning, at point of sunrise.'

She smiled. This captain, this good man who was their friend, always he wanted everything to time.

There was another surprise for them: the Father Abbot came with a woven pannier in his hands, one that was made on the island. 'For you,' he said. 'The men have salvaged what they could and they give you this as your share, because you gave them their lives.' There was some gold and silver, some trinkets. Blue nodded his thanks. 'That will help us.' He thought briefly of the beautiful indigo-dyed cloth he had so carefully bartered for. The treasured, rare fabrics he had acquired, no telling how. Gone now, a gift to the sea. God's Will. Allah's Will. Ill-gotten gains? May'appen. They had been granted their lives.

'There is this as well.' The Father Abbot held out a sea-stained blue bonnet. 'The sailor Muhi found it and Brother Theodore has tried hard to rid it of stains but perhaps it is as well to be reminded of your salvation.'

Hatice's gaunt face beamed. She took the sorry little bonnet gratefully into her hands. 'This was a gift from my man when I most needed it. I have treasured it because of this, and now because, as you say, Father, it reminds us that our lives were spared.'

'That is good,' the Abbot said gravely. 'There are two more things. This is for Niko.' He held out a *daf*, a beautifully constructed *daf*. Its frame was wooden and wide. Goatskin was glued on to the frame, and pins set behind the frame to keep the skin tight. Hooks in the inner part of the frame, and rings that would jingle in the playing. Nothing at all like the crude one he had made from the rim of a barrel, goatskin stretched across it, secured then wet and dried in turn.

'And a leather band,' said Father Abbot. 'The maker of this instrument says it helps if you play for a long time.'

Niko could hardly believe his eyes. He hardly dare stretch out his hand to take the *daf*. Surely this could not be for him? This beautiful instrument made for him? God was indeed good.

Father Abbot nodded, well pleased. He turned to Mehmi.

'And for you. It is given by the sailors with love and gratitude and in hope it will in some way restore your loss.' He held out a shining instrument. Not a *tanbur* but an *oud*; pear-bellied like the *tanbur* but bigger, and its neck was shorter. It was inlaid with mother-of-pearl.

'How did you do this?'

'Not us. The men. They did it. With what they salvaged from the sea. There is a man in the village, an Arab. He has the gift of making these instruments.' The Father Abbot smiled. 'God's gift,' he said. 'You gave your *tanbur* to the sea; now the sea and God gives back an *oud*. Not the same, my son, but take this and give thanks.'

Mehmi's eyes streamed with tears. 'Father Abbot, this is a miracle. I am not worthy.'

'You must make yourself worthy, my son.'

'Yes. You are right. I must make myself worthy.' Mehmi stretched out his hands for the *oud*, felt it bind with his body, felt for the strings and the neck and the sweetness of the swelling pear-belly that was pregnant with song. He ran his fingers across the strings; felt and heard them vibrate and whisper, deep and resonant. 'I must make myself worthy.'

'You will. God go with you, my son.'

18

Ieper
April 1337

O snowy mountain that bars my way like a highway robber.
I am parted from my beloved; will you still block my way?
(Yunus Emre: 14ᵗʰC)

It seemed he could not live. They willed it, prayed for it, but fever racked his body and his soul.

'He was tortured. That way, they thought they would learn the truth. When has torture ever brought truth?' Thomas wept. That stern, sardonic, dark-faced man wept like the child in the night he had once been. But now there was no pot boy to bring him comfort. 'We brought our witnesses and forced them to listen. The nephew of da Silvano, he came to give evidence, though he was in grave danger. He had been in hiding since his uncle was taken prisoner and killed. There was no one he could trust. But then Dafydd gave him hope, as he gave hope to the people of Murano. One by one, then in groups, they came to give evidence. And so it was proved that there was a conspiracy, and Marco Trevior and his conspirators were guilty of the very crimes da Silvano was accused of.' Thomas stopped. He tried to speak.

'Take your time, Thomas. These have been terrible times for you both.'

'Father Mertens.' Thomas stopped again. He had used the name that Kazan used, and Rémi. It was not his to speak.

Heinrijc Mertens laid his hand on Thomas' head. 'Tell me, my son. You have brought my Davit to safety and therefore you are my son. Tell me what happened.'

'The Council of Ten found Dafydd innocent, and Pietro da Silvano innocent as well, though little good it did him since they had executed him.' An innocent man, thought Thomas. It seemed all would be well, but Marco Trevior escaped. 'I think they did not want to see him executed. Perhaps. Perhaps not. I do not know. Only that he escaped into the *calli*. He had friends enough to hide him and protect him. All those young nobles who thought they were above the law.' Thomas' voice was bitter in remembering. 'Dafydd was recovering in the *casa* of the da Ginstinianis; I visited daily and I was not happy to see him there. The sister, she was his enemy but she bided her time. All smiles and fair words. Francesco, the fool, believed she agreed with him that perhaps a marriage was no longer possible between the two families. He believed her when she said she was grateful to Dafydd.'

'And you, my son? Did you believe her?'

Thomas shook his head. 'Never for a moment. There was that in her voice…something…perhaps I had been long enough with honest folk. Even Kazan, fooling us all into believing she was a young man – boy, more like – her voice rang true. All of us with our dark secrets hidden from the rest and yet we were honest. Isn't that strange?'

'Perhaps not.' Mertens grimaced. 'Who knows where the serpent hides? What happened?'

'She betrayed him. Betrayed Dafydd. She was the one who secretly let Marco Trevior into the *casa*. It was late one night, long after the curfew. It was by God's grace that Francesco was awake. He was not sleeping well, he was so troubled. And he heard them. Even so, he was not quick enough to keep Dafydd safe. Marco Trevior stabbed Dafydd as he slept. He hurt Dafydd badly. Very badly. It was Francesco da Ginstinianis who killed his would-be brother-in-law. He saved Dafydd but any hope of marriage between his sister and Jacopo Trevior was ended. Francesco said he would never have his family name allied with that of Trevior. It would bring shame on them all. It would dishonour them. His sister was furiously angry. What a vixen! I was there by then, and she ranted and raved in front of me. Shameless! I felt such sorrow for Francesco. She would have left her home and married Jacopo Trevior if Francesco had not prevented her. The old father, old Trevior, he saw it was impossible. Poor old man. One son disgraced and dead, the other... well, who would marry into such a family? In Venezia? If he lives out another year, it will be long enough for him.'

'And Davit? He was badly wounded, you say?'

'Yes. He was lucky to escape with his life.' Thomas sighed. 'Another of his lives. How many are left to him now?'

'Enough. He will survive this, my son. Believe this.'

'There is always faith?'

'Indeed there is.'

Thomas gazed into the red caves of the hearth fire. 'Winter was on us,' he continued, 'but Dafydd insisted we travel over the mountains though he was barely recovered. It was a difficult journey. Then the weather warmed and the snow softened. We were warned about the danger of avalanche but Dafydd was like a man possessed. He could think of nothing but coming home to you.'

'To Kazan,' the old man corrected him.

'To both of you,' Thomas said, 'and Rémi.' The boy was sitting silently by them. It was not often he could be persuaded to leave Dafydd's side but Matje had raised her hands in protest and demanded to know if he was so jealous that he would not let anyone share the tending of Davit? Did he think her so incapable of looking after Davit who they all loved? And so he had given way and coaxed Matje out of her indignation. She had smiled to herself, satisfied because Heinrijc Mertens had been worried for the boy, Rémi, sitting hours by Davit's side, not caring for sleep or food, until it seemed he, too, would sicken.

'Leave it to me, Master Heinrijc,' she had said.

Good food and good sleep; the boy would be well enough. And there was that girl of his asking every day after him and Master Davit. That would be enough to cheer his soul.

Now, Mertens and Rémi exchanged smiles: of course it was Kazan Dafydd wanted but it was impossible now to send word. First there were spring storms and no ships put out to sea; then the French blockade started, and it seemed impossible for anyone to slip past and across the *Manche* to the English coast. Just once they'd had word from Edgar, news of the Wordmaker's death, but too late for the girl to know of it. Mertens had sent back news of no news. And now here was his boy, his son, and near to death. Even if he could, should he send word of this?

'What happened, Thomas?' Mertens asked quietly.

'We were overcome by an avalanche and it seemed we must die.' Thomas was silent, remembering. The roar of snow rushing towards them, a huge snow wave crashing down on them, sucking them under, dragging them on towards the tumbling crevasse. He remembered grabbing Dafydd's legs and hanging on. They were suffocating in white-dark oblivion. He remembered how angry he'd felt. Angry. Angry with a God who could let such things happen. Dafydd rescued twice from death and now this white-cold horror engulfing them. He could not remember ever feeling such anger. He lashed out with the stout staff he still gripped in his hand. 'The staff I was still holding got caught against a tree stump. It stopped our fall. I managed to get hold of the stump – get my arm round it. Only God knows why it hadn't been swept away with the rest.' He had pushed the staff upwards through the snow until its end was free, and a trickle of air made breathing possible. He had heard Dafydd breathe, 'Kazan, *cariad*', and then nothingness until the *marroniers* found them and pulled them free of their ice prison. Dafydd's wound had broken open again but he was a man who seemed without reason. He would go to Ieper. He would not rest. He insisted they travel onwards.

'Yes, you are right, Father Mertens,' Thomas said ruefully. 'He wanted to reach Kazan. After the avalanche she was his only thought.' Thomas frowned. 'It was as if he believed she knew what had happened. As if she had seen it and perhaps thought him dead.'

'Perhaps she did know of it. Love is more powerful than any of us can imagine. It is the strongest power in the world. Isn't that so, Rémi?' Mertens smiled down at the boy. Boy no longer. He was fast becoming a man, and would soon bring his Enna to live here and cheer an old man's last years.

Rémi nodded. 'She knows he is alive,' he signed.

Thomas grunted. 'You are very certain, boy.'

'As certain as you are of your God and His son.'

Thomas nodded. 'Belief is everything,' he agreed.

Mertens stirred. 'You were to join the Friary and yet you have travelled with him.'

'Of course. What else should I do?'

'You are a good man, Thomas. You have saved the life of my Davit. We are in your debt, Kazan and Rémi and me.'

Thomas hesitated. For the first time he put into words what had troubled him since his arrival. 'But she is not here with you.'

'She and Giles have gone to England to find her grandfather. She said she had promised her *Nene* and so must go.' Heinrijc Mertens considered the sharp, dark face of Thomas. 'Rémi is right. She tells herself Davit is alive and so she can live. Do not doubt her love, my friend.'

Thomas sighed. 'I do not doubt it.'

'Then do not doubt our friend Davit will recover.'

There is always room for faith.

'How could I doubt it?'

Heinrijc Mertens nodded and smiled. 'But, my friend, how I wish my good friend Jehan were still living. He was a *chirurgien* I trusted with my life. He would have known what best to do for our Davit.'

'He was the man who gave back life to Rémi?'

'Yes.'

'Then he will give back life to Dafydd. Those who follow him have his wisdom and knowledge.'

The brown man tossed and turned in his bed. He sweated and shivered. He cried out in strangled, incomprehensible words. The stab wound inflicted by Marco Trevior broke open again and festered. His body was weak, weakened by days of torture and weeks of relentless travel through the snowy fastness of the high mountains and incarceration in the deep snows of the avalanche. 'You can survive this, Dafydd,' Thomas told him again and again. 'You must live.'

19

Bradwell
April 1337

Thou givest thy mouth to evil,
And thy tongue frameth deceit.
Thou sittest and speakest against thy brother...
(Psalm 50, *Authorized Version*)

'I know she wished to travel to the far west, see Dafydd's homeland – perhaps find his brother and sister, those who were alive when he left.'

'But we cannot go, Edgar. Kazan herself says this. We cannot leave you here in danger. It is unthinkable.'

'It is what you must do. These villagers have prepared themselves for attack, and you have helped them where I could not.' Edgar shook his head. 'Such skills, Giles. I had no idea.'

'Knowing how to make a longbow? I'm from the Marches; there are times when we don't know if we are in Wales or in England. It was a Welshman who taught me how to make a long bow when I was a young boy. It's the tillering that's the difficult part.' He flexed his shoulders. He'd spent hours making sure the bows would come round smooth and straight. Lucky for him Bernt had proved to have a good eye and hand and muscle enough. He said, 'Staves from the bole make a better bow but there's nothing amiss with bough stave bows. Plenty to be said for them – especially for us.' Edgar frowned; he didn't understand. Giles laughed. 'It's like this,

Edgar. Bough stave bows can be made straight from the tree, no seasoning, no time wasted, so this has helped us. In time, the bows will season, gain in weight. That's good for the boys; they start lightweight and learn to draw a heavier weight.' He shrugged. 'Elm is good. Powerful. Ash is good too but follows the string if braced for too long.' Edgar tried to follow Giles' reasoning. 'Yew is the best. Difficult to work but the best. Whenever you can, have yew bows made. Above all, they must train for part of every day, these villagers of yours.'

Edgar nodded. They had trained, when his father was alive and the old reeve was in charge. Luke told him so. Then the old lord died so suddenly, and the old reeve was dismissed, and the manor had gone to ruin. Training stopped. Why bother? Who cared? Not the young lord, new married; not the new bailiff; not the men. Too hard staying alive, see? But now, with the young master, they'd be wide awake for training.

Edgar had held a meeting with the men of the village, told them of the threat of Cedric Hayward. Luke had risen to his feet, their spokesman. The young master was not to ride out alone. It was dangerous. He needed protection. And the young mistress as well. She was the one who had unmanned Cedric Hayward, and he was not a man to forget and forgive.

Edgar agreed to their protection. Agathi in danger? He forbad her to venture out from the village. He was frowning, dictatorial, so much the lord that she laughed and protested. 'You must do as I say,' he insisted then he was Edgar again. 'Please do as I beg you, my Agathi. There is danger.'

'And for you, sweetheart. You must also do as the men say. They are right. No more riding the boundaries alone.'

'This is not for ever, Agathi.'

'I know, my love.' She waited, a heart's beat. 'Are you going to visit Roger de Langton?'

'Giles goes with me.'

'And Catley Priory?'

He flushed, nodded. 'I thought it advisable, Agathi.'

'In case Philippa and Alfred are behind this?'

Edgar sighed. 'I am afraid so. I cannot take the risk.' He tried a smile. 'I thought we should invite Roger to our Easter feasting.'

'And your brothers and their wives must come too. Both brothers.'

'And both wives. And the children. I know.'

Meanwhile, the training was underway. Giles had taken the training on himself.

Set your left leg before your right. Make your arrow nocking sure with your right hand. Not stooping but not standing straight. With your left hand a little above your right, stretch your arm out easy… easy….draw your arrow to your ear…when you've sighted your target let go your fingers…

'They must look after the bows as if they were living,' said Giles. 'I've told them so. Kazan's said the same. Keep them oiled. Use beeswax on the strings. But don't fret, Edgar, I'll make sure they're a fit, fighting force before we leave. Until then, we stay.'

Edgar sighed. 'You and Kazan, you are both so obstinate!'

Giles laughed. He thought of the morning she had appeared dressed once again in her plain blue *kaftan* and *gömlek* and *şalvar*. 'I shall come with you, Giles, to teach these villagers to shoot straight.' And she had, shocking them into silence first because of her outlandish, unwomanly dress; then because she amazed them with her prowess with the strange, curved bow.

'I wish I knew how to make a bow like Kazan's,' he confided to Edgar, 'but it's beyond my skill. I know it's a blend of horn and wood and sinew, and it's this that gives it such strength. And it's so much shorter than our long bows – this is why she can shoot while riding but it's a rare skill.'

'A skill and a bow that saved my life,' Edgar reminded him. 'Even so, Giles…'

'What's to do, Edgar?'

'Kazan must go to Dafydd's country,' he repeated, doggedly. 'It will give her peace of mind.'

'And you call us obstinate!'

'You must go with her. For her protection and,' Edgar added thoughtfully, 'she tells me you have it in mind to go to your own home in the Marches. It's a good thing to do, make peace with your father while he's still living.'

'It can wait.'

'Giles!'

'It can wait.' Giles was tight-lipped in a way Edgar had never seen before. 'How can we leave you, knowing you're in danger? Have some sense, man. We left Dafydd behind and now we have no idea what's become of him. What do you think Kazan would feel, leaving you and Agathi in danger? It's more than she could bear.'

Edgar stared at him, suddenly comprehending, his heart wrenched for Giles because his love for Kazan was hopeless. 'I see,' he said quietly. 'Of course, you must stay.'

Giles avoided his eyes. 'There may be word of Dafydd, come the spring,' he said.

The April days passed: the smaller trees put out green leaves and dawn bird song grew loud and sweet; fields were greening; lambs and kids had become sturdy; new-coppiced and pollarded trees were flourishing. Easter was close. There was no more news from Ieper.

Roger de Langton was resolute. He offered his men as security. 'We need a way to communicate,' he said. 'Our pigeons?'

'I'll send word should we need your help. But you must look to yourself. Who knows what's in their minds?'

Roger de Langton hesitated. He watched the sombre face of the young man sitting by his side. 'My young friend, I do not think your brother is responsible for this'

'Do you not?' The question was eager.

'No. Perhaps his wife? Perhaps that is a naughty thing to suggest.

This Cedric Hayward is a bad man, and bad men will do evil deeds, without any other to set them on.'

Edgar sighed. 'I hope you are right, Sir Roger.'

'Please, dear boy, call me Roger, plain and simple.'

Edgar shook his head. 'I cannot.'

'Then try your lady's name: Father Roger.'

Edgar smiled. 'That I can do. Father Roger.'

'I give thanks to the good God that you are returned, my boy.'

The journey to Catley Priory was on a day when it seemed spring had hidden itself behind chill winds and stormy skies. Sudden squalls of hard hail made the journey unpleasant. Giles went with him. They rode down the sloping hill to the flatlands and fenland and the Priory. 'And this is Blue's country?' Giles said.

'Something like. Mine as well,' Edgar said. 'If you think this is drear you should see Croyland.'

'A desert,' said Giles. 'A wet desert.'

'Not at all, my friend. It's teeming with life. A larder of good things. All manner of sea birds and their eggs; eels, pike, perch, roach, turbot, lampreys.' His mouth watered at the very mention. 'Samphire in summer. Then there are sedges and rushes, for thatching and basket making. Salt-making, of course. There are many salt works and it's very profitable. This is a great and wonderful place.'

Giles started to laugh. 'Blue should be here,' was all he said when Edgar asked what the joke was.

Catley Priory was in dire straits; that was clear. Poverty smacked them in the face. 'We owe so much in taxes,' said the Prior. 'I do not know how we shall survive. But how can we help you, my sons?'

He frowned at the news, this ascetic old man with grey-white hair and gaunt face. 'Of course, we hoped you would return. Your father was very distressed when he knew you had fled and there was no trace.' He sighed. 'A good man, your father, but only willing to listen to his own reasoning. It was only after you'd gone that he confessed his wrongdoing.'

'He confessed?'

'Yes, my son. Here in this Priory, to his Prior, in the confessional. He was a man who abased himself. He longed for your return.'

'Then I am sorry I grieved him.'

'It was his grief, my son. That was why he gifted you Bradwell. He said he should have loved you better.'

Edgar felt tears come. He bent his head. 'I wish I could have known him better.'

Giles moved uncomfortably. He thought of his own father, and the way he had renounced his older son, and Giles too when he had supported his brother. What had become of his father? Was he still alive? If so, better to beg forgiveness than be like Edgar, home, and his father dead. But, he reminded himself, he was committed now to this manor. He had to stay. He had no choice.

They were leaving the Priory when Edgar stopped. He watched the men at work. Tilers, working at a kiln. 'What are they doing?' he asked.'

'They are not of us. They have come from Hanworth – Potterhanworth, they call it – to work here and then they will leave. As well for us – they are not God-fearing men.'

'But they have the skill of making tiles.' Edgar picked up one of them. It was part of a length of piping. He smoothed his hand over the round pipe. 'What is this for?'

'The latrines, brother. They need repair, though we have little money to pay for the work. It is necessary and so the work must be done.' He shrugged. 'God will provide.'

Edgar hardly heard the Prior. He stared down at the round piping. Surely they could do something with this? He tried to recall the intricate piping of the *hamams*. Couldn't they channel hot water and cold? Blue would know, he thought. He wished again the big man were here with him. Protection as well, he thought. They needed Blue. Time he sent a message, now the snows were melting in the high mountains. Perhaps, if they chose to come, they could be here by the year's end. Too late for the baby's birth but if they were here...

And then it was Easter and Alfred was regretting his choice to join Edgar and Agathi at Bradwell. His choice? Philippa was avid with curiosity to see the changes made to the manor. So here they were, arrived on Holy Saturday for the third of the Tenebrae church services held late at night in the dark hours. Father Emanuel was in his element. He loved the drama of the late night services; the candle holder that they called the hearse, with its lit candles extinguished one by one, after the readings from the Psalms, from Lamentations, from Jeremiah...then the last, single candle hidden behind the altar, the mighty clap of the slammed book that represented the earthquake after the crucifixion; the single candle returned.

Have mercy on me oh God according to your unfailing love; according to your unfailing compassion blot out my transgressions. Wash away all my iniquity and cleanse me from my sin.

Alfred stood with tears streaming down his face, and Philippa could not prevent it.

Easter morning before dawn, and the villagers were already gathered before the little church. They watched the sun rise and sang loudly, lustily, songs of joy. They could be heard in the hall where Edgar and Agathi and their guests prepared themselves for the Easter morning service. In the little church, all the black cloth had been removed, and carved wooden figures of the Risen Lord and the disciples and Mary Magdalene were prominent on the altar. *Rejoice! The Lord is risen! He is risen indeed.* The sun streamed in through the east window scattering bright motes through the one modest window of stained glass. It lit up the walls in notes of yellow and blue and red, and the walls showed Christ in Glory: Alfred's heart was deadweight.

He had ridden home shamed after that Lenten visit. His youngest brother, so badly treated by their father, now so much grown, and so much the man; no longer the girl-faced boy he had been, but a man who had travelled in the far countries, who had had adventures, married a Greek girl of great beauty…and what he had done for the manor! Philippa must see that this was for the best. She must see that Edgar was a worthy lord of the manor. And that dangerous man, that Cedric, and Eudo's gang, they must not harm his brother and new sister-in-law. He could not acknowledge, not even to himself, that Cedric's escape owed anything to Philippa. She could not wish their brother harm. Surely not. But eating away at him was the worry that she could, and would. She was vengeful if she did not get her own way; he had found that out in the first months of their marriage.

The visit during Lent was bad enough. Edgar had invited them to confession in the little, black-hung church, and he had refused; he said he had promised Philippa they would go together in their own church, but in truth he hadn't the courage to face Edgar and Eric in the ritual before they went to the church and the priest; to bow to each member of the household and to any sinned against; to say, 'In the name of Christ, forgive me if I have offended you.' To have Edgar respond, 'God will forgive you.' No, this he could not do. And so he let the moment for truth and forgiveness escape him, and now here they were, invited to the Easter feast. The boar that he had frowningly said was killed out of season and that had all but killed his brother; that would be the centrepiece. He spared a thought for the villagers crowding into the hall. No important men. Not Sir Roger, who was laid low again. Alfred sighed with relief and contemplated Philippa's sour expression. Perhaps it would do her good to see how ordinary folk lived. Perhaps she would be the sweeter for it.

But her chin was raised in disdain; she was ostentatiously reluctant to muddy the skirts of her gown as she crossed the yard; she smiled tightly at the assembled villagers; then there was her astonished, jealous scrutiny of the rich tapestries and silken cushions. No sweetening here. Alfred wondered why he had been persuaded to marry such a proud, disdainful daughter, and so many years older than he was. He sighed. Why fool himself? Her father's lands and manors had persuaded him, and his father's urging. And there was the prospect of winning favour from the King himself. He must not forget that. It would make up, in some part, for this marriage that was doomed to be barren.

Alfred looked about him at the crowded hall and wondered at the sight. So much joy and goodwill, and all for his youngest brother. The courses were served, sometimes a little lacking in grace but these were the boys of the village who did this service, beaming with pride, trying to remember the rigorously taught table skills. Oluf was one of them, young but given the honour because he had been the one to attempt to capture the boar. The insignificant sub-cook Philippa had been so ready to send to this lowly manor – what was his name? William? What an artist! The boar's head was served with much reedy fanfare and flourishing on a bed of bay and rosemary, celery to represent the tusks, and strangely there was rosemary in place of its ears. Eric had provided the Pascal lamb. There were chewets of chicken; pigeons stewed in a rich herb and garlic stew; grain pottage preceding the meat; braggot and mead and ale and wafers fit for the highest table. Over all was the sense of comradeship. A group of musicians – villeins, surely? – struck up a lively tune.

'We'll have dancing later,' Edgar said in his ear. 'Thank you, brother, for leaving us the gift of the eggs. Our boys and girls, tell the truth, had much fun this morning.' Alfred had refused the offering of Lenten eggs. 'Let them be given to our villagers as the Easter gift,' he said. He was surly, refusing thanks, his conscience pricking him. The older eggs, hard boiled, were too old to eat. Now, Edgar was smiling, telling him how the children had searched for the gaudily dyed newer eggs; how they had rolled the old eggs down the hill, as if rolling away the great stone from the sepulchre, but whooping with glee and rolling after them. 'And Kazan joined them!' Edgar laughed. 'She has never seen anything like it. She enjoyed herself enormously, and I am glad for it. She has been so sad, waiting for news of Dafydd. Now, Easter brings hope to all. It is the Resurrection and new life, brother. The old life is dead and gone, and we should give thanks for this.'

'So we should.'

That morning's service had not been filled with the Easter Laughter Edgar remembered from the past; Father Emanuel was a cautious, sober man who preferred the drama of the Tenebrae services, suffering and death, more than the joy and jokes and laughter of Easter Sunday. *Then our mouth was filled with laughter and our tongue with shouts of joy,* he had intoned, and the villagers moved restlessly, crammed together in the tiny nave, releasing the heady sweet smell of new-strewn herbs and spring flowers. No rank odour from them, either; all new-washed and best clothes on and, since the new clothes had been gifted before Easter, there were additional gifts of stockings and shawls and bonnets and hats with curly brims festooned with feathers and flowers. Today's feast, Edgar promised, that was when they would celebrate Easter's Great Joke of life over death; and then they would have their *Risus Paschalis.* He fingered the two pouches containing the salted, dried ears of the black boar. There was a third pouch containing the tail. He would enjoy giving these to Oluf and Kazan and Giles. A pity there was no Mehmi to make a song in honour of the killing; Mehmi would have enjoyed it as much as any of them.

Alfred looked along the high table to Philippa. He hunched his shoulders uneasily. She was deep in conversation with Agathi and he worried. He knew that expression of hers; it meant mischief.

'Agathi, my sister,' Philippa was saying, 'I am so very happy to find you amongst friends. You seemed so lonely when I first met you, such a newcomer to our country, such little knowledge of our language. You must have felt a stranger here.'

Agathi inclined her head. 'But that seems long ago now, sister.' She wondered what was coming next. She distrusted Philippa's cat-and-cream smile.

'I am glad your friends are here. Kazan and Giles are your very good friends, I think?'

'Yes. Kazan and Giles are our family.'

'Hm. I wonder, Agathi...' Philippa paused, patted her mouth with her napkin.

'Yes, sister?'

'Kazan and Edgar...are they not very close? Closer than you would like them to be?' She nodded across to where Edgar was helping Kazan to another delicious wafer, another goblet of wine. He was laughing, teasing, and Kazan was protesting that she wanted no more. 'I have seen how it is with them.' She covered her sister-in-law's hand with her own. 'I know how you must hate this. I feel for you.' She gazed into Agathi's eyes, soulfully, waiting for the flicker of unease. It didn't come. Agathi gazed at her, amazed, unable to hide her contempt.

'What are you saying, sister?' Agathi asked in a voice that was dead calm and even. 'That Edgar – my Edgar – is unfaithful to me? And with my dear friend? Shall we ask him? Here? Now? At this table?'

'No...no...he would deny it.'

'Of course he would deny it. He would deny it because there is no truth in it. Kazan is our beloved sister and our saviour. We owe her more than I can tell. More than you can understand. Of course Edgar loves her. And so do I.' She drew a deep breath. Philippa was looking less assured. Agathi didn't care. 'I remember you wondered today,' she continued, 'if Ellen's baby was truly her husband's, or if it was John Reeve's after all. Of course it is Bernt's child. Perhaps you might wonder if my own dear baby is Edgar's. What a sad creature you are, to so want to destroy the happiness of another. But I think you must be very unhappy, you who have no child. I am sorry for you.'

Philippa froze. This was not how it was meant to be. 'Forget what I said, sister. I meant only to be of help.'

'No you did not,' said Agathi. 'You wanted to hurt us, me and

Edgar. Ellen and her husband. Kazan, who you do not know. That is why I say you are to be pitied. And your husband, my Edgar's brother, he is to be pitied also.'

Philippa toyed with a morsel of wafer. She lifted the goblet of wine to her lips, put it down untasted. 'I am the daughter of a great Lord,' she said. 'You have no right to speak to me like this. You are a foreigner here.' Her mouth tightened. 'You are a heathen.'

'Have more hippocras, sister,' Agathi said. 'It is sweetened with honey and spiced with cinnamon and ginger and grains of paradise. It is a wine that is very soothing and *douce*.' Philippa did not answer. Agathi gestured to the boy who was wine-carrier and who came sprightly with importance to fill their goblets. 'You know I am no heathen. But let us not quarrel on this happy day. In truth, Edgar and me, we have good friends who are Muslim. Christian or Muslim, what does it matter if the heart is true?' She considered a moment, decided. 'Prepare yourself for a shock, sister. Edgar rescued me when I was a slave. He saw me and loved me when I was a pathetic creature, in rags and chains. Do you think I could ever doubt his love? Or he doubt my love for him?'

'You? A slave?' Philippa was aghast.

'Yes. I was taken captive. So it is in my country. You are lucky here, in this cold, flat land of yours. There is no one to come to your home and kill your mother and father and take you as slave.'

Philippa was silent, intent on the brimming goblet. Agathi watched her. 'They took my little brother also. Then he helped my Kazan to escape when she also was captured. We are bonded together in a way you cannot comprehend.' Agathi considered the woman sitting next to her. 'I am sorry for you,' she said again. 'But it is Easter, and a time of rejoicing, and so we shall not talk about this anymore. Listen now to these musicians of ours. We are proud of them.' Though I wish we had Mehmi here, she thought, who sings and plays like the angels themselves. Dear Edgar, she thought, we are in a dark place and we need our friends about us. All our good friends. She glanced across the length of the table, saw Edgar was talking eagerly to Eric and Giles; Alfred was gravely watching her. She nodded, not smiling. How tired he looked. How wearied with this great trouble that weighed on him, heavy as millstones. How can we help him? she wondered.

But now it was time for the joking and laughter and music of the Easter feast.

20

Ieper
April 1337

Gull, see whether you may spot her
…I love her
(Dafydd ap Gwilym: 14thC)

The sky was bright blue with white clouds floating like boats on the sea. A seagull flew past the open window, dazzle-bright, strong-flight but the man saw nothing of it. His eyelids were shut fast. A mutter and murmur of voices. Stronger. Shouting. Matje. The name came to him, floating with the clouds. Who was Matje? He heard Matje's son laughing. Her son? How did he know that? A voice louder than the rest hushing the boy's laughter. The man stirred. Where was he? He stretched, felt the dim rumour of pain run through his body. He sighed. Somewhere close someone spoke a name. 'Dafydd?'

He was tired. Too tired to answer. His eyes were heavy-lidded, too heavy to lift. He sighed again, shifted slightly and fell asleep. In his sleep he dreamed of a beautiful maid fashioned out of gleaming gold-copper-bronze; a maid with shining golden-rimmed eyes. A shining maid, a lovely girl, as bright as daylight, whose eye was a glowing ember. How he longed for her. 'Kazan,' he murmured. '*Fy nghariad.*'

The man sitting by the bed felt tears start to his eyes.

He was dreaming. Broad blue skies and racing, rain-threatening clouds. Wind whipping across his face. A girl riding a piebald mare, mane blowing in the wind. A girl with gold-copper-bronze hair blown by the wind. Rain clouds racing across a broad blue sky. He shouted to her, the girl on the piebald mare, but no sound came from him. He shouted again, barely a croak. Again, but the wind blew his shout away into the racing clouds. Again, and he thought she heard him because she reined in and threw up her head, listening, tilting her head so that her hair, that gold-copper-bronze hair, was blown back from her face. She laughed. Kazan's joyous laugh. He opened his eyes the better to see her.

It was dark. Candlelight cast flickering shadows. Next to him, a slumped figure on a cushioned chest. Head back against a painted wall. Snorting snores. Rémi? What was Rémi doing here? Where was here? He closed his eyes, shifted slightly, fell asleep, longing to go back into the dream.

Rémi woke suddenly. What had woken him? What was it he had heard? A cry? Dafydd? No. He was sunk deep, unconscious still. The door of the chamber opened. Thomas. 'Is all well?' he asked.

Yes, Rémi signed back. Thumbs up.

'No sign of him waking?'

Rémi shook his head.

'He muttered – something – earlier when I was sitting with him, though he didn't wake. Just now, I thought I heard him cry out.'

I was asleep but something woke me. I thought it was Dafydd I heard. But see – he has not woken.

Thomas sighed. How long will you stay in your far-off land, Dafydd? How many lives are left to you, Dafydd? At least he was quiet now. His breathing was even, calm. No more dreadful whistling and gasping for breath and nightmare muttering. He laid his hand on the brown man's forehead. No burning. No fever. His face, thought Thomas, was serene.

'Rémi – see – he is sleeping. Just sleeping.'

21

Venezia

May 1337

...a man
Who would welcome me into his mead-hall,
Give me good cheer
(The Wanderer: *Anglo-Saxon*)

Plain sailing. That's what they called it. No storms, no contrary winds, clear skies all the way along the coast until they were nosing their way through the islands of Venezia. They turned past the island of San Giorgio, past the high walls of the Benedictine monastery where the bells of the newly built *campanile* clanged out the morning call to prayer. So strange, these bells; not the call of the *muezzin* from the giddy height of the minaret, though they had grown used to the bells of the monastery on the island. They entered a broad channel, the *Canalazzo*, which wound its way through the whole of the floating city. They stared in amazement. This they had not expected. Where were the walls and gatehouses?

'The sea protects us,' said the captain, 'by God's will. He has preserved us so that we may live in these watery marshes. He has enabled us to raise a new and mighty Venezia.'

Like my land, wattery like the Fens; same but different. The Fens were open, honest and open to God's eye. Here were narrow streets and dark canals and high buildings. *A don't trust this place. Bad deeds can be done in a place like this.*

They docked, and it seemed the whole city had turned out to greet them. This was a winter homecoming safe from the sea. Blue and Niko and Mehmi lurched down the gangplank on to the quayside. Here we are, Blue thought helplessly. What now?

'We must ask about our friends,' Mehmi murmured. 'Surely someone must have news of them.'

He nodded, grateful for the sensible advice. 'We need lodgings an 'all,' he said then, in sudden alarm, 'Where is Hatice?'

'There is lodging for all foreigners,' the captain had told him. 'I shall give you directions. But if you are friends of the Gistinianis, as you say, then perhaps you will stay with them?'

He was doubtful, suspicious of these poverty-stricken strangers, even if they had been shipwrecked. The Gistinianis were rich and powerful. What had these peasants to do with them? He had taken them on board as a favour to his friend, the Muslim Abu Hazim but a friend for all that, but they could barely pay their way. They had kept themselves to themselves the whole journey, and that was good. Now he wanted to be rid of them.

'The Gistinianis? You can tell me who they are?' It was the woman who spoke. She had not left the ship with her friends. He wondered whether to ignore her, as she deserved, but she was capable of making him listen and speak. He knew that. She was an unwomanly woman who did not know her place.

'Yes, *siorina*. I know who they are. See? That tall man standing in the arch? That is Francesco da Gistinianis. He is a very rich and important man in Venezia.' Too important for you, he wanted to say, but she was already down the gangplank to join the rest of her friends and pointing towards the *sior*. Well, let them approach such an important man. They would learn how the Venezia treated such low creatures. Then he was staring, astounded. *Sior* Gistinianis was smiling, taking the big man by the hand, embracing him. The heathen – the Muslim who played the strange instrument – he too was embraced. And – God protect us – the woman as well, and the small boy who did not know how to keep a still tongue. Greeting them as if they were good friends – or family.

'You are welcome, again and again,' said Francesco da Gistinianis. 'You arrive too late to see your friends. They are all gone across the mountains to Flanders.' He sighed. 'I have much to tell you.'

'Not all good?' Hatice asked.

'Not all good, Mistress. No. Some of it not good at all. But come. You must stay with me in my *ca'*. Oh, it is very good to be with friends of Davide and Giles and the good Thomas. And our Kazan of the bright gold eyes. And those two beautiful angels, Edgar and Agathi. And the little silent one. Rémi? That was his name? Yes? Indeed, there are merchants leaving tomorrow; they will travel over the mountains to the north countries but there is still snow and the threat of avalanche. Must you leave so soon? You must be tired after your long voyage. And shipwreck, you say? Yes, I understand. Of course you must go. But let us make this night one of rejoicing.'

22

Bradwell
May 1337

Sumer is icumen in
Lhude sing cuccu
(Anon.: c. 1260)

Oluf was sulking. He'd been sent with two younger boys – a pair of recklins – to gather new-grown stinging nettles and dandelion leaves – 'the brightest green from the centre', as if he didn't know – and fresh-sprouting wild garlic and young hawthorn leaf buds. It was what the youngest were sent to do. It didn't make it any better that he was in charge of these two young boys. He deserved a more important job now. Look at what he'd done for the manor! It wasn't fair. He wanted to make arrows. Jack Fletcher said he was good at making arrows but his da had cuffed him for cheek and said he should learn to know his place. Oluf had glowered at him and there were sharp words and sharper waps. Joan had watched him pass by and he made a great show of being in charge of the two young 'uns. She lifted her chin and the bucket she carried. She had been set to feeding the hens and finding their eggs.

Ellen watched the three boys trudging up the track that led to the north field and, after that, the Long Wood where they were told to go so far but not as far as the pond; that was forbidden until they knew it was safe. She sighed. What was she to do with the boy? He was becoming impossible. He wouldn't obey her this morning. It was his father who had forced him to do as he was bid and sent him off with a scarlet cheek and ringing ears. She didn't like to see the boy chastised so, and there had been harsh words between husband and wife before Bernt also raged from the house, reminding her so much of his son that part of her had to smile. She hoped both would return in better humour. She hoped this child she was carrying would not bring as many problems. She caught herself up. What did the problems matter against a living, healthy child? She had lost the last two bairns, one in the womb, the other only weeks after birthing. A terrible loss. She couldn't bear to think on it, even now. It was something they never spoke of, she and Bernt, but she knew he had grieved over the little lost ones, and was anxious now that all was well. She felt well. Better than last time. Happen because life had been easier with the coming of Edgar and Agathi – warmth, and food in your belly, and not worrying where the next bite was coming from.

Meanwhile, she had promised to take Agathi and Kazan to the Long Wood in search of healing plants. Not far into the wood. Not as far as the pond. There must be no risk of danger. They would keep in sight of the men working in the fields, and Kazan would have her bow. But they had need of the new spring growth after the hard winter. She hadn't expected the small, dark girl to be interested in such things but it seemed her grandmother had been a wise woman, and Kazan had learned healing from her. Her *Nene* would have been interested in the plants that grew in the cold countries, Kazan said. Full of surprises was this small, dark, foreign girl.

'Like my mother and grandmother before her,' nodded Ellen. 'They passed down their knowledge to me, though Hilda knows more than I do. She can't walk as far or as easily these days so I do the gathering and we share the preparing.'

She looked after the three figures, dwindling now into the far distance, the two younger boys bobbing after her son's longer stride. Perhaps she would see him later, when he'd had time to get over his anger. She saw Agathi and Kazan come down the outer staircase of the hall and cross the yard to the track, where the villeins' cotts began, and went to meet them.

It was peaceful in the Long Wood. The day was warm, the warmest this spring that had been so long in coming. A willow warbler trilled from a high branch. Such a tiny bird, such quiet colours, such a loud song, thought Kazan. This, then, was the English spring Blue had yearned for: so many shades of green; so many different kinds of leaves and plants and bushes and overnight it seemed they grew more and more. The air was sweet with the scent of foliage and flowers. Ellen knelt beside a patch of spindly plants bearing small white flowers.

'Stitchwort,' she said. 'It's a healing plant, good for wounds. My grandmother used to pound it with acorns and steep it in wine and honey but it's just as good mixed with goose fat.' She heaped the stitchwort she had gathered into her basket. 'And this one. It's celandine. See – such a beautiful yellow. We say it is loved by swallows and they come down to it to make their eyesight better but,' she laughed, 'I do not know if this is true for swallows see everything. But for us poor people, yes, it is true enough. This flower, boiled together with gill and daisies and the water of roses, will help the eyes. My mother said to apply it with a feather. The old grandmother has found much relief from this. Alas, it cannot cure her but it helps.' She dimpled suddenly, changing from serious teacher to mischievous young woman. 'See – if I dig up a root – look.' She showed them the little clustered bulb-like roots. 'We also call it pilewort because these roots look like piles.' She pursed her lips, said very seriously, 'Master John Reeve asked once if it would be help for him.' She gave up the attempt to be serious and the three young women rocked together in laughter. Ellen wiped her eyes. 'Now,' she said, 'with spring here we need a good cleaning of our bodies. And this clinging little plant is very useful.'

Kazan laughed. Just growing, and already the creeping little plant was catching at her clothes.

'Cleaver,' said Ellen. 'It catches all that is rank in our bodies. There are others that do the same. Bramble shoots and young nettles are good and I plan on making a good drink for us all. That way, we say goodbye to the winter and welcome the spring. With your permission, Agathi, I would like to serve it at our next meal.'

'Ellen, that is an excellent idea. What is this?' Agathi asked. She touched the silvery bark of a tree that already shivered with green leaves.

'Silver birch. That is our physic tree. All parts can be used. The leaves I shall add to my spring drink. The buds are good mixed with honey for the children. The sap as well. The bark – ah the bark – is so good for plasters for sore knees and stiff necks.' She smiled. 'One year, a Norse man came to the village selling his wares. I was very young but I remember he had such pale blue eyes and fair hair. He had cooking pots and baskets and they were made from the bark of this tree. We do not have the skill but I have often thought of trying to make the same.' She gestured towards a small white fungus growing on the tree trunk. 'See – a horse hoof. That is what we call it. This one is small but there are some that are very large. See inside this hard shell – how soft. We make a hole inside and light these to keep away the summer flies and stinging insects.'

They walked on through the woodland. Ellen stopped and gathered and explained. Plantain, again and again, especially useful for wounds. Burdock. 'The children know the leaf is good for nettle stings but if you heat the leaves they are a wonderful remedy for sprains and aching joints, especially with barley flour added.' Somewhere, a cuckoo called. *Cuccu. Cuccu.* 'Listen,' said Ellen. 'Now I know spring is here. These are strange birds. We never see them; we only hear their call. Bernt says they turn into sparrow hawks in winter but I do not know if this is really so.' She smiled. 'I think they fly away until winter is over but I do not say so to Bernt.'

She stopped by a tall pine. 'This is a special tree.' She rubbed her hand across a cut in the trunk. 'Smell. Isn't it good? Once Bernt had a rusty nail in his foot and Hilda put this juice from the tree trunk on a cloth and warmed it until it was softened. She put it on Bernt's foot and pulled out the nail and all the badness. He was better in days. The pine needles are not yet sprouted but we shall come back to gather them. They are delicious.' She sparkled. 'You will see – and taste.'

Agathi breathed deeply. 'How good it is to know the winter is past and summer is to come.' Her hand cradled her belly, swelling now. Spring and summer. And then? If only this terrible blackness did not hang over them, how happy she would be. Ellen was singing quietly to herself.

Sumer is icumen in
Lhude sing cuccu;
Groweth seed and bloweth med
And springeth the wude nu.
Sing cuccu!

Kazan wondered away from the two girls towards a tree that had been coppiced long ago. Tall graceful trunks rose around the great dead centre, towering high above her head to where bright green foliage flickered and swayed in the slightest of breezes. She rested her cheek against one of the trunks and stared up into the branches. *If only he would come,* she thought. *Or even a message from Father Mertens. Something – anything – other than this terrible waiting.* She stroked the smooth bark beneath her fingers. *But I know you are alive. I feel it, as surely as this tree is alive beneath my hand.*

'Ah,' murmured Ellen. 'So you have found our Queen of the Forest. She is our heart tree. In June, she will flower and the perfume then is so delicious. I come here when my heart is heavy.' She glanced at Kazan's face but said nothing other than a quiet, 'Agathi and I shall walk a little further along this track. Only a little. It is not safe otherwise. We shall wait for you.'

'Give over blating, yer maddocks,' Oluf snapped at Will and Simon. 'O' course nettles'll sting if you don't grasp 'em hard.' He blew out his cheeks. He was tired of their whining. He'd made them come further than he'd been told, out of spite. 'No further than the very beginning of the Long Wood,' his da had said. Well, they'd gone further, much further – as far as the Old Wood, where hardly anybody went. He'd never been as far, and all the time the boys protesting. There were boggarts and sprites in the Old Wood, they said.

'Frittened o' boggarts?' he sneered. 'Soft as shit, you two. There's no boggarts here.'

But he shivered himself, all the same, and looked about him. There was a quiet stillness here that should have been peaceful but he felt edgy as his da's sharp dagger. A cuckoo called, the first he'd heard that spring. *Cuccu cuccu*. Strange birds. Never seen, just heard. Come winter they'd change into sparrowhawks, his da said. He thought how his mother would sing the cuckoo song whenever she heard the call. *Cuccu cuccu*. He'd a memory of her singing it to him when he was just a tiny bairn, and how he'd joined in. *Sing cuccu*. He remembered her smiling face, and how she kissed his cheek and stroked his hair. Then he remembered her face this morning, streaked with tears, willing father and son to stop their fierce quarrelling. It made him feel bad. Just here, where his heart was.

Rapid drumming of a woodpecker. Somewhere a tiny wren shrilling loud song. Bracken was pushing up through the blanket of last year's oak leaves, leaf-ends uncoiling like a serpent's tongue. No leaves on the oaks, yet. *If oak is out before the ash then we're in for a splash…*the rhyme ran through his mind. *If ash is out before the oak then we're in for a soak.* Were the ash trees greening? As yet the tall trees were mostly bare of leaves. It was the smaller trees and bushes that had greened overnight, it seemed. He felt himself jump when a blackbird shrilled loudly close by. Simon was moaning again, rubbing nettle-reddened hands.

'There's birdseed ower theer,' he relented, pointing to where dock leaves poked through bramble briars. 'Grab a hand's hold and rub it ower yer nettle stings. That'll cure yer.' He pointed to a patch of bright green grass spiked with marsh plants. 'Keep away from there, 'less yer want ter be mud up to yer middle.' He snickered. 'Up ter yer necks, two maggots like you be.'

He wished now he hadn't brought them this far. Like an ambush, this place, he thought. Little wonder folk didn't come much to the Old Wood, though they'd made their way through easy enough this time of year, even though there were stinging nettles in plenty, and thorny whippy mayflower branches and great thick bramble briars higher than their heads that clawed their faces and tangled their hair when they pulled at the new young shoots; purplish-green thistles barely a thumb's height as yet but savage with prickles; hidden roots and stumps of rotted trees lay in wait to trip them; worst of all, runnels of deep water hidden by grass and all seeping into a great pond of brown water. Dried stalks of sedge grew near the edge, and stumpy rushes. It gnarled him that the two bairns might fall in and get tangled in the weed that lurked under the dark surface before he could get them out. They were whining now that they were tired and hungry. He was hungry himself though he wouldn't tell them that. He jerked a thumb at a hawthorn tree sprouting new bright leaves.

'Theer's bread-an'-cheese fer yer,' he mocked. 'Bite on that. Mind you don't go nodding off under it else the fairies 'ull fetch yer away.'

The three had all but filled the reed baskets they'd had pushed into their hands. A few more handfuls and then they'd go back. Simon was opening his mouth to whine again when Oluf heard the blackbird shrill again: a warning. In the same split second he realised what had been gnaggling him: yes, the way had been easy. Too easy. There was a track already trodden, and recently. His heart hammered.

'Whisht,' he hissed, and clapped his hand over Simon's mouth. He pulled them all to a halt and listened. It was Will who first caught the muted sound of muttering voices. Any of the village men, they'd not be in the Old Wood, thought Oluf, and if happen they were, they'd be clattering about, not stealthy. He froze, remembering the warnings he'd heard in the village. He wished then he'd taken heed of his da.

'Whisht,' he breathed again to the boys. 'Not a yaup out of yer. Lie down smack-smooth.' He pushed them down into the undergrowth, not caring if they fell on nettles or thistles. 'Stay hidden. I'll give yer a great ding i' the 'ead if yer make one sound.' He crept closer to where the voices came from. He carefully pushed aside branches of green-leaved hawthorn. He pulled his hood over his bright silver curls.

'I'm told you know how to make a living hedge, Bernt.'

'I do. Who told you so?'

'Luke.'

'What do you wish, Master?'

'What do I wish? I wish to restore the pleasure garden for our wives. I want it to be a beautiful place for them to sit and be at peace. I think it will ease their months of bearing our children. What do you say? If you make the hedge right, and we tend the garden that was here, wouldn't that be a good thing?'

Bernt nodded. He was still smarting from this morning's fierce quarrel, first with his son and then with his wife. It made it harder that she was right; he had been too harsh with the boy. And he should know better than to wap the boy about his ear. Wasn't that how Simon Weaver's son came to be stone deaf in his left ear? Hadn't Simon blamed Lord Alfred? Last spring, after the old lord died, Lord Alfred came riding into the village and the boy was in his way so he'd wapped him across his head. Ever after, the boy heard no sound in his left ear. Stone-silent.

He shook the memory from him. What the master asked was a good idea. It would please the mistress, and Ellen would be pleased that she was pleased – and a place for them both to rest! If Ellen lost this child she would be saddened beyond bearing. He studied the overgrown hedging. Hazel. Whippy new branches had sprung up. This was a good time of year to train them again into a layered hedge. He considered again. There were some lengths of timber that he could use as supports for an arbour. Hazel poles in plenty to stretch across them. Enough timber to make a seat inside the arbour. He set to work. Edgar had brought the wicker baskets that had once been used to contain plants and trees in this pleasure garden. Hilda came with him.

'Do you know how to prune the roses, Maäster?' she asked doubtfully.

Edgar smiled. 'If you teach me, Mistress Hilda.'

She folded her arms across her breasts so that they bulged together. They heaved with her sigh. 'I remember when there was peach trees grew here, Maäster, before the bad years of famine. Your mam was living then. She liked it here in this garden. The old Lord had it maäde for her. Now yer abaht the same fer the mistress. It's as it should be.'

'My father had the garden made?' He tried to imagine his father and mother in this pleasure garden, walking about a flower-studded lawn or sitting together under an arbour hung with sweet-smelling roses. He couldn't.

'He used to bring you here after she died, poor laädy,' Hilda said.

'He brought me here? To this garden?'

'Happen you were too young to have a memory of it, Maäster Edgar. Eh, I can see you now with yer bright curls and blue eyes begging a pear from that owd, half-dead tree ovver theer. He'd hold you up in his arms for you to pick the one you fancied.'

'I think I do remember that, Hilda,' Edgar said, slowly. Being high up and reaching out for the fruit through leaves that turned this way and that. Dappled shadow. 'It must have been harvest time.'

When had his father's love turned to hate? As if he'd asked the question, Hilda said, 'Your brother was that jealous of you. We could all see that.'

'My brother?'

'My Lord Alfred. Not Eric. He was always a sunny little lad, not much older than you and glad to have you for a plaäymate. But Alfred! What peevish tricks he used to play on you, in your cot and then when you was toddling. A tale-teller, was Alfred.' She caught herself up as she remembered who she was talking to. 'Though I says it as shouldn't, begging yer pardon, Maäster Edgar. Best forgot, innit, now yer hoöme and all brothers together again.'

'Yes, best forgotten.'

Hilda sighed gustily again. 'I'll be best pleaäsed when we've laäid that Cedric by the heels, and that gang he's tekken up with.'

'You and me both, Mistress Hilda.'

She shook her head over the villainous Cedric and the straggling briars. 'Now see look, this is what yer mun do, young Maäster.'

A small clearing and at first he thought a fallen tree but when he looked closer he saw there was a small shelter cobbled out of broken branches. Nearby, four men sprawled against the trunk of an ancient ash. Cedric Hayward was one of them. Oluf eased himself closer. He didn't recognise the other three. Two were not village men and the third had his back turned.

'Wiv Easter ovver and guests gone we'll 'ave our opportunity,' Cedric was saying. 'De mistress will reward us hif we dispose of dat cock's egg of a bruvver. I promise yer dat. She 'elped me escape, remember?' He chuckled quietly. 'She's a rare 'un, me Lady. Couldn't bear to let goldy-locks inherit the manor – better destroyed, she ses.' He imitated her high, harsh voice. 'Now it's in good fettle, reckons it's easier to get rid of goldy-locks dan de manor.' He was sharpening the end of an ash branch with his bright knife. Oluf caught the glint of sunlight on the blade as the man moved it up and back, up and back, whittling the point to sharpness.

'Eever way, good fer us. Pickings to be 'ad 'ere now.'

'What of our new brave lord? What does he say? Thick as thieves, all three brothers together, from what he says.' The speaker was a short, dark man, barrel chested, with muscular arms and legs. He kicked out at the fourth man, silent against the bole of one of the tree trunks.

'Doesn't want the manor to go to goldy-locks. S'why ee's said nuffin' about dat Will.'

'But the young lord and lady visit Roger de Langton. She's often there. He must have said something.'

Cedric gritted his teeth. 'Trew, but we know nuffin' 'bout dat. 'Sides, ee's an old man. Could peg out any time.' A slice of the knife blade. 'Better sooner dan later.'

'Does the new lord know about your Lady's plans?'

'Yer joking? Yer tink ee'd agree to putting 'is bruvver away? As yer say, fick as fieves. No stomach fer it so 'ee knows nuffin'.' He held up his knife in warning. 'And 'ee never knows nuffin'. See?'

'Think we'd go running, Cedric?'

'I tink it would go some way to winning yer a pardon, Eudo.'

Eudo! The short, dark man was Eudo!

'I doubt that,' Eudo said. He held up a flagon, tilted the neck towards his mouth. He swallowed so loudly Oluf heard it from behind the leaf screen; the liquid guzzled down his throat, his Adam's apple working up and down. 'So it's agreed? We get rid of goldy-locks and – well – the manor's looking good for the taking, eh, boys?'

Oluf was shivering. He gulped back the bile that rose in his throat. He stepped back, heard the sharp swish of the branch as he let it go, its clatter. He froze.

'Wot was dat?'

'Never heard nothing, Ceddy. You getting nervy?'

'You getting careless? Sure yer weren't follered?' he shot at the hidden man.

A grunt, another hawking cough. 'Not me.' A low growl.

One of the men gestured towards a scampering creature, red-tufted ears alert, bushy tail coiling and uncoiling. 'A squirrel, for sweet Mary's sake.' It paused above their heads, chattering a warning, then leaped away from one narrow, springy branch to another, high in the tree tops. Its mate leaped after it. Further away, a buzzard lifted silently from the branch of a tree and soared skywards. Somewhere invisible, the woodpecker drummed and the cuckoo called. *Cuccu cuccu.* Cedric Hayward grunted. 'I like a town, me. Knows wot yer dealing wiv. Now, we need a plan. It's 'ard while dese cursed friends are 'ere and training de villagers. An' de light nights coming.' He snorted. Spat. 'Dat unwomanly creature, dat furrener, prancing 'bout wiv a fancy bow.'

'She's a dead shot, Cedric. Our friend here saw how she took that boar in the throat.'

'And another through its eye.'

The hidden man snorted and hawked fat phlegm that splatted on dried brown leaves fallen in autumn. Oluf squirmed closer, trying to catch a clep of him.

'Ah, wot I'd giv to subdue dat one as she deserves.' Cedric breathed hard. 'Still, once dose two are gone, dere's nuffin' to stop us. Wench-faced Edgar? 'Ee's a pretty boy. And dat wife of 'is? How did 'ee ever get 'er wiv a brat in 'er belly?' He tested the sharpened point against the tip of his thumb and grunted with satisfaction. 'I've a score to settle wiv 'er. Oh yes, 'ow I'll see to 'er. A good seeing to, dat's wot she's asking for, boys. And after dat – let's look to riches, bruvvers.'

Oluf rolled silently away and slithered back to the boys.

'Say nowt,' he gritted. 'Uppens, and come away wi' me.'

He made them go silently through the woodland, making scrutchings on the trees so that he'd recognise the place again. When they were a clear distance from the Old Wood he hurried them down the hill track and back to the village.

It was Ellen who saw them first, stumbling down the hill; they all three watched Oluf stop to let the smallest one climb on to his back then he was lurching along, young Will clinging hard on and Simon trotting close beside them. No sign of the baskets she'd sent them with. 'Something's wrong,' Ellen breathed. She gripped tight hold of the woven basket, glad it was pannier style and slung on a woven strap across one shoulder, She would have run after the boys except Agathi grasped her arm, stopping her.

'Take care, Ellen,' Agathi cautioned. 'The ground is uneven here. Do not risk falling. We cannot catch up with them. We can only go as fast as is safe for our bairns.'

Ellen nodded. Understood. So difficult not to hurry. Kazan held back her instinct to run after the boys. Instead, she kept pace with the two slow-moving women.

The younger boy was mulfered. 'I'll pag yer,' Oluf said, and squatted down so the tired little legs could hoist themselves on to Oluf's back, and skinny arms wrap themselves round Oluf's throat. 'Not so tight, Will, else yer'll throttle me. Simon, yer mun run along o' me.' Simon gazed up at Oluf, adoration in his eyes, blood oozing from a deep scratch on his cheek.

'That's all right, Oluf,' he said. 'I'm not tired. It's Will who's fazed like.'

Oluf hardly heard, didn't see Simon's awe. Da, he thought, da will know what to do. The morning was forgotten, and the cuffing. He thought only of the comfort of his da's strength and purpose. 'Say nowt o' this,' he cautioned the boys. 'Mebbe yer'll need to tell me da or Maäster Edgar. Nob'dee else, now.' Will shook his head, frightened by Oluf's vehemence, by the presence of the bad men, by the thought of having to talk to the Maäster. Simon nodded. 'Whatever you say, Oluf.' They passed by Joan without seeing her. She stared after them, then ran fleet as a hare to the place where she knew Hilda was, and the Maäster, and Oluf's da.

'Is this true, son?' Bernt was stern, not sure whether to believe his son. A storier, when it suited him, but…

Edgar had sent the two younger boys away with Joan and Hilda; let them settle themselves, have their scratches cleaned and salved, be comforted. First they would hear Oluf's story. He led the boy and his father into the manor house. The sun was shining through the windows, shutters opened now for air and light. Shadows danced along the floor and dust motes flickered in the light. Best leave them together, he thought. Bernt will call me when he needs to. He settled himself at the further end of the hall.

'I heard 'em, da,' Oluf insisted. 'I heard 'em. They thought as nobdee wasn't there but I heard 'em.' He was shivering with fear. He tried to hide it. His father was so strong, such a hero, how could he show fear to his brave father? 'I couldn't stay longer. There were the two young'uns to get safe. I couldn't trust 'em to stay safe hidden and quiet like I told 'em.'

Bernt considered. Yes, he believed the boy. The harsh words of the morning were forgotten. He'd been expecting sulks from his son: not this. The boy's face was as pale as his curly hair and his hazel eyes wide with shock.

'I'm sorry, da.'

'Sorry?'

'I disobeyed you. I took them two to the Old Wood though you told me not to go no further than the pond in the Long Wood. Then when I heard the men I should have stayed. Heard more. And we left the baskets behind though we'd filled 'em.'

Bernt shook his head in disbelief at the string of jumbled confession. The baskets? Devil take the baskets. 'My son…' He stopped. Closed his eyes. Tried again. 'My son, I am angry because you risked your life, and the lives of the two boys, in going to the Old Wood.' *I love you.* He tried to say the words but they stuck in his throat. 'Your mother and I,' he said, 'we want you to be safe in these dangerous times.' He sounded pompous. What would Ellen say? She would say that she loved him and was proud of him. Why couldn't he? 'You did what was best, what was right, to bring those two back safe. I shall take your information to Master Edgar.' He stopped again, longing to take his son in his arms, hold him close, comfort him, thank God for his safe delivery from the gang and that brute of a hayward. If the man had taken him... Bernt felt again the vicious blows the man had dealt him until he couldn't breathe, could only curl up against the next and the next... He tried again. 'You were brave.'

Oluf felt his eyes brim with tears. He wiped his sleeve across them before his da could see but it was too late. He saw the horrified look in his father's eyes and burned with shame.

'My son,' said Bernt. His hands came up to the boy's head, closed on the precious silver curls, drew him close against his own strong body.

Oluf clung to him 'I wasn't brave, da,' he choked. 'I should have listened more but I was frittened.' The tears were rolling down his cheeks leaving runnels of dirt and grime. 'I'm shamed.'

'My boy, my son, I am only glad you are safe.' He sighed, bent, rested his cheek against the boys' head. 'I am sorry for this morning. I should not have hit you. I love you.' It was easy, he thought. Not difficult at all but easy. *I love you.* My Ellen, my wife, we are blessed again and again despite our lost bairns. His son sobbed and sobbed with fear and relief and Bernt held him tight.

Unseen, Kazan, Agathi and Ellen came into the hall. Edgar heard the sound of their footsteps. He held up a warning hand to stop them coming closer. He had heard the tale of this morning's quarrel; heard how Oluf was becoming too hot to handle. Let his father deal with him now.

'I wanted to be brave like you.' Oluf rubbed away snot and tears.

'Boy, I'm not brave.'

'You are! You are!'

A man who could not protect his woman and child? Who was

rescued by a foreign, fragile creature? Brave? 'I am not brave, son. I am a man. That is all.' He grasped his son closer. 'Listen. When Cedric Hayward took me prisoner, I was helpless. Your mother tried to help me. The young master's wife kicked his...' He hesitated. 'Kicked his make-water and so he was abless. But not through me. I am not what you think me.'

'You are. You are my da and you make things good.'

Bernt sighed. 'I try to, my son. That is all. That is all any of us can do. Try to make things good.' He rubbed his cheek against his son's head. 'Now, with Master Edgar and his lady, we have a chance of making things good.'

Oluf stirred. He raised his head, wiped bleary eyes. 'They said as it was Maäster Edgar as was to have the manor, da. That it was the old maäster's will.'

Bernt took his son by his arms, held him in front of him. 'You are sure of this?'

Oluf nodded. Yes. Of this he was sure. But the fourth man? The one who had heard and seen so much? 'There was another, da, but I couldn't see his face. His back was to me. I tried to have a clep of him but I saw nowt.'

'His voice?'

'He said nowt much.' Oluf frowned. The shivering had stopped and he was trying to think, remember. Now his da believed him, he had to remember all he could. 'He saw the boar killed. And he knows about the visitors – I mean, he knows they are good friends and about the training.'

Bernt looked at his son. Oluf's gaze was honest and open. He shifted his gaze across the hall to Edgar's.

'I think there must be a spy in this manor, Master,' he said.

23

Journey to Ieper
May 1337

O tresses of cloud on top of the snowy mountains
Will you untie your hair and shed tears for me?
(Yunus Emre: 14thC)

The high mountains and some of the passes were still blocked with snow.

'But we can travel now?' Blue insisted. They had stayed far longer than the night they intended.

Francesco da Ginstinianis sighed. 'You can. But there is still the danger of avalanche. Better to wait a week – two weeks – longer.'

Blue thought hard: Da Ginstinianis knew the trade routes, knew the dangers, but Dafydd and Thomas had travelled in dangerous March. God willing, they would be with Heinrijc Mertens by now. Should they wait or travel? He asked Hatice what she thought.

'Let us go on, husband.'

Always she wanted to go on and on. It seemed she would never rest until she was with her daughter again: the adopted, slave daughter she had taken as her own. Mehmi too wanted to travel on though his was a different wish. 'I do not like it here, Blue. There are many different peoples here, and trade with many different places, but I do not feel comfortable. And after what happened to Dafydd…' No, that was beyond bearing, no matter how profuse the apologies of the élite, these nobles of Venezia. They had tortured him, their Dafydd, trying to make him confess to what was not. *Barbar*, this land-sea country. He longed to be rid of it.

As for Niko, his was the response of the young, the daring, the foolhardy. 'Let's go – why have we waited so long? Edgar and Agathi will be so surprised to see us. And Kazan. I want to see Kazan. Let's go now!'

And so they did. There was an afternoon when it seemed an avalanche would sweep them away. They were easing their way over one of the fragile wooden bridges that crossed over chasms too deep for reckoning. The flimsy structure swayed and jolted under the weight of the pack animals and their human cargo. The mountains were higher than any in Anatolia, their tops reaching into the heavens, lost in mist. They heard the slow, loud roar and looking up saw the high snows began to slip. The *marronier* cried a warning and urged them on to the further side. Quick! Quick! The *marronier* pushed them behind rocks, animals and all, kept them safe. They watched, open-mouthed, as the tumult of debris, of bouldered snow and rocks and torn-off trees and branches, boulders, flying stones hurtled towards them. The noise of it hurt the ears, the teeth, drowning out all human voice. The snowstorm raged close past them. Too close.

Under his breath, the *marronier* muttered imprecations against the fools who travelled when there was still the threat of avalanche and who did not know how to keep themselves safe. It was not so many seasons since his friend had been engulfed by an avalanche. A miracle he was saved from under the snow. His wife was with child and she refused to believe he was dead. One day in the spring he came back to her. He had made an air hole through the snow and so survived, on breath and water from handfuls of melted snow. He said his unborn child spoke to him in his icy prison and it was this that gave him courage and faith. She refused to believe he was dead. Only two months ago there were two foreigners, two men, struck down by an avalanche. It was a miracle they had halted their fall before they reached the crevasse. One had the sense to poke his stout stick up through the snow and so they had breathed and lived and were rescued, though one was badly hurt, he had heard. Better not to be buried in the first place. He scowled at the travellers. They were gazing back at the beautiful, still, white sea. All quiet now, all calm, all still.

'A sign, my husband!' Hatice crowed. 'We are safe and so are our friends.'

''Appen so,' said Blue laconically, but he was impressed. That white storm of snow and rocks to sweep past them and leave them unscathed? This was a miracle. May'appen his friends were safe and waiting for them the other side of these high mountains. Mog on, then, he thought, best mog on.

24

Bradwell

May 1337

Ich hem habbe itrodded in wrethe and in grome,
And all my wede is bespreind with here blod isome
(I have trodden them down in wrath and anger,
And all my raiment is spattered with their blood together)
(William Herebert: 14thC)

'He is not guilty, Giles.'

'He knew of your father's Will, Edgar, and he kept it silent.'

'But that is different. That is the choice of a foolish man.'

'He did not honour your father's wishes. That is not a foolish choice, and you know it,' Giles said, impatiently.

It was almost twilight. Somewhere, a late blackbird trilled and warbled. The drenching rain had stopped but leaves splattered heavy drops so that it seemed it rained still. The evening was fragrant with the fresh, moist smell that comes in spring time after heavy rain. The setting sun sent rays of light glancing through the window, and the flickering shadows of branches. It should be peaceful, thought Edgar, and yet it is not. He sighed.

'He did not know of the plan for Cedric's escape,' he reminded his implacable friend.

'And he had no idea of a plan to murder you?'

'No! Oluf has said so. Giles, we are talking of my brother,' Edgar protested. 'He is my brother.' *There is always room for faith.*

'And you think brother does not murder brother?' Giles was sardonic. 'And you five years with the monks?'

'I know. Cain and Abel. But there was never such jealousy when we were young.' He stopped. Was that true? Hilda had spoken of jealousy. Jealousy and resentment because it was Edgar whose birthing had killed their mother. 'I don't know, Giles. My head can't think.'

'I understand, my friend. These are difficult matters.' Edgar heard the pain in his friend's voice. Yes, he thought, this is Giles who had to make the choice between his father and his brother. Choosing is never easy.

'I must find out if Eric knows anything of this.'

'Yes.'

'Until then, Giles, we must fend for ourselves,'

'Yes,' he said again. He was silent a moment, watching the sinking sun and the dappled light of leaves on the old stones of the window. 'We thought, Edgar, it might be a good idea if we pretended to leave.' Giles regarded his friend's face. 'You know, we make all the gestures of leave-taking, packed mules, fond farewells...'

'And then what?'

'We go to Sir Roger's and wait for the gang to attack. And they will, once they know the manor is not defended.'

'Defended by you?'

'Yes, Edgar. By me, by Kazan, by all of your villagers. Does it matter? Without us, you are without a guard.' Giles pursed his lips. 'This is no time to be precious about your pride. There's no time to lose now Philip's made it official he's confiscating Edward's fiefs in France. Edward will be commissioning fighting men before summer's over. Sir Roger is in danger as well, Edgar.'

'What do you mean?'

Giles sighed. 'Edgar, you are my good friend but I would lie if I said you were a good soldier – and you know it. Your skill lies in a different way. Let us each to our own, altar boy.' Another time he would have laughed at Edgar's outraged face but not now. 'I envy you, Edgar; you are skilled in making harmony where there was discord, making a destroyed land grow again – making a baby, for Mary's sweet sake. And you are frowning because your skill is not destruction and death. What an idiot! And here was I thinking you a clever man of learning.'

Edgar laughed, reluctantly. 'If you were not my friend, Giles…'

'Yes, I know, it would be swords for two. And I would win hands down. And Agathi would be husbandless and your child fatherless and Kazan would denounce me for a murderer and…'

'All right, Giles, all right. For Mother Mary's sake, I understand. What's your plan?'

Kazan halted by the girl who was piping a tune on a crude elder pipe, playing notes like the birdsong Kazan had heard in the Long Wood. The girl was far-off in her thoughts, her strange greeny-yellowy eyes dreaming.

'Joan,' Kazan said. 'Do you think you could play this pipe?'

She held out the swan pipe that gleamed like moonshine. Joan put down her own pipe and took the swan pipe in her hands, curious and careful, her fingers caressing the smooth bone.

'Not never seen a pipe like this. Seven holes. More n' mine. Still, different but same, mistress,' Joan said. 'Should be able.' She blew into the pipe. The note was clear and bright and caught on the air and mixed with the swallows' chittering. 'It's a lovely sound, mistress.'

'It is my grandfather's pipe,' Kazan said. 'I wish you could play this song.' She hummed the tune that Nene had said was Ieuan ap y Gof's. The girl followed her, tracing the notes on the swan pipe, at first hesitantly then with more assurance then in disbelief.

'This was the song of the Outlaw,' she said.

'It was the song of Ieuan ap y Gof, the great *pencerdd*, and the music master of my grandfather's brother.'

Joan's yellow catkin eyes were wide in disbelief. 'It is the song of the Enemy,' she said.

Kazan stared at her. 'How can this be so?'

'It is what my father said, and his father before him. His father was with the old Edward who led the great army into Wales. He said the Welsh music man was a troublemaker. This song of his called the enemy to him so they would fight.'

'But he was a good man,' Kazan said, slowly. 'My Nene told me so and she was never wrong.'

The little girl's face set in stubborn lines. 'It's not right to play his song.'

Kazan sighed. The girl played well, and it was wonderful to hear the notes of the swan pipe. A miracle, a voice calling her from a long-gone past. 'What about this song?' she asked. 'This song was made by my grandfather's brother, made especially for my grandfather. My grandfather is dead now, and I think the brother also. I would like very much to hear this song.'

The girl nodded. She wanted to play the pipe again. So rich a sound, so beautifully made. 'Sing it for me, Mistress Kazan.'

Kazan hummed the first low notes of the song. The girl's fingers faltered at first and the notes squeaked out in disharmony. She frowned. 'This is a difficult tune to play. More difficult than the other.' She tried again, and a third time and this time the notes came out pure and true. 'A lovely song,' Joan said, 'but sad.'

'It's a praise song,' a voice said behind them. Simon Weaver the villein, whose wife was dead and whose son was stone deaf in one ear. Simon Weaver coughed and hawked up phlegm. None of Hilda's and Ellen's salves and potions had cured him of his winter sickness. The women of the village helped him as best as they could, when he would let them, and then only for the son's sake; the men too, but it was hard going for the man and his son. They all said so, and pitied the two. Now he halted by the young girl and the girl not-so-much older.

'You know it?' asked Kazan.

'I've heard it.'

'How?'

'I've not lived here in this manor all my life, girl.'

Kazan ignored the man's rude roughness.

'Where then did you hear this?'

'What does it matter to you?'

'It matters because this is the song Ned made for his brother Will who was my grandfather. I did not know them. I know only what my Nene – my grandmother – told me. When I went to find my grandfather in the spring, it was too late. He died in the winter cold. I never heard this swan pipe until now Joan plays for me. She is very skillful, I think.'

'Aye, she's a right enough little lass.' The man's face was surly. 'Spit of her ma, she is. Pretty face and pretty ways yer ma had, little lass.' He snorted back phlegm. 'Yer've more sense than she had. Go on – play the tune for this one.'

'But where did you hear it?'

The man grunted with laughter. 'Nivver give up, do yer? Scotland, girl, fighting for Edward. Which one? Does it matter? Same – different – war's always the same for the little man. Hard and brutal and now there's to be another. Heard yer song one night. Minstrel brought in for the men – keep us sweet, see. He played it, the brother. Nivver forgot. Not nivver. Aching sweet it were. Made you long for things as you couldn't nivver have.'

Joan raised the swan pipe to her mouth again and played the notes sweetly and sadly. Kazan felt tears prick her eyes. *Made you long for things you could not have.* Dafydd, I long for you. Shall we ever meet again? She realised Simon Weaver was wiping his sleeve across his eyes, and his face was surlier than ever. A man who hid his true feelings; a sad man.

'Did yer ever hear this one?' he asked suddenly. And his hoarse voice rasped out a song that should have been soft and gentle. He broke off, hawking up phlegm.

'Yes,' Kazan said. 'It is the song for Angharad.'

A song I sang for Angharad before she died.
Gold girl, bright sun face, gift of goodness,
Gentle magnanimous girl
May she not want, may she find heaven…

'My Nene said she was a lady of great goodness and beauty who lived again through music as if the Saint Beuno had breathed life back into her. Like Saint Winifrede whose presence was always known by the sweet smell of frankincense and violets.'

'Eh, yer know all this, though yer be frim folk?'

'It is my family,' she said. 'We know of many things, from many countries and many gods.'

'That's blasphemy, girl.'

'Is it?' She stared at him, and he ducked his head, not wanting to meet that golden gaze.

''Appen not,' he agreed.

'No. Same but different. That is what we say, me, my dear friends. We are Christian and Muslim and good friends.'

'That's good to hear, mistress.'

He lurched to his feet and shambled away across the yard. Joan and Kazan looked after him. They heard him coughing and spitting.

'He is a sad man,' Kazan said.

'Shall I play for you again, mistress?'

'Yes. Can you teach me to play, Joan?'

'May'appen, mistress.'

Kazan and Giles left the following morning. They travelled light, leaving the packhorse behind at the manor. Besides, the horse had mostly carried gifts for Agathi and Edgar. The villagers followed them as far as the new bridge, waving and cheering, sad to see them leave, though the tight circle of trusted men knew what was happening.

'You'll see Roger de Langton?' Edgar had urged, in front of all the villagers.

'Yes, we owe such courtesy to Lord Roger, Edgar,' Giles said. 'But we cannot stay long. We must be on our way westwards. We have a long journey ahead of us.'

'Goodbye, my dear friends. God go with you. When you return, Dafydd will be here for certain.'

Edgar watched them leave. He wondered who was watching here with them, who would take the news to Eudo. When would they attack? He wished Agathi were better protected. He insisted she stay in the solar, with Ellen. He remembered Oluf's tear streaked face as he told his story, and how he spoke of Cedric Hayward's determination to hurt her. He would not. Edgar would not let that man harm her, his beloved, his wife – nor their child.

It was quiet after they'd left. So quiet. Only those two were gone, the man Giles and the strange woman they called Kazan, yet their going made the manor seem empty. That afternoon Oluf lurked behind the kitchen door. Rain was setting in again. Gentle rain, summer rain, good for the crops. He watched it sweep over the low hills. He'd promised his da he'd watch over the growing crops in the south field. Protect them from birds and vermin. Terrible dull work but he'd offered. He was trying to be good. But when he set out, he saw Simon Weaver crossing the yard. Nothing odd about that. But then the man hawked and coughed and spat. He always did but now it reminded Oluf of the man in the Old Wood. The unseen man. The informer. The traitor. Could it be Simon Weaver? Not possible. Simon Weaver was their friend. When his da was ill, and his ma weeping, it was Simon Weaver who had helped them. When his da was locked away and accused of killing the bailiff, Simon Weaver refused to believe it. No, he must be wrong. Besides, Simon Weaver's son had the deafness in one ear and Oluf's ma gave him potions to help, and for Simon Weaver and his bad chest. Then Simon Weaver coughed and hawked again, and muttered an answer to the old grandmother sitting outside in the May sunshine. Half blind she might be but her hands were still quick and sure, weaving rushes into baskets, and her hearing recognised the sound of Simon Weaver's footsteps on cobble. She called him by his name. It was him; no mistaking that low mumble any more than the hawking and cracking of gobbets of phlegm in just that way.

Oluf slid away from the door into the shadow of the kitchen wall. He watched Simon Weaver's round-shouldered trek up the track to the Long Wood; saw the furtive glance cast behind him. Should he follow? The boy who had thought to herd the escaped boar back to the sty said yes; the boy who had led Will and Simon into the Old Wood urged him on. But it was a different Oluf who had returned from the Old Wood, bringing the boys back to safety, and this Oluf shook his head. This was no time for puffed-up pride. Best tell his da and Master Edgar. Let them decide what was best to do. But they were away up in the coppiced wood checking for signs of trouble. Mistress Agathi was in the solar with his ma. He'd go to her.

Someone moved by the dairy; he twisted round sharply to see who it was, wary as the yard cats. Joan was loitering there, drying her hands on a scrap of cloth. She lifted her face to the sun. She looked tired. Her bright hair was scraped back from her face and bound with clean linen. It threw her thin face into sharp profile. Churning butter, probably. Maybe cheese making. Plenty of milk now there was lush grass for the cows to eat. A hard job for a young girl. He hadn't thought before how hard she worked, doing any job that came to hand, and no complaining. Not like him, all sulks and bad temper if he didn't get his own way. She'd done well, that day he'd come stumbling back from the Old Wood. Never a word to ask what he was about; just went to call his da and Master Edgar from the garden they were making for the women. Never a word after, though she gave him one of her straight, sharp looks. Same thing that wintry day, long ago now it seemed, when he'd followed Mistress to the undercroft and screeched for Joan to bring Hilda. Suddenly, he wanted her by his side when he went up the steps to the hall and into the solar. He wanted the comfort of her. She'd believe him. She'd back him. She always did. He called to her and saw how her face was wary. Well, he'd given her cause in the past. She came across from the dairy towards him.

'What's to do, Oluf? We're busy in there. I've to go back sharp.'

'Will yer come wi' me? I need ter talk about matters wi' the mistress and ma.'

She stared at him without speaking. Strange eyes. Like catkins in the sun. She nodded. 'If that's what yer want.'

Oluf breathed out the breath he hadn't even realised he was holding tight inside him. He grabbed her hand and pulled her with him to the hall stairs and hurried her up them. The door was open to let in the breeze so he went in. He thought at first the big chamber was empty. Sunlight danced through the windows and cast flickering shadows on the beaten floor. It lit up the carving on the hearth hood. Rain cloud chased it away. His mother was standing in front of one of the aumbries, opening its wooden door.

'Ma?' he croaked.

'Oluf? Why are you here?' Ellen's surprised gaze flicked past him to Joan. 'Both of you.' She sighed. 'More trouble, Oluf?'

'I'm not sure, ma, but I think I should speak with the mistress.'

'She's resting, Oluf. This is her first child, remember.'

His glance flickered over her body, saw how her belly was swelling. 'You need to rest as well, ma,' he said. It came out more pugnacious than he meant. He saw her smile, her lovely smile, lift the weariness in her face.

'But you mean to trouble us both, my son? You must think it important. Come.' She beckoned the two children across the length of the hall and into the solar. Mistress Agathi was half-lying in one of the cushioned window embrasures, watching light and shade, light and shade, turn and turnabout, of the sun in the orchard trees, and the rain clouds shadowing the line of the low hills. She looked up when Ellen came in.

'Two visitors, Mistress,' she said, and stood aside so that Oluf and Joan were there in the doorway.

Agathi smiled. They looked so small and young and nervous. She registered the determination in Oluf's face and sat up, very straight. 'What is your trouble, Oluf?' she asked.

It was easier now to understand her. She had learnt much of their language though the words were still strange on her tongue. He gave a little clumsy bow.

'Mistress,' he said, 'I think I know who the traitor is.'

He saw how her hand went at once to her belly; saw his ma's hand do the exact same thing. First thought was for the bairn. That's how it was when she carried me, he thought. Strange and wonderful, that's how women were. He realised he was still holding hands with Joan and he didn't care who saw him.

The night was dark and still and warm though it was still early May. Edgar couldn't sleep. He was restless at every sound. 'You must rest, husband,' Agathi said drowsily. 'We have guards enough.'

'I know, sweetheart,' he murmured. But he did not sleep. Oluf's thunderclap sounded in his ears. Simon Weaver? He would have staked his life on Simon Weaver. Happen Oluf was mistaken, this time? He sighed and turned. No. The child would not have spoken unless he was certain. But how? The way the man coughed and spat? His voice, low and muttering? As fragile as spun webs in a gusting wind. And yet. And yet…the man had a grudge, true enough, against his brother. Luke had said so. Cause enough, a child whose hearing was damaged by a careless blow. Grudge, then, against him?

'And now you are so tired,' Agathi teased him the next morning. 'Sleep today, dearest.' She chuckled. 'Then you can stay awake all this next night.'

She might smile and tease, he thought, but she too must have been wakeful though she had given no sign. He had thought her asleep. This morning she was pale cheeked and under her eyes were soot-smudgy shadows. He didn't ride Sorrel around the manor that afternoon but sat in the solar gazing out through the window at the cloud-laden sky and the land they had tended so carefully. Barley and oats were shooting up now, and the furrows of wheat. The pease fields were doing well. Fruit had set on the trees in the orchards. It should be a good harvest this year. Cattle and sheep and pigs, all healthy. Calves and kids and piglets, almost all born alive and lusty. Everything promised a good year. They'd talked together, him and Roger de Langton, about grazing more sheep now that King Edward was intent on maintaining the ban on export of fleeces to Flanders. The Flemish weavers would be without work. Perhaps they would come here? Set up a weaving industry here in Lincolnshire? Was it a wild thought? It was a heady thought. Heinrijc Mertens would be the man to consult. Except now there was Eudo's gang, and Cedric Hayward, and his brother Alfred's wife. And Simon Weaver who he would have trusted with his life. Round and round it went in his head, like the carols they sang at feast days but without their joy.

The next day they brought Simon Weaver to him, his arms tight-bound behind his back. The man was white-faced. 'I was coming to you, Maäster,' he said frantically. 'I was, Maäster, truly I was. Ask them where they found me, and if I tried to run away.'

Jack Smith shifted his feet. 'True enough, Maäster Edgar. Can't say otherwise. He was coming down from the Long Wood, creeping secret like. When he saw us he waited for us to come up wi' him.' He glared at the men with him. 'True enough?' he challenged them.

They nodded, muttered, uneasy, anxious. They all liked Simon Weaver, and were sorrowful for his boy. And him with no mother, and Simon wifeless. She'd died last winter, worn out with work and cold and not enough to eat.

'Untie him,' Edgar said.

'Nay, Maäster, yer mustn't.'

'Let him go. He means us no harm. Do you?'

'No, not any on yer. I didn't know as what they were set on doing.'

'Tell us.'

It was as Oluf had said: an attack, and the village razed; Edgar killed and his wife; the manor ransacked.

'My folk, Maäster, my folk. I couldn't have it.'

'Who wants this?'

'The Maäster's missus.'

'And the Master? Does he know of this?'

'No, sir; that he does not.'

Edgar breathed again. Alfred did not know. His brother did not know. God's gift.

'When do they plan their attack?'

'I'm not right sure, Maäster. May'appen tonight or the next night but soon. Before the full moon. That I'm certain on.'

A hand muffling his mouth. 'They are here,' breathed Agathi. He was awake instantly. 'Bernt has seen them.'

'Stay here, love.' He kissed her quickly on her mouth, felt her kiss him back.

'Take care.'

'I shall, sweetheart.' He grabbed hold of his sword and belt and hurried through the solar and across the stirring hall. Only women and children here now, and those few men on guard. The rest of the men and older boys were all in their new-built cotts or watching, as they had been instructed, turn and turnabout. He eased open the great door and slid out on to the head of the outer stairs. A shadowy figure was there. 'It's Bernt, Master. I sent word there were men about.'

Edgar gave a quick jerk of the head that Bernt probably couldn't see. 'Agathi woke me. Where are they?' His fingers fumbled on the belt fastening. The weight of the sword was heavy. Somewhere near an owl was calling. A flutter of pale wings swept by them.

'Long Wood. Coming down by the field track.' He glanced at the man standing next to him. 'Best cover yer head, Master. Bright as moonlight, yer hair.' Edgar felt his face redden, was glad of the dark night to hide it, pulled his hood over his head. That nod of his head, then, had been visible.

'We thought as they might fire the fields,' Bernt went on, 'but they haven't. Happen they plan to fire the village.'

'Can we stop them?'

'If Master Giles and Mistress Kazan have done their work, yes. Sir Roger promised us armed men.'

They watched. The bellying moon moved clear of cloud cover; in its half-light, fickle shadows flickered over the village. 'There,' breathed Edgar. They saw a shape flit from barn to stable. And another. 'Is it sure Sir Roger has men on guard?' he asked again.

'I'm certain of it, Master Edgar.' Another glance. 'We'll keep the mistress safe, never fear.'

'And Ellen.' And the babes they carried in their bellies. Neither man spoke of this.

'See there, Master? Look beyond the barn, if you can, into the shadows. That's where Sir Roger's men are. We'll see them stir themselves now.'

Eudo and his gang advanced into the yard, sure that they had surprise on their side. These villagers? Asleep. No idea of the planned attack. And then there was a warning cry, and horsemen bearing down on them, drawn swords glinting in the light of blazing torches where seconds before there had been no light. Not Sir Roger's men. These were streaming in from the northern track, down the marshy hillside. Plashy sounds of horse hooves came clearly to the two watchers then change to thudding as they gained firmer ground. Who were they, these armed, fierce men who were routing the gang? Above the clamour there was a halloo, a whistle, a shout. 'Stay close, Edgar. No need to show your head for shooting.'

Eric. It was Eric! And riding close beside him was Alfred.

Torchlight lit up his face, stern and fixed. Edgar saw horse and rider bear down on one of the gang. The horse reared and the man's arms came up to protect himself from the flailing hooves then he stumbled and was under the belly of the horse. His screams were loud, even above the tumult. Then the horseman was wheeling away, sword raised high.

'What are they doing here, my brothers? How did they know?'

Bernt didn't answer. There was no answer. He was as mystified as Edgar. Nothing had been told of the danger they were facing at Bradwell.

From out of the shadows of the barn came Sir Roger's men. Despite the dark and desperate fight, Edgar glimpsed Giles. And Kazan. Who had allowed Kazan to attack with the men? He answered himself. No one. Kazan was a law unto herself. Her bow was taut and an arrow unleashed, unerringly finding its mark, despite the night darkness. Then she was lost from view.

'Stay here, Master. Make sure the men are guarding the hall.' Bernt was gone, leaping recklessly down the outer staircase and melding with the fighters in the yard. Master, he had said, thought Edgar, but it was an order he had given. A sound order, but a true lord of the manor would be down there fighting with his men, not cowering up here in safety. All the same, he went back into the hall, made sure the men were at their posts, bows already strung and drawn. Agathi and Ellen were there amongst the women, he saw, helping them hush the frightened bairns. He went back to the great door and dragged it open. There was turmoil below him in the yard and beyond, into the village houses. Should he stay here, protect the women and children? Should he join his men? He hesitated, his sword drawn from its sheath. He hadn't felt its weight in his hand since Attaleia, and that desperate attempt to rescue Kazan and Niko from the house where they had been imprisoned by the slave trader Veçdet.

Clink of metal on stonework. Muffled grunt. Movement. Stealthy movement. A dark shadow creeping up the stairs in the darker shadow of the wall. Cedric Hayward. Edgar recognised him at once, by his shape not his face. Then the hayward gained the topmost step and Edgar saw his face grinning with glee. A bare blade was in his hand, held waist-height, slanted upwards ready to strike a man in the belly. Edgar stepped forward, his own sword raised and ready. The hayward laughed. Edgar understood instantly; his sword arm and the sword were too close to the stone wall; he had no room for manoeuvre. Cedric Hayward had the better plan of approaching with his sword levelled, not raised, and it was in his left hand.

'Well, Master Edgar, and 'ere you are, 'iding away wi' the women.' He giggled. 'You cock's egg, you blond curls, you woman.'

The man lunged forward and Edgar swung back against the door. The sword thrust went past him, the man following its sweep. He would have been inside the doorway except that Edgar twisted and stretched out his leg so that the hayward stumbled and would have fallen but he was agile and quick and saved himself, bringing his sword up close to Edgar's face. But Edgar had his own sword ready now and parried the stroke. As at Attaleia, the ringing blow shuddered through his entire body but now Edgar ignored it. Cedric Hayward must not enter the hall. Agathi was there. Agathi must be safe. He shifted his grip, felt the shaft in his hand, lashed out at Cedric Hayward with the hilt and saw him stagger. He lashed out again and this time struck the man full in the chest. Cedric Hayward fell backwards down the stairs, down and down, until he was a heap at the bottom. He lay motionless. Edgar started down the steps towards him. Eric was shouting his name. Bernt was there with sword ready. Then Cedric was up on his feet and staggering into the darkness.

'Are you safe Edgar?' Eric's voice.

'Yes.'

Alfred's voice. 'Let's have more light here. See who we have.' A pitiful round-up of the remnants of the gang, broken and bruised, and their dead comrades. There were losses too in the village. Mourning for more than one household, Edgar thought. But Eudo was dead, and ten of the gang, and only three of the villagers killed. Alfred had a gashed forearm and Giles bruising down his face. Luke was badly hurt. Simon Weaver was there amongst the wounded, nursing a shoulder wound. He was weeping.

'But you warned us, Simon Weaver. Without you, there would have been no warning.'

'He fought with us, Master Edgar.' One of the villeins spoke out.

'But he is a traitor all the same,' Alfred said.

The man's head came up. 'It's you ruined my son,' he said. 'I wanted to ruin you.'

Alfred grunted, disbelieving. 'I? Destroy your son? What fantasy is this?'

Edgar said, 'It's true, Alfred; you were the one who ruined his son's hearing. A moment's anger. A sharp clout across his ear. That's all. But enough to ruin the boy.'

'What? This is nonsense. When did I do such a thing?'

'Last spring, my Lord. When you were here with your wife. I saw it happen.' The villein's voice was even, flat, deliberate.

'You are insolent.'

'He is truthful, Alfred.'

Alfred sighed. 'If I did so I am truly sorry for it.' He sucked in his breath through tight teeth. 'But the man admits he plotted against us.'

'Don't be a fool. Alfred,' Edgar said sharply. 'The man is sorry for what he has done.'

Alfred hard-stared him. 'And so you would pardon him? You are more of a fool than I thought.'

'Better a fool than a murderer.'

Brother stared at brother. Never before had his young, golden-haired brother stared so into his eyes. So adamant. So determined. Such blue eyes. Blue like their mother's. Alfred dropped his gaze.

'I don't know what you plan, brother.'

'Why, brother, justice. That is what I plan.'

Alfred closed his eyes, breathed hard, nodded. Of course. This was how he had always been, this brother of his, always one for justice. Then Giles was with them, muttering urgent words.

'Kazan isn't here,' he said. 'She rode off after Cedric Hayward.'

'Is anyone looking for her?'

'Bernt's gone with some of the men.'

'Not you?'

'You need me here.'

Yes, thought Edgar, I do need you. I need Blue and how I wish Dafydd were here. Where are you, Dafydd? She won't believe you are dead, and neither do I, but we need you here. Come back to us, Dafydd. This man, Simon Weaver, I think he truly repents, but what should I do? Is Alfred right after all? There is the boy. What justice would it be to make him fatherless as well as motherless?

'Best get the wounded seen to,' he said. 'That's a bad weal on your face, Giles.'

'There's blood on your sleeve, Edgar.'

Edgar looked down, saw where the cloth was turning red. Strange, he hadn't felt the blow, didn't feel the hurt even now. 'More work for Ellen and Hilda,' he said, and felt the blood leave his face. Shameful, to be carried to his bed. Shameful, to be laid low while his men were wounded. He braced himself against the door frame. 'It's nothing – a scratch. What's happened down there?'

Giles slanted a long look. He talked of the wounded and the dead, of Eudo's gang finished. Around them, Ellen and Hilda tended to the wounded, wincing at the sight of a deep gash in Luke's thigh, the cloth of his hose and breeches embedded in the wound, chips of bone speckling the cloth. Another gash across his temple.

'I s'll have to hurt you, Master Luke,' Hilda said. The old man nodded. It was as much as he could do. He couldn't speak. Hilda breathed a sigh of relief when he sank into unconsciousness. 'Best fer him, Ellen,' she said. 'Let's be doing. Your man too, Mistress.

Looks white, he does. Get him over here.'

Edgar heard her voice as if in a dream. The doorframe was no use to him now. His arm had started to throb and blood was pouring down his arm.

'Find Kazan,' he said, and fainted.

She had seen the man tumble headlong down the stairs; seen Edgar at the head of the stairs; seen his sword hilt a cross against the lighted hall. Golden curls aureoled his head. An avenging angel, she thought, come to see justice done. And the wretched, creeping creature that had caused all this? He was away into the dimness of dark before dawn. She wheeled Yıldız around and followed the shadow. There he was! She flung herself off the mare, raced after the man, but he had heard her, was ready with a short dagger. He didn't speak. His face was twisted with fury. He grappled her to the ground and pointed the dagger at her throat. Even in this dark light she could see the savage glee in his eyes. She twisted, bit down hard on the fleshy part of his thumb, taking him by surprise but he stifled his gasp. She writhed away from him, but not far enough for safety. Her breath was rasping, and his as well, but there were no words spoken. He grabbed her again by her hair, pinned her down by it so that she choked with pain. The dagger was at her throat again. Except there were hoof beats and shouted warnings and the yelping and barking of the manor hounds closing in on him. His head came up. He scented the air like a wild beast, then thrust her hard back into the undergrowth and was gone into the darkness of the Long Wood.

Bernt was there first. He tumbled down from his horse. 'Are you hurt, Mistress Kazan?'

'He's getting away, Bernt! He's getting away! You must follow him!' She gasped out the words in Turkish but the sense was clear, and the way she gestured frantically to where the hayward had vanished into the Long Wood. The hounds were circling her, sniffing and growling, waiting for commands.

The three men riding with him had caught up. Bernt nodded at them and they urged the panting, plodding farm horses onwards in pursuit, the hounds loping alongside. Not that Bernt expected them to find the man. Too many places for him to hide, and once he was in the Old Wood not a hope of tracking him down, not even with the hounds. Too many stretches of water where the scent would be lost.

'You are safe, Mistress. This is what your friends wish for most. Come. Your horse has gone. She will be back in the stables, I think. Meanwhile, come up with me.' In his own language but the sense was clear and he reached out a hand to her, pulled her up in front of him. A foolhardy, fearless, courageous girl, this one. He felt how her whole body trembled against his. Not fearless, then. The more courageous for it.

'I owe you my life. He would have killed me, Bernt.' She tried to find the words in his own language and failed. 'Thank you,' she managed. He didn't answer only held her more closely against him.

A clatter of hooves in the courtyard. Bernt was back, with Kazan. Giles reached up to Kazan where she still half-lay in the curve of Bernt's arm. 'Is she hurt?'

'I don't think so. No blood. We got there in time but he would have killed her, no doubt about it. Has her horse returned?'

'Yes, just now.' Giles breathed freely at last. He lifted her down, kept his arm around her. 'We were worried, Kazan. You shouldn't have followed him, and alone.'

'I could have taken him.'

Bernt snorted with laughter, relief combined with admiration. Giles flung him an angry look. Eric grinned. 'I'm sure you could, Kazan. If anyone could have caught him it would have been you.' He asked. 'What happened to the hayward?'

'Gone into the Old Wood,' Bernt said. 'I sent the boys after him, and the dogs, but I doubt they'll find him.'

'Maybe not this day but we'll find him,' Alfred said, grimly.

It couldn't be helped, Giles thought. And truth be told, he cared nothing now for the man. All that mattered was that Kazan was safe. And Edgar and Agathi. Nothing more they could do now except tend to the wounded and the dead. Tomorrow was the time for questions and answers. But tomorrow was become today. Already dawn was creeping in and the hedge birds were cheeping. A pearly grey dawn with mist clinging to the beck and spiders' webs stretched from bush to bush. A blackbird shrilled from a high branch. A black cloud of crows lifted from the Old Wood and flew chuntering towards the mill. Yesterday had become today and today there were questions to ask and answers to be given.

Edgar roused himself. His arm was bound in white linen. It throbbed still but the pain was dulled and this was no time to play the wounded boy. He had insisted on getting up out of his bed, joining the group of men deep in discussion. His brothers, Eric and Alfred; Giles; Bernt. Not Luke. He was badly wounded, the gash inflamed and reddened. A fever, Hilda said, frowning. No help then from Luke, his man of sense, and such anxiety for his recovery. Wearily, he turned to Alfred. 'You must tell me why you are here, brother,' he said.

'Because you needed me,' said Alfred. He shrugged. 'That is all.'

Edgar looked down. He knew he must ask. 'Is that all, brother? You knew our father made me heir to this manor and yet you denied it to me.'

Beside him, he heard Eric's sharp breath.

'Was this attack known to you?'

'No!' Sharp, heartfelt, honest. Edgar felt his own heart lift. 'I had no idea that this was planned. You must believe me. I would never do you harm.'

'But you have.'

'Not like this! Never like this!' Alfred was heavy hearted, shamefaced. 'Yes, I resented you,' he admitted. 'Our mother died and I blamed you. It was wrong of me but a young boy's foolishness, Edgar. I never wanted father to send you to Croyland. Never.' He sighed. 'When you escaped I wondered if you might come here. You always loved this place as much as Father. But there was no word of you, no sign. Father was…' He stopped, staring into the past. 'Grief-stricken,' he said at last. 'He was determined to secure the manor holdings for you, Edgar, should you ever return. Then he proposed Philippa as a bride and it seemed a good match. I wanted only to please him.' He sighed again. 'It was a bad day's work.' He laughed, short and harsh. 'A worse night's work.' His head came up; he looked Edgar straight in the eye. 'I would never harm you like this. You are my brother and I love you. You are the image of our mother and I love you for that also. You have come here and made this manor a profitable place again, and its people happy. My wife?' He laughed again, the same short and harsh laugh. 'I have no wife. I heard her talk with the hayward. That is when I knew of her plans. I ordered her to get back to her father. I came here as quickly as I could and, thank the good God, in time to help. That is all, Edgar, and I say this before our brother and your wife and your people.' He looked around the men standing in front of him. 'I am ashamed.'

Eric stood dumb foundered. He had had his own suspicions after that Easter meeting. He had arranged for messages to be sent by pigeon, the fastest means, and both his own manor and Rochby kept excellent dovecotes. When his man had spotted Cedric Hayward lurking by the bridge, he had sent a message of warning, and so Eric had ridden out, with his men, to Rochby, and Matty went with him; she would not stay behind. He was driven by he knew not what. A sense of danger. Worse, Matty agreed. His sensible, practical wife agreed. What to do? They'd ridden hard to Bradwell, and just in time. He wished Matty was with them at this meeting, and all the company of women; calm Agathi, bright Kazan, gentle Ellen, even the stalwart Hilda. Women, he thought, who had more sense than war-driven men. But this was Edgar, gentle Edgar, and already he was embracing

Alfred, kissing him with the kiss of brother and friend.

'You are my father's eldest son and his rightful heir. You are my lord and I owe you allegiance. You are my brother and I love you.' He spoke as formally as Alfred, pledging himself to his brother, as Alfred had pledged himself. Edgar looked around the men standing in front of him. 'I say this before our brother and my wife and my people.' He looked Alfred in the eye, equal to equal. 'I am sorry for your loss,' he said, as if Philippa were dead, not cast off.

Later, the three brothers walked across the yard, past the fishponds and the orchard to the church. Agathi and Kazan were with them. Alfred wanted to light a candle, pray to God for forgiveness. He paused outside the porch. His hand traced a grooved pattern. 'I saw this at Easter,' he said. 'Do you remember it?'

They did. It was the graving of a hobby horse – a stick horse, the mason had called it. He'd been working on the east and west walls, making a place for new windows for the church, and new glass. He had watched the young brothers' pretend-fighting, astride stick horses with wicker heads. It must have been after some festival and a mock tournament. 'The porch because it is not allowed in the church,' he had told them. 'Remember this day,' he had said, 'when you were young and made only a game of fighting.' His face was serious. 'May it always be so.'

A game of fighting? Eric remembered how Alfred had lunged at his youngest brother; he had missed, caught Eric's shoulder and laid him flat on his back in the duck pond. 'Remember, brother?'

Alfred blushed as red as hearth bricks. 'That is true. I remembered all through the Tenebrae service. And there was the Judgement painting on the wall.' He heaved a great sigh. 'And still I said nothing.'

'That's all past, brother,' Edgar said. 'Come – look at the carving of the sailing ship. Remember that? I looked for it soon after Agathi and I arrived here.' He halted by one of the fat round pillars in the aisle. All three brothers had taken a hand in carving a sailing ship low down on one of the pillars. They had intended it to be a cog. They'd seen such sailing ships in Boston Haven. It was a good likeness. He traced its outline with one finger.

Kazan came up to him. 'I have seen the same in our churches,' she said. 'But there the sails are set differently.' Her face was sad. She was pale and drawn this morning. Agathi had said to him that Kazan was more shocked by the night's happenings than she would admit.

Alfred said suddenly, prompted by the carved cog, 'They say Philip's warships are raiding our southern coast. Attacking and looting. There've even been French ships seen at the mouth of the Thames. Our merchant ships are at risk, some captured. He's attacked Edward's castles in France, and he's trying to invade Gascony. It is intolerable! Edward has as much right to the throne of France as Philip. I'm taking my men to join the King very soon now.'

'That explains why Heinrijc Mertens has sent us no word.' Edgar saw that Kazan was gazing at a line of Latin inscribed in the doorway.

My hope is in God because, O Christ, I trust in Thee.

He translated for her. He hesitated. 'He will come.'

Sunlight flashed through the east window lighting up the little stained glass Christ in Glory, sending flashes of blue and yellow and red across the chancel and nave, across their faces and arms and hands. Kazan's face was suddenly, gravely, ecstatic. 'I know he will.'

They were only just returned to the hall when the messenger arrived. He was exhausted, white-faced, bedraggled with travel stains. His horse was trembling with the exertions of the journey.

'Trouble, Rudd?'

'Trouble, my Lord.' The man shuddered. 'Terrible trouble.' He hadn't wanted to be the one to bring the news. 'He trusts you,' they said, and so he was mounted and sent on his way with the image still burning in his head.

'Tell me,' Alfred said. 'Don't be afraid.'

'No, my Lord.' But he was. They all knew of the wild anger between their lord and lady, all the servants; they had talked of it, secretly, behind screens and closed doors. Many were glad that she was to be sent back to her father but others, her own people, spoke out angrily, defending her. All for nothing. Not now. This terrible thing had happened. Who could have foreseen it?

'Your wife, sir, she is dead.'

'What?'

'She is killed sir, murdered by her creature, the hayward Cedric.'

There. It was out now. Now he must bear the consequences. What a message to be charged with. He dared not look the master in the eye.

'Rudd, you have always been an honest servant, an honest man. Tell me what you mean.'

The man swayed on his feet, heard my lord Edgar call for wine and Lord Alfred's sharp exclamation. 'Sit down man. What time did you set out?' A cup was pushed into his hand and he drank from it, grateful, hardly aware of where he was. He was sitting on one of the window seats in the great hall, he reminded himself, and Lord Alfred standing over him. 'Tell me now. What has happened?'

The man Rudd took a steadying breath. 'It was sometime before midday, sir. We were all about our business. The Lady Philippa, she was in the solar, sir, with her women and the Lady Matilda. We didn't even see him come, sir. I swear we didn't. First we knew, the women were screaming murder. Mark Bailiff was first up into the chamber, and me, I was right behind him. My lord, such a sight. She was all bloodied and her throat sliced open like a stuck pig's.' He remembered the pooled dark blood and her face distorted and mouth open in a soundless scream. He shuddered. 'I'm that sorry, my lord, that sorry, but it unmanned me it did. Mark Bailiff, he was the one. He'd his sword out and he ran it through that man, that creature who killed her.'

'What man?'

'Why, Cedric Hayward, sir. It was him.'

'Brother.' Eric laid his hand on his brother's arm. 'Matty?' he asked the messenger. 'Is my Lady safe?'

'Yes sir, I swear it. She said to tell you, my Lord, that she stayed to set all to rights, as far as she was able; her sorrow to you, my Lord Alfred, for your loss; to you, my Lord Edgar, and to your Lady, for your troubles.'

Sorrow for his loss? Matty was more likely to be thinking it was all for the best, this death, and the shame of a wife packed off back to her father. But Matty was safe. His Matty. His dear wife. She was spared. He could hardly breathe. But his brother – ah – there was the thing. Philippa was dead, murdered, her throat slit wide. He saw Agathi move closer to her husband, half understanding the news. Edgar's sound arm came round his wife, holding her close. Together, united, combined against anything that was thrown at them. Yes, these two would survive anything and everything. His little brother, the runt, the weakling, Alfred's target. It was Edgar who would protect the manors; who would create harmony and prosperity for their people.

'You did well to get here so fast with this news.'

'Mark Bailiff said as I must get here as fast as I could, Lord Alfred.'

'Thank God for Mark Bailiff,' Eric said.

'A good man. He has always been a good man. First for my father and now for me.' Alfred's voice was too calm. Eric couldn't guess at his thoughts. A horrible end. An unimaginable end. But it released Alfred. Even now, with the news come so suddenly, he knew that. He glanced at Alfred and saw that he knew it as well. A fitting end, a murderous end for a woman who had plotted murder, but it was not Christian to think so, let alone voice to any other soul.

'We must send word to her father,' Alfred said suddenly. 'She died defending the honour of the manor. That is what he must know.' He turned to the messenger. 'Rudd. You have done well. You must be exhausted. Go to the kitchen for food and there will be a place for you to sleep.' He cocked an eye at Edgar. 'If you agree, brother? You are master here.'

'Of course I agree,' Edgar said roughly. 'This man has stood enough. Time now for him to rest and recover.

❀ 258 ❀

25

May 1337
France

It was mine owne strengthe that this bote wrought
(It was my own strength that brought about this rescue)
(William Herebert: 14thC)

It was the forests that all but did for them. France, and close enough to journey's end; close to Troyes, where the roads met and parted, one heading towards Paris, theirs towards Rheims and Bruges, and the last few miles of the long journey through the gladness of Maytime trees and blossom.

Close enough and glad enough to let their guard down. Robbers. Shouldn't be surprising but surprising them. 'Here's an infidel!' Blue heard the shout. 'And an English.' Frenchies. He recognised their tongue. Infidels and an Englishman? 'Infidel?' He roared his anger and charged the gang. 'Infidel? A'm a Fenman!'

He launched himself at the gang.

'Get yer selves out of 'ere,' he yelled. 'Get 'ome to yer maästers. There's no infidels here excepting yerselves, ungodly sons of Satan.'

Afterwards, he could never remember what happened. Not clearly. The robbers scattered. He remembered gashed heads and arms and shrieks. Then Mehmi laughing and binding up Blue's wounds. Hatice severe, shaking her head then kissing him and hugging him. Niko, wide-eyed.

'You are his hero, Blue Efendi,' said Mehmi. It was the first time Mehmi had used the title.

'Infidels and English,' Blue had fumed. 'They've no right. No right.' Then he collapsed.

26

June 1337
The Marches
For this son of mine was dead and is alive again;
he was lost and is found.
(Parable of the Prodigal Son)

A week later, and they were leaving, Giles and Kazan.

'Must you go?' Edgar asked Giles, but he knew the answer.

'She is determined to find Dafydd's family, if any are left alive.'

'And you, Giles? You go to find your family?'

'Yes.' A terse answer but behind it was the rift between himself and his father, the tearing apart after the terrible burning death of his Franciscan brother; the mother he had not seen in years; his brothers and sisters; the girl-cousin he remembered from her young days. The in-between world of the Marches, neither Welsh nor English. 'Yes. I must go to see my family. But first we shall search for Dafydd's brother and sister.'

'If they're still alive.'

'Yes. If they're still alive.'

'And you'll not see your own family first?'

Giles shook his head. 'Kazan's need is greater.' He sighed. 'If only Heinrijc Mertens had sent some message.' Kazan. Always there was Kazan.

'We may have word from him very soon.'

'I know. We will come back, Edgar, before the autumn. I pray there'll be news before that.'

'Take care, Giles. Eudo's gang is not the only one in these dangerous times. They say the Folvilles have the run of the Wolds beyond Newark, and your road runs that way. They count themselves as above the law and since they were acquitted of the murder of a judge barely ten years ago it seems they have reason.'

'Powerful connections, more likely.'

Edgar nodded. 'Since then, Luke tells me there have been endless murders, rape, robberies. They destroy property for payment, just as Eudo's gang did. This country,' Edgar said despairingly. 'What is happening to this country of ours? Never-ending wars, famine, pestilence, violence…'

'And the Four Horsemen appearing over the horizon?' Giles suggested, flippantly. 'Not yet, Edgar, not yet. There's good in this world yet.'

'And all shall be well?'

'There's always room for faith. Don't fret. I'll take care of her. I'll make sure we travel in company.'

Brent was giving the same warning to Kazan. Agathi clutched her hand, listening in horror.

'It's four years now since they abducted Sir Richard Willoughby and held him for ransom. 1300 marks. That's what they demanded – and got. And untouched by the law.'

'Peter Peddler said as how they wouldn't get away with it this time,' said Hilda. 'There's talk of them brothers being sent to war – Scotland and Flanders. Let's hope they die there.'

It wasn't fear of the gang that Kazan felt as they travelled along the Wolds road. They were in safe company, a caravan of merchants all with security in mind, and armed men, mercenaries, travelling with them. No, it was the emptiness of the land, its lack of trees, its huge skies grey with cloud. Desolate enough in summer; what would it be like in midwinter? As well, there was the sense of other lives lived long ago. Mounds where the ancient ones were buried; ungodly men, a friar told them, but Kazan could not believe him. Perhaps they had not worshipped the Christian God but a god of their own, and as holy to them as God and His Son Jesus and Mother Mary were to this brown-robed friar. There were crumbling churches that had been sacred places long before the Normans came to this land; now thatched roofs were destroyed, walls collapsed, and once-tended ground weed ridden. Even the road had been built by the old ones, paved and carefully made; now it was robbed of much of its paving and only the constant traffic of men and horses and carriages kept the track clear.

The journey took four days travelling from one castle to another, castles that protected one town after another, one lodging after another. Where roads crossed there were shrines or chapels or ancient crosses writhing with strange carvings. Whenever they entered forested lands there was the constant sound and sight of tree felling because the country was at war, and war demanded timber and plenty of it. Slashed and burned stumps of oak and birch and elm; heaps of branches hacked from the bodies of the trees; no birdsong. The charcoal burners were busy because the country was at war and war demanded iron and plenty of it. The air shimmered with heat. The men's faces were grimy and burning red; their eyes were black-rimmed. No smiles or jokes or song to cheer their days.

'It is a sad sight,' Kazan said.

There was a stonemason and his family, wandering like the *yürük* of her own country from place to place in search of work. This family was heading for Coventry. The man stopped again and again to catch his breath. He was like an old man though barely into middle age. His wife told Kazan, 'It's the job, see. All that dust. Gets into his body. He'll be stone himself afore long.' Her face was drawn, old before her time. 'I don't want my lads going into the same work but I don't see as they can do no different. That's the way it is, young miss.'

A knight escorting his family home, almost as far as Leicester, offered them hospitality but they refused and travelled the few miles further to Leicester, arriving just before the gates were closed for the night. The High Street, they'd been told; that was where they would find the best inns and lodging for the night. 'Look out for the signboards.' The street led up to the High Cross, houses on both sides, their gable ends to the road and separated by orchards and gardens and small fields. Pretty enough but...

'Giles, how it stinks!'

Newark had been bad enough but here heaps of filth were piled outside the houses in the street. It was putrid, a suffocating stench that tore at Kazan's throat. 'How do you English live in such squalor? It is *barbar*.'

'I suppose we are used to it, Kazan.'

She wrinkled her nose in disgust. 'Me, I cannot live in such a place.' No free lodging at a well-protected *han* with its well-run kitchens and stables and *hamam* with its piped water and efficient latrine. They passed a church, a hospital, a gaol where the stench was even worse.

The next morning she reined in Yıldız by the bank of the river. They were well away from the town and its castle. 'This river – this Soar, you call it? I shall bathe here, where there are shallows. I shall make myself clean. You must watch out for me.'

Giles kept his eyes diligently averted from her but he couldn't help imagining that slim, naked body and her hair, longer now, falling past her shoulders, gold-copper-bronze in the early morning sun, spread out on the surface of the water. He remembered Dai saying he had first seen Kazan in the *yürük* camp when her hair was gloriously long, falling to her waist. And then she had cut it off, all that gold-copper-bronze loveliness. She had told them so herself. 'Snip snip snip, like that,' with her *Nene*'s scissors. 'And my head so light I thought it would float from my shoulders.'

'What did you do with your hair?' someone asked. Thomas, perhaps.

'I burnt it.' She said no more. It was final. She had cut her hair and burnt it. But she had mourned its loss, Giles knew. 'And then I came searching for you and I found you.' She was triumphant, happy, this courageous boy-girl.

She was shouting to him from the riverbank. 'Now you Giles. You must bathe. You must wash the stink of this English town from you!'

And he laughed. So fastidious. But...did he really stink? He immersed himself in the cold river water and washed thoroughly.

From Leicester they fell in with a band of pilgrims travelling to St David's in far west Wales. 'Two pilgrimages to St David's,' one of them told her. 'That's equal to one pilgrimage to Rome, and so much more in the saving of our souls.'

The land was rising-falling now, and hills were smudged on the horizon. They came to Coventry, an important town, with a great north-south road through it that crossed with their east-west road. The townspeople and the Prior had been granted permission, barely ten years earlier, to collect taxes to fund the building of a stone town wall to replace the earth banks and wooden palisades. 'An ambitious project,' said a Coventry merchant who was travelling with them. He'd been months away from home. 'So many gates and towers are planned I wonder if it will ever happen.' But there was a beginning – he saw it straight away – scaffolding and builders and the just-started stone foundations of a town wall. 'See! Oh, this will make our town the greatest in all England.' He was smiling, certain of himself, certain that he was a man who came from an important place. 'It's the cloth trade,' he said, 'and with the blockade that can only get more important. Our workers are in the cloth trade – drapers, tailors, dyers, weavers, fullers. We're a match for the Lowlanders, indeed we are. And now King Edward has decreed the tax on exports to the Low Countries, with our own industry we are bound to triumph!' Then there were the leather workers, the saddlers, shoemakers, glovers. And the other crafts – the carpenters, the coopers, the goldsmiths. As well as the butchers and bakers of course.

Of course. A town had to eat.

'But it stinks, Giles, all the same. All these towns stink.'

The castle was half ruined. It was a sign of times to come. No castle but a manor house south of the town. And a Franciscan friary, and friars walking about the town in their grey gowns.

'You are thinking of Thomas,' she said.

'Yes. I hope he has found a peaceful life with the Franciscans.'

'He was your very good friend.'

'None better, Kazan.'

Left behind in Venezia. Dafydd left behind. No use thinking of that now. Sometimes thinking did you no good.

They picked their way through marshland, still in company with the pilgrims. They passed a French family, a noble man and his wife and two young boys, dazed with shock. Philip of France had declared Edward of England's fiefs in France confiscated; Edward's answer was to wreak reprisals on the French land-owning families in England. Bereft of their homes and lands, grateful to have their lives spared, what could they do but return to France?

They passed the great castle of Kenilworth where the second Edward, that unhappy king, had been imprisoned. 'Where he was forced to resign the throne,' Giles said.

Onwards, travelling towards the south-west on the old road made so carefully many, many years ago, and all but ruined by ransacking. 'All the way to the west country, to Exeter. I've never been that far but I know soldiers who have.'

'Is it not strange,' she said. 'We are following the roads the old ones made? Perhaps they were the same people who made the roads in my country – see how these roads are made in the same way? If so, they must have been powerful people.'

Yes, he thought, it was strange, but not thought of until Kazan had spoken of it. Roman roads, here and as far as the far country of the Turks. Same, but different.

They took the road to Gloucester. 'The second Edward's shrine,'

Giles told her then he laughed. 'A strange thing we heard, not long after we'd set out from Ieper. I'd forgotten about it till now. A strange story told us one evening by a traveller coming from the High Mountains. He said the second Edward was not dead, not buried in his shrine in Gloucester. He was alive and living in some monastery in Italy. He'd escaped, and another man was buried in his place. Sounds impossible but this traveller was certain it was the truth.'

'A very strange story,' said Kazan.

'Thomas was persuaded it was the truth. He questioned the man for so long we all went to our beds and left him.'

'Did he find out any more?'

'If he did he didn't say. You remember what he's like when he clamps his mouth shut? Nobody can prise anything out of him.'

Kazan laughed. She remembered.

After that, there were tracks and overgrown roads and more forest and the hills grew steeper. Clouds gathered. They crested one of the steep little hills; at its high point there was a break in the trees and a distant view of a line of blue hills. 'See that? It's Wales.'

Wales! Dafydd's country, that remote, mysterious, blue line of hills.

'Still a way to travel, Kazan. We can stay at Deerhurst tonight.'

'Do you think, Giles,' she asked, 'when we return to Bradwell, he will be there?'

'I am sure of it, Kazan.'

'You are a good friend, Giles. What would I do without you?'

'Well enough, Kazan. Well enough.'

She smiled back, that confiding smile that wrenched at his heart. Then they were crossing the Severn that the Welsh called the Hafren and that became like a huge sea itself before it met the real sea. The weather was changing. Storm clouds chased in from the west. The air grew chill and the wind rose. She was shivering. 'This is your English summer, Giles?'

'No, Kazan, it is a Welsh summer. See – the clouds are piling in from the west.'

The rain was pitiless. They were drenched, and a full two hours before the next town. He looked at her, doggedly urging on Yıldız. He gritted his teeth. 'My father's manor is close by, Kazan. We can go there.'

'Close by? Close by! We are passing your home and you would say nothing if it were not for this rain? This Welsh rain?' She was angry, spitting the words at him, rain running down her face and into her eyes, clogging her lashes together until she could not see.

'Maybe so,' he said. 'Don't expect too much.' He shrugged. 'We may be sleeping in a barn if we're lucky.'

She blinked the rain from her eyes and tossed her head. 'You are a fool, Giles.'

They left the high road, travelling into a narrow valley. 'A *cwm*, we say here.' She remembered Dafydd telling her that, long ago it seemed. 'It's a beautiful valley, the most beautiful in all the Marches. The hills rise above it, rounded and green, and a little river rushes through it. The church tower was built square and solid, to defend its people against attack – from Norman and Welsh alike. War and peace. That is what we know in the Marches. Peace and war.'

'I think you love this place very much, Giles.'

'It is my home. It was my home.'

Beautiful even now, with rain obscuring the hills and the swollen river noisily crashing over rocks and boulders.

And then there it was, his father's manor, and the land that Giles knew from his childhood. They rode down the steep valley. The *cwm*. There was no bridge. They splashed across the fierce-flowing ford and into the manor precinct. The hall itself was built of wattle-and-daub, the timber silvery-grey and the panels a deep ochre. Nearby was the church, solid and stout, as Giles had said, its tower built square and wide for worship and protection. Dogs surged out from the manor enclosure, barking madly. A manservant followed them, an old man, stumbling on the rain-glossed stones that paved the yard, trying to stay upright.

'Eh – Master Giles. It's Master Giles. Welcome to you, young master. Too many years. Too many years without you, young master.'

'Walter. Is my father well?'

'He's alive, young sir, but not so well. Never since your brother…' He broke off, cleared his throat. 'And then you were gone, and your mother so saddened. But come now, young sir, and make them all glad.' He shouted towards the stable block and a young boy came stumbling towards them. 'Take my lord's horse, Gareth.'

Giles swung down from his horse. He stood up straight, his shoulders back like a soldier ready for battle. He and Kazan walked up the steps to the great hall. The servant went ahead. He started to announce the visitors but a woman was there in the wide space of the great hall with torchlight flickering over her. Years after, Kazan remembered that moment: the high timbered hall, the sconces lit against the dark day, the woman standing there, one hand clenched against her heart, the other gripping the door frame. A young girl moved to stand close to her, shielding her, it seemed.

'Is it you, Giles?' She didn't move from the doorway. She didn't reach out towards him.

'Yes, mother.' He was stiff-straight, stiff-mouthed. He had, after all, warned Kazan there might be no welcome for them.

'My son.'

He saw then that she could not move. If she had tried she would surely have fallen. Afterwards, he couldn't even remember moving; just that moment when he reached her and his arms were round her, this small, bird-boned woman who was his mother. 'Yes, it's truly me come home. What of my father?'

'Walter has sent for him.' It was the young girl. A plain young girl, very slender, with dark eyes and dark hair and a frowning face.

'Esyllt?'

'Here he is now.'

A man bent with age and trouble, his close-cropped hair silver now, not the ginger-red of Giles' hair, but he could only be the father they were so alike. He came into the hall slowly. 'Giles?' His voice faltered. 'Truly you?'

'Truly, father.'

He stumbled across the space to where Giles stood with his mother. 'Thank God. Thank God you are here. Thank God you are returned to us. My son.' He reached up skinny arms to hold the big, broad body of his despised youngest son. Giles enclosed his father's frail old body in a young man's embrace. All was forgotten, forgiven in that moment.

Kazan watched and wept.

For this son of mine was dead and is alive again; he was lost and is found.

There were tales to tell, and Kazan to be explained. News to be told. Giles' brothers and his two sisters were married, living in other manors. One brother was in England. 'Some good connections,' Giles' father crowed, 'on both sides of the border.' Not land, here in the marches, but protection. 'Robert ap Gruffudd has offered for Esyllt. He is a powerful Marcher lord,' he explained to Kazan, nodding complacently. 'A good match. An excellent match.'

Kazan watched the face of the young girl who was the companion of Giles' mother. A ward, the girl-cousin, orphaned daughter of the lord of the neighbouring estate. Yes, a frowning face. Blue eyes, she realised, dark blue, like the stormy sea of her winter childhood. Giles' mother and father welcomed the return of the lost son but this young girl was angry. Not the face of an about-to-be betrothed. This girl kept her place behind her lady. So stiff. So angry.

Giles was bewildered. 'I've known her forever, Kazan, since we were children. She used to follow me around – a nuisance sometimes but she was a lonely little thing. Besides, we were friends. Why should she be angry with me? And as for Robert ap Gruffudd! Why, he is more than twice her age. That is no match. No match. She is too young.' He was angry, this phlegmatic man who rarely showed any feeling. 'This is my father's doing. You can bet on that. She cannot want to marry him!'

Best ask the girl. Kazan waited in an arbour in the pleasure garden, blowing on the swan pipe and pleased with herself because there were the beginnings of a song.

'We have always kept this carefully,' Esyllt said, 'despite the raids by the English and the Welsh. That is what it means, living here in the Marches. We do not know who will attack.'

'Giles said so,' Kazan said. They both spoke a careful Anglo-French. 'War and peace – peace and war. Always, here in the in-between country.'

The girl shrugged. 'It is what we know. It is easier now, with the third Edward, but who knows what will happen, when we are at war with France.'

'Perhaps it will be easier now Giles has come home.'

'If he means to stay.'

'I think so.'

The girl shrugged. 'And you? Will you stay?'

Ah, thought Kazan. This girl, her anger, her rudeness, now I understand. 'I go in search of my man's family. Giles has said he will come with me, to protect me. He made this promise to my man. It hardly seems fair when he wants to stay here.'

'Giles is not your man?'

'No. Never.'

'I thought he was.'

'You are mistaken. He is my very good friend. That is all.' She watched the sun shine out from behind the clouds. A plain girl – until she smiled. Then she was frowning again.

'But he may not choose to stay. Who knows with Giles? He is a soldier. He will fight for the King.' Esyllt picked a spray of sweet scented honeysuckle. 'Lord Robert will never leave here. He will always be here to protect my family.'

Do you love this Robert? Kazan longed to ask her. *Would you give your heart and soul and life for him?* No. She would not. Kazan knew it with all her heart, the heart that was given to Dafydd. With her soul. But would this Esyllt give heart and soul and life for Giles? She did not know. All the same, she thought it best to tell Giles that the girl did not love Robert ap Gruffudd.

Giles frowned. 'I know that. It is not a love match. How could it be? She has some idea of it being best for the family.' He shot a glance at Kazan. He loved her. He loved her courage, the way she braved all odds. How, then, could he dream of another girl? A girl whose dark hair flowed past her waist; a girl who glowered at him from eyes that were as dark blue as a late summer night; a girl he had known since she was knee high. A foolish, infuriating girl.

And Kazan? She was smiling, serene and certain and so remote from him. She was the unattainable. Hadn't he always known that? But now here was this mortal female, angry and confused and entirely loveable and desirable, and about to be betrothed to an old man.

'What should I do, Kazan? How can I prevent this marriage?'

'I think you know the answer, my dear friend.' Her hand went out to his, pressed itself on his, and he wondered if she had ever known of his hopeless love for her. She smiled, Kazan's mischievous smile. 'You are her love and she is yours. Yes, it is so, my dearest of friends. You must tell her so, though you have been absent so many years.'

'Too many years.'

Kazan shook her head. 'Never too many years. When two people love, time is not important.' Her face was sad. 'Time is not important. Believe me. The beloved is all and always they are together, those two, the loved and beloved'

Giles squeezed the hand that lay over his. 'He will come, Kazan. I know it.'

'And so do I, my friend, but sometimes I am so very tired.'

'There is always faith.'

'I know. I try. Sometimes God seems so very far away.'

The confession shocked him. He who had renounced faith when his brother was burnt alive. 'You are wrong, Kazan. God is here and he hears us.'

'You think so?'

'I am sure so.'

She smiled, but it was fleeting. 'I am glad of that, my friend.' Glad as well because this friend of hers who had renounced God, after his brother's cruel death, was ready to welcome God back into his heart and life.

He walked that evening in the pleasure garden that had been so carefully tended by his father, and his father before him. Scents of lavender and thyme and fennel. The full moon hovering in the sky above him. Half-moon, when they had routed Eudo's gang. Such a short space of time; such an eternity between that night and this. Home was around him. He had not thought he had missed his home so much. Esyllt. She was so much a part of his home, his growing-up. How could he have forgotten? Her voice, shouting to him. 'Come and see, Giles! Come and look!' And there would be some small wonder – a new born chick, a flower, a bird, a rainbow. She took nothing for granted. And now she was full grown and no longer his shadow. But still he remembered her voice. *Come and see Giles! Come and see!*

He kicked moodily at the stump of a tree. Did she love him, as Kazan said? Surely not. She was angry because he had stayed away so long and had distressed his parents. He glared at a bed of thyme. And she would be betrothed to Robert ap Gruffudd. A good man but too old for her. He stopped short. There she was, ahead of him, sitting in the arbour that his mother had always loved above all others.

'Esyllt? I didn't expect to see you here.'

'Why not? I often come here.'

She was surly. He approached her cautiously, stopped by her side. He didn't know what to say. And then the question: 'Are you truly going to marry Robert ap Gruffudd?'

'Why not? He is a good man. He is a man of property. It is a good match.'

'He is too old for you.'

'There are many good marriages made between young women and old men.'

'Esyllt, this is not for you.'

'Not for me? How dare you say so? It is nothing to do with you! You have been home barely a day and you – you not even my brother – you dare tell me what I must and must not do!'

He was angry. She was nothing but a pert young girl, not even pretty, despite her dark hair and dark blue eyes. Kazan was wrong. Esyllt had no love for him. He wondered if she had love for anyone. She had grown up spoilt and selfish. He shrugged. 'As you say. It is nothing to do with me. I am sorry. I should not have spoken. Goodnight.'

He couldn't sleep. It was the strangeness of being here, he told himself, home again. He woke early and rode up from the *cwm* to the hilltop where there was the great *cromlech* of the giant's grave. Grey sky swirled over grey stones. The fierce wind had dropped and soft rain was falling so that the hills were outlined in grey and darker grey. Here was where Arthur of All Britain killed the giant, and there was the imprint of the giant's elbow where he had fallen. Long ago, Giles had terrified Esyllt with this tale of the giant, and she had shuddered and looked about her in case the monster appeared. And King Arthur? It was said he slept somewhere underground with his men, and he would come again when the country most needed him. But the country had needed him, and he had not come. A story, then, for silly girls and credulous boys. There was no great hero who would come to rescue the world.

He clambered up on to the great capstone, his feet and hands scrabbling at familiar holds. The stone was dark and slippery with rain and moss. He sat on its top feeling the cold wetness penetrate through his breeches. The persistent drizzle had already soaked his hair and the shoulders of his cotehardie. He stared out over the valley and grey-on-grey hills. June, and as windswept and grey-clouded as if it were winter. He should never have come here. Oh yes, his mother and his father were overjoyed to see him. Messengers had been sent to his brothers and his sisters and no doubt some or all would soon arrive and there would be feasting to welcome home the Prodigal. Not all. Simon was dead, burned alive for his faith. Simon would never return home. His choice, Giles reminded himself, to give his life to save a child. Only Giles-the-Prodigal had returned home. Home? His home was with Dafydd and their band of travellers. This was no place for him. Not now. His dismal thoughts went round and round. He didn't hear the quiet approach of horse and rider until the jingle of harness made him look up. Horse and rider came closer, almost eye-level with him, perched as he was on the top of this great *cromlech*.

'Do you remember,' Esyllt said, 'when you told me about the giant and I was so frightened?'

'I was thinking about it. Why have you come here?'

'I saw you ride this way. I knew you would come here. I wanted to make my peace with you. We have known each other many years, Giles. We are brother and sister and I should not have been so angry with you last night.'

'We are not brother and sister.'

That dark blue gaze levelled at him. 'You hate me.'

'Never, Esyllt. Never. Why do you say so? I say only you must not marry that old goat.'

'He is not an old goat. He is a good man.'

'But not for you.'

'You are so stubborn, and your stubbornness has all but destroyed your mother and your father.'

'Do you think I could have left my brother to die alone?'

'No.' She turned her head away to look out over the spreading country below them. 'What you did then was right and good, Giles. But after…your mother was so very unhappy.'

'My father disowned me, Esyllt. What else could I do but go far away?'

'For so long? To leave us for so long?'

'What else could I do?' he said again. 'Yes, I missed my home. I missed my family.' He risked it. 'I missed you, Esyllt.'

'But not enough, it seems; to stay away so many years.'

'Did you miss me? All those years? Did you wish for me to come home?'

'I saw your mother's suffering, day after day after day. Season after season. Then it was year after year, and still she grieved. Of course I wanted you to come back. For her sake.'

Day after day after day, here in this sad manor, while he had travelled the wide world and seen strange sights. He had met Thomas, that handsome, dark enigma of a man who had become his great friend; he had met strangers who had become his new family. He had known adventure and danger. This girl had known nothing like that. She had lived here, day after day, season after season, year after year, caring for his grieving mother. He had seen the miniature mosaic in his mother's room, set in a wood panel with gold and multi-coloured stones and gilded copper. A rare work. The Virgin and the Christ Child, she lovingly embracing her son, and her mournful gaze looking forwards to His sacrifice and death. There were candles and incense. Never-ending sadness.

He felt scalding pity for the girl. Little wonder she saw marriage as an escape. To be the lady of a manor was to have a sort of freedom. Yes, this he could understand. But the nights when her aging husband demanded his rights: had she thought of this? He felt his guts heave at the thought.

'You have lived through a difficult time, Esyllt,' he said. 'My mother must be very grateful to you. You have served her well.'

'I love your mother. It was no service.'

'I didn't mean it like that!'

'Like what?'

'As if you were a servant. You know I didn't.' He was almost gritting his teeth in exasperation.

'I don't know what you mean. You are not the same. It has been too many years.'

'Never too many years. When two people love, time is not important.' He remembered Kazan's sad face, her longing for Dafydd, her conviction that he was alive, and suddenly he was calm and determined. 'Listen to me, Esyllt,' he said. 'These people I have travelled with, they are good people who have taught me so much. So very much. One thing I learned is that time is not important. Believe me. The beloved is all, and always they are together, those two, the loved and the beloved.' Kazan's words were ringing in his head. He hardly knew that he was repeating them. 'I love you. I want you for my wife. I cannot bear the thought of you with…' He stopped the words 'old goat'. 'With Robert ap Gruffudd.'

She was silent, not looking at him. The mare she was riding moved restlessly and she stroked the mane, patted the head between the ears, brought her quiet again.

'Do you hear me, Esyllt? I say I love you. I say I want you for my wife.'

'I hear you. The whole mountainside hears you, and the valley.'

'And what do the mountain and the valley say in return?'

'They say Esyllt loves Giles. They say she wants him for her husband.'

Yes, thought Kazan, this plain girl is beautiful now she loves, and knows she is loved in return. Lucky Giles. Lucky Esyllt.

'But I shall come with you to find news of Dafydd's sister and brother,' Giles said. 'No, Kazan, don't play the idiot. You need me with you. Esyllt knows this. She would not let you travel alone.'

'But you should stay here, my friend, to celebrate your betrothal and your marriage.'

'We know what we want. We have waited a long time, and we can wait a little while longer.'

Kazan heaved a huge sigh. Esyllt must wait again? Giles, she thought, you are a fool. That is the talk of a soldier, not a man in love. 'Why does she not come with us?' she asked. 'Esyllt speaks Welsh more readily than French. You speak little Welsh, for all this in-between country is your home.' Mischief lit her eyes. 'Esyllt,' she said thoughtfully, 'would be more use to me than you in Dafydd's country.'

'Is that so? And would Esyllt's sword arm be more use to you than mine?'

'I have my curved bow and my straight arrows.'

'And you are the best of all your tribe. I know. What astonishes me is that no one has wrung your neck. Yet.' He hummed a tune she recognised: the song of Kazan the Hero, the song that Mehmi had played so long ago, it seemed, after her boasting ride, galloping fast, then the sideways slip and up again balancing the bow in her hands and a shaft ready to loose. And another to follow the first before galloping back to the watching men and pulling on the reins so the mare reared up, dancing her forelegs in the air.

'*I am the hero Kazan whose boasting words fly faster than arrows,*' Giles sang softly.

'He was so angry,' Kazan said.

He watched her downcast face a moment. 'I'm sorry, little blue brother,' he said. 'I meant to make you laugh, not give you pain.'

'I know.'

'He was frightened for you as I am frightened for Esyllt. It might be a dangerous journey.'

Kazan snorted, more boy than girl. His face flushed. 'All right, Kazan, so you and Agathi were in great danger. You may still be in danger.' She said nothing. Eloquently. 'You think she would want this?'

'Ask her, not me.'

Ask her he did. Her answer was simple. Giles' father's answer was not so simple and not calm but when he saw how his wife smiled, how the grief-lines in her face were smoothed out, how his ward's eyes pleaded with him, his fierce refusal faltered. Esyllt spoke Welsh more easily than French, Giles said, and they needed a Welsh-speaker where they were going. Dangerous? No – how could it be? They were travelling into Wales, into Dafydd's country, but it was subdued now. No skirmishes, no revolts. The whole country was quiet. His eyes met Kazan's. Later, he thought, he would light a candle and pray for this sin of half-truth. As for the honour of his ward, Kazan had travelled with him alone and safe, as Dafydd had known she would be, but he would prefer to travel with Esyllt as man and wife. The two women would be company together, with him as escort. Not always comfortable travelling but the wife of a soldier would have to accustom herself to that. Esyllt's eyes opened wider as he pronounced this in a stern, unyielding voice but his father saw the sense in it. Reluctantly, he agreed and sighed over the loss of a good match with that respectable man of property, Robert ap Gruffudd, but privately, not even to his wife. He agreed if they obeyed him in following the route north through the Marches; that way, they could rest with Giles' brothers and sisters at their manors. When they turned west, towards Tegid, there was his own sister Ceridwen. 'Remember your Aunt Ceridwen, boy? And Uncle Eifion? They'll make you welcome. Make sure you stay until the weather is good enough for the journey over the mountains.' Giles nodded and agreed and said nothing of the Anatolian mountains, nor the high, treacherous, snow-covered Alps. Besides, the Welsh mountains might be dwarfs in comparison but they had their own dangers. Water-logged they were; lose the track and you found yourself sinking into waist-high peat pools.

But his mother could not lose Giles so soon. Besides, there was the hand-fasting and celebrations. His eldest brother John arrived with his wife and half-sprung children; John was running to fat, Giles saw with surprise, though John had always been an energetic hunter and falconer. His younger sister arrived with her Welsh husband and two babes-in-arms. Copper-headed, like himself. 'Our manor is near Clun, brother. You must stay with us on your journey.'

A week passed before they rode out from the manor on a morning that welcomed summer's return. A cavalcade, thought Giles; his brother and his family and servants; his sister and her family and her servants. His new wife, excited and nervous in equal measure. He grinned at Kazan, recognizing her carefully concealed impatience at their slow progress. Unseen by the rest, she pulled a face.

They splashed through the ford, riding towards the blue hills that were Dafydd's country.

27

Ieper
June 1337

Cydfyhwman marian môr
Cydaros mewn coed oror…
…Cydadrodd serch â'r ferch fain
(Together to be wandering on the ocean's shore,
Together lingering by the forest's edge…
…Together talk of love with my slim girl)
(Dafydd ap Gwilym: 14ᵗʰC)

Walking wounded. That was what the soldiers call it, isn't it? Walking wounded. Dai cursed his weakness. No sooner out of his bed than longing to be back in it. Two steps and the floor swinging up at him and Thomas gripping his arm as if he were some new-walking *dwt*. Autumn, winter and spring since he'd seen her leave in the flat-bottomed boat, and the summer passing him by. *Leaving. What is that? While the heart remembers, there is no leaving.* But his heart remembered, and still her leaving left him aching, as archers had told him they ached with the emptiness where their lopped fingers used to be, or war veterans their lost limbs. A part of him was missing. More than a part. Not a finger, nor a limb but his very soul. At least she was safe in England, and Giles there to keep her safe. Now they were on the brink of a new war, and the seas between Flanders and England raided by the French, and few boats willing to run the risk since merchant ships had been captured and the men taken prisoner. There was a man he knew, had a fishing boat, small it was but big enough for the crossing to England. Big enough for a few other ventures. Best not speak of that. Big enough to take him and Twm across that stretch of dangerous grey water.

He'd already sent Rémi to search for the man in his usual haunts, and Rémi had found him late one night. Not drunk in some tavern; an austere man, this one, who was never drunk, not even sheep drunk. Sober as a Muslim. His crew had to be sober when it came time to sail – or suffer his punishment. Not one of them had arrived drunk for sailing for years. Not out of fear of their leader, see, but respect. A strange man he was; a rogue and a villain, said the respectable burgers of Ieper. The more money-grabbing they were, the louder their outrage. Others – Heinrijc Mertens amongst them – laughed quietly at his exploits and, equally quietly, sometimes had use of his services.

There might be berths, the man had told Rémi, and a sailing before the end of the week. Too soon to say. Come back in the morning. Dai had said nothing to Twm, nor Heinrijc. Time enough. There'd be an outcry, of course. Best save his ears until he was certain. For over a week now he'd been allowed – allowed! – out of his bed to sit in the inner solar. The window looked out on to the summer garden, herbs in full flower and the orchard trees well-set with fruit, leafy branches rustling in the breeze that always seemed to flow around this town. The sky was clear, pale blue; not the brazen sky of the eastern world. Colours here were soft, muted like those of his own wretched, poverty-stricken little country with its grey, moss-covered rocks and tumbling, darksome rivers and shadowy oak forests. Except on those days of blazing blue: blue sky, blue sea streaked with green and turquoise. Gorse scorching his eyes with its gold blossoming. The Mawddach and Cader Idris and all the lands in between the mountains and the sea. Soon he would see it again. Except…he'd give it all up just to be travelling again across those wide flat spaces with the girl at his side and a *han* at the end of the day, and the marvellous gold-copper-bronze, bright-as-dawn girl lying close to him at night so that if he stretched out a hand…no… not so far as a hand's breadth away. He wanted to lie with her in his arms, her slender body cradled against his, her soft breath on his face. He wanted to know she was his. *Cydadrodd serch â'r ferch fain.*

'Dafydd? Is the wound paining you?'

'It's well enough.' He heard how curt he sounded, and to this most loyal of friends. He forced a grin. 'Stop mollycoddling me. Heinrijc's fussing is bad enough – not to mention Rémi's. They're like old women.' He saw Twm frown. 'It's what you said once, to me and Giles, after we'd met with the bandits. Remember? You'd a fierce arm wound and a temper to match.'

Twm's face cleared. He laughed but his look was shrewd. 'I remember. It was the day Kazan and Mehmi joined us.' He came to stand by Dafydd, looked out of the solar window into the courtyard below and the orchard beyond. Matje's son was there, kicking moodily at the cobblestones. 'Rémi will be longer than you expected,' he said casually. 'I sent him on an errand for me. No doubt he'll bring news from your dubious friend all in good time.'

Dai pulled a face. 'You know then?'

'Of course.'

'Did Rémi tell you?'

'Rémi? Is that likely? No. It's only what I expected, once you were up and out of your bed. It's too soon for you to travel, Dafydd. You know that. You'll undo all the good that's been done.'

'I have to go, Twm.'

'A few more weeks, Dafydd. Wait a few more weeks. Still summer. Still calm sailing, despite this wretched war. You know she's safe with Giles and Edgar and Agathi.' He watched Dafydd's face, said in exasperation, 'You're a stubborn man, Dafydd.'

'So you have always said. You should be used to it by now.' Dai leaned his knee on the window cushions, staring through the window, trying to see why below, down in the courtyard, there was a sudden clamour of voices: Matje's son's shrill squeals; Matje herself, wiping her hands on the cloth she kept wrapped around her, shrieking as loudly as her son; Heinrijc's bright robe, his arms raised in flamboyant welcome. And surely, unmistakeably, that was the broad dialect of a Fen man. Not just any Fen man. 'It's Blue,' he said.

Twm knelt beside him in the window embrasure, squeezing closer to see through the window opening. Rémi's beaming face was staring up at them and next to him…next to him…Blue, Hatice, Mehmi. Niko, wide-mouthed-laughing with delight.

'But how are you come so soon?' Twm asked later, after the greeting and hugging and exclaiming, and Matje had rushed away to the kitchen to prepare tasty food for these weary travellers. 'We know Edgar sent messages begging you to join him but they must only just have arrived. Did you come on wings?'

'Not wings but watter, and ower much of it. We know nowt of messages. We missed you all so we caäme looking. And here we are, saäfe and sound at last, though we've had our share of adventures. What's this about our altar boy? Why's he so keen to have us there? Nowt amiss, is there?'

'Nothing except Agathi with child and needing her Hatice – and Edgar needing your hefty shoulders at that manor of his.'

'Nay, do yer say so? Agathi bearing a bairn?'

It wasn't Blue who spoke: it was Hatice. Dai and Twm stared at her in amazement then burst out in loud laughter. Blue grinned and nodded and hugged his Hatice to him.

'A've made a Fen woman of her,' he said proudly. 'Niko and Mehmi an' all. Don't yer take no heed of these two frim foölk, my lass. Yer'll do well enough with Edgar's people. They'll not be proper Fen foölk but near enough.'

'Frim folk?'

'Foreigners,' Blue grinned. 'What do yer think on that, Welshman?'

'A marvel, Blue.'

The big man's face changed as he looked at the frail brown man sitting in front of him. 'Eh lad, but yer scathed. A nivver thought as A should see it. *Sior* Francesco said as it had been *gravemente male* fer yer, but there's been time enough for yer to shape and yer looks as if yer'd dwine away.'

'We had an encounter with an avalanche in the High Mountains,' Twm said.

'Eh, is that it, then? So did we but it passed us by. Our *marronier* said as there were two English – were that you, then? One as near dead?'

'Dead certainly if it had not been for Thomas here,' Heinrijc Mertens said.

After that, an evening spent in news from Venezia: Elisabeta da Ginstinianis was married after all to Jacopo Trevior. There had been pressure on Francisco and his father to heal the wounds between the two families. The great sea-city mattered more than any one family. 'May'appen,' Blue said, 'Francisco realised as there were nobbut Trevior to take the wench on. Brrr.' He shivered and rubbed his hands together. 'She's as cold as a fish's tail, that one. He's well rid. His part of the bargains was as they'd not live in Venezia. They'll go to the Veneto. Maybe as far as the Great Lake. It's the father A'm that sorried fer.'

There was tale-telling, adventures and near-escapes, wondrous encounters, admiration for Mehmi's *oud* and Niko's *daf*, and for their playing.

'Foölk at Edgar's plaäce, they'll nivver have heard the like,' Blue said proudly. 'Who'd ha thought as our two *giovane* would make sich a joyful sound together.'

'Dafydd has plans to travel to Edgar's "place",' Thomas said.

'Aye well, that's right,' Blue said. 'So he should.'

'As soon as he can arrange a sailing.'

Blue cast a look at Thomas, saw he was at his most austere; at Dai, expressionless; at Heinrijc Mertens, anxious, imploring. 'Ay well, A

❀ 285 ❀

reckon as Dai will have his way. Always does, Tom lad. No need fer fretting. It's doable. We'll be there – keep him safe like. He'll be better for being in England with our little lass. Though they do say as it's hard to get a boat across that pond these days.'

'Dafydd has a way, if Rémi has news.' Thomas' voice was resigned.

Rémi looked at him anxiously then at Dafydd, who nodded. 'Seems they know all, Rémi – except what news you have today.'

A sailing on Friday night, moonless.

'If any man can steer by the stars and keep us safe from the French, it's Jan Cloet.' Dai said.

'Room fer us all?' Blue asked.

'May'appen,' Dai said, at his most imperturbable.

28

July 1337

The Manor of Lord Roger de Langton

Girat, regirat garcifer;
Me rogus urit fortifer;
Propinat me tunc dapifer
(The kitchen-lad turns and turns the spit again;
The pyre burns me fiercely; Now the steward serves me up)
(Carmina Burana, 12*th*/13*th*C)

'Swan for Lord Roger's dinner? Don't talk daft, boy. When does he ever have swan on his platter? Any more than your own master's kitchens.'

'If he does…when he does…'

'Oh aye? Pigs flying, boy. Have done wi' yer chelp.'

'What's this then?'

The old man had crept up on them, quiet despite his bulk. He liked to tour his kitchens, ask Peter Cook what was broiling or baking or roasting, taste a little, savour titbits. If he had little life left to him, how better to use it than in pleasure?

'Sir. Lord Roger. It's this nuzzling lad from Lord Edgar's manor wanting to know if you'd be supping on swan.'

'Swan? You seem very eager for swan meat, child.'

'Not the meat. I want a swan bone. A swan's wing.' Oluf stood his ground. He stared the old man in the face. 'There's none to be had at ours.'

'A swan's wing bone is it? And what use do you have for a swan's wing bone?'

'A pipe,' Oluf said, his eyes bright, eager. 'They say you can make a pipe from the swan wing and when you play it, it sounds like the angel it once was.'

'And when – if – you have the wing, how will you make the pipe?'

Oluf's face was stubborn. 'I don't know but I'll find out how.'

'And when you have made it, do you know how to play it?'

'Not me. It's not for me. It's for Joan. She played Mistress Kazan's pipe that belonged to her grandfather's brother, the music man, and she loved it so, though he was an enemy of King Edward. I want to make a swan pipe for her.' He chucked up his chin, belligerent. 'She deserves it.'

Sir Roger chuckled, working his way through the confused explanation. 'So young. So chivalrous. Of course you must, young sir. Maybe my own minstrel can help you.'

Guillaume was a little rat-faced man, ancient now, a Gascon who had been with Sir Roger for many years. Minstrel he was called but truth be told too old now, and his fingers stiffened and bent. He was a lute player – used to be a lute player – but he knew how to play a pipe. 'I am called Guillaume after *mon père, et son père* before him.' Even after all these years of living in England, his speech was throaty, difficult to follow.

'My father, he give me a pipe of elder when first he come back from the Welsh war. The first Welsh war. A tale so strange. The pipe, it is made by a halfwit. A simple pipe of elder but the sound is true.' The old man's face creased into a grin, and suddenly Oluf could see the boy he had been. 'At first, it sound like – how do you say? *Lâcher un pet*?' He blew out noisily and Oluf giggled.

'Like a fart,' he smirked.

'*D'accord*. Like a fart. It make me laugh. But then, me, I practise and *mon père*, he know I am good. But never so good as the halfwit, he say.' He shrugged, the shrug of a man of Gascony. 'Not a halfwit, say *mon père*, that one, but he had not the use of his tongue.'

He was one of the *parti* being taken to Wales, this halfwit who was not a halfwit, to build the first of Edward's great castles in Wales, his Ring of Iron. They were brave boys, the one who made the pipe and the young brother who looked after him. 'Never am I forgetting what he tell me, *mon père. Pauvre petits.* Taken to war like that, and the younger a boy about my own age. I wonder what happen to them. So long ago. *Mort*, I suppose, and me, I am well on the way to my grave. *Dieu soit béni.* Ah well. Lord Roger, he has the need of a new minstrel but still he keeps me here. A difference, having a good master. You wish for a swan pipe? *Le bon Dieu* knows you do not ask for much, do you, *petit coquin*!'

There was a swan, of course; Roger de Langton made sure of that. He was beguiled by the boy's unswerving purpose. A villein's son a *chevalier*? When Edgar came visiting, he found Lord Roger determined to hold a feast with the mutilated swan at its glorious centre. The old man was absorbed in discussing its roasting with his cook. The largest iron spit, the square one, that would be best; easier to turn, better for carrying the heavy weight of the swan; and iron made for quicker roasting than wooden spits. 'That's my advice, my Lord Roger,' Peter Cook said. 'Well larded and basted to keep it moist.' He'd always thought that strange; a waterfowl's nature was moist and wet yet a swan was dry and tough unless it was well larded.

'And with Chaudron sauce?'

'Of course, my Lord.' Peter Cook's face spoke what his tongue did not: what else but that sauce made with the swan's entrails ground with bread and powdered ginger and galingale, coloured with blood, well boiled and strained and seasoned with a little vinegar.

Edgar listened to the two men, both in the autumn of their lives, and just like Kara Kemal. He wondered if the thoughts of all old men were set on food, then remembered Dafydd, and Thomas' joking 'mind always on your stomach?' Perhaps it was those who had lived through the Great Famine years who never forgot starvation.

'Edgar my boy, we haven't had such a treat in this manor for too long now. Blessings on the head of that young rogue of yours.'

'My young rogue?'

'That boy of Bernt's. What's his name? Oluf? Came begging a swan's wing to make into a pipe for that little maid he's so fond of.'

Edgar started to laugh. 'Oluf did that? For Joan?'

'Don't mock the boy, Edgar. He's a fine young man.' He shot a sharp glance at Edgar. 'Says young Joan finds kitchen and dairy work hard going. Too heavy for a young lass like that – not much meat on her.'

Edgar nodded. 'He's probably right.' He hadn't even thought of it, he who so prided himself on caring for the people of his manor. Joan was small and slight. He remembered now how he'd seen her slumped sometimes in the yard, her copper hair screwed back from her face, bracing herself when she was shouted for from the dairy or the kitchen. A young girl, not more than – what – eight summers? And still she'd found time to teach Kazan to play the swan pipe. 'So Oluf has his swan wing?'

'And busy with it now.' Edgar raised his eyebrows. 'With Guillaume, who was the best of minstrels until age had him by the tail, just as it has me.'

The two of them worked together, an old man irritated by his own useless hands, and the young peasant boy used only to manual work. Together, they cleaned the hollow bone, inside and out, until it gleamed like moonshine; then the careful measuring and drilling of the seven holes. 'This must be true, *petit*. There must be not one mistake.' Four low and three high. Then the mouthpiece, bevelled securely to the distal end of the gleaming bone. At last it was done. Guillaume and Oluf stared at each other. 'Now it is the pretty Jeanne who must blow *esprit* into this wing of the dead swan.'

Roger de Langton held his marvellous feast. He made sure the girl was there, though she was red-faced-sweating in the kitchens. Oluf served at the tables, subduing his excitement so that he would be worthy of the honour shown him by this kind old gentleman. Such kindness. Such unlooked for kindness. His da and ma were somewhere in the hall because Sir Roger had invited all of the manor of Bradwell, sokemen and villeins and cottars alike. 'In the fashion of the old days,' Guillaume had told him. Oluf knew his ma and da were watching him walk with the other waiters behind the Marshal and Sewer to the top table. He bowed, keeping time with the rest, and turned to kneel by the Carver. All the same, it was a struggle to contain himself until the moment when Lord Roger called for silence. And then for music. He demanded that the girl Joan come forward. 'She is responsible for our mutilated swan,' he announced. 'Yes, call her from the kitchen,' he said impatiently.

She came, her red hair frowzled by the heat and steam, her shoulders sagging from the heavy labour, small and shy amongst this grand company.

'You can play the swan pipe, they tell me,' said Lord Roger.

'Only what I've played for Mistress Kazan,' the girl murmured. She glanced nervously around all the great company there at the tables, and her own kind sitting at the lower tables. There was Hilda, and there Oluf's ma and da. She was red-faced with it all, hating being the centre of attention.

'Then you can play this one.' Lord Roger beckoned to Oluf and he stepped forward, proud and smiling, holding the swan pipe before him. Guillaume was behind him, his thin rat's face proud and anxious.

Joan gasped. 'This pipe? My Lord?'

'This pipe, my girl, made especially for you by this young man of yours and my old friend Guillaume. Ah, what it is to be young.'

The girl took the pipe in her hands. She was no longer sagging-shouldered. She stood upright, as if at a command. Her eyes were glinting green-yellow like catkins in the spring sunshine. Her hair gleamed coppery-red in the torchlight. Just once she looked at Oluf and her small, tired face lifted in a glimmering smile. She raised the pipe to her lips. She breathed life into the dead bone and a thread of wavering notes spilled out into the hall until the pipe sang like the angel it had once been.

29

The Marches
August 1337

I love the sea coast of Meirionnydd
Where a white arm was my pillow
I love the nightingale in the green wood
In the sweet vale where two waters meet.
(Hywel Ab Owain Gwynedd: d.1170, trans. Tony Conran)

They were not high mountains, not like those in the Great Plateau of Anatolia, nor the High Mountains they had crossed in late autumn, but there was a sense of space and of being very high. The roof of Wales, she thought. I am on the roof of Dafydd's country. That morning it seemed the sun had not risen so black were the clouds, great towers of them, swirling above and about them, and the edge of the mountains even darker against them. A brooding, alien world, this country of Dafydd's. Later, much later, as they neared the highest point of the pass, the darkness thinned to greys with lighter grey and in places a white sky. *Oerddrws. Bwlch Gwynt.* Windy Gap. It lived up to its name. The dark mountains were green now, with dark splotches that were the peat bogs they had been warned of. *Keep to the paths* they had been told. *There's peat bogs as will suck you in if you strays.* And so they kept to the route, well-trodden because this was the way the pilgrims came on their way to Saint David's. *You should be travelling in a pilgrim party. It's not safe elsewise. There's bandits between Oerddrws and Mawddwy.* In the end, they were joined by a solitary pilgrim. 'You must call me Huw,' he told them the first morning. 'This is my second journey to St David's in the far west of this country.' Two journeys to Saint David's were equal to one to Rome. That was what he said; what they had said, those pilgrims they had travelled with in England. But there was range on range of high hills between them and the comfort of an inn. Suddenly sharp sun shone through a cleft in the clouds and there was a flash of rainbow. They stopped to look, gazing back the way they had come. Dark clouds, and the rainbow an underbelly turning the underside of the clouds into rainbow colours.

'That is surely a good omen!' Esyllt breathed. Esyllt was a good girl, Kazan acknowledged. It had been all holiday at first, travelling from manor to manor of Giles' brothers and brothers-in-law, and then they had left Giles's wren-like Aunt Ceridwen and her placid husband Eifion in their manor near Tegid. 'All these brothers and sisters and aunts and uncles,' Kazan said. 'This is like Amir, and his cousins of cousins of cousins.'

'Not so bad as that,' Giles said, and they laughed, and told Esyllt the story of the guide Amir, and how he had cousins of cousins of cousins in every part of Anatolia. They told her of the journey to Attaleia, and Esyllt's dark blue eyes opened wide and wider. It was after that Kazan found her saddened.

'How can he love me, Kazan? I have done nothing. I have been nowhere. How can he love me?'

'He loves you. You are his wife. And you have been on a journey as great as his. Do not mistake that. A different journey but difficult for all that. Now your journeys are ended and you meet and your meeting is sweet. This is good, Esyllt. Your souls and your hearts meet, and your bodies make an even sweeter meeting.'

The girl blushed fiery crimson. 'That is not for maids to talk of,' she said.

'But it is the truth.'

They started the journey along the banks of the great lake,

following the track that would lead over the mountain pass. At first horrified by their solitary travelling and often rough lodging, Esyllt had become accustomed to it, had enjoyed new-found freedom. Everything was astonishing to her. But Giles, she reminded herself, had been in stranger places, had met stranger people. Kazan was glad to see the girl's better understanding of her new husband.

Now here they were, riding the pilgrim route across the roof of the Welsh world and it was summer, she told herself, a Welsh summer. This is Dafydd's country, and it is beautiful, but so cold and so wet.

The track levelled out across the summit of *Bwlch Oerddrws* then began its downward journey, past the great cross that had marked the parting of the tracks for long time past. Here and there were stone huts, *hafotai,* the summer dwellings, built alongside fast-running streams and with small sheep folds close by. They were hailed at one, and welcomed, and asked the questions all travellers were asked. Where have you come from? Where are you going? Best not tell too much, Giles had warned the two girls, but the lie that they were pilgrims travelling to St David's, that stuck in Kazan's throat. 'To Cymer Abbey,' she said.

'Then you've not far to go,' the shepherd said. He shared sheep's cheese with them, and bright, clear water. 'There's a spring higher up,' he said. 'It never dries up.'

Not surprising, Giles thought, with so much rain. Did God have rain clouds especially for this country of Dai's? He shook the blasphemy from his thoughts and muttered a prayer for forgiveness. The shepherd was grinning at him, weather-beaten face creasing. 'It's not always like this, young sir. Some days there's blue sky and white cloud and God smiles on this land of ours.'

Giles' ruddy face reddened even more but he laughed back. 'Frowning today, is he?'

'Frowning on our enemies more like.' The man's mouth clamped shut after that.

They travelled downwards, sheer rock rearing high above them, dark against the shifting grey cloud-mist blown by a chill wind that funnelled through the valley. High above, the cloud-mist shifted again and white cloud gleamed through, lighting the whole valley. High above, tiny on the steep sides, a man's bent figure stood silhouetted against the pouring light. A turf-cutter. In this country, the pilgrim Huw told them, they relied on peat turves for fire and warmth but the land was too steep for horses and so the men toiled up the mountain sides to cut the turves and stack them and heave them on to a hurdle – a *glwyd-fawn* – that they would coax down the steep mountainside. A perilous work. Brave men lived here.

There was lodging in the village, Huw said, at the foot of the pass. It was the place of the *hendre*, the winter lodgings, and there was an ancient church where pilgrims such as himself could receive blessing. Travellers too, like themselves. As for him, he would spend a day here with an old friend who wanted to journey with him to St David's. 'Tomorrow, you must follow the river to Mawddwy. Anyone there will give directions to Cymer.'

It was a fast-rushing river that tumbled clamorously along its rocky bed and tumbled white-edged over rocky falls. Oak trees buffeted their branches together, green leaves writhing and hissing, but today there was no dark cloud mist sweeping the high tops; a white-over sky, true, but in its clear light they could see white falling water tumbling down clefts in the steep valley sides, leaping great grey boulders to swell the river they followed. Not far to go. The valley was already opening out, as they had been told. Soon the village would be in sight. Wasn't that the church? Giles had to almost shout to make himself heard.

They didn't hear the horsemen. They had no warning. It was too sudden for defence. Kazan fumbled for her curved bow and arrows but the leader laughed and plucked them from her. She lashed out, angry, determined to thwart these bad men, these robbers. He laughed louder and grasped her more securely, pulling her from

Yıldız and on to his own strong horse. He plucked the sharp-bladed dagger from her before she could use it.

'Giles,' she yelled. 'Giles. What are you doing?' He was making no attempt to defend them. She could not believe it of him.

'I'm not sure, Kazan. I'm not sure. They say we must go with them.'

She was smothered in the man's strong hold. He glanced down at her, grinned, and said something she could not understand. She writhed and bit down hard on the base of his thumb. He cursed but did not let go his hold. They were riding away from the river, away from Mawddwy, up a rock-strewn track then down into a narrow cwm and up again, up a steep, precipitous path, up another valley side. Trees tumbled down its sides, and beyond rose ridge on ridge of hills, jerking and jumping with the movement of the horse. Up, to a levelled out plateau where there were make-shift dwellings of rough-hewn stone: longhouses with room for animals. Here they stopped. Kazan's rider flung himself off his horse, pulling her down with him and keeping her tight in his hard hold, his sleeve half-suffocating her. He was shouting something she could not understand but it was Dafydd's language, she was sure. Esyllt and Giles were close to her. No rough bandit holding them tight-close, she fumed.

Giles said, 'Kazan, I think...'

Her voice was muffled, angry. 'You think! You do nothing but think! You did nothing. These *barbar* – these robbers – you did nothing! Coward! I spit in your face.'

'Kazan, I think they are...'

The man who had taken her so roughly on his horse and held her roughly even now laughed loudly. 'Dai warned us you'd be trouble,' he said, but she couldn't understand him. Esyllt was smiling. Smiling?

'Now then, pretty miss, sure it's welcome you are.'

'I do not understand what you say and I do not know what you want of us, *barbar*,' she said haughtily in the French tongue Edgar had taught her and Agathi. The man laughed again.

'Nothing but your own sweet self,' he answered in the same language. 'That's all we're after.' He called across in Welsh to a man emerging from the nearest longhouse. 'Sure, you could have warned us, Dai. She's a snarling, spitting wildcat.'

'I did warn you, Conor. I told you to take her bow and arrows from her, first thing you did, and after that her knife.'

'It's a bitten thumb I have here. Bitten down to the bone.'

'More fool you. Greetings, Kazan. How is it with you?'

She stared and stared and felt the earth tilt under her. She felt as she had felt on the tilting deck of the ship when fierce waves surged under and around them. Coming towards her was the brown man, the quiet man who some called dangerous and who she had left behind in Venezia in such peril. The man who had been in her thoughts and her mind and her heart all these long, long months. *I would give my heart and soul and life for you.*

'You have done this,' she cried. 'You sent these *barbar* to take us! Shame on you!'

Above her the clouds swirled and shifted. Below her the earth heaved and bulged. The man in front of her was blurring then clearing then blurring again. Then there was only blurring and blackness. She sagged in the grip of the man who held her. Not such a wildcat, he thought, and held her secure but gently now.

Ages had passed. Could have passed. She had no idea. She was lying flat on the ground under a stunted, green-leaved oak tree. Its leaves flickered and danced. Dark. Light. Dark again. Somewhere in the distance was laughter. Giles' voice, and the hateful *barbar* who had held her captive. Esyllt's gentle voice. The clouds still swirled overhead but the terrible blurring and blackness had receded. Thomas? That was surely Thomas' voice and sharp laugh.

Warm breath on her forehead.

'Better now, my Kazan?'

Not flat on the ground. She was lying on a rough blanket close to Dafydd. She put a hand to her head, trying to make sense of this new world.

'Still angry with me, *cariad*?'

'Is it you? Truly you?'

'Truly, *fy nghariad.*' He was stroking her hair, smoothing away fear as he had done that terrible night in Attaleia, but now he was smoothing away his own fear as well. Safe now. Safe. His own sobbing in terror in the blackest night. His fear that he would not live to see her again. She was nestled against him, her face burrowed against his sleeve as she had that night in Attaleia, that night of terror.

'Am I your *cariad*?'

'Always. Forever.'

Somewhere there was male laughter and a woman's voice speaking in Welsh, answered by Esyllt. Then Giles' voice stumbling over Welsh words, and Thomas speaking slowly, carefully in Anglo-French, but she was conscious only of the roughness of Dafydd's tunic against her face, of his arms holding her close against him.

'Never let me go. Never again.'

'Never again. Never.'

No more words. No need for words. This Welshman whose language turned out crooked just when he needed it most; this time he had no need of words. She was his, this gold-copper-bronze maid. Bright Kazan of the golden eyes was his, heart and soul, and the promise of her slender body cradled against his in the night, her soft breath on his face: the promise of knowing she was his. *Cydadrodd serch â'r ferch fain.*

Old man, Kara Kemal, how did you know?

Later, there were stories exchanged. Thomas told of the terrors of the High Mountains. Dafydd was silent. Kazan shuddered and remembered that strange day in Ieper when she had felt such suffocation she could not breathe, and the black whiteness, and she wondered though she said nothing. Giles told of their journey to

Ieper, and then to Swineshead and Boston, and the news of her grandfather's death, and then the ride to Bradwell and rescuing Edgar from the wild boar. Dai remembered that moment when he had roused from his deep sleep and tried to call her name and she had heard him, and he wondered though he said nothing.

There was the story of the three brothers to be told, and Alfred's shame, and his wife's wickedness, and how Edgar was now lord of his own manor.

There was Kara Kemal's death to be mourned all over again, and the story of Blue and Hatice and Niko and Mehmi to be wondered at.

'You mean they are here?'

'In England, at Edgar's manor. Hatice has taken charge of Agathi. Blue was planning a new barn when we left. He was eyeing over the black poplars that grow on the manor grounds. You know the ones?'

Giles nodded. The very ones Alfred had intended for the new build at Rochby.

'What of Niko?'

'Happy to be with his sister, Kazan, but disappointed you weren't there to greet him. As for our Mehmi, he is a great success.'

Tom laughed. 'There's a little girl, a scrawny little copper-knob…'

'Joan,' Kazan said.

'That's it. Taught you how to play your grandfather's swan pipe, from what I hear. Got one of her own now, thanks to her young man.'

'Oluf? Oluf made her a swan pipe? But they are babes!'

Tom shrugged. 'As you say. Babes. But not too young for heart burning. The joke is that Mehmi's much taken with her, and Niko. Say she's a true musician. So the three of them play together – pipe, *oud*, *daf* – and the young swain's eaten up with jealousy. Now there's a story to unravel, Kazan.'

'But that is not a joke, Thomas. That is very sad.'

'Then you'd best get back there and sort it out.'

'Oluf and Niko, they are enemies then?'

'That's the strange thing. Start, yes, they eyed each other up and down as if they'd like to *tek a poäke* at each other, as Blue put it.' She laughed at his mimicry but fondly. She loved the big, blue man-mountain. 'But then,' Thomas continued, 'it was as if they'd known each other all their lives long. Close as close.' He grinned. 'Twice the mischief.'

She shook her head, disbelieving still that here was dark, handsome Thomas, here with Dafydd, and not in some distant friary.

'Not made a monk of you yet, Thomas?' Giles asked.

'Not been the time, these past months,' Tom said carelessly, 'what with this one needing rescuing and the rest of you scattered the good God knew where. Later. Time enough.'

No word spoken of Dafydd's imprisonment and torture; no need to see his slight shake of the head. But Kazan knew. She had seen his weakness, his fatigue, though his spirit kept him vital.

'Thomas,' she asked later, 'is he well enough?'

'Well enough, Kazan, but that is all. He insisted on travelling here. He knew you were heading here. He came for you but I won't lie to you. It has exhausted him.'

'I am grateful to you for taking such care of him, Thomas.'

'And I am grateful to you who love him and have given him life.'

'You do not doubt me now, Thomas?'

The dark man shook his head. 'No, Kazan, no doubts. I am happy for you both. I only hope you are not angry with me for what I said to you in Venezia.'

'Never!' she cried. 'Never! You are our great friend. Without you, he would be dead. Without you, I would never have known he loved me. We need you with us, Thomas. Must you truly join the friars?'

'Truly, Kazan, I must.' He smiled, his dark face lit with happiness. 'May'appen, as friend Blue would say, it is enough to be with the friary in Lincoln. Then I can do God's work and still see my little family at Edgar's manor.'

'That is a good choice, Thomas.'

Time enough as well for Dafydd to tell her of his journey. He had not found her at Edgar's manor. She had gone, travelling on to find what trace she could of his family, seeking to do what he had determined to do himself. And so he had followed her. First to the old home, deserted now, walls tumbling, shaped stone robbed out. Dark it was. Forlorn. *No fire, no light. Grieving overcomes me.* Dafydd had stood silent, the words of the old song in his head. *It wounds me to see it, with no roof, no fire. Dead is my lord yet I live.*

She had not been here. He knew she had not been here. Where was she?

'Where now?' Thomas asked.

To the Abbey of Cymer where Dafydd was remembered with affection. But she had not been there.

'Still the same poverty-stricken abbey that it always was.' Father Abbot sighed. A *Sais* abbot but bound up with this strange country of the *Cymro*. 'So troubled by Edward's last war. The first Edward, I mean.'

So much trouble, Thomas knew, that Edward had given £80 in compensation. Compensation! For lives lost and this holy place desecrated.

'Because it was loved by our last prince,' Dafydd said. His crown, the *talaith*, given into the safe-keeping of the monks of Cymer but taken from them by the first Edward, as he had taken the *Croes Nawdd*, that sacred relic of the Holy Cross, to be paraded in London as proof that he had vanquished the hated Welsh. So long ago. So many years in between: before the terrible years of famine and Dai's father dead in that hopeless revolt against the *Sais* and for him the moon and the stars had shifted and slipped and his world had tumbled.

'We have wanted to build a tower to the glory of God for so many years,' Father Abbot said wistfully. 'Perhaps it is God's will that we have never done so. Perhaps it is His wish to remind us that we are humble before Him.' He smiled at the two weary men. 'You must be tired after all your travelling. Come. Rest and food and drink. This is what you need. We do not have riches but what we have we share.'

'Sharing is riches, Father,' Dafydd said. How lucky he had been, he thought, to have met such men as Heinrijc Mertens and Kara Kemal of blessed memory. How they had honeyed the bitterness of his life. And these friends of his, these loyal, loving friends: riches shared indeed. And Kazan…no, don't think of her gold-copper-bronze beauty, her gold-rimmed eyes…don't think or he would be lost indeed. Was she here? Would she come? Aiming for his home, Edgar had said, for Dafydd's home and his family, if any were left alive.

The Abbot's blue eyes were penetrating, intent on Dafydd. 'You have suffered, I think, my son, and your wounds still trouble you. Our Brother Tanwg will see to that. Come. Let us make you comfortable. And you also, Dafydd's friend, for I think you have suffered much for his sake.'

Later, after they had rested and eaten, he told them what he knew. 'Your brother died but your sister lived. She is married and has a child. A boy.'

Alive! One at least out of all this wreck was living, and with a son. Except…

'She married one of the English lords,' Father Abbot told them. 'His manor is not far from here. Close to Dolgethley. It has a market now. It promises to be a wealthy town.'

Dolgethley, the town of the bonded men, the villeins, the un-free; valued now because it was so well placed, between the rivers of the Wnion and the Aran, and close to the mouth of the Mawddach and its sea routes. The next day, lowering and dull as any Dai remembered, they splashed across the ford, safe crossing place on this rushing, dark Wnion, and into the land beyond the town. They found the manor easily, nestled into a *cwm*, stone-built like so many in this place, hefty, fortified against attack by the Welsh because this was the manor of a *Sais* lord and while the Welsh were suppressed who knew when these treacherous peasants would rise against their lords?

Dafydd's sister was alone. He hardly recognised her. He'd last seen her as a *dwt*, a scrawny, starving *dwt*, and now here she was, the blooming wife of a wealthy man, and with her own *dwt* in her arms. She wasn't pleased to see him.

'I thought you were dead. What are you doing here?'

'Come to find you, little sister. Our brother too, God have mercy on his soul, poor child.'

'It's glad I am to see you alive, brother, but you can't stay here. If my husband knew about you – the past – the bandits – you can't stay here, Dai.'

'No need to worry, *cariad*. It's happy I am to see you alive and living well – and with this little one, this *dwt* who looks so much like *Taid*.'

'Don't hate me for marrying an Englishman,' she said, suddenly.

'I don't,' he said. 'How could I? Twm here is *Sais,* and my great friend. I owe him my life twice over and more. Time we forgot old enmities, isn't it?'

Thomas understood only part of the rapid exchange of Welsh. Dafydd told him the bare facts. It was enough. It had always been enough, even in Ieper. Restlessly insistent on journeying to England; in England, even that joyful meeting at Edgar's manor, as soon as Dafydd knew that Kazan and Giles had left for Wales, nothing would do but to follow them, find them. Once, it had been important to find his family, or what remained of it, but now it was Kazan he searched for, as she was searching for what remained of his family. They were riding through the pass between Cymer and Dinas when the bandits encircled them. Menacing, tough, careless, hopelessly out-numbering them. Dafydd was weakened by the journey and yet he laughed.

'Put that sword away, Conor *bach*,' he said. 'Stop your swaggering.

You're no more descended from the Kings of Ireland than I am from our Last Prince. Don't you recognise me?'

'Dai bach? Is it you? Sure, fancy that now. What are you doing here, Dai bach?'

And so they had taken shelter with Conor's gang of bandits and waited for news of Giles and Kazan. 'Sure, we'll hear the word, Dai. We always do. We couldn't have survived if the *gwladwyr* did not help us.'

So they had waited and waited and wondered that the journey could take so long. 'They should have been here weeks ago,' Dai fretted.

'There's been bad weather, Dafydd. All those storms and those wild west winds of yours. They've taken shelter, for sure. Remember Edgar told us how Giles talked of visiting his family?'

'But *after* coming here, Twm. *After.*'

Thomas shrugged. 'Like I say, may'appen they hit the bad weather. Giles wouldn't take her on in that.'

'May'appen,' Dai agreed but he was still frowning.

Then there was word that two women and a man had been seen travelling the pilgrims' path over *Bwlch Oerddrws*. 'Not pilgrims, Conor, though there's one of the praying sort with 'em.' *Two* women? It couldn't be them. But it was. The shepherd at the *hafoty* had recognised them as the ones looked for, and had sent swift word, and so Conor had set out with his men to intercept them, and bring Kazan safe to Dafydd.

'But you, my friend Giles, have kept her safe all this time.'

'Of course. I promised you.' Best kept to himself forever his secret love for bright Kazan. Not even for the confessional. He would confess to God himself, and his crucified Son, and pray forgiveness. Perhaps he was forgiven? To be rewarded with his own Esyllt – surely that was for sins forgiven?

As if Dai had read his thoughts he said, 'And you found yourself a wife!'

'Isn't it astonishing? Kara Kemal would say *Allah has decided.*'

'Always room for faith, eh?'

'Always.' Giles sighed. 'So long since we left you. Was it very bad?'

'Yes.'

'I am sorry I was not with you.'

'My dear friend, you did the best that could be done. You got them to safety. You kept them safe. We were relying on you to do just that.'

'All the same…'

'All the same…thank the good God for Giles!' Thomas laughed and, after a moment, Giles laughed with him.

30

Cymer
August 1337

Woe's me that foul misfortune felled him,
Woe's me his loss
(Gruffudd Ab Yr Ynad Coch, c. 1282)

That night there was feasting and singing and dancing. Drinking as well. Conor was known as a drinking man and the more he drank the more he sang, off-tune and out of key.

'As bad as Blue,' Giles complained.

'You wrong our man-mountain,' Thomas said. 'Blue's a reformed man. As sober as a Muslim.'

'A shame this Conor of yours had no dealings with our Muslim friends, Dai.'

'Each to his own,' Dafydd said. He felt intoxicated himself but not by drink. If he glanced across at her – as he did now – and caught her eye – as he did now – he rejoiced again and again that she was his, promised to him, and soon she would be given to him in the presence of a good God he had all but ceased to believe in. *Who are you to decide what is and what is not to be? Only Allah the all-compassionate, the all-knowing decides.* Allah – God: the thinnest of thin gauze between them. Who was to tell which was the greater? Who was to tell which the greater believers? Impossible and useless. Same but different. Different but the same. All he knew was that a great good had led this gold-copper-bronze, golden-eyed girl to him;

had given her to him. He gave thanks to all the gods there were for this great joy, and if the priests declared there was blasphemy in his joy, the good God would forgive him. All the gods would forgive him. He smiled, content. Thomas dropped down beside him.

'Will you stay here?' he asked Dafydd.

'I don't think so. My sister is well married and does not need me.' He shrugged. 'Let's be fair now, I'm an embarrassment to her. If it were known I was come back here, and it's remembered I was once one of this gang of bandits, it could only do Branwen harm. I could only give Kazan the life of an outlaw. They both deserve better than that. Then there's Heinrijc. He's grown old these last years. I owe it to him to go back to Ieper, especially now with this new war beginning.' He sighed. War. Always war meddling with lives.

'What does Kazan want?'

'Kazan wants to be with Dafydd.' She spoke from behind them, came to stand in front of Thomas. 'That is all Kazan wants, Thomas. Where he goes, I go. Where he stays, I stay. His people are my people and his God my God. Where he dies, I die, and there we shall be buried. Is that priest talk enough for you?'

Thomas took her hands in his and, turning them, kissed the palms one by one then folded her fingers over them and kissed the folded fingers. 'More than enough, Kazan, dear sister, dear woman and promised wife of my true friend Dafydd. I give thanks to our good God and his son Jesus that you came to us.' He grinned suddenly, his serious face vanishing. 'And I give thanks as well to the good Allah and his son Mohammed.'

Dafydd threw back his head and laughed and laughed. 'Those friars, Twm, they don't know what they're getting now, do they?'

Thomas shrugged and laughed with him. 'I don't think they do.'

'And you, my friend, where will you go now?'

Twm laughed again, happier than they had ever seen him. 'I have told Kazan I think perhaps back to Lincoln. There's a Franciscan house in the town and I may as well be there as anywhere. Close enough to Edgar and Agathi, should they have need of me. We can all travel together, see Giles and Esyllt home, then back to Bradwell, may'appen?' He was smiling, his dark face handsome and glowing. 'Or is that not pleasing to two pairs of turtle doves?'

Kazan darted up and kissed his cheek. 'It is very pleasing, Thomas,' she said. 'I so want to see the new barn Blue is building. And Agathi and Ellen must be big with their babes by now. I want to hear what new mischief Niko has he got up to with Oluf.' She fingered the swan pipe. 'Perhaps Mehmi and Niko and Joan will let me play with them.'

'Play for us now, storyteller's granddaughter.'

'I do not play so well.'

'Neither did your grandfather, by all accounts.' Conor leaned across, grinning foolishly at them through a haze of ale. 'It was his brother who could coax the angel out of the swan pipe. So my *tad* said. A better bard than even Ieuan ap y Gof himself, and himself a *pencerdd*.' He hoisted his wooden cup into the air, splashing ale. 'All the same, play for us, savage little thumb-biter.'

She chuckled then fingered the drilled holes in the length of the pipe; her fingers rubbed along its smoothness, felt the scarring marks that had come there in its other life. Then she raised it and started to play, a thread of wavering notes spilling out into a night sky that was cloudless now, and bright with stars that were cut and crumbled from the fat old moon. It was the song of Ieuan ap y Gof, and the men and their women listening felt their hearts ache with sadness for their broken country.

The next morning was as bright blue as Dafydd could have wished. 'See what it's like, Kazan, on these blue-gold days!' he exulted. 'All the rain and wind and black skies – isn't it worth it for a day like this?' He kissed her joyfully 'I want you to see the Mawddach, the most beautiful river in the whole wide world, and the most beautiful meeting of river and sea.'

She smiled to see his boyish pleasure. It was a Dafydd she had never seen before. And truly, on a gold-blue day like this, it was a different country. Glad summer had returned, and with it swallows that swooped and dived after the milling insects; an invisible lark trilled high in the sky; a pair of buzzards mewed and circled high and higher on warm winds.

They were a small cavalcade: Dafydd and Kazan; Giles and Esyllt; Thomas and a head-clutching, groaning Conor; Sion his brother scarcely in better health; and Sion's woman Mair, soberly disapproving. They rode over the mountain almost as far as Cymer's gatehouse then trekked up the steep sides to the very top of the tall crag. There they stopped. And looked. No need for crooked words.

The Mawddach rolled down to a sea that was glittering in streaks of silver and dark blue, and blue and periwinkle and green like new apple leaves. It was a cloth of light. It was beautiful. And this – this – was Dafydd's country. She stood silent. It was as beautiful as the sight of the glittering blue of the sea far below her when she sat on the highest, loftiest, topmost point of the ruined city close by the *yürük* summer camp. Far below was Cymer Abbey; nothing grand about it, not even a crossing nor a tower for its church, but sturdy and enduring for all that. Around them rose the mountains. Nothing like the high mountains of her own country, nor the terrifying High Alps, but sturdy and enduring for all that. Mair said, 'See that mountain? Cadair Idris, it's called – the Chair of Idris. Whoever sleeps on that mountain through the night wakes a poet – or a madman.'

'May'appen that's what I should do,' Dafydd said. 'May'appen a night on the mountain would make a poet out of me.'

'May'appen a madman,' Twm said, at his most sardonic. 'Best keep what wits you've got left to you, Dafydd *bach*.' He mouthed the Welsh word carefully, making them laugh.

'Sure, if it got rid of this vile head of mine, I'd be spending the night there.' Conor rubbed bleary eyes. '*Pen mawr*, thumb-biter, that's what it is now. *Pen mawr*.'

Kazan nodded. 'I know,' she said. 'A terrible head. You deserve your pain.'

'It's a hard woman you've taken, Dai *bach*.' But he was smiling. He liked this fiery little foreigner with the sharp teeth and golden gaze. She'd make a good Welshwoman. And if she could shoot as well as Dai claimed...' There'll come a day,' he said, 'when there'll be a man to lead us. A man of courage and honour. When that day comes – and come it will – all who long to be free from tyrants, all the little men and women of this country, will rise with him, and follow him.'

There was silence after he finished speaking then Giles said, 'You must have slept on that mountain already, friend.' He gestured down the steep way they had come. 'One of your abbey friends, from the look of it.'

Dafydd's gaze followed his pointing finger and fixed on the lithe, brown-clad figure scrambling up a steep gully. He shook his head. 'Not one of the white monks,' he said. His gaze narrowed. The figure had stopped, was crouching behind an outcrop, peering cautiously out from behind it, looking back towards the abbey. Then he was coming on again, rapidly – too rapidly for such a steep climb.

'That's Ceri!' Conor craned closer. 'Wynn's boy.' He grunted. 'One of the abbey's now – went as one of the lay brothers last summer.' He exchanged looks with Dafydd: two friends with a history of dangers shared. 'Those wits left to you – sharp today, are they?'

'Sharp enough. Your own?'

'Grinding, *bach*, grinding.' No time now for *pen mawr*. Time now to be sober. Time now to be alert. He turned back to the small group. 'Best keep out of sight – keep those horses silent till we know what young Ceri's about. Might be nothing. Might be all holiday with him, and his Father Abbot in the dark.' He nodded to Dafydd and the two men stealthily tracked downwards to where they could see the boy again crouching and peering. Close enough to hear him panting for breath. Perhaps he sensed their presence because his gaze swung round and up, searching the crag side with fearful eyes. 'Conor?' It was the faintest of sounds, the breath of a name. 'Conor?'

Conor's hand came warningly on Dafydd's. He jerked back his head and Dafydd nodded and edged closer into the rock shadow. Conor moved cautiously into the sunlight. 'What do you want with me, Ceri *bach*?' His own voice hardly stirred the air.

The boy sighed with relief. Half-grown, not yet old enough for even faint fuzz on his face, but agile as a mountain goat and as skilful at keeping himself hidden... That's what Father Abbot had said. Just the one to go up the crag to find them. 'Brother Aiden saw you ride by,' the boy said, breathlessly, 'so we knew where to look for you.'

'And why would you be after looking for us now, *bach*?'

'Soldiers, Conor, soldiers coming for you and Dafydd ap Heddwyn ap Rhickert.'

Conor nodded him back into the niche of the rock, nodded to Dafydd to join them. 'Trouble?'

'Might be.' Conor nodded at the boy. 'Better tell us what you know, and quickly.'

'Father Abbot had word from Lady Branwen. From your sister.' The boy glanced at the brown man sitting so close to him. He'd never thought to be so close. He'd heard the stories about the man but he'd never seen him. 'Her husband knows you are here. A *Sais* servant who has never trusted her betrayed you both. He told Lord William of your visit to your sister and she had no choice but to tell Lord William who you are. No – she is safe, and the child – but she tells you she is sorry to betray you, and the Father Abbot. She told him, you see. Father Abbot knows where the bandits have their camp. She says her husband is determined to have you all in one sack and make a present of you to the King himself. She begs your forgiveness and hopes you will escape to safety.' He stopped. The hastily memorised message was ended.

Conor and Dafydd measured looks. Lord William had soldiers

well trained for war – ready for war with France. Armoured knights on horseback; foot soldiers well equipped; war dogs; tactics for dealing with peaceful monks. For sure they would find their way to the camp. May'appen they were there now. May'appen they knew the men they searched for were above them on the crag.

As if in answer to the unspoken question, the boy added, 'There's more. I crept out quiet, like Father Abbot told me, and round by the back of the abbey wall. That's when I saw them – Lord William and his men.' His eyes were wide with the remembered sight of the fierce-some company, their helmets and armour and lances and swords sheathed but ready, and the morning sun glinting off the metal so it seemed they rode in fire.

'Foot soldiers?'

The boy shook his head. 'All on horseback but they had a pack of hounds with them.' He hurried on. He'd seen Brother Luke standing, waiting, talking, gesturing up the crag…and he had hurried as fast as he could, this goat-boy who knew the steepest, shortest, quickest ways up the crag, listening, always listening, for the clink and jingle of armoured men and horses. For the panting, padding, treacherous, fierce dogs…

'There's a way we can take,' Conor said. 'Dai, remember the hollow way we used in the old days? They never did find it, these *Sais*.' They had re-joined the rest, were making hasty plans. Ceri was gone, promising he would be safe – he knew another way down the crag; too steep for most, and for horses, but not for him. 'Remember the hollow way?'

Dafydd nodded. He remembered. It led into the wild country beyond Cymer. An escape route where they'd never been – never would be – caught. But the track was halfway down the crag. 'Best be moving, then,' he said.

Conor laughed softly. 'Unless it's wanting to say *bore da* to them, now?'

Kazan shuddered, suddenly reminded of Father Heinrijc's stories of the *Clauwerts* against *Leliaerts* and the brutal *goedendags*. No prisoners taken.

Dafydd shook his head, his glance taking in the three women: Esyllt trying to hide her fear; Mair sturdily prepared to defend her man; Kazan, who had already suffered so much, ready to suffer more. Get them to safety. 'Too few of us, too many of them, Conor *bach*.'

And Dayfdd still so weak it would take all his strength to use that peasant sword of his to any purpose, thought Thomas.

Conor nodded. 'There may still be time to warn them at the camp.'

'If we get to the hollow way, Conor, I know all the short cuts.' Sion's glance at Mair. Enough. She knew what must happen.

'*We* can use the short cuts,' she amended. If they reached the hidden hollow way in time.

'Then go but keep a good look out. Keep out of danger. If the camp has been found…'

If it's hopeless, Conor meant, but how could he mouth the words? They hurried back down the crag, leading their horses, keeping as low as possible and slowly, so slowly, picking their way. They were almost to the jagged outcrop and shattered oak that marked the start of the hollow way when there was the glint of sun on metal shields and swords and helmets. Conor turned to Dafydd. 'They truly are well armoured, these Sais soldiers,' he said. 'A fierce-some sight for the French but not best for these hills of ours. Heavy-going. Dogs, now, there's different. Best you go fast, Dai *bach*. I'll hold them up long enough. Get to the river and follow it down a way – shake off your scent.'

'Leave you?' Dafydd asked.

'Yes.'

Dafydd shook his head. 'No. Of course I do not leave you, *cyfaill calon*.'

'You stayed behind in Venezia, Dafydd,' Twm said. 'Now it is your turn to leave.' He nodded. 'I'm staying with Conor.'

'Leave you both in danger? No.'

'Remember?' said Conor. 'The track leads down the stream bed. You're hidden by the earth banks and tree roots.'

'No.'

'The bushes and trees are well grown enough to hide you all. Then it's marshy land, remember, so go carefully.'

'No.'

Thomas said carefully, 'You are not recovered, Dafydd.' He watched for a moment the troop of disciplined soldiers advancing slowly, steadily, up the track towards them, dogs straining at their leashes. As yet, they were unseen, unscented. 'Too few of us, too many of them, as you said. You must get Kazan safe away, Dafydd.'

'No, Twm.'

'Don't argue. You're wasting time.' He said in desperation, 'You have Kazan and Rémi and Father Mertens to look out for. Giles has Esyllt and his family. Sion and Mair must get back to the camp. Me? There is nobody for me.'

'You have us. We are your family.'

'Dafydd man, do you think I want you to die with me? Kazan and Esyllt to die here? For the good God's sake, for Mary Mother's sake, for Father Mertens and Kara Kemal and all those we love, go, Dafydd. Go!'

'No.'

'So stubborn. Your conscience will kill us all.'

Conor said, 'Sure, it's sorry I am for this, Dai *bach*, but Twm's in the right of it.'

Hardly a blow – not even a tap – but Dafydd collapsed in a heap. That tough brown man downed with less than a tap. 'But it's feeble he is now,' Conor grinned as he hoisted Dafydd's inert body across Sadık the Faithful's broad back, 'and this is our way.'

Thomas remembered how he had seen Dafydd do the same to Blue, so long ago now – a whole year ago – when the big man was reeling drunk and ranting abuse. He'd collapsed mid-word and so did Dafydd now. Thomas sighed with relief. 'Get them to safety,' he told Giles. 'Get them to safety.'

It was what Dafydd had told him in Venezia, Giles thought. His fate, always to take his friends to safety. Never to stay and fight.

'You have a wife, Giles, and you must take Dafydd and Kazan safe home. Promise me this.'

'I promise.'

'My friend,' Thomas said. 'We have had a good life.'

'Nothing better.'

'Then no sadness, no grieving. This is my choice.' He smiled suddenly. 'May'appen, as Blue says, you'll remember me sometimes.'

'Always. Always!'

'Go now – quickly – no time.'

They followed the stony stream bed down between the high earthen banks, down to the rushing river that washed away all scent of them and their horses; crossing it then up, up and out into the safety of the marshland. Above, the bright blue day and golden sun mocked them. Behind, Conor and Thomas; a peasant, half Irish, half Welsh, and an English knight's son, were fighting a hopeless battle.

31

Bradwell Manor
September 1337

I shall sing songs in your praise
Man of peace,
Man of honour,
Man of courage in danger,
Man strong and steadfast.
(*Will-the-Wordmaker:* Lament for Dick – *Flint, September 1277*)

A misty morning at the very end of September; mist wreathing over the beck and breathing over herb garden and pleasure garden alike so that trees and bushes and late flowers dripped with moisture. Spiders' webs hung from branch to branch, leaf to leaf, glistening in the early morning light. In the high tree tops, magpies chattered, and in the lower branches robins were already challenging their territory.

The new barn stood proud and weather-tight, harvest safe-stored. All the gifts of autumn had been harvested. Ellen gloated over the haul. Elderberries and blackberries, sloes and hawthorn, rosehips and hazelnuts. Good wintering this year. Apples and pears and quinces, medlars and plums… The herb garden had yielded sage and rue and feverfew, hyssop and lavender, rosemary and thyme…an abundant harvest. Only last week Oluf and Niko had come back from the good God knew where, both gibbering with excitement. Black coneys! Black coneys in the warren! Wasn't this good news? Yes, at least four pairs and half-grown babes.

Best harvest of all was the girl-child, born weeks early on a night of new moon. A good omen but Bernt wild with worry, and Oluf no better. It was the women who arranged it all. Her dear friend Agathi and Agathi's Hatice, her own Hilda…and a healthy child, red-faced and squalling, already a crop of pale curls. And such a hungry mouth! She bent over the nuzzling bairn, rejoicing in the painful pull on her nipples, and her milk-swollen breasts.

Agathi was calm, serene, her body swollen with the child she carried. She stared out at the misty morning. Another moon – less than a moon – and she too would hold her child in her arms, God willing. It was Edgar who was anxious. She was not. Such unlooked for blessings this year. And greatest of all – no, not greatest – that was Edgar – but next greatest was that her family was here with her: her brother Niko safe and happy, making mischief with Oluf but both of them growing now to be serious, strong young men; Mehmi, whose music gave such happiness to the soul; her dear Hatice, her rock through all the bad times – and Blue.

Blue! That man-mountain, that one-time drunken nowter… 'Need a new barn,' he'd said that first day. 'This un's no good fer yer. See daylight enough through the planking fer Kingdom Come.' It was like the Creation. God forgive me the blasphemy, she thought. First day, black poplars eyed up, Edgar and Bernt consulted; second day, trees chopped; third day, stripped, shaped, smoothed; fourth day, wooden timbers erected… Stone walls to waist height – keep the vermin out, Blue said – then lath and plaster. 'May'appen we can build the rest in stone later, Edgar.' He'd called him 'Maäster' at first but Edgar had been as angry as Edgar could get. 'Never that, Blue. Never, between thee and me. No master, no servant. We are friends, you and me, working together for all our good.'

All the men working together, villein and sokemen, and Father Roger's men hauled in to help. 'Though they are your men now, Edgar, my son.' Father Roger was an ill man. He didn't expect to live out the year. 'No weeping for me, bonny girl. I've had a good life –

a better life since you and Edgar came home. I hope only that God spares me to see the child. That is all I wish.'

Luke as well was lost to them. The wounds, the fever, his age had all been too much. He had died and was buried in the church yard close by the East End so that Resurrection would find him there amongst the first. Edgar mourned him.

After that, after the harvest, Blue had looked at the bath huts and talked with Edgar and Jack Smith and travelled down to Potterhanworth. Now he and Jack Smith were crooning over the water pipe channelled from one of the springs down to the smithy where the pipes were heated by the roaring furnace until the water coursing through was steaming hot, scalding hot…not terracotta pipes. They cracked. Not as useful as Edgar had hoped. Lead pipes. That was it! Soft and malleable. And so very efficient. Such hot water! A second pipe channelled cold water.

With them was Simon Weaver, recovered now from his racking cough. Brought back into the village and welcomed. A life given: a life taken away. Simon was still wary. Still worried that he was seen as the enemy. His son didn't worry. He was happy, learning to sign with Edgar; learning to be a wayward boy with Niko and Oluf. But not so wayward. Those two had learned hard lessons.

And golden-eyed Kazan and the quiet, dangerous Welshman were together again, married, one body, one soul, one heart. A year ago Agathi had been a miserable slave held captive by the evil Veçdet. No hope of escape. Now here she was, free wife of the lord of the manor, her beloved, the father of her child. All the same…

She watched Kazan walk in the early morning mist through the sodden pleasure garden. Such loss. They had returned, Dafydd and Kazan. Giles and Esyllt? Those two had stayed behind in the Marches, with Giles' mother and father, and years of agony to be reconciled. 'Let there be a child,' Agathi breathed. A child would heal all wounds.

And here in her own manor – hers and Edgar's – her beloved Kazan and the dangerous, gentle, contradictory man that was

Dafydd were blissfully reunited; desperately unhappy because their great friend Thomas was dead. Killed protecting them. Another dead to give him life, Dafydd said. How could she help them in their bitter anguish? They would not stay here: she knew that.

Edgar's brother Alfred had already left, gone to join the third Edward's army against the French. He had left his manor in Edgar's care. 'Should I not come back,' he had said, but they had known what he meant. No coming back. Death and maybe glory but no coming back.

'What glory?' Edgar said, but once only, and she was not sure she was supposed to hear him.

'Agathi? A feast for our friends.' Edgar stroked her smooth silver-gold hair. 'They are to leave us.'

Long summer evenings had given way to dark nights. A full moon shimmered above the shallow valley. It glanced across the old stone manor house and gleamed through the arched window openings. Inside, lit sconces shut out dark. The whole village was gathered together to celebrate the finishing of the new barn, and the harvest safely gathered in, and Ellen and Bernt's bairn, but in truth it was a sombre gathering.

'Where?' Dafydd said. He leaned across the table towards Agathi. 'First back to Ieper and Heinrijc and Rémi – and Rémi's wife. Can you believe my little reckling has taken a wife? After that, we shall go to the far countries. Kazan and me. We both want to see those wondrous worlds. That land of Sakoura's…the holy city…we want to see those places.'

Years of travelling. When would they be together again?

'Always we are together. How can it not be so? We have seen so many things together.'

Kazan was serious. *Leaving? What is that? It means nothing. While the heart remembers there is no leaving.* But it was wisdom hard-learnt. Leaving meant everything. The sound of a vanished voice, the touch of a hand, the familiar, fragrant smell of the beloved;

the day-to-day living of petty argument, foolish laughter, meaningless talk… *Leaving? What is that? It means nothing. While the heart remembers there is no leaving.*

Nene, Sophia-the-Wise, I hope you are right. These are my dear friends. Already I miss Giles who faithfully looked after me for so many months; his wife Esyllt that good, brave girl who followed him into danger; my dear Thomas, the beautiful man I once thought was Bamsi Beyrek of the Grey Horse. And perhaps you were, dear Thomas. You kept my Dafydd safe; you saved us. We shall mourn you for ever and ever. She looked up into the sky with its bright full moon and paler stars. It was Nene who taught her the names of the stars in the vast sky. Nene's soul was a star high above, watching over her. There must be somewhere the stars of her grandfather, the Wordmaker; and Thomas, that dark, handsome man who wanted only to be a peacemaker.

'Come, Kazan.' It was Mehmi. 'Let's sing and play together for our lost ones. Let us honour them.'

Mehmi who was also bereft and whose joy was in making music.

Let the white horse come
Let it go free
And let go of your grief
Set that free as well…

He laughed, rippled the strings of the deep-bellied *oud*. 'For my warrior boy-girl,' he said to them all. 'For our Kazan.'

Warrior on the prancing Arab horse
What warrior are you?
Shame it is for a warrior to hide his name from another.
What is your name, warrior? Tell me!
I am Çiçek, granddaughter of Sophia-the-Wise
I am Çiçek, granddaughter of Will-the-Wordmaker

I am Çiçek, who rides a bright star
I am Çiçek, who shines brighter than a thousand suns
I am Çiçek, wife of Dafydd the Welshman

The strings quivered into long silence. A sigh rippled round the room. Yes, this girl-warrior, this bright star, was truly the wife of Dafydd the Welshman.

Select bibliography

Cooking and dining in Medieval England by Peter Brears, Prospect Books, 2008

Giotto: new concepts of space and sense of reality by Matteo Cecchi, ATS Italia Editrice, 2011

Giotto and 14thC painting in Padua by Davide Bansato, Marselio, 1998

Giotto by Arnim Winkler, Uffici Press S.A. Milano, 1968

Life in the Middle Ages, selected, translated and annotated by G.G. Coulton

Lincoln: a place in time by David Vale, FLARE, 1997

Lincolnshire Dialects by G. Edward Campion, Richard Kay, Boston Lincs, 1976

Lincolnshire Dialect Dictionary: Wodds and Doggerybaw by J.M. Sims-Kimbrey, 1195

Lincoln: Wigford; historic Lincoln south of the city edited by P.R. Hill, Survey of Lincoln, 2000

Lincoln: south-East; Canwick Road, South Common, St Catherine's & Bracebridge edited by Andrew Walker, Survey of Lincoln, 2011

Lyrics of the Middle Ages edited by Hubert Creekmore, Grove Press Inc, New York, 1959

Making the Boughstave Longbow by Don Adams, FLARE (Friends of Lincloln, Archaeology Research and Excavation), 1988

Medieval English Lyrics edited by R.T. Davies, Faber, 1963

Medieval Gardens by Anne Jennings, English Heritage, 2004

Venice; the Biography of a City by Christopher Hibbert, Grafton Books, 1988

Venice; a guide to the principal buildings by Anotonio Salvadori, Canal & Stamperia Edrice revised ed 1995

Venice; Pure City by Peter Ackroyd, Chatto and Windus, 2009

Violence in Early Renaissance Venice by Pro Guido Ruggeiro, Rutgers UP 1980

Francesco's Venice (BBC DVD) 2006

ABOUT HONNO

Honno Welsh Women's Press was set up in 1986 by a group of women who felt strongly that women in Wales needed wider opportunities to see their writing in print and to become involved in the publishing process. Our aim is to develop the writing talents of women in Wales, give them new and exciting opportunities to see their work published and often to give them their first 'break' as a writer. Honno is registered as a community co-operative. Any profit that Honno makes is invested in the publishing programme. Women from Wales and around the world have expressed their support for Honno. Each supporter has a vote at the Annual General Meeting. For more information and to buy our publications, please write to Honno at the address below, or visit our website: www.honno.co.uk

Honno, 14 Creative Units, Aberystwyth Arts Centre, Aberystwyth, Ceredigion SY23 3GL

Honno Friends
We are very grateful for the support of the Honno Friends: Jane Aaron, Annette Ecuyere, Audrey Jones, Gwyneth Tyson Roberts, Beryl Roberts, Jenny Sabine.

For more information on how you can become a Honno Friend, see: http://www.honno.co.uk/friends.php